MATHEV

The continuing voy

CW00799144

ALAN LAWRENCE

I was born in Cornwall's haven, steeped in wet salt air;
As a boy I roamed the coast, every day with ne'er a care;
I fished the pilchard grounds, my youth a marvellous trance;
As a dare I crossed the Channel, sailed over to far France.
Happiness and hot summers, long days spent with my brother,
I cherish those memories still, I thought they'd last for ever.

As a young man I plied the oceans, the winds ever a merry dance,
Whilst I served aboard the packet, striving for my chance;
Until pressed into a frigate, war a fright and thrill,
My brother lost to roaring guns, a bitter memory still.
Doubtless of great value are the blessings of the peace,
Boney gone at last, I was grateful for release.

My days afloat now but a memory, no longer any hope,
Not the least prospect of a ship, and all I do is mope;
Now too old to serve, I gaze across the chop and waves,
Sitting on the Falmouth quay, to sail again the dream I crave.
I cling to blessed recollections and will ever wonder: was I wise?
Until that final day comes at last when I will close my eyes.

The Tide of Life
Alan Lawrence

MATHEW JELBERT

The continuing voyages of HMS SURPRISE

As wave is driven by wave
And each, pursued, pursues the wave ahead,
So time flies on and follows, flies and follows,
Always, for ever and new.
What was before is left behind;
What never was is now;
And every passing moment is renewed.

Ovid

A tale of the struggle for Greek independence by
ALAN LAWRENCE

Mainsail Voyages Press Ltd, Publishers,
Hartland Forest, Devonshire
www.mainsailvoyagespress.com

MATHEW JELBERT

The continuing voyages of HMS SURPRISE

This edition is copyright (c) Alan Lawrence 2018. Published by Mainsail Voyages Press Ltd, Hartland Forest, Bideford, Devon, EX39 5RA. Alan Lawrence asserts the right to be identified as the author of this work in accordance with the Copyright, Designs and Patents Act 1988. The reader may note that this book is written by Alan Lawrence. It is not authorised, licensed or endorsed by Patrick O'Brian's family, agent or publishers. There is no association with any of those parties.

ISBN-13   978-0-9576698-7-1

Story text typeset in Times New Roman 11 point.

Cover painting by Ivan Aivazovsky: 'The Wave';
Book cover comment by Larry Finch, New York;
The Reef Knot graphic in this book is courtesy of and copyright (c) United States Power Squadrons 2006

The continuing voyages of HMS SURPRISE

The series:

The Massacre of Innocents   *(first edition 2014,
                                 second edition 2017)*

Freedom or Death   *(2017)*

The Fireships of Gerontas   *(first edition 2016,
                                 second edition 2017)*

The Aftermath of Devastation   *(2017)*

Mathew Jelbert   *(2018)*

The Tears of Despair   *(2019)*

MATHEW JELBERT

The continuing voyages of HMS SURPRISE

A FOREWORD BY THE AUTHOR

In this fifth book of my series I have continued the story of both actual historical events and the fictional adventures of my characters directly following on from the end of my prior book. That one concluded with the escape of *HMS Surprise* from the Bay of Navarino when the combined Turk and Egyptian fleets invaded the island of Sphacteria, it being the key to possession of the great bay. The Greek loss of both island and bay was fundamentally instrumental to the subsequent fall of their fortress of New Navarin *(modern day Pylos)* to the besieging Egyptian forces of Ibrahim Pasha. However, although this is a series and each book generally follows on from its predecessor, all of them may be enjoyed as standalone tales.

I would like to express grateful thanks to my helpers: Elaine Vallianou for her encouragement and local research on Kefalonia, Paul Jones and Geoff Fisher for help with book covers, Ivan Gorshkov for the Ivan Aivazovsky cover photographs, George Loukas for translation of Greek texts, Don Fiander for permission to use the reef knot graphic, Don Seltzer for sailing advice, David Hayes at *www.historicnavalfiction.com*, Peter Collett for technical advice on navigating Cornish waters, Helen Hardin for copy-editing, and my Sally for her support.

At the end of this book is a glossary of contemporary words occurring within the story with which the reader new to the naval historical world may be unfamiliar.

This book is dedicated to the serving men and women of all the navies of the free world - the *democratic* free world that is.

'Give you joy, shipmate! Come aboard! Voyage with HMS Surprise and share her crew's reminiscences in familiar old haunts, and revel too in their exciting new adventures! Come aboard! Swiftly now, there is not a moment to be lost!'

Alan Lawrence   *April 2018*

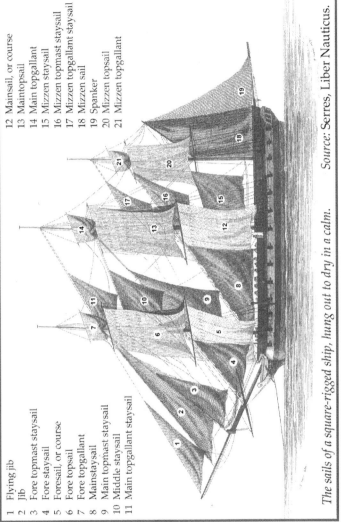

1 Flying jib
2 Jib
3 Fore topmast staysail
4 Fore staysail
5 Foresail, or course
6 Fore topsail
7 Fore topgallant
8 Mainstaysail
9 Main topmast staysail
10 Middle staysail
11 Main topgallant staysail

12 Mainsail, or course
13 Maintopsail
14 Main topgallant
15 Mizzen staysail
16 Mizzen topmast staysail
17 Mizzen topgallant staysail
18 Mizzen sail
19 Spanker
20 Mizzen topsail
21 Mizzen topgallant

The sails of a square-rigged ship, hung out to dry in a calm.   *Source:* Serres, Liber Nauticus.

MATHEW JELBERT

The continuing voyages of HMS SURPRISE

HISTORICAL NOTE

There is an inevitable and insidious effect on men at war, usually termed 'combat fatigue'. Generally unknown before the First World War, prior to which battles were fought in one or two days with the soldier able to recuperate for a relatively lengthy spell afterwards, the prolonged exposure to danger in the trenches of the Western Front inflicted traumatic changes on the infantryman. Robert Graves, who fought at Ypres, reported: *"At six months the infantry officer was more or less all right; by nine to ten months he became a drag on the other officers; after a year or fifteen months he was often worse than useless."*

In the Second World War, Brigadier G.W.B. James, a regimental medical officer and holder of the Military Cross and bar, reported: *"Prolonged exposure to killing and the threat of being killed wore men down such that by late 1942 (in the Western Desert campaign, starting September 1940) there was complete and utter exhaustion... while brief periods of rest did little to restore the cumulative effects of constant mental strain."*

One widely-recognised study of such effects is by *Swank and Marchand* on US infantry in north-west Europe, written in November 1944: *"The first symptom of combat exhaustion made its appearance at D-Day plus 25 to 30 in most soldiers. It could not be relieved by 48 hours of rest. The soldier lost confidence in himself and sleeplessness became evident despite his exhaustion. By D-Day plus 40 to 45, emotional exhaustion appeared as a slowing of mental processes, memory defects became extreme and there was also a lack of concentration. In some men they suffered physical symptoms such as paralysis of an arm or visual defects. For 98% of men, after 60 days, they were tense, sleepless and irritable. Some were emotionally unstable to the point that they became angry or cried at the slightest provocation or became irritated towards their friends for trivial reasons. Some became anxious, hyperactive and restless."*

The more complex detail of these effects on soldiers is beyond a book of fiction such as this; however, these issues rarely, if ever, make an appearance in fiction, and that hardly does justice to the story or delivers authenticity for the reader. In my own books I have striven to write with a degree of attention to these cruel realities.

Alan Lawrence   *April 2018*

Historical and *present day* place names:

Modon is *Methoni*

The Morea is *the Peloponnese*

Nauplia is *Naplion / Nafplio*

All dates referred to within this book are of the Gregorian calendar.

Chapter One

Those days immediately succeeding every battle were always hard; win or lose they were ever black days, particularly so when men had been struck down, when unfortunates had died; and painful thoughts of those hapless victims who had become casualties, whether wounded or dead, lodged like the most persistent of ethereal visitors in the tormented minds of all those more fortunate souls. The prior day had seen the most tearful, distressing and heart-rending funeral ever conducted on the deck of the shabby, much damaged, English frigate, and the lingering mood in the great cabin was wretched, few words ventured over an unusually spartan table as the anxious steward, Murphy, hovered silently at his captain's call whilst serving a simple first breakfast in an ambience of unrelenting, terse gloom.

The much crippled and mutilated ship rocked gently at double-anchor on the slightest of swell, imperceptibly so to its dejected men who, scores of them in much the same mood, thronged the gun deck, the waist and the foc'sle in melancholy, in abject misery and in near complete silence, save for the morning routines, all conducted exceedingly slowly and by rote, no thought given to anything except the recent events, no man able to cast aside his distressing recollections.

The death of one man in particular, Mathew Jelbert, long-serving veteran of many years and master gunner, had hit extraordinarily hard, for he had been a reliable friend to all aboard, a steadfast helper in times of difficulty and a confidant for troubled minds in those fraught hours of personal dejection and acute anxiety which had afflicted many a homesick man from time to time. Indeed, it was also his experience as ship's gunner of many years and his technical expertise which had saved the grievously battle-scarred *Surprise* from catastrophe a bare few days beforehand as she had sought to flee the confines of the great bay of Navarino whilst blockaded by the combined

Turk and Egyptian fleets. The wind, for almost all that terrible and massively destructive breakout, had been unhelpful, feeble, barely a breeze as the frigate had fought for four hours to escape through the gulf's narrow entrance mouth in a roaring, flaming, destructive orgy of hundreds of great guns firing, a fiery cataclysm which had left her stricken with broken yards, battered and fragmented bulwarks, ripped and torn rigging, shredded sails and numerous gaping holes smashed throughout her hull, several of which leaked water at a prodigious rate despite the carpenter's best efforts to plug them, the pumps attended frantically and without let up, day and night. Had the Turks been even half-decent gunners, Patrick O'Connor, *Surprise's* captain, had harboured not the least doubt that she would not have survived, could never have emerged from the howling torrent of shot and grape pouring in upon her from all sides; and then, when the Turk firing had reached its shrieking crescendo, when the shadow of death and devastation had assuredly and finally come upon them, Mathew Jelbert, in their darkest hour, had emerged from below with his secret weapon, one devised during the voyage out from Falmouth: huge incendiary shells, filled with inflammable pitch, packed with highly reactive sulphur and best red powder, the shells fabricated to detonate upon impact and then to fiercely burn, the sulphur assuring that the flames could not be extinguished, the target recipients would be impotent as their vessel was consumed all about them. The shells had delivered a brilliant but wholly unexpected success, so much so that O'Connor and all the Surprises, every man anxiously watching and hoping beyond dwindling hope for salvation, could not believe their eyes: the fiery explosions had immediately ignited to set aflame and consume the tar-soaked oakum caulking between the Turk deck planks, the volatile sulphur setting afire great expanses of rigging - all soaked in highly flammable pine resin - the flames swiftly lighting up sail canvas, receptively tinder-dry in the hot sun. The result was immediate and catastrophic for the attacking Turk vessels: intense flames roaring aloft in sheets of flickering orange-red fire, brightly illuminating the raging devastation in the dim light of the late evening and spreading swiftly from mast to mast, from sail to sail. The sight had frightened all other astonished enemy captains so much that their ships had hastily shied off, and their blockading line - a constricting death grip around the battered frigate's throat - had thereby been prised open, allowing a severely wounded *Surprise* to inch painstakingly away from assured destruction, gradually pushed by the weak wind, the ship's progress barely faster than drifting as she crept away to the south to skulk into the cover of blessed darkness as night, thankfully, brought down its welcome curtain upon the most fraught and despairing battle of Patrick O'Connor's life.

Fortunately, thanks to the woeful ineptitude of the enemy gunners, only two men had been killed, albeit a score of her crew had been wounded, until Mathew Jelbert had unleashed the fiery incendiary furies from *Surprise's* quarterdeck carronades; this despite the near stationary frigate being a sitting duck, scarcely shifting a cable during four desperate hours, a virtually immobile target for the blistering hail of iron ruination pouring in upon her from all sides. Subsequently, in the closing minutes of firing, as the enemy vessels hastened to shift away from the terrifying nemesis hurling explosive shells from close within their midst and as fragile hopes of escape began to flicker in the terrorised minds of exhausted men, then came the so shocking death of their saviour, the stalwart veteran, Mathew Jelbert. Sadly, just when the prospect of escape seemed at last to be before them, their desperate hopes flickering once more to life, one of the final few of the Turk cannonballs had struck the bulwark alongside the quarterdeck where Jelbert had supervised the loading and firing of the incendiary shells from the carronades. A particularly large and jagged splinter had penetrated deep into his chest where, lying prone amidst a river of blood, much of his chest flesh ripped away and his head propped up in a horrified Captain O'Connor's arms, the ship's surgeon had hastened to his aid, but, in instant and crushing diagnosis, Doctor Simon Ferguson had stared aghast, in abject distress and futility, recognising his utter inability to help his patient, a hopeless case, plainly not the least prospect of saving him, his wound so

3

irreparably severe: the master gunner's life was ebbing away in broad red rivulets flowing from his chest, more blood trickling from his mouth as he gasped weakly for air, and within a very few distressing minutes Mathew Jelbert, desperately struggling for breath, coughed for the last time, spattering with a thousand bloody spicules the anxious faces of a half-dozen of his despairing comrades who were crouched all about him.

All firing had wound down as blackness had succeeded the weak light of the gloaming and, despite her many and varied wounds, *Surprise* had made good her escape, the freshening wind just sufficient to fill her topsails - rent and torn that they were - to carry her away from the increasingly disinterested Turks, the frigate catching up in the darkness of a thankfully tranquil night with the preceding small Greek squadron as they too bore away for safer waters, all together gaining the sanctuary of Calamata in a brilliantly clear morning under a fierce sun.

The mood of all aboard had since sunk into deep despond, the loss of Jelbert the subject of unceasing gloomy talk amongst the men, for he was - perhaps without exception - the only man of the lower deck regarded by a unanimity of his shipmates, both officers and men, with adulation and with an infinity of respect which verged on reverence; indeed, it might be said that he had been perceived by all as the benevolent father of the ship.

The late morning of their arrival had concluded with a reunion ashore with those comrades who were the crew of *Eleanor*, a Garmouth-built schooner which belonged to Patrick O'Connor personally and which served as *Surprise's* tender. The afternoon passed with a meeting with Prince Mavrocordato, the representative of the Greek government. He had also escaped the bay aboard *Aris*, a Greek brig, together with *Surprise's* First officer, Duncan Macleod. They had been rescued by *Aris* from the island of Sphacteria, which bordered the western side of the Bay of Navarino, in a last-minute scramble to escape the redoubt as it was overrun by the Egyptian invaders. On the succeeding day, the 10th, in the calm waters off Calamata and in the warmth of a bright noon sun, Mathew Jelbert, master gunner and hero, had been buried at sea, every man aboard without exception in varying states of dismay, an ambience of depression and sadness prevailing throughout the frigate. It lingered still within the great cabin where two silent figures sat in abject, silent misery at the table, the breakfast barely picked over without the least of Pat's customary relish.

'God damn and blast, how I will miss that man!' exclaimed O'Connor eventually in a tone of angst and despair, stamping his coffee mug hard upon the table, splashing much upon it and looking up to gaze at his silent companion from bloodshot red eyes, deep-sunken within lined black shrouds.

'You are exceedingly hipped this morning... low in your spirits,' offered a startled Doctor Simon Ferguson quietly after a momentary evaluation and in that consoling murmur of voice medical practitioners customarily call upon when speaking with those not long for the world. 'I venture you refer to Jelbert. Pray be so good as to elaborate on your vexing perturbations if you will.'

'God strike me down!' declared Pat with undiminished vehemence, distress shrieking from his every word; 'Yes, Mathew Jelbert gone... and died in my arms, he did.'

'It was, sure, the vilest of setbacks,' murmured Simon, a shiver passing through him as he vividly recalled the ghastly event. Murphy, similarly taken aback and looking on from the end of the table in obvious dismay, nodded in mute accord.

'... and his son dead before him... struck down last year... and both killed on *my* quarterdeck... *both of them*...'

Simon recalled with another surging flush of distress that young Annan Jelbert had actually been killed whilst serving his gun within the great cabin, the painful memory of rushing to attend him where he had fallen still very vivid, his tiemate and shipmates all about him. He had not cared to move him from the deck where he lay in his agonies in the brief few minutes before he had died. However, Simon did not care to contradict his friend in his angst and confusion, determining to do his best with consolation, 'It is a cruel burden, I make no doubt, but you are to consider that it was the earnest wish of both men to serve... to serve with *Surprise*... to serve with *you* most particularly. I

5

collect that you told me that it was Mathew Jelbert himself who brought you to your own conclusion to sail again... in this gallant vessel, our dear *Surprise*... Was that not the case?'

'Yes... yes... and now he is dead,' Pat sighed again and his head slumped into his hands, his spirits sinking to a new low.

Murphy, staring with gaping unhappiness at his captain, turned in silent appeal, in obvious supplication, to Simon, the surgeon struggling himself to think of something to add, to lift his friend's morale. From beyond the door, the prevailing, unusual silence of the ship was eventually interrupted by the shrill sound of the bosun piping the hands to breakfast. 'I collect that day... in Devonport... during the refit.' Pat ignored the rising sounds of activity. 'He pressed me to take him aboard... he bore me no ill will for the death of his son. Yes, Jelbert it was... who did indeed convince me... I was decided by his words, I was so... to come back to the barky... It was *his* words... *his own plea* to serve again... himself... and his son lost... which made up my mind when my every thought... until that moment... was all ahoo.'

'Let us not dwell on these distressing matters... of which we can do nothing...' Simon struggled with a persistence such as exists only between the dearest of friends for something, *anything,* useful to add, to console Pat. 'Will I prescribe a curative... a generous measure of Ward's Drop perhaps?'

'Certainly not, and I would be obliged if we might hear no more of Ward's Drop.' Pat scowled.

No further reply from Pat other than an enduring, caustic glare, Simon persevered, 'Then will we enjoy a warming tint, look to a bottle of whisky - that precious standby - before we consider of any other of the day's necessities?'

Pat looked up, belatedly recognising Simon's caring efforts to cheer him, 'I should like that of all things, I would so, but no, I could not. I venture a brace of bottles would not serve, save to encourage this maudlin grief... and there is a deal to do, much work to repair the grievous damage aboard the barky; why, two of her yards are smashed...' His voice, hesitant, unhappy, tailed off into a long, long sighing exhalation.

'The yards... I have heard the term for ever... as a descriptor of measurement, *of length...* but I confess I do not wholly retain the... *the nautical principles*; are they of significant importance to the operation of this vessel... particularly useful would they be?'

'Pretty useful, I dare say.'

'Would their absence - a temporary one I am sure - be very much of a loss, at all? I am no great navigator.'

'Their absence... a loss?' Pat looked up to stare at his friend with a face of absolute incredulity, 'Oh... yes... yes, of course... two yards... it is a loss of the first order, and there is also a splintered mizzen topmast in need of repair... and a brace of holes in her hull... a world of things to remedy.' He grimaced, sighed once more, his face a picture of strain, of dismay.

'You are most cruelly vexed, set back, your spirits low... it is plain to see... and... and whilst such is perfectly understandable in these... in these distressing circumstances...' Simon laboured his point, even cautiously half-raising a finger, the extreme measure one that he felt was warranted in the circumstances, '... you will allow me to say, brother, that it will not serve you well to linger in that... in that particular cerebral locus. The Dear knows, it is assuredly inimical for the humours... and it will most certainly impinge upon the confidence of the men... will surely be adverse for their morale.'

A thoughtful pause for reflection but no reply from Pat who did not give a stuff for the humours although he could see Simon's point about the crew and their morale. He continued to stare at his friend with deeply tired eyes, the cautionary finger, still raised, passing entirely unnoticed. He coughed and took another swig of the cold remnants of his coffee. 'Did he... Jelbert... did he have kin... in Falmouth?' he uttered eventually in little more than a whisper.

'I believe there is a wife... *a widow*, the poor soul; bless her.'

'May God and Saint Patrick preserve her,' Pat sighed again, drank the final dregs from his near empty mug, spat the coffee grounds back into it and smacked it down, a minor liquid eruption showering the table. Murphy, staring in dismay, seized the mug, but instinctively reined back the replenishment inquiry on his lips, wisely judging his captain unlikely to welcome even the most innocuous of interruptions.

'Patrick is undoubtedly the most versatile of saints, there is no doubt of that...' Simon noting with acute concern Pat's repeated references to heavenly personages, 'but, listen my dear... I believe we may also usefully contemplate on more *earthly* endeavours. Allow me to say that there is a passage in Jeremiah with which I have long been taken; indeed, it may be said that I have taken it to my own heart.' Pat, remaining mute, stared at him with a blank expression, finally nodding, when Simon continued in mild voice, 'Let your widows trust in me.'

'Eh?' Pat looked up, pausing from the wringing of his hands. 'What does that signify, tell?'

A deep intake of breath and Simon spoke up, a little louder and in firm voice, 'You will collect that I have taken into my own Tobermory abode a widow...' Pat frowned, beset by confusion, and Simon quickly pressed on, ' I am not suggesting you do that yourself... no, of course not, but doubtless when we return home... that is to say to blessed Falmouth town... you will be able to make a settlement upon the unfortunate woman... upon Mrs Jelbert.'

'Yes, yes... of course I will... for sure I will. God bless you, Simon, it is the kindliest of thoughts.'

A knock at the door and a rather stout figure entered: it was Duncan Macleod. He was a longstanding and inseparable friend of both Pat and Simon, had been a shipmate for a very long time. With a slight gesture of his arm, Pat, wholly absorbed within his own thoughts, silently waved Macleod to a seat at the table, an attentive Murphy hastening to pour him a mug of coffee, spilling much on the table even as the steward's eyes, filled with concern for his compatriot the captain, both being men of Galway, darted anxiously back and forth, looking to the coffee, staring at Pat, and all the time wondering whether an effort to wipe the table might raise a rebuke or even opprobrium, even as he strived to listen attentively to every word, to every murmur.

'Good morning to you, Duncan,' murmured Pat, 'I trust I see you well?' adding after a momentary pause, 'How... how are our people this morning?' This was whispered in a voice that plainly carried a world of sadness.

Macleod, ever the unperturbable rock and always a pillar of strength even in the most distressing, the most adverse of circumstances, replied with conviction and authority, his words spoken, as ever, in reassuring tone, 'There is plentiful relief that only three men were killed...' a hesitation, 'though I find, too, a deal of anger... with the Turk...' Macleod's voice, heavy with the accent of the Isles, wavered, became harsh, cold, his own feelings of remorse and ire coming strong to the fore, 'Aye indeed... plentiful anger... Jelbert being lost.' He shook his head as if to dispel his own angst before resuming in a warmer, more comforting voice as he strived to restore his own equilibrium, to return to the essentials, 'It pleases me to say that... that the wounded are as comfortable as can be... *thanks to Simon here*... and - *allow me to say* - that is plain to all aboard the barky.' Murphy, staring, nodded emphatically himself in silent consensus as Simon exhaled with a heavy sigh, acutely difficult thoughts of his wounded patients pressing hard upon him. Macleod, nodding himself, turned to and smiled at his fellow Scot, 'Aye, we are all grateful for your presence aboard, nae doubt of that.' He picked up his coffee, 'Thankee, Murphy.' He gulped down the lukewarm liquid in one long draught and set down his empty mug, his roving eye catching sight of a trio of mutton chops congealed in a pool of white fat, the cold breakfast remnants. 'Might I ask, are those chops spare? I am mortal hungry.'

'Could you eat another one, Simon?' asked Pat quickly before Duncan might seize the tray, Simon having eaten very little and Duncan's prolific appetite never satiated and oft remarked upon within the cabin. 'May I help you to another chop, eh?'

'No, my thoughts are turned elsewhere,' murmured a downcast Simon in low voice, a long and heartfelt exhalation escaping. 'I must away directly... step downstairs... to the wounded... and without further delay. Doubtless Marston and Jason are toiling still with our patients, and I cannot countenance lingering here.'

'The men are dosed and settled, auld friend; have nae worries,' offered Macleod, who had already seized the tray. He had prized out one of the chops and was consuming the attached fat with obvious pleasure. 'Marston is moving amongst them with his attentions... and a deal of kindly words.' Without delay he bit into the meat and began to munch, chewing vigorously and with intense satisfaction, the Greek mutton a precious treat after the recent return to salt pork and salt beef, much of it too long in the cask. Its taint of spoil, the hint of the beginnings of decay, was an unwanted flavour the Surprises were long accustomed to, but it was always loathed despite the cook's best endeavours to disguise it with copious garlic and vinegar.

'There is a plentiful pile of eggs under that lid,' Pat conceded, Duncan's pleasure very evident.

'Why, I do believe I can hear the wind,' announced Simon with a pleased lift in his voice, looking up and aft, a gentle zephyr blowing in through the glaring absence of the damaged stern gallery, the glazing shattered and swept away in the recent battle, barely a pane remaining. 'Perhaps it will carry us far from this place... to peaceful Cephalonia... What say you, Pat?' The question was offered more in hope than expectation, Simon long accustomed to disappointment, many a straw frequently clutched but with precious little success, 'I venture to say, so many minds aboard this gallant vessel being so cast down... so greatly set back, such a change would answer tolerably well. Indeed, a better remedy for all our ills cannot be imagined.'

Pat slowly looked up from his own ruminations, appeared to ponder the suggestion momentarily before a seemingly reluctant reply, 'As to that, perhaps you are forgetting that we still carry the Greek coin press. Once that infernal device is delivered, we will away, I make no doubt.'

'When will that be, would you think?' asked Simon despairingly, a sinking feeling already chilling his heart. 'I only throw out the enquiry.'

'Why as to that, I must inspect the barky... The lads are attending to her damages... That is to say, as best as can be with precious little of stores in the hold. The boats all be mightily damaged, my barge the only one I am minded will float. As for the ship herself, well... the bosun remarked there be plentiful smaller holes in her hull which he ain't yet attended... every one of 'em calling for a deal of work....'

'A great deal would it be... a plethora of holes perhaps?' asked Simon despondently, his vision and hopes of tranquil and safe Cephalonia fading fast. 'How many holes?'

'A prodigious number... the plethora of the world.' The gloomy silence returned, spirits sinking generally.

'Do we know to where we are to carry the press?' asked Duncan tentatively, swallowing the last of his chop and seizing a second with alacrity in case Simon might change his mind.

Pat coughed, his throat still sore from the after-effects of hours of burned and unburned powder particles swirling about his quarterdeck, and raw from hours of shouting frantic commands amidst the incessant roar of thundering guns during the recent battle of long hours duration. He picked up his coffee mug, set it down with an audible clunk, still empty, the disappointment in his eyes catching the attention of Murphy who immediately stepped forward to pour from the pot. 'Prince Mavrocordato mentioned Aegina. Being an island, it offers protection from Turk land forces. Doubtless Ibrahim with his Egyptians will endeavour to head north and east from Modon, sweep through all the Morea and towards the Greek place of government at Nauplia. Though the island is in the general line of their path, it is close to the Greek port and fleet at Hydra... and such is surely Aegina's best protection.' Neither Simon nor Duncan having a great knowledge of Greek geography nor exhibiting the least interest in Pat's predictions, he ceased to speculate and looked to his steward, 'Do you care for another pot... of *hot* coffee, eh? I fancy I do. Murphy, kindly light along there to the galley.'

'Will we beat to quarters this morning?' enquired Duncan, grasping a boiled egg as casually as could be.

An indistinct shouting from the deck, a resonating thud against the frigate's side and Pat's interest was caught, his thoughts shifting in an instant to speculation about what was undoubtedly a small vessel coming alongside. Duncan half rose from his chair as if to leave to investigate, and then there came a knock on the cabin door when Lieutenant Codrington, his demeanour cautious yet plainly excited, stepped in. He nodded towards Pat, 'Beg pardon, sir, a Greek caique has come alongside... visitors be 'ere. It is Admiral Miaoulis....'

'Miaoulis... the great man himself!' exclaimed Pat, his attention wholly engaged in an instant. 'Why, show him in, Mr Codrington... and without the loss of a moment... *and send for Mr Jason,*' he declared loudly, springing up from the table and hastening towards the door, his mind switching to something more near his customary active mode. Simon rose in Pat's train, welcoming the beneficial distraction for his friend's sake.

Duncan, wholly unperturbed himself and fully seated again, stared for a wistful few seconds at the solitary remaining chop. The most momentary hesitation, a cautious eye to his friends - both exiting the cabin, not the least interest in the table - and he swiftly wrapped it within his handkerchief and stuffed it into his pocket, a brace of boiled eggs quickly following.

The senior Greek admiral, a Hydriot, was the acknowledged leader of the disparate Greek squadrons, as much as anyone was ever recognised as such. The fiercely independent Greeks of the islands of Hydra, Spetses and Psara were rarely, if ever, happy when acting in concert with their compatriots. Somehow Miaoulis had brought accord, had created a willingness within the Greek factions to accept his direction. Perhaps it was because this famous patriot had pledged his own three brigs and his every penny to the cause of Greek independence; perhaps it was that he personally had fought in nearly all the battles at sea thus far; or perhaps it was simply his strength of character, his presence, for he was not a young man, aged in his mid-fifties, greying and full of figure. His appearance suggested a man comfortable with himself, at ease with the world, with his lot; but, as Simon had previously remarked, that was entirely misleading.

Pat stared at him as Miaoulis stood on the gun deck near the boarding ladder. The admiral, in his recall, had never affected any airs or graces, yet he certainly exuded a plentiful natural authority, his two aides maintaining a pace behind him as if in deference. He possessed an air of intelligence and, despite the very considerable pressures upon him - the severity of which might well have crushed the spirits of many a lesser man - he retained a countenance of humanity and exuded a benign air of good nature. Four score of *Surprise's* crew looking on, Pat shook hands with him, both men holding each other in the greatest of respect, for the Greek was well aware of *Surprise's* participation in many an action; in fact, they had met for the first time after *Surprise* had carried off plentiful fleeing refugees from the tiny island of Psara in the course of a bloody Turk sacking, the island utterly depopulated as a consequence, those of its people not murdered by the invaders being carried off to a bleak life as slaves. Since then the English frigate had fought to defend the island of Samos, near the Turk coast, with the massed Greek squadrons of Hydra, Psara and Spetses, routing the Turk invaders in a series of battles which had driven them away only to return some weeks later, together with the numerous fleet of their Egyptian tributary. Even so, the Greeks, fighting once more with the help of *Surprise,* had prevailed again: the island had been saved for a second time and there had been no Ottoman naval actions against it subsequently; rather, the Egyptians had decided upon easier and more fruitful pickings, having invaded the Morea, landing and capturing Modon on the southern coast, their army moving a very few miles north to besiege the town and port of New Navarin for months. And then came their invasion of Sphacteria, the long hill of an island guarding the west side of the great bay of Navarino, the best natural harbour in all of south-western Greece.

The Egyptian invasion had been fast and brutal, overrunning the small island in little more than an hour, those few Greek brigs within the bay running before the Ottoman blockade of the great sanctuary could bottle them up within. The Greek brig *Aris* and the frigate *Surprise* - a mile in *Aris's* wake - were the last to leave, to fight their way out in a protracted four hour battle, just prior to which *Aris* had rescued the Greek minister, Mavrocordato, from the island, where he had gone to bolster the morale of the men at its weak defences. His subsequent escape aboard *Aris* had been a minor miracle, *Surprise* in her wake capturing the interest and attention of much of the enemy fleet as the Greek brig before her fought her way out through the massed enemy ships.

Admiral Miaoulis, with the collective Greek fleet, had been incapable of intervening, being some way distant to the west, the wind barely the feeblest of zephyr, leaving the admiral's brigs utterly unable to close and engage the combined Turk and Egyptian armada. The loss of the island and consequently the bay was a fundamental disaster for the Greeks, for besieged New Navarin could no longer be resupplied by sea, and hence it was sure to quickly fall to its besiegers.

Pat, accompanied by his visitors, returned to the cabin, Murphy hastening in with two large coffee pots. The customary introductions and cordialities swiftly executed, the assembly sat at the table, lingered for a minute or two in thoughtful assessment whilst they sniffed their coffee, its delightfully aromatic fragrance rising as all sat back to gaze at each other, an overriding sense of enquiry filling the cabin, the frigate's officers all curious as to the visitors' purpose. Murphy, too, was standing near the door, listening attentively for any word which he could rush to reiterate to his mates within the crew. Pleasantries were exchanged, as was usual, but the atmosphere was strange, a strong sense of tension prevailing within the Surprises, even a little of apprehension in the presence of this important Greek.

'Sir, if you please, what can I do for you?' asked Pat eventually, skipping further formalities. His question was uttered with foreboding, for he could see no particular reason - at least no military one - that Miaoulis should grace his badly damaged ship. His words, therefore, were uttered as much as a convention as a meaningful enquiry, for the poor condition of his vessel and the wearied state of his men still pre-occupied all his thoughts. That the much mutilated frigate's deteriorations were severe was obvious to all, and - it occurred to Pat - undoubtedly Miaoulis would have seen that as he approached her; they were such that they surely must preclude the provision of any further substantive assistance for the Greeks. 'Was that why the admiral was here?' Pat silently asked himself the obvious question with a fresh wave of anxiety rising up within him in a fierce surge of discomfort. He reluctantly reminded himself that *Surprise* was, at least officially, a Greek-flagged letter-of-marque, the frigate only ostensibly belonging to Pat himself, and as such she was obliged to act under Miaoulis's orders. Unofficially, she was in reality the tool of the British Foreign Secretary, Canning, and she still belonged to the Royal Navy, though neither the Admiralty nor His Majesty's government wished that to become public knowledge, having not the least inclination that the Porte in Constantinople should discover London's tangible support for the rebellious Greek provinces of the Ottoman Empire.

Pat's words were translated by his purser, Abel Jason, Miaoulis speaking little, near nothing, of English. Jason had originally joined the present ship's community as an Admiralty messenger, but he had stayed ever since. His several abilities included considerable language skills; indeed, he spoke both Greek and Turkish fluently. He was also willing and competent to assist the surgeons when they were overloaded, and had done so on many occasions. His help was highly valued by all aboard, particularly by Simon Ferguson and his assistant surgeon, Michael Marston; the latter was also the ship's chaplain.

'Captain O'Connor,' Miaoulis replied after a thoughtful half-minute, Jason translating, 'I am minded that if New Navarin is to hold out then the besieging fleet must be driven away and the island of Sphacteria recaptured; its well is also the only water source for Old Navarin, across the narrow channel to the north of the island, for there is none within that fort.' His thinking and his intentions brutally revealed, Admiral Miaoulis sat back and began again to sip his already replenished coffee, gazing all the time at Patrick O'Connor's countenance, staring at his unblinking eyes, studying the effect of his words, very alarming words indeed to all the Surprises present, certainly so to Pat.

Pat, shocked by the implications, the exceedingly unwelcome ones, of Miaoulis's pronouncement, strived to show no expression on his grimy, tired face even as his mind whirred frenetically, his pulsating heart close to panic. He was sure he could feel his blood coursing around his head, carrying his frantic and anxious concerns, for what could he, his tired men and his severely damaged ship really do? Indeed, what could they *reasonably* be expected to do? What contribution were they actually capable of making? The excruciating questions were burning like fires within his mind, the jagged dagger of anxiety within his heart twisting again; his face flushed red and he felt the sweat running down his chest and under his arms. These were not *reasonable* times, he reluctantly conceded to himself even as Miaoulis continued to stare at him in pointed anticipation, as was everyone else at the table, silent expectancy hanging heavy in the air. Pat's thoughts continued to race even as his unmoving eyes, taking in all before him, registered the fascinated close attention of every person present. The bloody flight from the Bay of Navarino had heightened the general awareness of everyone aboard ship to a sense that these were the most desperate of times. Pat reminded himself that for the defenders of New Navarin they certainly still were, being cut off from resupply by sea with the loss of the bay and concurrently besieged by land. Yet even with all his urgent concerns for his ship and his men, Pat could not dispel from his mind one particularly unpleasant recollection, a memorable event in the past, one when his crew had protested when asked to soldier on, to persevere, to fight the fast approaching and second battle to defend Samos against the imminently expected Turk and Egyptian fleets acting together. He recalled, with another surge of anxiety, that it had been an hour of the most extreme delicacy before the protest - he would never refer to it or even think of it as mutiny - was calmed, the men brought back on side, when they had returned to their duties to face the invasion fleet. That disturbing event, the demonstration of their heartfelt wish to go home, their conviction that they had done enough, done all that they were capable of, had been engraved indelibly within Pat's memory. He recalled most vividly the desperate, long minutes when any satisfactory conclusion to the protest remained in doubt. Many months on, many hours of reflection since, he had no wish to experience any repeat of that distressing event. He prolonged the final draught of his coffee for as long as he could, his thoughts groping for a clarity he could not find within a confusing mental darkness, his mind struggling for some semblance of a statement - *some reason* - to credibly explain why *Surprise* could not participate in the next Greek engagement. Perhaps an explanation of the dismal state of his ship, of his inability to take her again into battle in her evident disrepair, might suffice for the admiral? Perhaps the telling of his men's exhaustion, the escape from the bay being so recent, might serve? He did not care in the least to refer to his men's protest, to their conviction that they had done all that could be asked of them or, indeed, to their heartfelt belief that they had done enough. Time, before his tired, sore eyes, appeared to be passing at a snail's pace, and the evident expectations of his guests - and his own officers too for that matter - were pressing heavier than ever upon him. Absolute silence reigned in the cabin, every face around the table was staring at him, polite, patient, waiting. Still floundering without conclusion, he sought to stall, to give himself more time to consider, and he spoke at last, 'Sir, of the veracity of your thinking I have not the least doubt... Would you care to enlarge a trifle upon your plans... your *immediate* intentions most particularly?'

The Greek admiral stared intensely at Pat, scrutinising his face for the least sign, the smallest indication of his thinking, the silence enduring for what seemed an age to all around the table before he eventually spoke - Jason translating - in an unwavering voice that carried not the least hesitation, 'I have received reports from my scouts that an Egyptian squadron has withdrawn to the port of Modon. It is, as you know, a very few miles to the south of New Navarin and little more than half a day of sailing from here. It is where Ibrahim first landed his invasion. It is likely that they are revictualling their ships there, for they surely maintain plentiful stores in that place for their army.'

Pat, increasingly uncomfortable under Miaoulis's intense scrutiny, looked to Jason as the translation was uttered, all the time acutely conscious of the spellbound gaze of Duncan and Simon remaining focused upon him, and sure in his own thoughts that Simon most certainly did not care to see another battle with any more of its inevitable, accompanying casualties. 'Doubtless so,' Pat murmured, prevaricating still, his spirits sinking.

'I am departing, Captain O'Connor, for that place,' declared Miaoulis, raising his voice a little, perhaps striving to coax some meaningful statement from Pat, 'My ships, my men... we are leaving... at first light... We will attack the Turk on the morrow... in Modon... with fireships.'

A deathly silence settled again in the cabin, the admiral and his two aides gazing intently at Pat and self-evidently waiting for his reaction. Both Duncan and Simon were similarly anxious, their eyes fixed upon their friend. Codrington, lingering at the door, stared with unconcealed apprehension. Murphy, the steward, remained motionless, hardly daring to breathe in case his continuing presence might be remarked and he be expelled. Pat allowed the tiniest of sigh to escape his lips, instantly regretting it and chastising himself in case the admiral thought ill of him. He sensed the importance of the admiral's statement; he had realised in an instant, of course, that the visit was neither a social one nor was it without the admiral's own hopes resting upon it: Miaoulis surely wanted his help, was asking for it, *obliquely* perhaps *for the moment*. There was no other explanation, and that sat hard with him, his mind torn savagely between the wish to spare his exhausted men, to preserve his much reduced and damaged ship, and his desire not to let down his ally, one who plainly attached infinite importance to his help; for the admiral could not conceivably have missed *Surprise's* severe deteriorations. What to do? What to say? His stomach turned over with the unease thrust upon it, his heart beat ever faster, his thoughts pulsated with anxiety; he could feel the acceleration of his breathing, the colouring of his face, even as he strived to contain the physical changes pressing upon his own exhausted body, upon his tired mind. Sweat coursed down his body like a tide, puddling on his chest; his shirt was soaked and sticking uncomfortably. What on earth *could* he possibly say?

The ship's bell clanged dolorously, the unusual and somnolent tone of its *"ding-ding"* attracting no-one's attention; the total lack of any response from anyone exacerbating Pat's awareness that all were waiting with singular focus for *his* words.

Miaoulis, if he was aware of Pat's rising anxiety and discomfort, ignored it. He enjoyed neither the benefit of superior ship numbers nor the inclination to leave aside the most powerful vessel available to him, for *Surprise's* guns were of a heavier calibre than the lighter array of various types within his own brigs, invariably a mélange of disparate prior captures. The admiral, perhaps tiring a little of Pat's hesitation, perhaps perceiving it as procrastination, came to the point, his still quiet words instantly translated by Jason, a tremor in the purser's voice. If the admiral's request was reluctant, his own words carried no hint of that, for such was a luxury Miaoulis could not afford, 'Captain O'Connor, I beg you will aid us.'

This time, Pat could no more contain his heavy sigh than he could slow his fast breathing or his rapidly pumping heart, a long and deep exhalation revealing his heavy concern, his burning dilemma, the most dreadful predicament, one which he would wish on no other man. He looked momentarily down, a few seconds passing; he stared again towards Jason. His translator was of no help at all, exhibiting a face of the gravest concern, and such mute inability took Pat's own despairing thoughts no further. From the corner of his eye, he caught a glimpse of distress and consternation upon Simon's face. His heart and spirits sinking fast, he turned back to Miaoulis, the bitter sentiment of rejection strong in his mind, 'Sir, you will have remarked upon the damages... many and varied... to my ship as you came aboard...' Jason's translation was near concurrent and the admiral nodded gravely. 'For four hours we fought the Turk before escaping the bay... *four hours*, sir, and there is precious little of powder left in her magazines... perhaps one barrel... of the lowest quality, and as for shot... why, I doubt we possess of a score of balls.'

Miaoulis nodded again but held his tongue, the admiral seemingly reflecting on the paucity of firepower remaining to the English frigate.

Duncan, keenly aware of Pat's dilemma but also cognisant of the two attendant stewards - Freeman too having entered the cabin - and their likely purpose in lingering, interjected, speaking very quietly as an aside to them, 'Murphy, get away to the galley and fetch more coffee... perhaps a tint of brandy too. Freeman, pray go and help, cut along there.'

Another painstaking minute elapsed in silence, an age passing so very slowly, before Pat resumed his litany of concerns, his words plainly an effort, 'Admiral, my ship has prodigious damages to remedy... a brace of broken yards, a splintered mast, the sails a calamity to behold... and her rigging is in tatters, shreds... why, I doubt Nelson himself would care to take her to sea.' This latter point was mentioned in the lightest of tone, Pat striving to lift, even if only by a very little, his gloomy verdict on his vessel and to introduce the smallest, the gentlest intimation of his necessary refusal.

Miaoulis nodded once more but said nothing immediately, the table falling once more into gloomy silence, one which endured for another long pause, every man present wondering to what conclusion things were leading. Eventually the admiral spoke again and in mild tone, 'Captain O'Connor, I did have the great fortune of meeting Admiral Nelson... I did, only once. It was in the year 'two; I was off Cadiz and running the English blockade when I was caught by the great man. He was in the mind to string me up as a pirate... yes, I see his face, his condemnation within it, all these years on... but then we talked and I believe he recognised in me that same characteristic which he knew very well was in himself: that is... the intention of getting the task done... whatever the cost might be... and whatever the tools at hand.' Miaoulis smiled for the first time, 'We parted on the best of terms, Nelson bestowing his blessing on a young Greek ruffian... I was so, and... and in my recollections of that moment I am also minded that there was a place in his heart for Greece, even in those days long before this war.'

The Surprises listened with great interest, all pondering those qualities common to both admirals, undoubtedly the attributes of great men. Still nothing at all was spoken by anyone as they reflected, and then the stewards returned, racing through the door and to the table with the coffee replenishment and brandy bottles, both men determined to miss as little as possible of the hugely significant discussion. 'Well, 'ere it be, sorr,' declared Murphy in positive tone. Even the steward was striving with what little he possessed, in a rare moment of amiability, to lift the enduring black mood. There was not the least reply from anyone. In the painful silence the stewards set to to refill the mugs and poured generous measures of Greek brandy into the glasses, handing them out about the table, but none of the seated recipients moved in the least, not even to any acknowledgement of the refreshments; indeed, Miaoulis pushed his own glass away, untouched. Pat simply nodded his mute thanks; at that moment he had no belief that he was himself a Nelson, none at all.

Silence reigned at the table, heavy, oppressive, the cabin ambience one of gloomy apprehension. All present stared fixedly at the two principals, Pat and Miaoulis, but neither of them spoke, both men thinking, both wondering how to break the painful deadlock. Much to everyone's surprise, one of Miaoulis's aides, a young man who until then had said nothing at all, spoke up in barely more than a whisper with a tentative plea, pulling a scrap of paper from his pocket, 'Sirs, will you allow me to offer a very few words?' Mute nods from the table, Pat grateful for the interruption, and the young Greek spoke out in nervous tone,

'Until when, brave warriors, shall we live under constraints,
Lonely like lions, in the ridges of mountains?
Living in caves, viewing wild tree branches,
Abandoning the world, due to bitter slavery?'

21

Faces around the table stirring, looking up, the impassioned orator raised his voice,

'Losing brothers, country and parents,
Our friends, our children, and all of our kin?
Better an hour of free life,
Than forty years of slavery and jail.'

Greek heads nodded; hearts and minds, painfully prompted, raced as the unexpected speaker looked towards and spoke directly to Pat, 'It was, sir, the precious words of Rigas Feraios, the apostle of our revolution... and I am... myself... I am an aspiring poet.'

Pat nodded, offered a weak smile, but found himself still unable to speak in that instant. For another painful minute of expectant, resonating silence in the cabin he said nothing before he found his voice at last, speaking to Miaoulis with hesitation and extreme reluctance, venturing towards the acute subject which concerned him the most, 'Sir, my people have fought hard to help your cause, fought bravely... and we have lost more than a score killed and three score wounded these two years gone...' A lingering hesitation, no reply from the Greek, and Pat took the fearful plunge, 'They are uncommon weary... dog-tired, a score more of them were wounded... escaping the bay... and it is far from sure that they... *quite fagged out as they be*... that they will be minded to answer the call. That is to say...'

At this point Miaoulis interjected, the admiral plainly allowing his own anxieties to rise and his personal spring of unfaltering patriotism to colour his thinking; his voice edgy and tinted with more than a hint of impatience, he spoke out with steely conviction, 'Captain O'Connor, for myself I answer only to God.'

The general cabin anxiety surged to new heights even as cold silence returned, desperation plainly seizing its grip upon all present. A minute more of private thoughts followed until three bells rang out, much louder and very intrusive, the *"ding-ding, ding"* this time catching the attention of the Surprises. It offered a welcome distraction to Pat, whose eyes flickered between his guests and his shipmates even as a vague notion began to take shape in his mind. All present sat mute, every man sunk in deep gloom. The two stewards fidgeted, in sympathy with the mood.

Pat sensed that a deeply regrettable exchange was looming imminently upon them all, one which would doubtless afflict the relationship between Miaoulis and himself for a very long time, and one which would serve not the least good. His mind painfully firming to an unwelcome conclusion, one reached with infinite reluctance, he blurted out his offer, one which the long spells of silence had allowed him to formulate as his last resort, a decision made with the utmost trepidation, with grave concern, and only offered under the immense pressure he felt weighing heavy upon him. He hoped with all his heart that it would not prove to be a decision which he would come to regret, 'Admiral Miaoulis, I venture we will assist you...'

There was an audible gasp from all the Surprises around the table, their faces instantly radiating dismay and incredulity. Pat resumed immediately, speaking this time without his former hesitation, his firming resolution plain in his voice, 'My ship, as is plain to all to see, is in the most severely damaged state; indeed, she is in a truly parlous condition... and I have reported that there is a lack of powder and shot...' Miaoulis simply stared at Pat as he strived to hear Jason's translation, the interpreter's voice falling off to little more than a disbelieving whisper. 'However... and fortunately... we do still possess sufficient men to fight her...' All the Surprises reacted with a start to Pat's last words, unexpected ones and so greatly shocking. Pat blinked, glimpsing the look of undisguised dismay on Simon's face; his mind racing, he desperately hoped that his men would fight if they were called upon. He continued quickly before anyone could interrupt, '... at least that is how it will look to any Turk vessel she may encounter.' Jason reiterating in translation, the Greek admiral nodded cautiously, sensing the emerging essence of Pat's thinking as he continued. 'Mindful of her *true* state, that is to say *her damages*, I must tell you that we are able to help you only *with her presence*... sir, but I doubt *with her guns*... even were your ships to provide powder, for I venture your own shot is too small for our eighteen-pounders... and so, sir, I regret that we could not... we *could not* be in contemplation of any engagement served only with what little we still possess... no, I could not countenance that. We *will* attend your squadron, sir...' Miaoulis was nodding more emphatically, '... but expect not the least of firing from this vessel, for that is plainly beyond our powers at the present time. As she is, she may deter any supporting Turks from engaging with you... that is to say *only until her mettle is tested*, when, sir, we must away... depart. I regret that is all that is left to us to offer you. I trust it may be of some small service to you, Admiral, for I say it plain... *I can offer nothing more...* nothing!'

A collective exhalation of breath reached Pat's ears, Miaoulis too looking all about him; perhaps it signified a relief of the claustrophobic tension and fearful apprehension every man was gripped by, their sighs something of the sound of their escape from very considerable anxiety: Patrick O'Connor, a captain possessing of infinite respect in the eyes of all his crew, had pulled a rabbit from the hat; perhaps it was, in reality, only a dead rabbit, but it had apparently satisfied Miaoulis, for the admiral, still unspeaking, nodded sagely, rose slowly from his chair and stepped around the table to offer Pat his hand. Everyone else rose as one in the strangest ambience of an amalgam of shock and disbelief somehow melded with a general and profound sense of relief. Patrick O'Connor had found his way, and no words were spoken until Admiral Miaoulis offered his thanks; his words, spoken in gentle voice, professed an understanding of *Surprise's* status and her limited capabilities. The highly-charged atmosphere in the cabin deflated, the acute unease falling away, a swift and welcome inrush of sensory abatement settling in the minds of all present.

Despite the admiral's grateful words of thanks and his appreciative sentiments, the customary post-amble of farewells seemed brief, the air still strained somewhat, few further words being offered by any man, certainly nothing of note being raised. Simon in particular remained mute, the potentially distressing implications of Pat's commitment taxing him greatly, the enormity of Pat's pledge and its potential for further calamity weighing heavy upon him, pressing down hard upon his fragile spirits. The Greeks, Miaoulis seemingly pleased and satisfied, moved towards the door, readying themselves to depart the ship, all the Surprises in close attendance, the party shifting out through the coach towards the gun deck.

Prior and brief intimations of the cabin meeting obviously having been disseminated by the stewards, who had already left in a great degree of haste, the officers, Surprises and Greeks together, began to emerge to the deck. They were greeted by a solid phalanx of the crew, two hundred men, all standing in expectant curiosity before them, excited murmurings rampant, but an air of dissatisfaction, of simmering anger, prevailed. Barely a man was absent save for the wounded; indeed, some of those, the more lightly afflicted, had come up from the lower deck to see for themselves what was happening. All stared aft in searching, anxious trepidation, for all the men present were well aware of the true state of the damaged ship, of the glaring absence of powder and shot, of the leaking hull, of numerous severe damages and countless other lesser physical shortcomings; and then there was the state of the men themselves, a score wounded, all others exceedingly tired, their extreme fatigue closely verging on absolute exhaustion. How could anyone contemplate taking the barky to sea, to go back into action so soon? It was simply beyond their ken, and they were vexed. Such was surely something that their captain, Patrick O'Connor, the man who had previously saved all their lives in battle and, later, from the full force of a hurricane, a man who all considered to be the most careful of trustees with their lives, would never consider? Yet was that fearful prospect, such an incredible one, now actually happening? They desperately wanted to know. Two hundred frantic hearts surged with racing anxiety; two hundred anxious, disturbed minds screamed out for the answer and four hundred eyes, simmering with displeasure, were fixated on the group of officers, who had all emerged from the coach and halted, blocked by the gathering to an involuntary standstill.

Pat, Miaoulis and all with them were astonished, indeed stunned, for there was no visible way forward to reach the ladder through the packed crowd, all resolutely standing firm, not a man yielding an inch, a dense press all about the officers. The stench of unwashed bodies was nauseous; not a man had found the least opportunity to wash since escaping the Navarino battle, few possessing a change of clothes; indeed, there had been precious little time to even catch up on sleep. Pat, the endemic foul odours very evident, presumed that he was in much the same stinking state himself. Worse, the mood of the crowd was, self-evidently, highly charged, bitterness and aggression bubbling only slightly below the surface but much evident nevertheless. Pat's spirits swiftly sank even as his own heart raced ever faster: how was he to explain his decision to his men, worn out and exhausted that they were? It was very much akin to that nightmare he had found himself in once before, when the men's protest had erupted before the second battle to defend Samos, save that then the barky had not been so severely damaged and she had preserved a goodly supply of powder and shot; but now she had none, or at least exceedingly little, and that was known to all aboard. What was he to say? How could he explain his pledge made to Miaoulis to all his men and expect to carry them with him a second time? How to do so in circumstances which all knew were much worse than ever before? His spirits descended to new depths and he silently despaired.

Chapter Two

A subdued, sullen muttering continued to resonate throughout the assembled Surprises, an awkward and plainly unpleasant aura seizing and settling upon the men; tired, red eyes blazed and flickered in searching gaze of one officer and then another, the uncomfortable stand-off prevailing, not a word of direct enquiry uttered by any man present, not the least instruction spoken by the officers. Admiral Miaoulis was certainly recognised by all of the crew, and it was plain that they had become aware of his purpose, of his intention of calling once more on *Surprise*; they clearly knew of his request that the barky should go into battle again, they understood the reason for his presence; and in the normal course of events not a man would have minded; indeed, none would have much remarked upon such an event, for that was their own essential mission in being here, as they all understood so well; but so soon after such a deeply destructive battle and without any ability to fire the barky's guns: how could it be?

Pat, rarely gloomier himself, called upon his own dwindling reserves and spoke up in determined voice, the endemic hubbub dying down but not entirely ceasing as he raised his hands. 'Lads,' he hesitated, searching for the appropriate message, the particular appeal, which might bring his men round. 'Lads, our Greek allies are in need...' Pat hesitated as a general murmur of disapprobation became loud protest.

Whatever the needs of the Greeks might be, they plainly left the Surprises entirely unmoved, a silence quickly returning, one founded in a defiance born of incomprehension. High tension prevailed. The faces of all the men that Pat could see standing before him were set as if cast in Portland stone, unmoving, not the least indication of the slightest willingness to hear more, nor any sign of mental faculty exhibited at all, save that their anger shone through their obduracy.

Pat tried again in placatory voice, 'You have all heard of Marshal Grouchy's decisive aid for Wellington...'

Not a man stirred, not a one showed the least recognition of having heard of the said aid, decisive or otherwise; nor did anyone display the slightest recognition of the essential incongruity of Pat's words nor any indication of willingness to listen to anything at all. Instead, from the back came the stamp of bare feet on the deck, a few men raising their objection in the only way they knew. Sullen faces, standing near, just the smallest of steps in front of Pat, seemed to him to be seemingly near to outright hostility, gazing with fixed vacancy at the officers immediately before them, vexation much evident.

'Lads, I say again... Admiral Miaoulis is in want of our help...' A mere second of silence and near all the men erupted into low chatter.

Pat seemingly floundering, the Greek admiral pushed one pace forward; he was not a tall man, many of the men before him towered above him; he stared for a long moment at the assembly, his eyes roving over the front rows of the crowd, and slowly, theatrically, he raised his arms. Such was the respect accorded to this renowned, fighting sailor that the crowd quieted, the foot beating ceased and the few men still muttering were urged to silence by their shipmates. With Jason standing at his side and translating, Miaoulis did not hesitate, he shouted out in loud voice and with blunt words, 'The Turks have kicked you out from Navarino...' A sharp and angry intake of breath followed from two hundred men, much louder chatter greatly evident to the officers, angry shouts coming from the back. 'My ships also...' The few continuing shouts of discord from the men were brief, Miaoulis taking not the slightest notice of them, '... and I understand that the Turks have killed several of your comrades...' A loud tide of resentful comment arose this time, a painful chord not so much touched as stamped upon. Pat's heightened awareness and attentive ear caught mention of Jelbert from several quarters, '... and many of my own countrymen... hundreds of them... lie dead on the blood-soaked earth of that desolated island, Sphacteria.' At that the swell of background noise greatly subsided and the Greek admiral raised his voice a very little, as if in so doing more substance, more importance, might attach to his next words, 'Well, now we are many more... All my Hydriot squadron are here with me... with others... Spetziots and Psariots too...' His words, increasingly upbeat, had plainly captured the attention and the curiosity of the Surprises, for a near silence now prevailed, '... and now I AM GOING TO GIVE THE TURK A GOOD KICKING!' A brief puzzlement was exhibited on many faces as Jason translated, valiantly raising his own voice to mimic Miaoulis's vehement shouting, and the words, in their primitive simplicity, struck a sympathetic chord, a few cheers echoing back, though it was by no means from the majority of the crew. Silence quickly settled again, and Miaoulis resumed in quieter voice, a sympathetic tone within his words visibly resonating with the men, 'You have fought well... You are much fatigued... I see that plain... You are... all of you... valiant friends of poor Greece; I know that... You fought with me before... at Samos... and I will not call on you until you are rested... when those of your wounded who were struck down by the Turk are healed... and until you have plentiful powder and shot once more... I WILL WAIT... I WILL WAIT... until your own spirits are restored.'

The admiral's message appeared to throw the Surprises into confusion, quizzical faces abounding everywhere, including Pat's, for the Greek appeared to contradict the rumour which had originated from the stewards and spread rapidly throughout the ship. What was up? Pat and those of his officers who had been present in the cabin were utterly confounded, but Pat said nothing, his own burning curiosity seizing hold of his thoughts: *what on earth was Miaoulis about?*

The admiral continued in measured voice, exuding confidence and calm, all his audience thoroughly bemused, completely quieted and seemingly now perfectly prepared to hear him out, 'We Greeks, we brave men of Hydra... with our valiant compatriots... the fighting men of Spetsis... with our brothers, the heroes of Psara... we are sailing tomorrow TO GIVE THE TURK A BLOODY NOSE... for the time has come when WE WILL SINK HIS SHIPS...' A general buzz of excitement rose up within the gathering, the praise Miaoulis had showered on all his various compatriots striking a chord with the Surprises, perhaps as the admiral had intended.

'Simon, old friend, it is plain that you are mightily cast down,' whispered Pat.

'I do not much care for our imminent direction.'

'WE ARE LEAVING FOR MODON IN THE MORNING...' Miaoulis's voice boomed out, echoed by Jason, valiantly shouting still, '...in the *early* morning. I know that place well... I have sailed in these waters since I was a lad of ten...'

'I am heartily sorry for your dismay... I am so.'

'Never mind me, Pat. I concede that you possess an inveterate mariner's obligation to do your duty as you see it.'

'WE WILL CATCH THE TURK IDLING... with an onshore wind so he cannot run away. WE WILL SET AFIRE HIS SHIPS... WE WILL BURN THEM TO THE WATER!' The endemic murmurings within the Surprises were rising, ever louder as the admiral pressed home his own anger, his burning determination very visible. He settled back to quieter voice, 'This is my homeland... and I will not stand by... stand idle... while those vile pigs desecrate it... while they live off Greek toil... sleep in Greek homes... while they steal our food... ravage our women... and take thousands away as slaves...'

'I am fully persuaded that we will do little on the morrow, we will keep our distance from Modon...' Pat strived to reassure Simon, '... and remain far from any engagement; we will serve only as a scout... an observer; I have made that plain to Miaoulis.'

'Would it be uncivil to suggest that the Turk may not be a party to your intentions, may indeed determine to set about us... and what then? What of your obligation in such an event? We will be, as you have yourself explained, a dog with neither bark nor teeth.'

'Oh, I would not go that far... no, no... I have no doubt a trifle of powder, a goodly measure of shot will yet be found... though for sure I am not in contemplation of more than a display... a demonstration of her teeth. She will bark, if called upon... and bite... Have no concerns about that.'

'That is precisely my concern,' Simon sighed, his despair rising like an incoming tide to consume him, his gut wrenched with the most violent tension.

Miaoulis brought his speech to an end with his final rousing declaration, 'I AM SAILING... in the morning... to serve the Turks out, TO KILL THEM... THE VILE DOGS THAT THEY ARE!'

After this, the admiral's apparent conclusion and his self-evidently heartfelt feelings, there was an eruption of vibrant chatter amongst the crew, a general consensus with Miaoulis's sentiments, a widespread groundswell of loud approval arising and a vigorous babble of endorsement, many arms raised with clenched fists, an increasing number of shouts of 'HUZZAY!'

Miaoulis, noting with plentiful satisfaction the effect of his words, unexpectedly raised his arms again to capture the attention of the crowd once more, 'MEN OF SURPRISE... FRIENDS... COMRADES... will you seek vengeance for your dead brothers?' Absolute silence for just the briefest of seconds before came more muttering about Jelbert. 'WILL YOU?' and in lower voice, 'Do you care to sail... to sail with me?' Jason, struggling hard, still persevering in full voice and quite frantic in his efforts to keep up with the admiral - with the rising tone of anger within the Greek's voice - translated, his own voice all but failing him, his sore throat harshly protesting, 'Will you see the Turk smashed, his ships burned and sunk? Do you care to see that? Eh? What do you say?' Miaoulis concluded with a passionate cry, 'WHAT SAY YOU ALL?'

Pat, Duncan and Simon looked on in utter disbelief: two hundred fists were waving in the air, two hundred voices were shouting; indeed, all the men in sight were screaming in raucous confirmation of the admiral's fiery sentiments. From the front, a big man climbed upon the capstan and shouted with all his voice, 'THREE CHEERS FOR THE ADMIRAL!' Clumsy Dalby did not care to pronounce Miaoulis's name, his confidence did not extend that far, 'THREE CHEERS! HIP! HIP!'

The bellow of reply was unanimous: from two hundred throats came the tumultuous roar of 'HUZZAY!'

'HIP! HIP!' Dalby, precariously wobbling, waved both his arms in the air.

'HUZZAY!'

'HIP! HIP!' Dalby, much excited, slipped off the capstan into the arms of his friends, Fisher and Mason.

'HUZZAY!'

'Well, what to do, eh? Will we take that man's name, Duncan?' whispered Pat at last, for he could not believe his eyes, certainly could never have conceived of the reaction of his men.

'I think ye will need to take the name of every man aboard the barky,' muttered Duncan quietly, astonished but finding himself much pleased by the unexpected turn of events, by the vociferous and general support of the men for Miaoulis.

The admiral, visibly gratified, raised both his arms again, the hubbub dying away, 'I thank you... every man... with all my heart. THANK YOU! THANK YOU!' There was a final cheer before bedlam erupted, a hundred conversations all concurrent, and Miaoulis turned towards a dumbfounded Pat, who was still striving to grasp what he had seen, what he would never have believed had it only been described to him: here before him was the evidence, the reason, that Miaoulis was the accepted commander of all Greek naval resources; the man truly was a considerable way beyond exceptional, and all who encountered him soon came to realise it.

Pat's gravest dilemma was resolved, his fear of protest had been dispelled, and his spirits swiftly rose within him. A great relief, a lift within his heart and mind surged up, bringing huge cheer to wash away his anxiety. His trepidation fast fading, he seized and shook Miaoulis's hand vigorously for a long minute, the two men staring at each other with a fiery renaissance of mutual respect, with the affinity of one fighting man for another. At last, Pat turned to his men, all his hesitations now vanished, his own voice resolute, 'LADS!' The hubbub gradually died down. 'LADS! LADS, WE ARE SAILING WITH ADMIRAL MIAOULIS!' Another huge cheer of accord erupted, only fading away as Pat raised his hands again, 'BUT FIRST... we must hasten to remedy her damages...' The deck erupted again into chatter, every man talking to his fellows, a vibrant turmoil of fifty concurrent conversations overwhelming Pat's intentions of saying more.

'LADS,' Pat, his mind still racing, resumed eventually, 'LADS... we will be with Admiral Miaoulis's squadron... but on his quarter, a watching guard. We ain't got the powder... nor the shot to do more...' The loud hubbub continued within the crew, a hundred men speaking at once. Miaoulis and his aides looked on, as did Duncan and Simon, the latter horrified at the turn of events, his face betraying fearful feelings which he could not conceal in the slightest.

'I must away, Captain O'Connor, for my own preparations,' pronounced Miaoulis at last, 'You have my grateful thanks. We will depart in the morning. If the Turk does lie at Modon and we catch him with the onshore wind which I anticipate, I believe we can strike hard... will gain a notable victory. It is in my contemplation that we shall truly achieve a day of glory... and I am greatly pleased that your ship will be with my squadron... Indeed, sir, I am humbled by your men.'

'As am I... *as am I*... Goodbye, sir,' said Pat, no other words could he find, the profound sense of disbelief lingering.

The admiral stepped to the side, Duncan and Jason in close attendance, ten more minutes passing as they talked further before the admiral clambered down the ladder to his caique.

Pat, meanwhile, shouted to the noisy crowd. He strived unsuccessfully to bring order and quietude to the deck. Failing, as a last resort, he sent Dalby up to the quarterdeck to vigorously ring the ship's bell, the shrill, violent clanging rapidly delivering silence.

'What to do with the broken yards?' murmured Pat. 'Mr Tizard?' Pat cast about him, his eyes eventually finding the ship's carpenter in the front rank of his men, 'Can ye fix the broken yards in the hours we have left to us this day?'

All eyes turned to Stuart Tizard, the carpenter plainly more than a little bewildered by the attention upon him. No conceivable alternative reply available to him, he shouted, 'Aye, sir.' Another roar rose up from the men.

'Mr Sampays...' Pat looked to his bosun, 'can ye remedy her sails?'

'Aye, sir, after a fashion like, though they ain't going to be at their best.' A more measured reply and a more muted chorus followed this time, the truth of the bosun's words sinking in with many, a little of the earlier enthusiasm fading; returning reality was extending its probing fingers, beginning to strike home.

'GO TO YOUR DUTIES!' shouted Pat over the enduring raucous babble. 'Mr Codrington, signal *Eleanor*; Mr Mower is to take off all our wounded without delay.' He turned to Simon, 'I venture we may yet need you with the barky on the morrow, and so I cannot consider of you shifting to *Eleanor*.' The surgeon's face was a picture of abject dismay, no words could he find. 'Will you be happy if Marston alone attends the wounded?'

Simon gazed at his friend with a face of the utmost reprobation, 'Happy? Why I doubt I will be happy until I set foot once more upon the blessed quay at Tobermory. As for the men with Marston, yes... there is no wound beyond his care; thankfully, all the unfortunates are removed from peril.'

'I beg you will attend them directly... without the loss of a moment, for Mower will be here within the hour, and I must ask that the men are disembarked the minute he arrives.'

'Of course, I will go downstairs... I will speak with Marston and Jason. We will prepare the necessary medicines for the men.'

Pat nodded his gratitude, prepared to break off, but paused to speak his few words of reassurance, 'Simon, it ain't in my contemplation to fight the ship... you do understand that?'

The surgeon stared for a long, uncomfortable moment, eventually offering the coldest of reply, 'Heat not a furnace for your foe so hot that it do singe yourself.'

'Eh?'

'*Shakespeare*... on revenge. It is a dangerous game, brother; I most dearly hope that all these men do not come to regret it.'

'The Turk has killed our men... *has killed Jelbert*, and I heard it from a deal of voices... before us, on the deck; the lads have said it plain: they wish to serve the Turk out. I am, myself, minded it is more akin to *retribution*... and here is the chance.'

'And before you embark on a journey of revenge... *before you embark*... dig *two* graves,' said Simon in little more than a whisper. Pat simply stared, mute. '*Confucius*,' added Simon. He halted abruptly as he started for the companionway, turning back with a puzzled look, 'Marshal Grouchy's aid to Wellington?'

'At Waterloo, his arrival in time... the battle in question.'

'I venture you meant Marshal Blücher.' With that his last word Simon turned away, intending to hasten to his patients, a vile consternation raging within him.

Pat, in turmoil himself, dismayed, wound up, excited and thoughtful, paced towards the forward companionway, to where his men had begun to drag spare canvas up from the sail loft. He walked amongst them, exchanging a brief word here and there with several, a frenzied cutting of scabby, well worn cloth already underway. He continued up to the forepeak where the carpenter and his assistants were already sawing timber with which to make temporary repairs to the broken yards. After a few minutes he walked slowly aft the length of his ship, staring closely at everything in passing, and he stepped up to his quarterdeck. Duncan was there and gazing at the approaching schooner, *Eleanor*. She was still flagged as English, and as such could reasonably expect unhindered passage through Greek waters, Turk and Egyptian ships of war not likely to trouble her. It was a small advantage, for she could fetch and carry both wounded, stores and communications without let or hindrance.

Twenty minutes passed and *Eleanor* came alongside; her lieutenant commanding, James Mower, scrambled up the ladder. Wounded most seriously in the first battle to defend Samos, shrapnel in both his legs, in one arm and his chest, he had been nursed to health over a protracted period of many months of recuperation in Cephalonia. The English-governed Ionian island had been the adopted base for *Surprise* when she had first arrived in Greek waters; both Pat and Duncan's wives, together with their children, had established a house in Metaxata, and there they had cared for the wounded of the frigate's battles.

'Mr Mower, there you are!' exclaimed Pat, seizing and shaking his hand. 'How do you fare? I hope I see you well.' Of all the people dismayed by the loss of Mathew Jelbert, Mower had been particularly struck hard, for the old gunner, more than anyone else, had sought to encourage the junior lieutenant whilst he was recuperating, cajoling him to strive constantly to recover his fitness, ever urging him on whilst offering comforting words when he struggled, weak with his wounds; to the extent that all aboard the ship had concluded that Jelbert had, *unofficially*, adopted the young officer as someone akin to a substitute for his own dead son. At Jelbert's funeral, an emotional Mower, whilst reading the tributes, had completely broken down, visibly streaming tears, recovering only with considerable difficulty to complete the oration.

'Plentifully well, sir,' declared Mower, pleased with his captain's so personal greeting and stretching the truth a long mile, for his wounds troubled him still although he strived not to let that show, and he had been most disappointed to exchange, on Pat's order, with Codrington when the latter lieutenant had formerly commanded *Eleanor*.

'We are sailing in the morning,' said Pat, 'to aid the Greeks. It is Miaoulis's intention to catch the Turk fleet with an adverse wind, a south-easter, against which their ships will be unable to leave the harbour at Modon. He believes... as we have oft remarked... that such is the customary wind direction in the late afternoon at this time of year. We will be... we will be *with* his squadron...' Pat could not but notice Mower's raised eyebrows, his look of astonishment. 'That is to say, the barky will be sailing as... *as an observer*... a scout.' Mower nodded cautiously, could offer no response. 'You are to embark all our wounded aboard *Eleanor* within the hours remaining to us this afternoon, and you will remain with us on the morrow... at a far distance, a league or more, standing off in case of any need.' Pat did not care to elaborate on that. 'For the moment, please to see Doctor Ferguson about shifting the sick... *the wounded*, if you will.'

'Of course, sir,' Mower nodded again, hesitated for a moment as if to see if Pat deigned to tell him anything else but, his captain's attention self-evidently shifting elsewhere, he hastened below without further words.

Pat, his mind consumed with practical matters, determined upon an inspection of his armament; he stepped down and walked the length of the gun deck once more, past the galley and so to the bow, looking for but seeing no shot at any of the great guns: things truly were in a parlous state. He descended the companionway to the lower deck, glanced towards the wounded in passing: Simon was already engaged serving the casualties. He hurried on, in case he might catch his surgeon's unwanted attention, down to the orlop.

Striving to ignore the foul air and the stench rising from the bilges, he went first to the forward magazine to assess the quantity of powder remaining. A cursory inspection, the magazine deserted, revealed his worst fears were entirely well-founded: one barrel was marked "sulphur", which he did not care to examine, but only a half barrel of powder remained. Gently lifting the loosened lid, it was plain it was old stock, visible traces of damp evident within it, the powder lumpy. He felt sure it must long ago have been condemned for use only for salutes.

His thoughts turned to the aft magazine and he pondered going back up to and along the lower deck, but he very much did not wish to encounter his disgruntled surgeon so soon. He stared, apprehensively, down the steps to the hold; even in the dim gloom he could see it was visibly awash with a foot of water, sloshing noisily as the frigate rolled gently on the slight swell, straw strands awash on the surface. The ever-present sound of the hand pumps, a continuous clunking noise and unceasingly repetitive, struck an unwelcome reminder of the many leaks in the hull. Pat pinched his nostrils closed with his fingers and drew short breaths through his mouth; he near gagged on the vile stink which filled the air, foetid and deeply unpleasant. He looked to the water with a deep reluctance but, his mind made up, set firmly against a meeting with Simon in passing in case he was pressed to declare to his friend the truly parlous state of ammunition and powder, he stepped with a grimace down into the uninviting black water of the bilges, intending to hasten through it the length of the ship.

The water was colder than he had anticipated, immediately chilling his legs to near his knees and, as he picked his way very carefully through the muck and filth below the water, the most unpleasant smell arose from it. Pat reflected that many of the wounded were too injured to venture as far as the heads to relieve themselves. 'Murphy will not be best pleased,' he thought absently as his pale trousers were immediately soaked to far above his knees and stained brown by the noxious liquid. Lit only by lanterns at the fore and aft hatchways, the light was poor, and so his steps were halting, his stance precarious; several times he tripped and just managed to prevent himself tumbling into the stinking filth. At the far end he could see a man crouching low in the water near the aft companionway. 'What on earth would he be doing?' he wondered. Picking his way carefully and regretting - the cold further chilling him - that he had not walked the length of the lower deck or even returned to the gun deck, Pat carefully approached the man in the water: it was Clumsy Dalby.

Dalby was a man for whom Pat always had mixed feelings. He was, as his nickname suggested, neither particularly agile - a useful trait on a sailing ship - nor indeed was he blessed with a surfeit of intelligence, and hence he was a man who regularly appeared on the Wednesday punishment parades. Yet, for all his failings, Dalby had qualities too; indeed, it was Dalby who had rescued Simon off the island of Kasos when the surgeon had been left behind, the frigate fleeing before an approaching Turk squadron; Dalby had been ashore with that search party which had eventually escorted Simon and Marston - with a crowd of refugees - to safety when pursued by raging Turk beserkers keen on their capture and death. Dalby had also saved Pat's own life, when he was in the process of being washed overboard, exhausted and powerless to help himself, during the worst of the hurricane as a damaged and sinking *Surprise* fought to reach home, to make Falmouth in the prior November.

'Dalby!' exclaimed Pat, curious, 'What are you doing down here... in this murk and filth?'

The giant stood up, shaking water from all about him, every stitch of his clothing soaked. 'Sir...' Dalby spat and shook the water from his hands, 'Mr Macleod sent me, sir... to look to the shot lockers...'

'I see... and did you find many of shot, tell?'

'No, sir, the lockers all be empty, but 'ere be about two score of ball in the bilges... All be long discarded by the gunners... That is to say, they be with defects.'

'Very good... and where are they... the shot?'

'I have carried 'em up as far as the lower deck, sir; Mason and Fisher be there, with 'em, cleaning off the rust afore we shift 'em to the guns.'

'Thank you, Dalby; *well done*, you have my best thanks.'

'Thankee, sir.' Dalby smiled a near toothless grin and shifted aside as Pat squeezed past him.

Pat stepped on, thankfully moving quickly up and out of the wet murk of the hold and to the aft magazine, finding two more of his men there, bagging into ready-use, six-pound sacks the contents of the one remaining barrel present, which at least had the look of dry powder about it. He stared all around the tiny copper-lined room, to every corner, noted a score more of filled sacks on the shelves. Chegwin and Penrose stopped filling and looked to their captain.

'Is that it, lads? Would that be all our powder?' The answer could hardly be in the negative for Pat had never seen the magazine so severely depleted.

'Aye, sir, that it is,' said Chegwin, 'Precious little... I dare say enough for two broadsides, sir... but no more.' His voice tailed off, not wishing to further dash his captain's hopes, Pat's face a picture of disappointment.

'On my life, we are sorely served,' whispered Pat. 'Carry on, lads.' He stepped out, his thoughts returning to a disagreeable recollection of Simon's prior cautionary words. 'Two broadsides... powder *and* shot... Why, here's a pretty kettle of fish,' he muttered to himself. He continued up the companionway steps to the lower deck, casting an inquisitive glance the length of the ship. Simon and Marston were both still engaged with their charges. Freeman - as was usual - was helping with his own attentive care, his good nature so greatly appreciated by his wounded shipmates. Pat's second steward was always a welcome presence with the surgeons.

A little later, in the early afternoon, dinner in the cabin came and went in silence, Pat eating alone, no sign of his usual table companion, Simon. He presumed that the surgeon was still engrossed in preparing the wounded to disembark aboard *Eleanor*. His meal passed largely unnoticed, without any of his customary satisfaction, an oppressive weight settling upon his mind as he steadily chewed his food, a grave concern occupying all his thoughts: the question of whether he had said the right thing to Miaoulis. Certainly, the enthusiastic reaction of his men had wholly surprised him, he could hardly believe it even now, but then Mathew Jelbert had been the most popular man aboard the ship. Perhaps a sense of injustice and a consequent thirst for revenge was understandable; after all, his men were not philosophers, almost all of them had received no education whatsoever, no learnings above what a Cornish youngster might absorb from his parents and his fellows; and yet he had always found them to be men of principle, a fundamental integrity common to them all, including even regular miscreants such as Dalby. And perhaps too that was the foundation of their passion: a determination to serve out those who had blighted them, who had brought about their grievous loss. 'Was that so very wrong?' Pat muttered aloud to himself. He sighed; he hoped with all his heart that his decision to help the Greeks once more, *Surprise* in such poor shape, so ill-equipped, her men so greatly fatigued, would not come back to haunt him.

The quietude of evening eventually arrived to overtake the afternoon, a splendid sunset going wholly unnoticed by Pat, still sitting at his table, deeply engrossed in thoughts of the morrow, a morose anxiety never far from his feelings. Would God protect them? He had no idea and held precious little belief in the Almighty. Perhaps Marston might offer something useful there?

His mind drifted to images of his wife, to his children, all such thoughts unsettling him further. He dearly loved them all, and he prayed with every vestige, with the tiniest remnant of all the hope he still possessed, indeed clung to with a passion, that the next day would see him and all his men preserved. Murphy, much concerned for his silent captain, entered with the coffee, Pat deigning a wave of thanks but no words. Another half-hour of difficult reflection and he settled upon his cot. An hour more passing and, failing to sleep, vivid conjectures whirling in his mind, he resigned himself to what might be; the new day would doubtless bring what it would and there was precious little he could do about that now: the mortal die was cast.

Thursday 12th May 1825   05:00   Calamata

The first inkling of the new day was not so much bright light as an emerging and gentle diffusion of grey; swathes of deep, dark shades were becoming faintly discernible, low in the eastern sky, slowly and inexorably climbing to prise away the night's enduring black grip. The sparkling profusion of stars were becoming less brilliant, dulling and fading incrementally as lighter shades seized a determined hold on the morning, many a man's dream ceding to apprehension in the waiting, expectant eyes of four score of the crew, the men of the morning watch sitting and dozing unobtrusively in somnolent reflection all along the frigate's scarred side, waiting patiently for the call to weigh anchor; even the brief and unusually gentle ringing of two bells seemed subdued, mournful even to the fanciful mind.

Pat had passed a sleepless night, a degree of trepidation about the forthcoming day, about Miaoulis's intentions, seizing all his thoughts whilst he turned over and over within his cot. He had resigned himself to sleeplessness long before the dawn, and with a feeling of resignation he stepped up to his quarterdeck, a muted greeting offered to the handful of men on watch. He was a passionate astronomer and stepped across to stand at the rail, sparing himself a few minutes before engaging in his duties. He stared upwards, gazing towards the heavens, its marvels fast fading, until he became aware of a silent Simon, who had

41

appeared at his side. Concerned for his friend, still self-evidently in an excruciating state of unhappiness, and cognisant of the fears plainly pressing upon them both, Pat strived for a cheering voice, 'A penny for your thoughts.' This was offered in a whisper, as if he did not dare to break the enduring contemplation of them both, not wishing to shatter the serenity of the emerging dawn, the sense of peacefulness all about them certain to be short-lived and of such great value to Pat himself in that precious moment.

'A penny... a penny indeed... most generous of you and, I venture, strikingly innovative.' The surgeon, barefoot and dressed only in a nightshirt, scowled but offered nothing more. He shivered in the slight, chill breeze, little warmth in the dawn so far; the light, just passing the cusp between the twilight and the dawn proper, was holding to that strange air of crystal clarity the Mediterranean alone seems to possess.

'Oh,' Pat sighed, 'as a lad in Connemara a penny was greatly valued and never spurned, oh no; and as for amassing the very great fortune of twelve of them, why, I could only dream of possessing a shilling... and as for a pound... now there was wealth for you, and far beyond my imagination it was!' Pat laughed out loud at the memory, the tiny relief that it presented.

Simon nodded, the bare trace of his own smile registering in Pat's scrutiny, and standing together they gazed across the bay, the indistinct shapes of a score of Greek brigs becoming ever clearer as the sun peeked higher over the mountains of the Mani.

'Brother, I beg your pardon...' murmured Simon.

'Eh? For what?'

'I spoke to you yesterday intemperately... on the regrettable nature of revenge... and man's passion for it.'

'Oh that, no, never in life; I paid it no mind. I venture you spoke the truth of the matter... were in the right of things.'

A silent minute more passed before Simon spoke again, 'Do you reflect, brother... in the brief spells of tranquillity such as this? Do you wonder... have fears for what this day might bring... for our shipmates, for all your men... *for yourself perhaps?*'

Pat sighed deeply, a long, long exhalation, his face wholly in sympathy with his feelings, 'Every day, old friend... not a one passes without I am in contemplation of what might befall us... all of us... and many a night I dream...' Another heartfelt sigh, 'That is to say, I am on occasion beset by nightmares.'

'I make no doubt that must be the most unwelcome affliction.'

'Why, for sure it is. In my sleep I sometimes recall the faces of those shipmates we have lost... Jelbert being only the latest of many. It is something of a... a *black* burden. In those hours... in the moments when I awaken I... I endeavour to turn my thoughts elsewhere... I dally in my cot - in discomfort, I grant you - seeking sleep again... I dream... *I imagine* a Galway hooker... sails filled and pressing her far over, flying in a westerly... out to the Arans...' Pat's face lost the mask of strain for the first time, '... or a calm day off the Gannoughs in a currach with rod and line... a brace of salmon in the basket for supper... Fergal with me and homeward bound... to my dear Sinéad... ' a wistful smile, '... for a supper by the fire... sitting in the warmth of the peat, a glass of whiskey at hand. Oh for such happy days, eh?'

'I would dearly wish to be with you in those precious hours... in those places of blessed sanctuary, I would so,' Simon spoke very quietly, his heartfelt aspiration plain in his voice. Another long pause, 'Tell me, is it ever in your mind to consider for how long we will endure... *will persevere* with this accursed Greek venture?'

'Oh, as for that... there is nothing to be done, save to fight... to fight this ship... *our ship*... to fight the barky. In Devonport I made my decision... that man Jelbert again, eh... and I am here, *we are here*... all of us, with the Greeks; we are bound to them... come rain or shine. One might venture that we are in the lap of the gods... *Greek gods now*... and precious little do I know of them,' Pat managed a weak laugh.

Simon sighed, an air of resignation overtaking him; plainly Pat's thinking was not to be shifted, at least not far and not today. 'Then let us hope we do not encounter that demonic sea goddess and are turned to stone.'

'Sea goddess?'

'The fearsome Medusa.'

'The gorgonzola?'

'The Greeks are hauling anchors, sir,' shouted Codrington in loud voice, sparing Simon any reply, his wit quite failing him.

'And so will we, Mr Codrington!' declared Pat. 'The time has come; carry on, rouse out the men!'

'Yes sir. Dalby, strike the bell!' Three bells rang out, loud, strident, so piercing that Pat thought the clanging must be heard on the distant Calamata quay. At once those men who were lingering over breakfast remnants at the galley began to pour from the companionways as Codrington barked out the most stentorian orders for preparations to get underway, three score of men climbing aloft to let fall the sails, others taking station to haul on the braces, two dozen and more moving to stand ready to push on the capstans.

'Do you care to join me in the cabin for breakfast?' murmured Pat, 'I venture Murphy might care to appear presently... to grace us with his attendance.'

'Yes, yes... thank you. I will attend presently... after I look to my patients...' Simon halted, recollecting that his wounded charges had disembarked to *Eleanor*. 'Yes, I will be there *directly*...' He hesitated, ran his fingers over his chin, '... though first I may shave, it is the week or more since I was blessed with the convenience of the least time to spare.'

'And perhaps you might look to your shirt?' offered Pat, the rare opportunity presenting itself, rather tentatively pushing the proverbial boat out in the friendliest of voice.

'Yes, yes I will; I blush to say that it has been in my contemplation to shift my clothes these two or three days... There is a deal of dried blood on my shirt and breeches. Murphy remarked it at breakfast yesterday.'

'Did he not also mention your old coat? I collect he was minded to suggest - *I venture it was when you was wearing it at dinner* - that it too would much benefit from a wash.'

'The wicked dog!'

Pat smiled, enjoying the moment and speaking with utter abandon, 'Indeed, in the broad daylight, it would seem he was in the right of things there... Why, have you been serving in the bilges... perhaps shifting coal for the cabin stove, tell?'

'I have not; the man is a fanatic... a confounded nuisance, he is so; the coat is perfectly... perfectly...' a searching look of scrutiny and a faltering conclusion which did not, to Pat's ear, ring true, 'Why, it will serve for an age yet.'

'Never mind, I beg pardon. I'm sure it will,' Pat's lying words wholly lacked conviction, his face telling a different story, which did not escape Simon.

His friend still looking extremely doubtful, the merest hint of condemnation enduring in his countenance, Simon continued in apologetic voice, 'Take note I do not care to wear it when I am attending my patients...' The plain look of disbelief crossed Pat's face, '... save perhaps for the more minor of procedures... a foot coming off and suchlike.'

Pat blanched, as far as such was discernible beneath his deep tan, and decided to steer for more comfortable waters, 'Where is the infernal man, Murphy, this morning? Breakfast is disgracefully late. Will you excuse me, Simon? I must go and look to matters on deck.'

Within five minutes the anchors were catted and fished, within ten the frigate was shifting slowly, wind abeam, her course one point west of south, picking up speed as she strived to catch up with the Greeks, *Surprise* already a mile in the train of Miaoulis's fleet, underway since the dawn. Pat stared through his glass to count twenty-six Greek brigs; he was minded that it was certainly a determined coalition of naval resources. He passed a few more minutes in looking all about him from the quarterdeck rail, observing that his ship's patched yards and repaired mizzen topmast seemed to be holding their own, though whether they would endure in much more than the present extremely gentle wind he did not much care to speculate. He looked to his men at the helm, stared momentarily at the master and the bosun, every man steadfast, determination writ upon their faces, confidence exuded generally; solid, imperturbable steadfasts, all of them. 'Would any captain ever be served by better men?' the striking thought lodged firm in his mind. He much doubted that, although, his stomach rumbling, he did harbour momentary doubts about his steward particularly, a few black words going unsaid. He took heart from his conclusion, nodding to Barton at the helm as he stepped past him and thence down the companionway to the gun deck. He looked along the length of it: men were already working at the great guns - their tompions had been removed - swabbing barrels clean, oiling trucks with slush begged from the galley, and strapping spare breeching ropes to better secure the guns in their ferocious recoil. He watched for a minute or two his lieutenants, moving all about the men with a nod here and a word there. His own enduring consternation of the night ebbing at last, he stepped through the coach and into the great cabin, Murphy appearing as if from nowhere and already on his heels with the flask. To Pat's great delight both Simon and Duncan were sitting at his table and engaged in conversation. He took his seat, grateful for the company of his friends and for the hot coffee, nodding his thanks to his steward even as his face exuded his confusion of pleasure and concerns.

'Well, will 'ee care for burgoo for breakfast, sorrs?' shouted Murphy as he exited the cabin without so much as a glance to the table, no opportunity offered for anyone to countermand his declaration. No one was inclined to do so, all their thoughts were focused on other, more worrying anxieties.

'That will serve, Murphy, ye rogue!' shouted Pat, to no avail for the door had crashed shut. He turned to his companions, another subject coming to mind, one that he had enjoyed no time to think or speak about, 'Duncan, did you find time to speak with Mower in Calamata?'

'Aye, we passed an hour on the quay... after Mavrocordato rushed away to look for the gold... to seek out the two villains, Peddler and Perkis... to ask their story.'

'What did Mower have to say, tell?'

'Perkis had declared to him... *to Mower...* that the gold must be offloaded from *Eleanor* in anticipation that the schooner would not serve... likely could not be made available to deliver it to its final destination; and so Mower brought her alongside the quay, when a shifty set of Greeks toiled to unload the gold. Mower's offer of the assistance of his own men was declined by Perkis. Mower suggested that all parties would be better served if the gold remained in *Eleanor's* hold until Mavrocordato himself arrived... or the barky did... but he was ignored.' Duncan halted for a draught of his coffee. Pat, deep in thought, stared.

'Pray continue,' interjected Simon, Peddler being a life-long friend from his childhood. The theft, as all had believed, of the Tsar's half-million pounds of gold, a loan to Greece, was still a matter he found astonishing, his revered friend's participation in the crime utterly astounding him. It had been carefully concealed in iron-plated disguise as ballast ingots and conveyed to Greece aboard *Surprise* before being offloaded to her tender when the frigate had been trapped in the bay of Navarino, and thence it had finally been delivered to Calamata aboard *Eleanor*.

'Mower shifted *Eleanor* off the quay and anchored her a cable away, the port always busy, plenty of Greek merchantmen and armed brigs coming and going. His further offer to station a guard of four armed men - half his crew - with the gold on the quay overnight was also declined by Perkis. In the morning he found no sign of anything, nothing remaining at all, no gold, and Perkis and Peddler had both gone. Neither could he find anyone to tell him when they had left nor to where.'

'Damn thieves,' exclaimed Pat, smacking his empty cup upon the table with vehemence. 'And what would I have reported to Melville, eh?'

'Thankfully, there is no necessity for that since Mr Sampay's exceedingly fortunate intervention,' said Simon with an audible degree of reservation, reluctant even now to condemn his childhood friend. 'We must be grateful for his shifting of the gold elsewhere... downstairs... at the bottom of this vessel... *the orlop* would it be? We must be thankful that the scoundrels made off in blessed error... with worthless iron metal.'

'Aye, that we must,' echoed Duncan emphatically, 'and when we do catch up with them... *when we do*, I venture it will give me great pleasure to ask their explanation; aye, indeed it will... the damnable rogues!'

'For sure it will,' said Pat wearily, tiring of the story about the abortive theft of the Tsar's gold, more pressing matters returning to mind. 'So, to today, eh? Duncan, the mistico that came alongside last night... I saw it approach, looking out the stern gallery; I heard the commotion as it came alongside... and the voices, of course, but I was so damnably tired that I stayed in my cot. What was that about?'

'Miaoulis sent his gift, a half-dozen barrels of powder and three score of shot... which he said was suited to our guns. Apparently, his brig possesses of a brace of 18-pounders. Mind you, the gunner... that is to say *Timmins*... you will collect that he was the friend of Jelbert... was not greatly impressed with the shot. There is a deal of rust which is being cleaned off, but it will serve... aye, it will have to serve.'

'Let us not look a Greek horse in the mouth, eh?' declared Pat. 'D'ye hear, Simon... a Greek horse... Hah! Hah!'

'And perhaps we should beware of Greeks bearing gifts?' muttered Simon, frowning.

'No, no... thanks be to Saint Patrick, his blessings are upon us: powder and shot from Miaoulis; that is the most welcome of news,' continued Pat emphatically. Simon remained silent, his thoughts plunged back into rekindled consternation.

A crash and Murphy returned, kicking open the door, his hands clutching a large tray with three steaming bowls upon it. 'Vittles is up, sorrs,' he declared in loud voice. Pat conceded the scent was satisfying and decided against any reprimand; he knew his steward would pay little heed to it save to sulk, when all subsequent meals would surely be delayed and likely arrive cold.

'Ahhh, oats...' cried Duncan with relish, 'A taste of the Isles, eh? What do you say... Simon? Oats... aye, 'tis burgoo!'

'The porridge does indeed smell delectable, a most pleasing aroma. Thank you, Murphy.' Simon's smile was a welcome relief for Pat.

Ten minutes later and the porridge all consumed with nothing more from Murphy, Pat reluctantly presumed that the burgoo had been his breakfast ration in full. He rose from the table, 'Let us go up, gentlemen.'

Murphy returned in that instant, empty handed. Pat scowled at him as they passed in the door, 'Murphy, *man does not live by burgoo alone*... ain't you heard of that famous notion? I am mortal hungry still... A few eggs, a tray of sausages perhaps... either would have served very well. D'ye hear?' Murphy affected to take not the least notice, scowled, looked away and busied himself about the table, his low muttering going unheard by all.

On the quarterdeck, the weather was fine and sunny, little cloud visible. The day was warming, pleasantly so, but the wind remained feeble. Though it was a south-easterly, it would be many an hour before they reached Modon. Pat wondered whether they would still find the Turk ships there. Gazing forward, he noted that *Surprise* had caught up with the Greeks, and she lingered close in their wake, all vessels making no better than three knots. He contented himself with the benign weather as the frigate smoothly sailed on, uninterrupted hours passing in steady progress, little heel in the mildest of winds, the sea calm, the most trifling of gentle swell hardly rocking the frigate in the slightest. All along the decks, at the tops and through opened gun ports, two hundred men gazed out to every point on the horizon, watching, staring, not a man off-duty caring to try for sleep. That they were sailing once more towards a battle in such benevolent weather conditions and mild sea state whilst near wholly bereft of powder and shot seemed wholly incongruous to many a mind, but the determination shown to join with Miaoulis lingered still, numerous conversations all about the ship overheard by the passing officers. A score of hands applied themselves to practical tasks: chipping rust from shot, stacking the cleaned cannonballs in the ready-use racks, and all the time a small rota of concerned men at the carpenter's direction constantly climbed the rigging to anxiously assess the state of the repaired yards and mast, the constant creaking loud and concerning, and to look to the fragile sail repairs, the sailmaker himself in a permanent state of nervous apprehension.

'Good morning, Mr Sampays,' said Pat pleasantly to the bosun, standing near the helm. 'Be so good as to pass the word for Timmins.'

'Aye aye, sir,' Sampays replied. 'Green... Green there! Find Timmins... he is wanted by the captain.'

A few minutes passed and Timmins appeared. 'Timmins, there you are,' declared Pat in encouraging voice. 'I am minded... minded that... with no gunner...' Pat swallowed hard, 'That is to say... since we are no longer blessed to have Mr Jelbert with us...' The eyes of every man on the quarterdeck, helmsmen and officers all, turned to stare at Pat, all ears instantly attentive. 'Mr Macleod speaks well of you, and I choose to appoint you to... to Mr Jelbert's position.' A silent Timmins unmoving, evidently thinking hard, Pat continued, 'It ain't official, of course... there is no warrant... not as yet, but I will be obliged if ye will serve as master gunner.'

'I will, sir,' declared Timmins, breaking into a huge smile, 'yes, 'tis an honour, it is so... and thankee; thankee, sir; I will do my best.'

Shouts of congratulation broke out from a score of men who had heard the exchange, for Timmins was popular in the crew; all aboard knew he had been a close friend of Jelbert, and he was a proficient gunner, perhaps the best in the ship. A half-dozen of his shipmates were immediately patting him on the back, the news spreading along the deck, many more men shouting vocal congratulations from afar.

Pat was pleased; he offered his hand, his pleasure evident. 'Well done, you have my best thanks.' The loud hubbub of widespread applause died down as Duncan intervened, holding up his hands in a call for silence, cognizant that Pat wished to speak. 'Thank you, Mr Macleod,' said Pat. He turned his attention back to Timmins, 'I collect that you worked with Mr Jelbert to fabricate the incendiary munitions... the explosive shells we fired in the bay.'

'Yes sir, I did so, working under his direction.'

'All were fired? Is that so?'

'Every one, sir.'

'I see,' Pat paused in reflection, adding after a moment, 'Those shells saved our bacon... saved the barky. Without them I doubt... *I am sure* we would not have escaped the bay.' The loud gathering of men who had coalesced around Timmins on the quarterdeck was reduced to silence. 'Would you think... is it... is it within your grasp to make some more?' His question posed, Pat stared intensely at Timmins.

'Well, there is a dozen or more we didn't finish... perhaps a score... no time to do so. Why, yes sir, I think it could be done... given plentiful time... and if there was no want of powder. There is the one barrel of sulphur still... in the for'ard magazine.'

'Excellent,' cried Pat. 'Please to start, lose not a moment. Mr Macleod, Timmins is to work solely on fabrication of the shells, and with all the help he requires. As to powder, you are to use one barrel of that which Miaoulis has gifted us.'

'Aye aye, sir,' Duncan nodded. 'Mr Sampays, you are to clear all... *everything*... from the bosun's store; the dozen shells are to be shifted there and the powder is to be moved to the for'ard magazine where Timmins will work. Am I plain?'

'Perfectly clear, sir,' the bosun hastened away with Timmins.

The morning passed in the incongruous ambience of tranquillity, *Surprise* closely trailing the Greek brigs, no Turk nor even any other vessel ever coming in sight, a still distant Koroni on the starboard bow at noon, the wind freshening a little as the morning ceded to the afternoon and yet more hours of slow progress under a bright, burning sun. When Dalby rang five bells in his customary strident fashion, it started a deeply pre-occupied Pat from his thoughts. He went below for a late dinner, Simon accompanying him whilst Duncan remained on watch.

'Pat, were you minded that Benjamin Peddler was a swindler?' Simon's words at the table were hesitant, as if he did not much care for an answer in the affirmative, Peddler being his childhood friend of many years.

'As to that, why... I failed to reach any conclusion, but as far as his friend Perkis is concerned, I would watch my last penny if he was about.'

'I always thought of Benjamin Peddler as a brother...'

Pat set down his knife and fork, and took a draught from his wine, 'It may be that he... Peddler, I mean, was influenced by Perkis. I doubt we will see either man again; indeed, I hope not... and 'tis a long way home from these parts.' He smiled, 'I would give a month's pay to see their faces when they find out they have stolen only *proper* ballast... iron pigs... *only iron*, eh! Hah! Hah!'

Chapter Three

Cape Akritas was passed at two bells of the first dog watch, *Surprise* making slow progress on a beam reach. Duncan, in command, observed the general change of course of the Greek fleet. 'We will bear away, Mr Pickering. We will follow the Greeks.'

'Aye aye, sir.'

Surprise began her turn to the north-west behind the brigs, all now running directly for Modon, the south-easterly wind astern but still weak. 'Square the yards, Mr Pickering,' ordered Duncan, the Surprises hastening to haul on the braces.

'Both sheets aft, sir,' reported Pickering a few minutes later. The frigate glided on, not the slightest of heel discernible.

Pat emerged on the quarterdeck, Simon accompanying him. The two men took up position near the stern rail to look all about them. 'Mr Macleod,' declared Pat, 'let us fly our best *Greek* colours aloft if you please.' He looked all about him; his men without exception were holding to the prior confidence and determination he had observed all day. 'Mr Codrington, would you care to see if Mr Timmins is set fair with his work on the incendiary shells?'

Ten minutes passed and the lieutenant re-emerged, an expression of uncertainty upon his face, 'It is a slow business, sir; a great care is needed for the mixing of the charges.'

'Doubtless so... Very well,' murmured Pat with an air of disappointment, 'We will leave the gunner to his devices.'

At four bells Shiza loomed large on the larboard bow, the sun hovering low in mesmerising fixity in the western sky and just above the island. All along the horizon its brilliant luminescence was fading to a residual orange wash, the day seeming much diminished for it despite the sense of imminent action looming large and ever more acute in the thoughts of all aboard the frigate. Men everywhere stared all about them, to their fellows; glances were directed towards the quarterdeck, to the near Greek brigs, a heightened sense of something close at hand prevailing, a subdued hubbub of a myriad low conversations audible all throughout the decks.

'Not long, Simon, not long before darkness... when I dare say the Greeks will go into action,' declared Pat.

'Will 'ee care for an early bite o' supper, sorrs?' asked Murphy, appearing near the helm. Pat waved him away, shaking his head, possessing not the least appetite, Simon also silent.

Surprise pressed on, the atmosphere of keenly felt anticipation rising within all aboard as the sun eventually disappeared below and behind Shiza, the much more muted light reinforcing the increasingly anxious ambience, tension rising, the frigate maintaining her distance at just a cable behind the Greek brigs. Another hour and a half of infinitely slow movement, a precious few more miles gained in the still slight wind and the north-east coast of Shiza lay on the larboard beam. In the final hour of weak daylight before the sunset, a most distinctive light in the Mediterranean, Modon's buildings had become distantly visible to the topmen, the masts of many vessels just discernible above the harbour wall, a bare five miles on the bow. A signal from Miaoulis invited Pat aboard his brig. The Greek squadron slowed to a drifting halt, all yards' braces slackened, deflated sails flapping feebly in the weak gusts, the warmth of the day rapidly fading to the cool of evening. Pat crossed in his barge, the Greek captains likewise all attending for a conference. The admiral held this on deck, no time afforded for the relative comfort of his cabin, no refreshments other than a glass of fiery brandy offered to his visitors, Miaoulis taking nothing himself, as two dozen and more of his senior officers assembled about him.

Wasting no time with formalities, the admiral commenced, 'Gentlemen, we believe the Turks remain within the Modon harbour; many topmasts were sighted before the light began to fade... and I have received no contrary reports from my scouts...' Pat staring directly at him in obvious enquiry, Miaoulis added, 'Fast misticos, waiting and replenishing on these near islands for signs of Turk activity...' Pat nodded. 'This wind will serve us well, onshore and at our backs. There is no means of escape for the Turk... none. Nothing can save him now from that which we are about to inflict upon him... FIRE AND DESTRUCTION!' Miaoulis shouted his final few words, a general and loud murmur of endorsement coming from his captains.

Pat admired the admiral's confidence, one doubtless founded on long familiarity with the layout of Modon's harbour and the customary seasons and times of the local winds and currents.

Miaoulis, exuding determination, turned once more to Pat, 'Captain O'Connor, here are six brave warriors of Greece. These men will captain my fireships...' Miaoulis made the introductions himself, 'Andros Pipinos...'

Pat shook hands with Pipinos and declared his earnest good wishes for success, Jason translating. They would surely need a deal of good luck, he reckoned, for the bruloteers enjoyed little or no opportunity to change tactics for any reason, to hold back their brig when prepared for immediate combustion if no immediate opportunity to tie alongside the enemy presented itself. They always held the advantage of the weather gauge but the reverse was also true: no retreat was possible, for such was to shift against the wind; perhaps that was just conceivable if they could make short boards and if they enjoyed plentiful sea room in which to do so, but such a desperate manoeuvre was difficult in the extreme within the small bay and its harbour, and likely would only be made whilst under fire from the guns of their target vessel; and, whether ablaze or not, the Turks would surely still be firing their guns at any fireship within range.

'... Anagnostas Dimamas...'

'I bid you victory,' said Pat, offering his hand. He studied the resolute face of Dimamas; he was plainly a man committed to the most dangerous of tasks; indeed, it was a near suicidal mission, for the volunteers, as they invariably were, necessarily abandoned their own highly incendiary brig when it was fiercely ablaze, no prospect of any vessel near at hand to aid their rescue, their only hope being to take flight aboard their small boat, to pull away frantically with the oars, and no opportunity to use any sail they might possess with the wind always against them, the very wind which had propelled their fireship to close on its victim.

'... Demetrius Tsabelis,' Miaoulis continued.

Pat shook hands with Tsabelis even as his mind wandered back towards the qualities of the men before him. The fireship captains and crew were young, were agile enough to undertake the most violent of physical tasks and fit enough to pull hard for the punishing time required to escape, for the heroes rowed in frenetic haste: panic was always close, death often closer.

'... Marinis Spahis...'

Pat declared his earnest support and his hopes for a triumph as Spahis seized his hand and shook it fiercely. He wondered whether, perhaps, such men lacked a deal of imagination, for their prospects were precarious, their chances poor, particularly so if their target evaded the fiery bourlota's intentions of crashing alongside and the enemy preserved some small mobility with which to seek revenge upon the fleeing boat. Any eventual escape of the bruloteers was assuredly difficult and dangerous; the fleeing crews of any who had taken to their boat were much exposed and without the slightest protection.

The admiral hastened on, perhaps mindful of precious time passing and the magnitude of the opportunity before them to inflict a significant defeat upon the invaders, 'George, the son of Theodosius... and...' Miaoulis hesitated with a discernible note of concern, of audible uncertainty in his voice, '... and Anthony... my own son.'

Pat shook hands with the last two of the Greeks, and with a wandering gaze he looked in turn to each of the faces of all six fireship captains; not a one appeared to waver. He was grateful that he could not conceive of ever joining the crew of such a desperate venture himself and he marvelled at the courage of the men who did. He was ever impressed by their bravery. Was it foolhardiness? No, he concluded, for the Greeks lacked the heavy firepower to destroy the larger Turk vessels: frigates, razees and even the occasional 74-gun ship.

'Captain O'Connor,' Miaoulis turned his own thoughts to what Pat with *Surprise* might do, 'I am minded that your ship will best serve if you remain a cable or two to the west of my squadron, to stand off to the south-west of the old Venetian fortress. From there any vessels scouting from the north, from Navarino, might be visible. I will say that I doubt you *will* see any... for sunset is nigh upon us and the Turk does not care to be at sea save in the full light of the day. Your ship out there will be a sure deterrent to any Turks that might venture south to see what is afoot.'

'Of course, sir,' Pat glanced to the west, the sun already well below and beyond Shiza, the faintest hint of its former brilliance lingering still in the sky above the island: sunset was imminent. Miaoulis had timed his attack perfectly: the dying of the light to a diffuse, subdued twilight would offer the Greeks undiscovered passage to Modon and assured tactical surprise when they arrived.

'Perhaps... with your heavy guns...' the admiral spoke again, his voice emphatically one of supplication, of suggestion, without the least shred of any overbearing tone of direction, '... you might care to fire upon the fortress? That would serve to distract the Turk gunners from our fireships as they approach the harbour beyond the wall... from the east.'

'We will do our best, sir,' said Pat cautiously, mindful of his limited powder, Simon's confession of distress also never far from his thoughts.

The admiral continued, 'We are afforded a half-hour of twilight and so will press on to Modon. Our attack will begin at nightfall proper... when the Turk will not know of our approach until it is too late; he will not see our bourlotas until they are aflame.'

Pat nodded, marvelling at the man before him and his leadership qualities, his ability to carry his men with him and more: to send them, the fireship crews at least, to a firm prospect of death, their rescue extremely doubtful.

The admiral turned to directly address the small group of his half-dozen fireship captains; he shook hands with each in turn, a personal gesture of encouragement, of thanks. 'Now, a glorious opportunity presents itself... and this day will be one of the most illustrious for you and for Greece. The Turkish fleet is at anchor; GO... and profit by the favourable occasion which God presents us of delivering us from our enemies!'

This was well received and much more handshaking followed, all the other Greek captains pressing their best wishes upon the six. Pat himself once more wished the six fireship captains well. Five loud minutes more of voluble farewells and all the Greek visitors had departed, Miaoulis and Pat alone remaining. 'Goodbye to you, Captain O'Connor,' said the admiral, holding out his hand; 'I thank you again for attending this venture.'

'Your most devoted, sir,' murmured Pat very quietly, for he had himself entirely taken to heart the authority of the man before him, the Greek possessing no uniform, no badge of rank, nor any distinction or decoration upon him; yet Miaoulis simply exuded an indefinable command presence, one so rarely found; Pat recollected that he had seen such an aura only once before, an age ago, and that was in Nelson, the great man himself.

Half an hour more of slow sailing until came sunset, all brightness fading from the light, the mood everywhere excited yet restrained with an enforced silence on every vessel save for Dalby's seemingly discordant yet subdued ringing of the solitary bell announcing the first watch aboard *Surprise;* and in the weak, fading dusk light before complete darkness, the Greek squadron entered the channel between Sapienza and the mainland, Pat bringing *Surprise* a little further to the west, as close to the island as he dared in the black unfamiliarity. Fifteen more tense minutes passed whilst he could, only with difficulty, just make out the lighter sails of the six fireships, the oldest of Greek brigs, all bearing away to the north to approach the harbour anchorage from the east, the bulk of Miaoulis's fleet staying on course to position themselves east of the Venetian fortress and the harbour wall. Any Turk ships which did escape the fireships and, with a miracle, get past them to exit the harbour with short tacks against a contrary wind would then encounter the waiting Greek brigs.

Miaoulis was right, thought Pat; fleeing from the harbour against even the weak breeze seemed impossible. The scene was perfectly set: the Turks must be destroyed; there was no escape for them that Pat could conceive of. What damage the fortress's guns might serve out to the Greek fleet was unknown, but the Turk gunners generally were lamentable; certainly their shipboard ones were, as Pat had oft observed, always to his great relief.

'Final preparations, sir?' prompted Duncan.

'Yes, of course. Barton, I would be obliged if you will take the milking goat and the precious pigs below,' declared Pat to his cox'n.

'Aye aye, sir.'

Simon paced slowly across from the companionway, his profound unhappiness plain to all on the quarterdeck to see, his countenance black, apprehensive, his face filled with despond. The sky had darkened generally and little more than weak vestiges of twilight remained. He glanced over the side; *Surprise's* passage was audible, the sound being the wash alongside her hull, a white froth within the black water, visible even in the dim light. He contemplated the prospect of more bloodied shipmates soon to be set upon his table, and his spirits sank in a cold resignation to inevitability. He leaned on the rail and pondered, the recurrent bleak question forcing its way to the forefront of his mind: for how much longer could he really endure, and if his inability to cope did return - he would never forget his acute and momentary mental collapse after the Samos battles - well, would he let down his friends and patients? He took a deep breath and turned about to look towards the helm.

'Do you care for a swift bite of supper, Simon? asked Pat absently, his gaze fixed upon his friend, Simon's discomfort apparent. The air temperature was falling away noticeably as the last of the twilight faded to the night proper. 'That is,' added Pat, 'to bolster our strength before we begin any engagement.'

'I do not,' the terse reply.

'Wilkins has prepared a prodigious fine pie,' Pat pressed on, striving to occupy his dear friend's mind, to distract him from unwelcome concerns, 'One of inestimable qualities... so says Murphy... A pie that would not disgrace the table of the King.'

'Hmmm... what kind of qualities?' this in a tone of deep scepticism, mellowing only slightly as, a few seconds later, Simon added in a voice with only the slightest tint of curiosity, 'What particular pie might it be?'

'Oh,' Pat was caught out, flustered, not really having the slightest recollection of his steward's words at all, 'the kind they eat in Heaven, so he says... the most glorious of pies.'

'Perhaps later we will partake of the pleasure; if, that is, I am not otherwise engaged... immersed once more in blood and gore.'

'Simon, I am heartily sorry for your unhappiness, and I do not care to sound unsympathetic, but my thinking must run on different wheels. I am forever mindful of the shocking cost we ever bear, I am so; but you are to consider that it is beyond our present capacities to enter into any conflict; little enough of powder and shot do we possess, and I have not the least doubt that - *if challenged* - the barky must bear away; and so it is not in my contemplation that we will serve other than as scout for Miaoulis, nothing more... and you may cast aside any notions of a deal of wounded men being sent below.' Pat stared at his dear friend's distressed face, unmoving, Simon silent. 'Is that a help?' he whispered, 'I pray it is.'

A thoughtful pause, 'You are an exceptional man, Patrick O'Connor,' Simon relented in an instant, staring full into his friend's face, 'Yes indeed... God bless you... and I am ever reminded of it when my own spirits are low, my nerve wavering. In the tumult of these recent times, I confess that I may have allowed my personal vexation to creep into our exchanges... I beg pardon... I offer my apology, brother, I do.'

Pat's ruddy face was a picture of relief, 'Oh, as to that, no; no apology is called for. I beg you will cast aside such silly notions. We are here together, you and me... and all our shipmates about us... we stand *together*,' Pat's hand was offered and gratefully accepted, the precious bond reaffirmed with a mutual iron grip.

Two bells rang out, the tension rising all over the quarterdeck, and Pat stared hopefully into the absolute darkness in the direction of the vanished bourlotas. Within moments his eyes caught sight of the fires breaking out aboard them; the flickering flames would soon be roaring up tar-soaked masts and rigging. The Turk captains, whether aboard their ships or in the town, must by now be panicking, Pat thought: fiery hell was come upon them. General firing broke out in clamorous announcement within a few minutes, bright flashes of flame jetting from a myriad guns, both Greek and Turk, all visible to the men of *Surprise*, the sound of their explosive crack and the bass rumble of their thunderous eruptions resonating all around the bay. The ambience aboard the frigate tensed further, the previously subdued conversations about the gun deck rising up to loud exchanges, to much speculation and the like about the Greeks' prospects.

Surprise herself was near stationary, having come about to face into the wind. With just the slightest of gentle drift, her braces slackened, she lay with her bow pointing east, a half-mile south-west of the old and tiny Venetian fortress. It was almost an island, save for the short and connecting pedestrian ridge to the mainland - just visible in the moonlight as a white-water wash at a foot or two above the insignificant swell. There was no reaction from the small fort as yet. Across the water to the north and west was utter darkness, not the least glimmer of any light whatsoever visible to sea; and the principal, more substantial fortress on the shore itself obscured any sight of Modon town behind it. In the weak south-easterly wind it was a distant five or six miles to New Navarin and the great bay, and certainly it would take many hours for any responding Turk vessels from that place to reach Modon against the feeble wind. Pat much doubted that any squadron would ever emerge from the anchorage to investigate the gunfire resonating loud in the dense, cooling night air, a barrage of sound which must be audible even in New Navarin. No, the Turks could not conceivably reach Modon for likely three hours by sea even with their swiftest vessel and, were they minded to respond, better to send cavalry

61

from their besieging army all about New Navarin to see what was happening at Modon.

Pat, hating every moment of the inactivity of his ship whilst comrades in arms were risking their lives, decided to investigate the near fortress, to observe the anticipated firing of the two guns remarked atop its walls. He reckoned he could bring *Surprise* back to her position as an observer of the waters to the north and west, if necessary, within an hour, and that afforded him the time to do what little he could to help the Greeks, to help Miaoulis particularly, the admiral's personal request and gratitude for *Surprise's* assistance still very much in his thoughts. 'Brace up, Mr Macleod,' he shouted; 'We will shift a trifle to the north and east, towards the projecting Venetian fort.'

'Aye aye, sir,' Duncan reiterated the orders to the hands, and the frigate within minutes gained the smallest of momentum, a little push afforded by the weak south-east breeze on her beam.

Near half an hour passed before *Surprise* could approach the old fortress, the frigate turning slightly into the wind so as to bring her great guns to bear. She slowed, holding as close as she could stay without falling off, close-hauled and near drifting once more, her progress no more than the slowest of crawl, a bare cable off the tiny island fortress, not really anything more than a gun tower. From the man with the lead line the water depth was shouted out from the side every minute. Pat had determined that *Surprise* must make a contribution to the attack, however small. He had decided she would fire a half-dozen of her precious cannonball stock, no more, at the old Venetian fort; perhaps in doing so *Surprise* might distract the much more numerous Turk gunners on the far larger town fortress proper. Judging the moment, no interest shown in his ship from the small fort's two guns thus far, he called to his First, 'Mr Macleod, tell Mr Codrington plain, from for'ard, six guns... *six guns only*... and one at a time, open fire!'

Macleod hastened down the steps. Another tense minute of waiting passed until, with a fiery orange flash and a thunderous boom, *Venom* spat out her destructive poison, followed by *Dutch Sam, Tempest, Hurricane, Delilah* and finally *Vengeance,* the deck shaking violently, the frigate's yards and masts quivering in reaction, frissons of vibration rippling through her sails. The gun smoke was ultimately swept away by the breeze, and Pat stared towards the fortress in the exceedingly dim light of distant fires. No visible damage could he see. It did not surprise him: the walls, though old, would be thick; the 18-pound balls doubtless would dislodge a stone or two, but nothing short of a direct hit through the apertures would worry the fort's occupants and their gunners. He contented himself with the thought that he was doing *something*; not that it was much but it was all that he could do. He could not see the main battle, for that was beyond the east-west harbour wall which projected from the land, akin to a breakwater, but the much increased magnitude and number of flames on the other side of that pier were readily visible, soaring high atop many fiery masts, brightly prominent above the harbour wall; the yards, rigging and sails of at least a dozen ships were firmly alight and the roar of guns was ever louder. He wondered how the fireship crews were faring. The Greek squadron of supporting brigs had shifted closer and were in an arc behind the fireships; Pat could make out their mast tops in the bright flash of guns, a score of brigs firing constantly in thunderous cacophony, hurling their barrage at the Turk ships within the harbour.

Her guns silent once again, *Surprise* inched on, ever eastwards, the old fortress left astern, both its guns firing in the frigate's wake without success. Pat determined he would climb to the mizzentop and better see for himself what was happening beyond the harbour wall. He swiftly climbed up, panting with the sudden exertion, to sit on the platform, from where he stared in something akin to disbelief. 'Oh my God!' he exclaimed, for the sight, to any seafarer, was shocking, stunning, horrific even: on the other side of the wall lay two score of Turk vessels, a dozen and more of them burning brightly, the light from their fires sufficient to make out in some detail the chaos prevailing. Most, on seeing the approaching fireships, had presumably cut their cables in an attempt to flee: in vain, for the south-east wind had driven many, indeed almost all, on to the beach and shallows below the fortress walls. Many were entangled together, alongside each other, yards entwined in the rigging of neighbouring vessels, their crews helpless to save their ships, and likely their own escape would also be very doubtful. 'May Saint Patrick help those men!' gasped Pat, utterly horrified. He could pick out two Turk frigates, four armed brigs and three corvettes, all in total disarray, fires burning on more than half of them; a gabarre was also blazing furiously. A few smaller vessels, seemingly merchantmen, had managed to get some sail aloft and were struggling to sail east, their only way past the harbour wall and so to the sea, but they must first pass directly into the mass of the Greek attackers, their passage painfully slow against the adverse weak wind, the short tacks they strived to make incredibly difficult in a space that was not so much restricted as strewn with burning ships. Great swathes of smoke, bilious great clouds of it, swirled above all the conflict, the wind pushing it on to engulf the town.

From atop *Surprise,* despite her being upwind, Pat could smell the stinking, pungently sulphurous stench of the reeking smog, choking his nostrils and burning his throat; what it must be like aboard the burning ships he struggled to imagine. In the bright light of the inferno of hundreds of roaring fires, he studied the catastrophic destruction before him - an annihilation of vessels on a scale he had never seen before. He counted again and concluded that there were twenty burning ships: six of them would be the bourlotas, all entangled alongside their victims. He hoped with all his heart - a sudden tremulation within afflicting him - that their crews were safely into their boats and pulling hard to the east, towards Miaoulis and rescue. The deeper bass boom of the guns of the principal fortress, to the north of the old Venetian one which *Surprise* had fired upon, caught his ear. A score of heavier guns, likely at least 24-pounders, were firing at the Greeks. A hit from one of those would inflict the most severe damage. There was nothing that *Surprise* could do; her own guns were exceedingly unlikely to score any direct hits on the Turk ones, firing from where she was, beyond the harbour wall, and were she to open fire then her limited powder and scarce shot would near immediately be exhausted. The Greeks would have to stay and suffer by themselves, for *Surprise* could offer no help. Pat dearly hoped that the fort's gunners were as poor as their compatriots who served aboard their ships.

A quarter-hour passed with Pat staying aloft, gripped by the gigantic spectacle to the exclusion of all else; his ears were pummelled by the thundering roar of guns, his nose was twitching in the stinking air, and his eyes were assaulted by the bright gun flashes lighting up the sky above the fort, the burning ships throwing flickering red illumination upon the walls and the near town. Pat was unable to shift his gaze from the fiery hell before him as a near stationary *Surprise,* just the slightest of way upon her, shifted on a little further east. He observed three surviving small vessels, escapees, close-hauled and struggling hard to sail out, striving to pick their way through the fiery maelstrom of their burning compatriots and between the lines of the furiously firing attackers. He watched for another ten minutes in absolute fascination as they passed through the front wave of the Greek brigs, emerging infinitely slowly to try for a tack to the south, all the time under fire. It was not unlike *Surprise's* own escape from the Bay of Navarino, he recalled, shuddering at the memory. That had been a day he was sure he would never forget. He looked again at the fortress, eruptions of flame flashing out in a constant barrage pouring from its heavy guns atop the walls, their thunderous, booming explosions unceasing. He fretted, becoming ever more anxious: some of their heavy shot must surely be striking the Greeks, and such - even a solitary strike - would inflict the most catastrophic damage, would rip unfettered through fragile wooden hulls.

The three fleeing vessels - they appeared to be merchantmen - had succeeded in their turn through the wind, and all bore down on *Surprise*, the three now heading south-west and converging gradually upon the frigate as they picked up a little more speed. Pat turned his attention to them; his closer scrutiny, albeit in the near darkness, confirmed his identification: they were not warships, and so he determined to hold his fire. Conceivably they might even be neutrals - he could see no pennants - and he did not care to risk firing upon them. He hastily climbed down to the quarterdeck.

Ten more minutes and the three fleeing merchantmen came closer to the frigate, all close-hauled, their turn to the north-west to escape the horror of the bay blocked by *Surprise* herself. 'Will we fire, sir?' asked Macleod.

'No, hold fire,' Pat sighed and shook his head wearily, 'We have precious little powder and near nil shot to waste on such minnows.'

From the rail, from the quarterdeck and the gun deck all the men of *Surprise* stared in silence at the grey shadows and blackened canvas of the three small brigs passing close by; even in the darkness it was plain to see that they were grievously damaged. Much shot had evidently smashed into them, their escape from the furnace and the Greeks a near miracle, a reminder of *Surprise's* own escape from Navarino bay, and hence many of the men had a great deal of sympathy for them.

Surprise crept forward on her north-east course, akin to drifting, as she approached the harbour wall, the light from the two dozen burning ships blazing ever brighter above it, their many projecting masts flaming fiercely; on *Surprise* went, the frigate ever closer to the loud origins of the firing, a more intense assault inflicted on the ears, all eyes wide in the grip of total fascination. Gradually she inched past the east end of the wall and could go no further, the massed Greek brigs all before her, every one blasting away fiercely, their guns roaring and flashing bright eruptions of orange fire, and all moving infinitely slowly in a confusing labyrinth of varying tracks, always near conflicting with others within the packed mass of vessels, both Greek and Turk, every one making short tacks, east to west, west to east, striving to hold off from the shore to the north, and all keeping back a cable or two to the east of the fiery inferno which was the harbour. Fortunately for the Greeks, and doubtless as Admiral Miaoulis had anticipated, the wind still carried the voluminous black smoke away, blowing it onshore, into the town and over the fortress walls, to some extent obscuring the vision of the Turk gunners, but despite the restricted view of their targets they continued to blast away with determination if not with accuracy.

'No shortage of powder there,' declared Pat, a vestige of envy in his voice. The smell of burning tar was overwhelming; the highly flammable materials employed in the construction of all the burning ships had ensured success for the bourlotas as soon as they had closed on their victims, who plainly could never have escaped their approaching nemesis. The men of the fireships had succeeded beyond their wildest dreams, for the inferno within the harbour walls, under the fortress guns, resembled the hell of the worst of nightmares. Pat dearly hoped that the bruloteers would not pay with their lives.

'What to do, sir?' asked Duncan.

Pat simply shook his head; he could not conceive of anything that his men or his ship might usefully do, save perhaps to stay and watch, and that served precious little purpose and would remain dangerous. He hastened along the gun deck and climbed this time to the maintop with his glass, seeking to gain a clearer view above the smoke. He stared through the telescope, peered between the shifting swathes of black murk at the town, the fortress walls and beyond, searching in the light of a hundred bright fires for any target, anything at all which might be worth firing a very few of his precious remaining shot. Before him was a vision of unmitigated horror upon fiery horror, a sight beyond belief, had he not seen it with his own eyes. In the quarter-hour that he watched, two of the burning Turk warships violently blew up; the raging flames had evidently reached their stores and exploded their powder, no one able or thinking to flood their magazines. The entire vessels simply disintegrated into fiery fragments, large and small, the blazing debris hurled high into the air, burning materials flying in every direction. Pat was stunned: there could not conceivably be any survivors unless they had long ago abandoned ship. He could not imagine the terror the men in the adjoining vessels must be experiencing. Thousands of flaming splinters were swept about within the dense airborne smoke plumes, burning wooden fragments - small bright stars - rising and glowing bright amidst the swirling black clouds of smoke, and the air was saturated with sulphurous particles of gunpowder, much only partially burned, a stinking, choking assault on the throat. Still the heavy guns of the fortress thundered on.

Pat watched, spellbound, for several more minutes, gazing in awestruck stupefaction at the widespread destruction before him, the vaguest of indefinable notions coming to mind and shifting his concentration when he identified the roof of a building behind the fortress wall. The two ships' detonations had started a train of thought; more minutes of crystallisation, of further consideration passed before he finally determined that perhaps there was something which might help the Greeks. He descended to the gun deck and hastened back to his quarterdeck, quickly calling to the bosun, 'Mr Sampays, go below... to the for'ard magazine at all speed. Ask of Mr Timmins if he has finished making any of his incendiaries, any at all... one or two will serve... *You may care to run!'*

'Aye aye, sir,' Sampays hastened away, returning within a few minutes. Pat stared at him with acute curiosity, mute, simply nodding as the bosun presented himself. 'Five shells are ready, sir.'

'Praise be to Saint Patrick!' shouted Pat with huge satisfaction. 'Take Dalby and another two men, and fetch Timmins... fetch him here... to the carronades... *and with his five shells*... as quick as can be.'

It was a full ten minutes before the men re-appeared, each with a shell; all bar Dalby were struggling with the heavy load, a canister in shape: doubtless accuracy would be very poor save for the shortest of range. 'Here, come to the side,' shouted Pat, the men toiling, their steps slow with their great burden. The shells were set down, to the visible relief of the five; even Dalby had much exerted himself. Pat pointed the length of the east-west pier; 'There!' he shouted over the ferocious tumult of the continuing firing. *Surprise* was lying barely fifty yards off the end of the harbour wall, and the constant screams of hundreds of distressed and dying men were audible between the booming detonations of explosions. A thousand men at least were in the water, twice that strewn about on the beach below the fortress walls, many trying to scramble north towards the town, all likely having escaped their burning ships. 'Look to the fort!' Pat pointed his finger above the harbour wall, the fortress wall prominent beyond it. 'See there!' he shouted, all eyes following his direction, 'Behind the wall is a large building. It may be that it is a barracks or perhaps a storehouse, we cannot know for sure... but I venture it is likely that the garrison is quartered in the town; doubtless that will better serve their comforts... and the structure I have seen from the maintop may prove to be their store, their magazine.' His men nearby all nodded their understanding, all save Timmins who was staring in abject fascination at the inferno before his eyes, for he had remained below deck until summoned, staying at his solitary, slow task of finishing the manufacture of the incendiaries. 'Mr Timmins,' cried Pat, gracing him with the customary title the ship's principal gunner was afforded, 'Mr Timmins,' said Pat again in lower voice, the attention of everyone present on the quarterdeck wholly engaged, 'Can you put your shells over the fortress wall and on to that building which lies beyond it?'

It was the tallest of orders, for of the building nothing could be seen from the frigate's deck. 'How far beyond, sir?' said the gunner a little nervously.

'Directly behind the wall, perhaps a trifle to the right,' offered Pat, perhaps reflecting that it really was too much to ask, the carronades being cold, the range most uncertain and nothing of the target visible. Any slight success at all could only be a minor miracle.

'Will we fire a few balls first, sir, to warm the gun?' asked Timmins cautiously.

'Yes, yes, of course. Dalby, Mason, the carronade... that one. Fetch the shot, a brace if you will. Tremayne, the powder... Go to the gun deck, to Mr Codrington, and bring a dozen cartridges of powder directly.' Dalby and his mate hastened to pick up two large shot from the other side of the quarterdeck, 32-pound monsters, for the carronades fired a much heavier shot than the 18-pounders lining the gundeck.

Timmins pulled a canvas bag from his pocket and scooped out half the six-pounds of powder from the cartridge prepared for the long guns, tipping it into his satchel.

'Is that sufficient powder?' asked Pat, looking doubtful as the carronade was charged, the powder and wad rammed home by Dalby.

'It will be plentiful for the first shot, sir,' said Timmins, 'For the carronades it is more than enough; the range is mighty short and the firing will serve only to warm the barrel.' Dalby heaved in and shoved the shot down the short barrel, Mason adding a second wad, both pushed in by Dalby with the rammer.

Timmins ripped into the cartridge with the vent-pricker before pouring the priming powder into the gunlock pan and snapping it shut. 'Stand back, sir, if you please,' he declared to his curious captain, standing much too close for comfort. 'Fire!' he screamed. Dalby, Mason and Pat leapt back a yard. Timmins himself yanked the lanyard, the gunlock snapped and the carronade exploded with an ear-shattering crack of a detonation, leaping back on its slide as it roared and belched a long jet of orange flame followed by a dense black cloud of smoke.

The Surprises all stared in eager, gaping anticipation. The heavy shot fell upon that brig which was beached and burning below the fortress wall, smashing a visible flurry of splinters from its target, the impact illuminated by the endemic, roaring flames all around it. The carronade was hastily swabbed and reloaded by Dalby and Mason, Timmins looking to Pat who nodded, and it fired again, the ball flying a little further from the warmer barrel, striking the fortress wall, that impact also visible in the light of hundreds of fires, smashing stones away to fly in all directions.

Flying, burning splinters were a substantial hazard to *Surprise's* own sails at this close range, and the stinking air was offensively noxious, filthy; the pungent, acrid stench of smoke was overwhelming, every man constantly coughing. The roaring prevalence of fires on a score of vessels, all flaming bright and wholly uncontrolled, could not be ignored. The constant and overbearing noise of the screaming of a thousand men, some drowning, many of them burning to death, was altogether utterly insufferable. The combination of all together, an agonising crescendo of destruction, was more powerful and louder than anything Pat and his men had ever experienced before, gripping their attention as a powerful distraction which they struggled unsuccessfully to ignore. No man could fail to see the bodies littered all along the beach between the burning vessels. No man could mask the sickening, nauseating stench of burning flesh.

'And now to the first shell, sir,' shouted Timmins, jolting Pat from his enduring stare at the scene of horror before them. The gunner was plainly enjoying the challenge despite the tension and discomfort which gripped every man present. Mason charged the carronade once more after Dalby had swabbed it, another half of a powder bag going in, a wad, the long canister of the incendiary shell with the second wad rammed gently home, a plainly nervous Mason cautious with the rammer and more than a little apprehensive of a premature explosion, the incendiary shell so greatly unfamiliar to him.

Every man of *Surprise*, the frigate rocking near imperceptibly with no way on her, had gathered all along the larboard side to stare, two score of men encroaching on the quarterdeck, the fiery, hellish inferno before their eyes something all could scarcely believe. The attentions of the nearer hands registered on Timmins' presence at the carronade, for his proficiency, learned from Jelbert, was known to all.

'Very well,' declared Pat, nodding, Timmins enquiring glance fixed upon him, 'FIRE!'

The gunlock snapped and the carronade charge detonated instantly, the gun leaping back on its slide and cracking to a brutal stop as the carriage gripped it firm, the flame roaring momentarily from the stubby barrel before flickering out amidst the eruption of powder, burnt and unburnt, a swathe of discharged and choking particles filling the immediate air around the firing party, all men present coughing violently. The shell had been no precise fit for the barrel, the materials at hand and the tools allowing no precision for its manufacture; none of which concerned the Surprises in the least, for every man gazed at the anticipated flight of the shell. It struck the top of the fortress wall and exploded in a bright fireball, one which briefly distinguished itself even amongst the light of the furnace which was the dozens of burning vessels below it.

The fortress gunners, their attention captured, replied at last, a brace of heavy shot flying over *Surprise's* tops, the attention of all aboard alarmed and turning to the tearing, ripping, screaming noise of the close cannonballs as they passed through the air a few yards directly above. Pat's thumping heartbeat leapt to a new high; he did not care to contemplate a ball of such heavy calibre striking his ship.

The second carronade shell flew over the fortress perimeter to no visible effect, no view afforded beyond the high stone wall. 'That is the general direction,' screamed Pat, his hopes rapidly diminishing, directing his shout towards Timmins, '... perhaps a trifle more to the right.'

A shot from the fort smashed through the bulwark, fortunately missing the men a few yards away as it ripped and teared hammock netting over the side with it. Eyes returned to the carronade and its third shell; like the second, it similarly disappeared into the night without result. By now Pat's mind was accepting the failure of his notion, his calculations hastily shifting to the pressing urgency of moving his exposed ship away from the Turk guns, another brace of heavy shot from the fort flying overhead, lower this time and with an audible hissing noise: closer, louder, more alarming still. The fourth shell also achieved no visible result, and the hopes of all the Surprises were fast fading. Plainly they could not succeed; it had been just a desperate notion after all. Pat's spirits sank to a fresh low.

Dalby and Mason, persevering, had reloaded the carronade with the final shell whilst Timmins stared long at the fortress wall, weighing the results of his first four shots, the range and the elevation of his carronade. Pat's hopes were now wholly extinguished; he admitted such to himself. It had always been a long shot, the target's position invisible and only generally understood by the gunner. Timmins, meanwhile, made a minor change to the carronade elevation before standing back to look to his fretting captain in searching enquiry; every man of *Surprise* looked anxiously to see the final shell fired, their last chance of striking a blow, *their blow*, a general air of urgency prevailing; hope still flickered, albeit weakly, within all their thoughts.

'There is not a world of time to spare, Mr Timmins,' declared Pat, coughing, his anxiety rising to new heights as bright, flaming fragments swirled ever closer about his topsails, sparkling against the absolute blackness which was the sky to the west.

'Never you worry, sir,' said the gunner, 'We'se ready to fire the last one.'

Pat gulped, nodded, the last of his hopes resting on the final shot. He shouted, 'FIRE!' The carronade roared, jumping back ever more violently on its slide as the burning, fiery orange flame roared out. There was a delay of a second, no more, before the detonation resulted, one on a scale Pat had never seen before in his life; a shooting pillar of fire roared into the sky whence it flashed in the most violent of instants into an expanding orange ball of flame to light up the whole night sky. A thousand large fragments of debris and a hundred bodies were silhouetted within it; its brightness illuminated the burning Turk fleet, lighting up the whole of the harbour and the fortress, the fires aboard the burning ships paling to momentary insignificance, the whole of Modon town lit up with the brilliant white light. Then came the thunderous rolling roar of the explosion: deafening, overwhelming. The two together, flash and detonation, smashed upon the senses of every man within miles. The Surprises recoiled in shock, and all firing from every gun in the bay ceased as if by magic, every gunner stunned by the spectacle of the visual and aural assault. The flames on the stricken ships continued to burn, the fires crackled, roared even, but nothing could anyone in the bay hear of them, for the explosion had been so gigantic, so loud, that all were deafened. Retinas held the white flash in every eye, seared by the brightness; not a man who had been staring at the fortress in the instant of the explosion could see properly, their vision so substantially impaired, and their ears no longer seemed to function.

Five more minutes passed and still not a gun was fired from either side, the enduring shock entirely stunning, overwhelming, every man dazed and stupefied. The sand glass ran out and Dalby rang six bells of the first watch with the fiercest determination. Pat shook his head as if to try to clear his vision and he rubbed his ears to coax them to resume working properly. He spoke to his men on the quarterdeck; he shouted at them, again and louder, all to no avail - not a one could hear any spoken word nor any other sound. The silence was absolute; the catastrophe of fire remained visible on the burning Turk ships but somehow everything was a little less prominent in the enduring absence of any noise at all. Pat cast about him to see if his men were similarly affected; he looked to the Greek brigs: several of them were already turning away, bearing off to the south, departing: their task was done, finished. There was nothing remaining to sink, burn or destroy, and dead bodies floated everywhere in the sea within the flotsam of destruction on a horrifying, gargantuan scale. The Greeks could never have imagined the size of their success; Miaoulis had scored a victory of unbelievable magnitude: perhaps half the immediate Ottoman fleet in Greek waters was utterly wiped out in the flaming, sinking devastation which was before their eyes; hell truly had arrived on earth this night, at least for the Turks.

With frantic gesticulations Pat managed to convey his orders for a similar direction - away to the south - to his officers who were standing, unmoving, all about him on the quarterdeck. At last the message was understood, *Surprise* must make a long, looping turn through the wind. Duncan Macleod, Lieutenants Codrington and Pickering passed instructions on to the men, many dazed and motionless, wholly dumbfounded, several quite incapable of returning to their tasks for yet more minutes. The double watch of all the crew on deck rendered the tasks in hand easy to carry out, the frigate's gentle easterly course building ever more speed until Pat judged it sufficient to bring her round in a sharp tacking turn to the south when she came up to the wind and a near stop, her sail edges flapping, her way just enough to carry her forward and through to complete her turn, south with one point west, as close to the wind as she could come, and keeping clear of the mass of the Greek brigs who were making their own tack a half-mile to the east.

Shock still abounding throughout the frigate, the destruction on a scale every man was struggling to comprehend, the Surprises went about their business in silence, just a nod here and a hand signal there to reinforce the unspoken messages and the customary practices of the men, all entirely familiar to them, spoken orders wholly unnecessary; indeed, it was doubtful that any man would have heard them, for the deafness which had beset all who had been on deck when the fort's magazine had exploded was enduring.

'Pass the word, Mr Pickering,' shouted Pat without delay. 'All hands to splice the mainbrace!' The call was welcomed everywhere throughout the ship, the gill of rum issued for every man serving to calm shot nerves, to cool burning anxieties, to calm the excitement enduring in tired bodies and within fatigued minds.

A half-hour of a semblance of returning normality and *Surprise* had gained a mile to the south. 'There is your revenge, *your day of glory,*' declared Simon in a voice of despond and with not the smallest trace of triumph, standing with Pat and Duncan on the quarterdeck, the trio staring aft, a crowd of two score of men all about them. The fires of Modon harbour were still brightly visible in the night sky. 'Thankfully we have lost no men... I pray the Greeks have fared as well.'

Pat simply nodded, his own throat sore from the vast volumes of noxious smoke he had inhaled whilst atop the mast and staring at the conflagration. Duncan put his hand on Simon's shoulder with a gentle press of friendship, saying nothing, no words could he find, none seeming to be in the least appropriate.

Slowly, *Surprise* sailed on, reversing her approach to Modon with frequent short tacks, barely enough way on her to come about, her sails shivering, several times falling off, until Shiza was left astern and she could set her course for the open sea. Another hour passed in absolute quietude, the hearing of all only gradually returning, the sole and indistinct noises being the working of the ship's timbers and the creaking of the rigging, until a long, looping turn brought her round, wind abeam and the barky set fair for the long haul to Calamata, every man remaining on deck to gaze astern for hours at the diminishing holocaust, the most confusing mixture of shock, joy and wonder filling all their minds.

Chapter Four

Twenty hours of slow sailing and a rising ambience of celebration endemic throughout the barky, and *Surprise,* trailing a mile astern of the Greek squadron, approached the welcome vista of the twinkling lights of Calamata in the subdued twilight, the weak vestiges of the gloaming fast fading, black darkness near. Despite the repetitive hard work of many hours to bring the frigate up to and around Cape Akritas, for the most part with frequent tacking against the weak south-easterly wind, every man had slept little save for cat-napping, the mood of the crew, both officers and men, remaining jubilant. It was plain that a momentous triumph had been achieved, a great blow struck against the perfidious Turk, and perhaps half of Ibrahim's squadron had been burned. However, the man most pleased was Doctor Simon Ferguson, for he saw matters quite differently: the principal factor to celebrate, in his opinion, being the absence of a single casualty amongst his shipmates. He sat in quiet reflection with his friends, Pat and Duncan, all amiably contented within the cabin, the three savouring with great pleasure a considerable quantity of wine, their supper having been the truly exceptional raised pie which Pat had promised, the pastry coffin filled with slow-baked goat meat, the food and drink enjoyed in a relaxed ambience, the general feeling being one of contentment as they approached welcome sanctuary, and that sat well with them all.

The second bottle of wine had been consumed, prodigious attention having then been devoted to the succeeding port and walnuts, and all at the table had fallen into silent contemplation, deep fatigue and the beatific absence of anxiety the benevolent, settling and soporific influences upon them all. 'Simon, ain't that the victory of the world, eh?' declared Pat at last in delighted voice, his own exhilaration still enduring, his fatigue determinedly held at bay.

A broad smile, the welcome descent from the grip of super-tension had reached even the surgeon, 'I congratulate you on your vanquishment, Pat,' Simon raised his glass, 'I give you joy of your day of glory.'

'Aye,' Duncan spoke up, great satisfaction also loud in his own voice, 'it was certainly that... nae doubt.' He raised his glass, 'And here's to Miaoulis, the great man himself.'

'To Miaoulis! Hear! Hear!' declared Pat loudly, pleased with the mention of the Greek hero of the day, more pleased to see a shard of relaxation touch upon his surgeon friend.

Murphy replenished the wine in the glasses and hovered a yard away, wholly cock-a-hoop albeit somewhat mentally diminished himself, for the grog ration had been doubled for all the hands; consequently, he had much appreciated the greater occasion to frequent the liquor store. Pat also had not skimped on the wine at the table, Murphy never failing to take his due portion as he saw it.

'It is the world's pity that the Greeks lack a leader on land of the stature of Miaoulis at sea,' Pat continued, allowing his thoughts a generous drift towards speculation. 'Doubtless Ibrahim will eventually move on from... *I venture*... a successful conclusion to his siege of New Navarin... to spread throughout the Morea with his army... and I doubt he will find a deal of opposition... at least precious little *effective* opposition.'

'Aye, that's the case,' murmured Duncan, 'I regret to say.'

'Do the Greeks wholly lack for a general?' asked Simon.

'Many are minded that their best man is the renegade, Kolokotrones,' Duncan replied, 'and he is locked up at present. You will collect he was the leader of the revolt during the civil war. He resides in a prison cell within a convent on the island of Hydra, but the man still has followers... though Mavrocordato is not one of them; indeed, the prince loathes him.'

'Internecine strife... and at such a time as this, bah!' Simon downed his glass and stamped it on the table.

'Shame on them!' exclaimed Pat vehemently, wholly in accord with Simon, for who but a traitor could contemplate engaging in civil war at such a time.

'What futility, what waste in our brief moment,' Simon murmured softly and with evidently heartfelt feeling, his friends quietening, long familiar with his moments of philosophy in the cabin, the real revelations of his mood. 'Life is but a day, one fragile dew-drop on its perilous way from the tree's summit,' Simon's bleak voice revealed his return to despond.

'Eh?' Pat set down his own glass, stared at his friend, 'Dew drop? Would that be Mower again?'

'No... a little-known poet, John Keats... I confess the phrase has stuck firm in my memory, simple as it is. He was a contemporary of Byron, from whom I first heard it... In Metaxata it was; we shared a deal of the most convivial of suppers in those last days... before his Lordship departed for Messalonghi. "The ills of the world are as nothing compared to the brute folly of man". I collect he said that to me... and how true it is.'

Silence persisted for a few minutes as Pat and Duncan pondered what to offer, to say, until further discussion was halted by Lieutenant Pickering's entrance to the cabin to announce imminent arrival at Calamata and the anchoring of the ship at some two cables off the quay, any nearer being quite impossible as the whole of the Greek squadron had preceded *Surprise* to anchor as close as could be.

'I fancy we will go ashore for an hour,' declared Pat, brightening and grateful for the change of subject, 'Duncan, I collect you wished to speak with Mavrocordato... if he ain't departed already.'

'I am minded that I will attend the Greek wounded,' declared Simon, pleased to find some personal purpose, even if it was so late in the day. Within a quarter-hour of anchoring, he was rowed across to the brig of Miaoulis, the admiral's aide coincidentally coming alongside *Surprise* in a small boat to request his presence to treat the wounded bruloteers of the prior night's action. Astonishingly, not a one had been killed, merely a half-dozen were suffering a variety of burns, wounds and injuries, generally light.

Arriving at the quay in the barge, Pat and Duncan walked along to the particular tavern which Prince Mavrocordato had been known to frequent. Within it, they were immediately engaged by a score and more of Greek captains, Admiral Miaoulis himself espied amongst them. It was a boisterous and cheerful gathering, the raucous victory celebrations already underway, many hundreds of Greek seamen of the squadron outside and liberally availing themselves of liquid refreshment, and the tantalising scent of roasting goat hung thick in the air all along the cobbled waterfront, several unfortunates already turning over charcoal fires.

'Captain O'Connor!' exclaimed Miaoulis, hastening to greet the welcome arrivals and, no gesture to protocol, seizing Pat in a fierce bear hug, conventions of rank entirely cast to the winds.

'Admiral...' Pat gasped for breath, stepped back to shake hands for a long minute, the admiral's grasp as strong as his own, mutual pain and bruising sure to follow.

'I thank you... I thank all your men...' Miaoulis offered in halting English, Jason not present to translate. He stopped, as if he could not quite believe events himself, and no further words could he find in his pleasurable confusion of language.

Pat beamed a wide smile of satisfaction, nodded emphatically, and then from within the crowd another man emerged to speak, 'May I offer my own congratulations, Captain O'Connor?' Mavrocordato stepped away from the garrulous noise of the ensemble. He turned momentarily to Duncan, 'Captain Macleod, it is exceedingly good to see you once again. Gentlemen, I hear that a most striking success has been achieved... a victory of impressive magnitude. Well done... well done indeed! I thank and congratulate you both most heartily.'

'Thank you, sir,' mumbled Pat, rubbing his right hand vigorously with his left before offering it, tentatively, to the Greek whilst thinking with some relief that the prince was, thankfully, a politician and not another jubilant military man.

A half-hour passed in cordial pleasantries, Pat and Duncan much enjoying the jubilant mood of celebration, a beaker of local wine gratefully accepted, Duncan sniffing and looking all about him with rising interest for the source of the teasing aromas wafting into the tavern.

'I must tell you,' Mavrocordato had returned and spoke again in a whisper, 'that I will depart on the morrow for Nauplia... our capital. I beg you will consider... that is to say, you would greatly oblige me were you to convey myself with the gol... *our precious asset* to Nauplia aboard your smaller vessel, *Eleanor*; and perhaps, Captain Macleod, you might be minded to accompany me? There are a number of persons of some significance for Greece at Nauplia to whom I care to introduce you.' The prince said no more, simply stared at an unblinking Pat, whose mind was by now turning very slowly, the copious wine of the evening having long caught up with him.

Duncan, with Pat's blessing, had previously attended Mavrocordato for some weeks in the prior year, acting as a liaison officer between *Surprise* and the Greek navy, during which time he had made himself absent from *Surprise,* ultimately rejoining her at Messolonghi when Lord Byron had been conveyed there by the frigate. In fact, Duncan had acted principally as an unofficial intelligence gatherer for the Admiralty on all such occasions. He had also been tasked with several other covert missions by the First Lord, Melville; the one of most significance being the collection of the Tsar's gold from Russia, departing Kotlin Island with it aboard *Eleanor* just ahead of the winter freeze in the Gulf of Saint Petersburg. Duncan, slightly inebriated himself, looked to his captain in enquiry.

'Why...' Pat collected his thoughts, racked his brain. What was in the air here? He looked to the prince, 'It seems to me that the barky, being in need of many a remedy... *repair*... will be here for some weeks... and, I dare say, we can manage without Mr Macleod. Yes, indeed; that will be in order, sir.' He nodded to Mavrocordato who was smiling, perfectly delighted.

It was long past midnight when, at long last, Pat's bargemen pulled away from the quay to return to the frigate; all of them, it could not escape Pat's attention, significantly the worse for wear; not that he felt any less debilitated himself, for the inexhaustible flow of Greek wine after the prior consumption in the cabin, after the prior night of little sleep and after the generous portion of roasted goat which Duncan had insisted they partake of, had altogether quite taxed his utterly expended reserves of energy and everything else as well, both men struggling to remain awake as the barge slowly crossed the calm harbour waters, the bargemen finding themselves also some considerable way below par. Arriving alongside, Pat tried to climb out of the thwarts with some difficulty, total exhaustion long settled upon him, several oaths escaping his lips as his men looked away diplomatically; until, assisted up the ladder by welcoming hands, he finally hauled himself aboard with a final effort, quite finished. He staggered across the deck, his head a complete fog, and he wobbled through the coach to his cabin, wholly ignoring Murphy's concerned attendance save for a dismissive wave, when he slumped gratefully into his cot, still fully clothed, to immediately fall asleep. Murphy fussed about him, removed his boots, Pat unmoving, already snoring loudly. Entirely oblivious to the world, he slumbered all night like the most contented of babies, not the least worry entering his head.

Saturday 14th May 1825   10:00   *Calamata*

Eleanor, Duncan in command and assisted by Mower, had completed the loading of her valuable cargo under the watchful gaze of a score of heavily-armed Greeks: stern, fierce men who, to Mower's mind, resembled brigands, every one sporting the most luxuriant and perfectly combed moustache the lieutenant had ever seen. Pat looked on from the quay without a deal of interest and nursing a greatly painful head as Mavrocordato approached him to say goodbye. The prince, whilst seemingly contented and striving to be affable, appeared to be also pre-occupied with some pressing concern, something of substance weighing heavy upon him, for his exchanges were unusually short, much unlike the man's customarily pleasant, often garrulous demeanour. Perhaps, Pat wondered, he was recalling his own narrow escape aboard ship from the hell of Sphacteria and the subsequent prolonged firefight to escape the bay, or perhaps he too had simply over-indulged during the prior evening. Pat did not care to speculate nor ask when the Greek shook hands with him before stepping aboard the schooner.

Mavrocordato offered a brief wave from her deck before swiftly taking himself into the small cabin without looking back. The hands cast off and *Eleanor* shifted quickly away from the quay. Duncan, standing on her deck, raised his arm to Pat in farewell salute as the vessel swiftly picked up speed and hauled away to the south, the Surprises watching and wondering, their attention captured, until she was no more than a distant speck.

Sunday 22nd May 1825   *13:00*   *Calamata*

Pat sat at the gunroom table, the guest of his officers, awaiting Sunday dinner, as was the Royal Navy custom. He was enduring a little of mental discomfort, knowing that he was the bearer of imminent tidings which, he much regretted, would spoil the social occasion, but he held his tongue for the moment, for a short while longer, sitting in some unease and keeping his silence only with difficulty. Abel Jason, the translator for the Greek bearer of the bad news, also knew, and he fidgeted most uncomfortably, saying nothing, occasionally glancing nervously at his captain. The loyal toast had been proposed, the bottle of sherry was already much depleted and the chatter, whilst the stewards were awaited with the food, was convivial, for the tremendous Modon victory was little more than a week ago and was still much discussed aboard ship.

It was a small gathering, a thin table indeed, Pat reflected, in comparison with the old days when they had fought against the Corsican tyrant. He recollected occasions aboard *Tenedos* and other ships when there had more usually been a half-dozen and more officers present, and at least four youngsters, midshipmen, all attending with awestruck reservation and keen ears; and then there would be the purser and on many an occasion the ship's chaplain as well, when the small table would be entirely filled, the small space crowded with diners, a stiff formality always the case at the beginning of the meal. He looked about him: to his left his only two lieutenants, Codrington and Pickering; to his right his purser *cum* translator, Abel Jason; beyond Jason sat the chaplain *cum* assistant surgeon, Michael Marston; he was also a violinist of exceptional talent. A short man, he was a little older than all others present, his hair thinning, and he sat patiently, listening to the ebb and flow across the table, rarely speaking unless prompted and always maintaining his rather serious demeanour. Pat had an infinite respect for Marston, had even on occasion been grateful for his companionship, his words of comfort being well received when Simon Ferguson, Pat's oldest friend, had been captured by the Turks. The chaplain was held in the highest respect by all the crew; indeed, he was also much valued for his attendance in the sick bay, assisting Simon as second surgeon when the heavy load had oft been too much for one man. Finally, there was Simon himself: learned, intellectual, a dedicated student of all natural things, both plant and animal; a man exceptionally gifted with many talents, principal amongst which was his ability as a surgeon of the highest calibre. There was not a man aboard the barky who had the least doubt of that.

These days, *post* Napoleon, *post* official Royal Navy service, Pat reflected - several voluble conversations proceeding concurrently - formality was in much shorter supply; indeed, he minded that not the least and was secretly pleased that such was the case, for he encouraged all his officers to speak their piece, to offer any thoughts of relevance to the table talk, even if such sometimes did seem more than a trifle remote, even perplexing on occasion, that being usually when Pickering volunteered his contribution. Pickering was the ship's wag, and he could usually be relied upon to offer an amusing anecdote, a jest or an inexplicable puzzle to the table, the solution invariably humorous and far-fetched; yet today the lieutenant had hardly spoken at all, save for the loyal toast, certainly had offered nothing witty, at least not yet; all questions directed to him at the table were invariably met with hesitation and little more than the most cursory reply, 'I will consider the matter further.' Perhaps, Pat pondered, his humour might return later, after the meal and with the port, for the lieutenant seemed mightily set back generally.

Codrington, yet another old *Tenedos* shipmate, had served for almost the whole of the Greek venture as commander of *Eleanor*. His origins were something of which he spoke little, near nothing. The general understanding was that he originated from some, hitherto unmentioned, island in the Caribbean; which one the lieutenant had never cared to declare. Indeed, he was somewhat swarthy of complexion and always sensitive if the table talk ever veered towards the subjects of slavery, tobacco and those parts where such remained prevalent. He was a particular patron of Freeman, a liberated black slave who had escaped his own particular hell, a Bristol slaver, to swim to sanctuary and fearful hiding aboard *Tenedos* in the Caribbean eight years previously, his presence discovered days later in the darkest corner of the hold whilst scavenging for potable water, thin, emaciated, hungry and exceedingly frightened. Codrington had coaxed him out, reassured him with sign language and friendly gestures, and over the many subsequent weeks and months the black African had slowly relinquished his nervousness and fear. With no sailing experience and few, near none, words of English, he had been seconded to Murphy's tutelage as second steward for the great cabin.

Codrington had subsequently exchanged with Mower, who had been most severely wounded; Pat was sure that he had yet to fully recover, and so he had been switched to *Eleanor*, out of any conceivable danger, the better to facilitate his complete recuperation. Mower was a poet of some talent, oft entertaining the table with his latest verse, and his presence was much missed. He was also an accomplished musician, playing the Spanish guitar, and on many an occasion was to be found in acoustical sojourn with the men, with whom he was exceedingly popular.

Pat's eyes fixed upon Abel Jason. The purser had served aboard *Tenedos* during the French war, as had they all, before joining *Surprise* in Greece, in the unofficial base for operations which was Cephalonia, the Ionian islands remaining under English rule, to where he had brought secret Admiralty despatches from London. Entirely comfortable speaking both Greek and Turkish languages, his contribution had been invaluable for close liaison with the Greeks. A fine shipmate, Pat thought, as were they all, a small swell of gratitude rising up within him. Biting his tongue, he decided he could wait no longer. 'Gentlemen,' he spoke up in authoritative interjection, the several conversations falling away in an instant, 'There is one matter I regret I must touch on without delay... Miaoulis's aide has brought the news but an hour ago...' All present and seated sat up straight from casual posture, the attending stewards' ears pricking up, an alerted Murphy hesitating as he was about to refill the sherry glasses, his hand frozen in mid-air. 'There can no longer be any doubt,' Pat resumed, 'New Navarin will capitulate to Ibrahim on the morrow.'

As Pat had known, it was the abrupt end of all comfortable discourse, gasps of dismay issuing from several seated at the table. Murphy, halted in the act of leaning over to refill the glasses, gripped tight the tray which had near shed its bottles, all sliding precariously as he shot bolt upright. Shocked silence: the news seemed utterly incongruous after the victory at Modon, but then Ibrahim had been besieging New Navarin for a very long time.

Pat raised his hand; this was not an occasion during which he intended to allow interruption. 'Murphy, are you now about the dinner? I am mortal hungry... and rouse out a bottle or two more of wine... anything will serve.' Pat waved his hand in dismissive emphasis, the steward leaving most reluctantly. 'It is my understanding, so Miaoulis informs me...' Pat nodded to Jason, '...that a number of vessels, foreign merchantmen, have been chartered... within which the Greek garrison of New Navarin will be taken off to be conveyed to this port... to Calamata... after they surrender. Ibrahim has promised to honour those arrangements.'

All present stared fixedly at Pat; the unwelcome news had deflated their good spirits utterly. 'Might that... that setback present something of uncertainty for our own circumstances... here in Calamata?' murmured Simon, his anxieties rising once more in an unwelcome and chilling mental and physical flood.

'With no longer any call for his army to stay in that place, it is sure he will begin his wider invasion of the Morea... and doubtless Calamata, the only remaining Greek port in the region, will be in his attentions... his *early* attentions, I make no doubt. Here we are... a mere forty miles from Modon... scarcely a day's ride for his cavalry...' Pat's gloomy prognosis tailed off; he was himself still coming to terms with the dramatic contrast with the recent and more buoyant spirits after the Modon victory.

The stewards arrived with the food, and the rising aromas wafting all about the small confines of the gunroom were divine, but all appetites around the table, unfortunately, were much diminished. A miserable meal followed, an ambience of dejection prevailing, and Pat took his leave with a final few words, 'Gentlemen, we will begin on the morrow to take on what stores we can find in this place, for we have yet to deliver that... *that machine* in the hold... *the coin press* it is. I venture we will depart in a very few days.'

Sunday 22nd May   18:00   Nauplia, Greek seat of government

'Captain Macleod,' Prince Mavrocordato whispered his words, as if frightened they might be overheard, 'New Navarin will... it much pains me to say... surrender within one or two days. The defenders can hold out no longer; they are without food and ammunition, perhaps a day of rations remaining, no more, and their powder is near all gone.'

'I am so greatly sorry to hear that, your Highness,' mumbled Duncan, shocked, his thoughts instantly flashing back to the desperate last minutes of his escape from Sphacteria, the island in the bay opposite New Navarin, fleeing with this man, with Mavrocordato; he recalled the frenzied rush for the last boat, Egyptian soldiers with bloodied bayonets mere yards behind them all the way to the water. A tremor of fear was rekindled throughout his body and his mouth dried in an instant.

'It is plain that Ibrahim will renew his efforts to capture the whole of the Morea... and Nauplia itself, we must conclude, is within his reach, for his present approach cannot be halted by such weak forces as we possess,' Mavrocordato sighed, the prospects of victory seemingly never bleaker for the Greek independence movement. 'There is, too, a resurgence of popular support for the rebel, Kolokotrones, and I fear... that is to say... it becomes ever more likely... that he will be released from his prison in order to assume command of such land forces as may yet be mustered to resist Ibrahim. I confess that I am affrighted that either monster may seize our precious reserves... *the gold.*' Duncan nodded cautiously as Mavrocordato continued his dismal assessment. 'I must ask of you... dear friend of Greece, if you will convey the gold in your vessel, your schooner... to a safer place... to a sure sanctuary, one which will be protected from those coming dangers and privations which appear more imminent by the day.'

'Of course, sir,' a shocked Duncan whispered, 'You may count on myself and my men to aid your intentions.'

'Thank you, Captain Macleod,' a tired Mavrocordato managed a thin smile for the first time. 'Time is of the essence. There are men since some days engaged in excavations all throughout Nauplia, searching for the rumoured gold, their purpose being to find it before Ibrahim's army arrives... as many expect it will. Our Roumeliot brothers are gone home and we are left only with mountain bandits and peasants. I fear our country's grain and flour is all before Ibrahim's path and it is far from certain that any defenders for it will be found. The prospects for a free Greece...' the prince sighed, '... I much regret to say... have never looked bleaker.'

Wednesday 25th May 1825   *14:00*   *Calamata*

Surprise had been becalmed all morning, and Pat was in dejected mood, the military gains made by Ibrahim weighing heavy on his mind. He was standing on his quarterdeck with Simon, patiently waiting for the *meltemi* wind which, long familiarity with weather in Greek waters led him to expect, would begin blowing off the land behind Calamata in the early afternoon. 'Perhaps it really is a wind of change for Greece?' was the disquieting thought which escaped his lips as he stared at the panorama of vessels moored about the frigate, vessels of many kinds and from all across the Mediterranean, all busily loading from boats which had pulled out from the quay.

'To what do you refer, brother?' Simon's question was gently stated, Pat's downcast demeanour plain.

'Oh, the *meltemi*... the wind... ' Pat sighed; 'Perhaps it pressages the advent of Ibrahim's re-conquest of all the Morea and further? Do forgive my despond... my tedious ramblings.' He recalled Mavrocordato telling him that it was here, in this very place, *this backwater* which was Calamata, where the Greek rising had started, back in early 'twenty-one. Four years on and the bloody pendulum appeared to have swung back with a vengeance. He strived to cast away a dismaying thought, one which he did not dare to voice, Simon studying him and listening attentively: had his own men really fought for two years in vain?

All along the deck scores of the men of *Surprise* gazed across the calm water towards the quay. That the town itself was far from settled had been obvious for the past few days; indeed, it was in a tumultuous state of panic; the arrival of Ibrahim's brutal army was expected imminently. The defenders of New Navarin had arrived as promised: crushed, tired and defeated men. Thankfully they had been conveyed to safety - Ibrahim had kept his word, safe passage had been assured; but even Calamata now looked increasingly like a temporary and exceedingly short-lived sanctuary. The merchants of the town had, in the past few days, sought to shift everything of value to the merchant ships which filled the harbour, their owners and captains demanding the most exorbitant of tariffs.

For the ordinary people of the port, Pat concluded gloomily, there was no escape: no ships to carry them away, nowhere to go to save perhaps for a perilous trek through the mountains; and who was to say that they would not encounter the invaders if they did attempt such? In any event, there really was no sanctuary to flee to, for the Egyptians enjoyed free rein to the north, where no Greek forces of any significance remained to oppose them.

'Is the war lost?' asked Simon, 'The Ottomans will now triumph; is that sure?'

'No,' said Pat gloomily, 'I do not care to think that, but I do venture that it is the case that the war can only ever be won at sea, for to my way of thinking there never will be a sufficiently well-armed, well-trained and well-led Greek army.' He simply could not see that happening, but at sea, well, that was a different matter, as Miaoulis, Sakhtouri, Canaris and many other brave Greek captains had demonstrated these two years during which *Surprise* had served with them and for a long time before that. Pat concluded grimly that it was of the first importance that he and all his own men continued fighting, that they persevered - *come what may* - even though the casualties were rising and the cost was so very high and measured in the blood of his own men, *in rivers of blood*. He shuddered, his spirits were sinking again. He looked all about him: many of his shipmates were standing attentively close by; his stalwarts were ready to depart; his dear comrades - for that was how he perceived them - were all awaiting his orders, not the least hesitation visible in their eyes, every man holding an unlimited confidence in their captain. He saw that plain, and in that stark moment he felt greatly humbled and more than a little uplifted from his personal gloom.

The wind was freshening, picking up, flicking strands of Pat's greying red hair about his eyes. He brushed the distraction away and put on his hat; wedging it firm, he turned to his First. 'Mr Pickering, it is time we departed,' he declared in loud voice, all his men instantly alerted.

'All hands, prepare to make sail!' shouted Pickering.

'Lay aloft!' the master picked up from him. Men everywhere scrambled up the rigging. 'Rig capstan bars... Bring to the messenger... Man the bars!'

Surprise was tugging on her anchor cables, the emerging *meltemi* beginning to exert its influence, the wind itself announcing the barky's departure, blowing a firming north-easterly, other vessels within the harbour similarly making their own preparations, a few already underway.

'Breast the capstan!' shouted the master.

'Up anchor!' ordered Pat.

'Up anchor!' Pickering echoed.

'Heave and a-weigh!' cried Prosser.

'Up and down!' the shout from Dalby at the bow.

'Thick and dry for weighing!' shouted Prosser.

The topmen, already on the yards, cast off the gaskets, gathered the canvas under their arms and waited as the tierers coaxed in the cable until stowed, when the anchor appeared, hauled up out of the water, shedding streams of mud.

'Standby aloft, let fall!' roared Pickering before a shrilling *peep-peep, peep-peep* whistle blown by Sampays.

'Let fall! Sheet home, SHEET HOME! Hoist away!' the master shouted. The topsails tumbled down, unfurled and flapping, and the men hauled on the braces.

Surprise began to shift, slowly at first as she gained way, her bow coming round to the south, towards the open sea, her sails pushing her on, a little faster, a tiny wake beginning to be visible astern, a gentle wash rising at her bow.

The deck crew heaved in the last of the anchor cable which was swiftly catted, and within five minutes *Surprise* was fully underway, all her sails under gentle load, the ship bearing south, to whatever events awaited her next; and all along her sides her men, their immediate tasks finished, stared at the familiar ribbon of bubbling white water.

Sunset and Cape Matapan off the larboard beam as *Surprise* made her turn, east with a little north, towards the strait of Cerigo. Pat was standing at the rail in solitary contemplation when he was joined by Abel Jason. The translator *cum* Admiralty messenger, like Pat, much enjoyed the final hour as the sun departed the day and the darkening twilight gradually introduced the night, their hopes always for a star-filled panorama. The *meltemi*, as was the norm, had much fallen away in the past hour and the frigate made little more than two knots on the feeble beam wind, the sea presenting not the slightest of chop. At least, Pat consoled himself, the slightest of heel to starboard - *insignificant* - made for a stable platform for gazing up into the heavens. He clutched his glass, waiting patiently; the fierce and former demands upon him of two weeks ago, an acute combat tension, lingered even now, but very gradually they were continuing to ease away, his mind stirring with precious and brittle inklings towards the beginnings, no more than that, of blessed relaxation.

Jason had acquired the passion for astronomy from Pat, a great aficionado of star-gazing, and - although the purser possessed no telescope of his own - he had taken to borrowing his captain's nautical glass, which was itself no mean device. The two men often encountered each other at that particular time of the day and, on many occasions, enjoyed a social discourse which, whilst ostensibly about the movement of the heavenly bodies, also oft opened to discussion on present and prospective events. Jason was always most careful not to overstep the tactful mark, ever sought to avoid treading upon his captain's command proprieties, and he had long recognised that Pat had no pretensions as a philosopher; rather, he contented himself with scientific observation and its associated discussion. However, such dialogue was never difficult, for Pat himself welcomed the gentle sounding board of Jason for his own mental explorations; and Simon, in these past weeks, had retreated to a much more insular frame of mind, a little of their friendly informality when within the cabin seemingly having slipped away, much to Pat's regret. For there were times when command was a lonely place, the burdens and responsibilities were very heavy ones, safeguarding the lives of his men being the heaviest of them all, and such was never wholly out of his mind.

'Good evening, sir,' said Jason in friendly voice.

'And to you, Mr Jason... a very good evening it is. Here, please to take my glass, if you will. I am minded that, the weather so, we will be blessed with a fine observation of Jupiter in an hour or two. I expect we will see it over there,' Pat pointed, 'south of Cerigo with a little of east.'

'Is that so, sir?' Jason marvelled at Pat's knowledge of the planetary movements.

'Saturn too is promised... in the early hours that is, if you are not sleeping. There is not the slightest of cloud, and I venture we may be fortunate.'

'Why, it would give me infinite pleasure to see that splendid marvel, it would so.' Jason stared at the emerging stars for several minutes before his question, 'To where are we sailing, sir?'

'Oh, to the island of Aegina... north of Hydra, south of Athens. I venture 'tis fifty more leagues distant and a few days sailing, if - that is - we are not greatly hindered by the *meltemi*, which is ever a northerly and not greatly advantageous for our passage, but we may hope it will not blow so strong as to hold us back. I am minded we may gain the island afore the sunset two days hence.'

'And after that, sir?' The question was asked tentatively, Jason sensing a little of indecision in his captain's subdued and hesitant demeanour.

Pat's indecision was never tested as, in that moment, Simon stepped up from the companionway and across to the rail to join them. 'Why, Simon, there you are!' declared Pat in warm voice, much pleased to see his friend, for he had not graced the cabin since they had departed Calamata.

'Good evening,' Simon replied in a somewhat dispirited voice. 'I am come to take the air before I must take to my cot... in that claustrophobic box... downstairs.'

'Why, you are welcome to mine... in the coach, if you care to shift. I will ask Murphy to make up another in the cabin... 'tis but the work of a moment.'

'Thank you kindly, that is most gracious of you, but I am sure I will survive, perhaps after a generous whisky dram or two from my medicinal flask... which Murphy has not discovered,' a long pause, 'at least I think not.'

'Weak would it be, at all?'

'Why yes, as you mention it; a little of the fire is certainly lost. I had thought it a trifle strange, perhaps the passing of time, an inexplicable natural decaying of the alcohol.'

'I venture it naturally decays greatly faster when mixed with water,' Pat smiled, 'You have doubtless remarked that the grog ration is three parts water and one of rum?'

'The rascal... Murphy it is!' a vehement realisation; 'I shall dose it with *cucubalus colocynthis* to serve him out, the rogue.' At this, Jason burst into laughter and the helmsmen all stared across, eyes wide, ears straining, humour a most rare event on the quarterdeck.

'Coco... cubis?' Pat stared at his friend, mystified.

'The pith of the bitter apple. There is a trifle remaining in my medical chest; it hails from Candia. It is the strongest of all the purgatives, and mixed with three parts beans crushed in oil will send him to the heads for a day at least.'

'No, no, no; I beg you will not!' Pat was horrified. 'Have a care and be minded of our food in the cabin. He is tardy enough as things lie, and I would not care to see worse.'

'Very well, Pat,' Simon smiled, both his friends were pleased to see. A few seconds more and he resumed, 'I collect, as I stepped up from... from downstairs, hearing Abel here asking of your intentions... after the press is delivered. Would you care to speak of them?'

'Why, as to that, I am minded that we must await the intentions of their Lordships at the Admiralty. A number of English frigates are in these waters, and doubtless one will bear Melville's order. When, we cannot know, of course; until then, a return to Argostoli is in my mind. The packet may yet bring our orders to that place.'

The rogue in recent question appeared at that moment, bearing a tray with three generous glasses of a white liquid. 'Well, sorrs, 'ere be a tint for 'ee, from a pal o' mine aboard one o' them Greek barkys... *lion's milk* he called it; 'tis arak with three parts water, white as 'ee can see.'

'And you are quite sure of its provenance, Murphy, that you have diluted it to the appropriate measure?' teased Simon with unconcealed pleasure.

'Oh yes, sorr,' Murphy looked extremely doubtful.

'I suppose you are practised in those arts, eh, Murphy?' said Pat, 'That is to say *with dilution*... and with whisky particularly, I venture, eh? What d'ye say?'

'Whisky, sorr? Oh no, I ain't seen a drop since Mr Macleod took his bottles away with him... aboard *Eleanor*. He did not care to leave 'em aboard the barky.'

'I wonder why?' Pat laughed, Jason and Simon laughing with him; Murphy scowled and skulked away.

94

Jupiter did not disappoint them, the trio having enjoyed lion's milk refills from a suspicious Murphy for another hour until all were in amiable, relaxed mood, the telescope passed round for each to marvel in turn. It was nigh on midnight, Pickering on duty, when the party retired, Saturn entirely forgotten, claustrophobia wholly dispelled and a goodly degree of peace of mind attained by all.

The Cerigo strait was transited during the night, the dawn finding *Surprise* emerging to the open sea, making her turn and setting up for the north, for Hydra and beyond, to Aegina. Pat emerged on deck to be greeted by Codrington, the lieutenant plainly much pleased to command the frigate. *Surprise* was heading two points east of north, the weak *maestro* wind a helpful westerly on her larboard beam and the rising sun low in the sky on the starboard quarter, a brilliant yellow orb in a sky bereft of any trace of cloud. Things could not be better, thought Pat, in good cheer; and long may it last, he hoped.

For once his wishes were granted, no vessels being sighted all day, an uneventful one of great tranquillity, until the islet of Velopoula was passed to larboard as the sun was finally lost over the mountains of the Mani, the succeeding soft dusk light bestowing its peaceful blessing on the grateful men of *Surprise*, a sense of quietude settling about the barky as the hours rolled by.

In the cabin Pat sat with Simon and Marston, the chaplain having joined them by invitation and looking exceedingly happy. He had brought his violin. 'You are in the moon, Mr Marston, I venture,' prompted Pat cheerfully; 'What do you care to play?'

Marston, despite his obvious contentment, seemed a trifle hesitant; he was sitting in silence, his first glass of port wine lasting an age and the Greek cheese after supper little touched. It had been some weeks since the last invitation and he did not care to be in the least presumptuous in any respect, though he did concede that the times had hardly been propitious for musical entertainment. 'Sir, will we try for a trifle of Boccherini?' he suggested. It was a little optimistic, he reckoned himself, for the trio had enjoyed precious little practice for as long as he could remember. 'Though we are only three and we lack for a guitar, I am in the way for an attempt upon his guitar quintet number six. Indeed, I am much looking forward to when Mr Mower might care to join us in that delightful composition, but for the present I believe we might carry it off without him.'

'A capital notion,' Simon smiled by way of encouragement to a doubtful Pat, the surgeon seizing his viola and bow in a fit of enthusiasm, nodding to his fellows, a rising contentment firming within him. For several minutes the trio tuned their instruments in an ambience of mutual pleasure, the discordant squealing and wailing resonating far beyond the cabin, Murphy waiting behind the door in the coach muttering to himself, 'Well, there ain't no bleeding peace for the wicked.'

A momentary hiatus, a consensus of silence and Simon nodded to Marston, 'Pray give the note.'

The music began with Marston leading, for his skill with the violin surpassed by far the lesser talents of Pat and Simon, both striving hard to offer a full background with viola and 'cello for the sharper sounds of Marston's violin, his playing recognisably that of a near master, a subtle and sweet contrast to the steady foundation offered by the 'cello and Pat's best attempts upon intricacy which, whilst fair if not quite rough, would never have attracted applause anywhere, save perhaps for his gracious companions in the cabin. The musicians applied themselves with enthusiasm and, the volume rising, the cabin filled with a musical jubilation, a sense of joy touching the trio, smiles and nods passing from one to another as all other thoughts bar their concentration on delightful sounds were expunged, Simon's fears fading in the soaring, exuberant and quite lovely music.

Though the precision of the rendition was somewhat doubtful; indeed, it might well not have been recognised as the master's intentions by any audience in the great halls of Vienna, Paris or Rome, for the three musical companions it represented a triumph nevertheless, delivering in that precious twenty or so minutes whilst it lasted the tiniest of indications that, after the bloodshed, after the enduring fear and grave apprehension of recent weeks, there remained some small interlude in which the treasured elements of life might be appreciated, during which the fellowship of valued friends could be enjoyed in the sublime release of music. Indeed, such convivial moments were, in the beleaguered minds of all three present, the foundations of worthwhile life itself.

On the quarterdeck, Codrington, on duty, was standing with Jason, the ship's movement through the water exceedingly gentle, just the merest hint of roll and not the least rise and fall of the bow in the calm sea state. Both were much enjoying the music as it rose up to fly through the glass skylight and the grating, the coach doors left open in the enduring warmth.

At the waist Pickering stood by himself, staring forward, listening intently, nothing disturbing his precious tranquillity and great pleasure found in the sounds, lifting his spirits mightily, for in recent months the spark of humour had left him, and because of that he had found himself downcast, the dissatisfaction of it lying hard with him, for he was customarily the most buoyant of souls.

On the gun deck Dalby stood, leaning on *Devil's Tongue*, Mason, Fisher and two score more of men with him taking in the melodic pleasures emanating from within the cabin, barely a word spoken as all absorbed the sonorous flow, waves of precious pleasure striking welcome chords in weary minds, the sweet sounds greatly in contrast with the thunder, the blood and the violent death of recent, frantic times.

The reluctant ending was reached eventually, despite all three players striving to preserve the pleasure of the piece with *ad hoc* additions, and it was followed by an enthusiastic round of mutual applause. Even Murphy, behind the door, conceded a smile to himself before he entered to attend his captain.

'Murphy, there you are,' beamed Pat, speaking in cordial voice, 'More toasted cheese for three, if you will, and we will have another bottle of port.'

In the cabin the cold cheese toasts were consumed, the residue of port wine was finished and the second bottle welcomed as Murphy returned and strived to fuss about the table, recalling the earlier comment about whisky and dimly aware that perhaps another of his nefarious transgressions had been discovered.

Later, after the coffee and in the dim yellow glow of the two Argand lamps, the three friends, grasping for a continuance of their rare relaxation, determined to play on, mutual nods exchanged from time to time as improvisations followed variations, all seized by the moment, all basking in the sense of tranquillity, the three gripped by a benign physical and mental relaxation, so rare, settling upon them all; and the delightful sounds resonated throughout the ship for further uninterrupted hours, a hundred men and more gathered on the deck outside the coach to listen. For all it was a blessed hiatus within a world of unrelenting strain, the precious time a gift of unfettered pleasure; the fatigue that all had long endured was held at bay, at arm's length. As time progressed, the musicians tired and the music slowed. The third bottle of port and the cheese reinforcements were quite finished and the lamps were guttering, their oil near finished. Wisps of smoke began to waft all about the cabin in the weakest of draught, no longer any glass in the stern panes, when all three friends gratefully crept off to their cots, each man in stronger spirits and resolved to better endure such tribulations as might likely come on the morrow. A little of the customary apprehension of the new day faded, a trifle more of inner strength was seized upon by all; so much the better to endure whatever they might be tasked with, a little more of fortitude found to face come what may.

Chapter Five

Friday 27th May 1825   20:00   *Aegina port*

Another day of uninterrupted sailing, blissful and so sublimely recuperative for all aboard, and Hydra was left astern to larboard as the northerly *meltemi* wind fell away and the sun began its descent towards the western horizon. Poros was passed as the sun kissed the mountain tops over the Morea and sunset came upon them as Aegina loomed on the bow, when *Surprise* made short boards to close on the island during the gloaming, passing Agistri to larboard; and in the dying of the light she slowed to a stop, all sails aback, to drop her anchor a cable off the quay at Aegina port, the scene before them one of absolute tranquillity.

'Sir, I do believe that is *Eleanor* over there...' declared Codrington with a modicum of excitement, 'Look, sir, a cable off and behind the caique. There, to starboard of the mistico.'

'Why, I do believe you are right, Mr Codrington... 'tis something of a mystery... I had believed she would be at Nauplio. What's amiss, eh? Mr Sampays, prepare my boat, if you please. I am going ashore directly.'

Pat's bargemen pulled across to the quay in darkness, bearing for the lights of the town, dozens reflecting on the still, black water, ten minutes of burning curiosity in the minds of all until the barge was tied alongside and they were standing on the quay when, from out of the inky shadows of a waterside building, Duncan Macleod, Mower and all the Eleanors appeared. 'Good evening, sir. We sighted the barky as she made her turn, a cable shy of Agistri.'

'Good evening, Mr Macleod, lads,' declared Pat happily, the reunion more pleasing in being wholly unexpected. The officers shook hands, the men clasped hands, exchanged loud greetings, all the Surprises pressing their fellows of *Eleanor* for an explanation of their presence.

'Sir, if you please,' prompted Duncan, 'Let us repair to the taverna over there where we can speak further.' This seemed an eminently sensible suggestion to all the Surprises, the men most particularly welcoming mention of the glorious prospect of liquor.

All were ensconced within minutes, enjoying rough, red wine and loud, jovial banter, when Pat and Duncan shifted to the privacy and quietude of the back room of the house. 'We are sent here by Mavrocordato to await your arrival with the coin press,' Duncan began, Pat simply nodding, his curiosity rising by the minute. 'We are carrying the gol... *the cargo*,' Duncan's voice dropped to a whisper. 'His Highness is minded that Nauplia is no longer the place for it, no prospect of safety for it there whilst waiting for the coin press and its foundry to become established here on the island.'

'Ibrahim... his advance through the Morea... would it be?'

'Aye, and there is a deal of activity in Nauplia since a week or more... excavations abounding everywhere and rumours of a treasure of gold being buried somewhere within the town. Neither does the prince believe that this island is secure... if, that is, the word of such a treasure leaks out, for it is a small place and, as you may collect from life at home, there are precious few secrets in such rural places.'

'What then does the Prince care to do? What does he wish for the... *the cargo*?'

'He has asked; indeed, he has begged... that we will convey it to a place of sure sanctuary until... until the military and political situation becomes plain. It may have reached your ears that Kolokotrones is to be released from his prison?'

'There has been much speculation, of course.'

'It is expected to happen on the morrow, and Mavrocordato fears that once he gets wind of the Tsar's loan... as is sure to happen, then he will demand possession of the gold to pay his men... and that will be the end of that, no new Greek coins, all gone into the hands of brigands and bandits for their personal enrichment.'

'I dare say there are many who would much care for enrichment,' Pat sighed, 'I would not be averse to a trifle of it myself. You do collect that we ain't seen any pay since we left

Falmouth? The men ain't happy about that, no, and Murphy's whingeing is the curse of the cabin, so it is.'

'Doubtless Murphy will be pleased to hear that the gold is coming back aboard the barky, Hah! Hah!' Duncan laughed.

Pat smiled, 'This place of safety... this sanctuary... Where is the prince minded that we will deliver the gold?'

'He is of the opinion that there is but one place in the whole of Greece, all its islands included, where it is sure it will be safe.'

Pat had already pondered for several minutes the perilous predicament of every part of Greece, everywhere either occupied or threatened by Ottoman forces on land or sea, until he could control his curiosity no longer and interjected, 'Where is this precious place, Duncan, tell?'

'With the monks... of the many monasteries abounding near Mount Athos, on the mountainous peninsula there... no roads in... save for the most miserable of footpaths... and plentiful hiding places.'

'Ahhh,' Pat exhaled, his mind trying to picture the Holy Mountain, as it was known by all, until an expression of deep scepticism slowly formed on his face, 'Will I say there seems but one almighty flaw in the scheme... if my recall serves me; that is to say... was not that place overrun by the Turk after independence was declared there.'

Duncan nodded, sighed, as if to say he could not quite believe his own words, 'Quite so, and much of the monasteries' treasures have been stolen by the Turk military since the occupation began, yet the Tsar has protested to the Porte, and the Sultan has subsequently promised a cessation, published an edict... that looting is punishable by death.'

'But to deliver half a million pounds worth of gold to... *to a place with a Turk garrison?*' Pat smiled, 'Come, come, Duncan; are we to cast all our sensibilities overboard?'

'It is... it is an idea which strains credulity, no doubt, but the Turk occupation and the remoteness of the monasteries ensure that no *Greek* brigand will venture to that bleak, barren place. The inhabitants... the *Greek inhabitants* are entirely monks, and we must presume they possess little interest in *earthly* treasures.'

'Mmmm... and the Turks will stand idle? The notion seems greatly doubtful, I will say.'

'I can only speak of what the prince has said,' declared Duncan, although his face betrayed his thoughts on the matter. 'Seemingly, the sanctity of the peninsula has been vouched by the Sultans in Constantinople for several hundred years... until the present troubles, and more recently the safety of the monks and monasteries has been guaranteed by the Tsar himself who, for some time, has sent aid to the Orthodox monasteries there. Hence, it is Mavrocordato's belief that the present garrison would not dare to touch again upon the monasteries for fear that the Tsar would hear of it, likely would intervene, and so such would bring war to the common border between Russia and the Ottoman Empire.'

'Come, come, Duncan; think now,' Pat was not persuaded, 'Did ye ever find a soldier - or a sailor for that matter - who was above a trifle of booty, a guinea or two of prize money, eh? Is not a measure of capabarre one of the navy's old traditions... *one of the oldest...* Did ye ever know a sailor who passed up an honest theft, eh?'

Duncan nodded resignedly, the scheme seeming ever less credible as time had passed. He persevered, 'The prince is minded that neutral vessels continue to deliver supplies to the monks, and so the presence of *Eleanor*, an English-flagged vessel, will attract no attention. We are to go to the most inaccessible monastery, the Great Lavra, on the east slopes of Mount Athos. There is a tiny strand nearby which will serve our purpose. An agent of the prince will ensure that... for every night of the next week... there will be a party of monks awaiting our arrival, at midnight... so that the cargo may be unloaded and swiftly shifted away to a secret place of storage, its movement unnoticed by any Turk presence.'

'Doubtless there is something in what the prince says,' murmured Pat without the least conviction, his mind wholly failing to dispel his own grave doubts. In fact, he was already thinking of the passage to Mount Athos, 'And what of the infernal coin press? What is to be done with that?'

'That will be the ostensible reason *Surprise* is come here, to this island, to deliver it. No word will be uttered about bringing or removing anything else.'

'Very well, we will unload the press in the morning. I am minded that may take some considerable time. We will speak further at breakfast of what to do next, of the passage until we fetch Mount Athos. Now, Duncan, to other... will I say... more pressing matters, Hah! Hah! Will ye join me for another whet? I am mortal parched since we let slip her anchor.'

Midnight and back in the cabin, Pat with Duncan settled for a nightcap of Greek brandy, Murphy in surly mood, prohibited from joining the shore party and tasked with cleaning the cabin, a deal of glass fragments, the tiniest of ones, lingering and shifting about the deck in the strongest of winds, as Pat had remarked since several days. As Pat lit up a rare cigar, quite unexpectedly Simon entered to join them, despite the late hour. Pat, even in the muted light of the lamp, noticed his tired eyes, reddened as if by rubbing.

'What's afoot?' asked Pat. 'Did you not care for sleep?'

'I would like it of all things,' said Simon, 'but of late it much eludes me and I have taken to promenading upon the... the upper deck would it be, where the prominent great wheel resides... *the quarterdeck; there, I have it!* Forgive me, I am not quite in my intellects this evening.' A tolerably credible explanation coming to mind, for he was not much given to discussion of his own feelings, particularly those in sad spells of personal distress, he elaborated, 'A perplexing contemplation on the efficacy of laudanum in a particular individual, one of the wounded it was.'

'How is he?' asked Pat.

'He will survive, I believe.'

'Could you do with a drop of brandy,' offered Pat with audible concern, 'a cigar perhaps?'

'No, thank you; I beg to decline, though I might care for the merest splash of hot coffee. Murphy, would you have the good grace and benevolence to make the smallest of pot for a tired man?'

'Well, I ain't slept a wink at all yet, your honour,' moaned Murphy in grudging voice, but seeing Pat's face he sniffed and quickly appended his salvation, 'But as it's yourself asking then I'll cut along to the galley d'reckly.' Sensing reprobation, he sniffed again and hastened out before Pat's remonstrance could be inflicted upon him.

'When I find myself on watch at the midnight hour, nothing doing, I am oft minded to think of bonny Scotland,' declared Duncan, equally aware that all did not seem to be well with his friend. 'A brace of grouse or a fish from the Minch, the turf burning brightly and a wee dram at the fireside table; there's satisfaction for a tired man, aye.'

'I am entirely as one with your sentiments, I am so... and - save for bonny Scotland - these days I would be hard-pressed to think of anywhere else as being home save for the dear bar... barky... *the barquentine.*'

'Simon, I pass over you calling the ship a barquentine,' murmured Pat quietly. 'I will concede that there is an equal number of masts, I do so,' a small laugh ventured but without gaining any response. 'Will I ask, were you engaged in any particular observation on deck?'

'I was contemplating on a brief poem which Mower delights in. He read it to me when I last attended his wounds... All such are healing most admirably, I hasten to add. The words have lodged with a goodly degree of fixation within my memory, and I was thinking of them just now.'

'Come on then, auld friend; let us hear it if you will,' Duncan spoke in cheerful voice, seeking to lift Simon's spirits.

'Very well; here it is, I have written the words down.' Simon pulled a scrap of grubby paper from his pocket. 'I will endeavour to recite the words with the emphasis Mower accords to them,

As wave is driven by wave
And each, pursued, pursues the wave ahead,
So time flies on and follows, flies and follows,
Always, for ever and new.

What was before is left behind;
What never was is now;
And every passing moment is renewed.'

'A most admirable poem indeed,' declared Duncan with a slight gesture towards clapping.

'Though a trifle melancholic,' said Pat, fretting, not caring to see his friend downcast, for such was obvious despite Simon's pretensions. 'Another of Mower's?'

'Ovid, it is; the great man of poetry and, so I always thought, a writer of considerable talent... the man possessing a commendable philosophical bent.'

'But... Simon, is there some other matter sitting ill upon your mind, tell?' Pat, not convinced, pressed, 'You have a greatly tired look about you, you do... as if you are bearing all the sorrows of Connacht... and - doubtless you will recall - there's no smoke without fire. What's afoot? I beg you will speak plain now.'

'Oh, 'tis nothing, the tiniest of blow to my nose as I stumbled and fell upon the... *the compass would it be*, the device within the binnac... *within that infernal box* on the floor... upstairs.' Simon's voice lacked the slightest conviction. 'It presented itself in the darkness as I endeavoured to reach the steps in an upright, seamanlike fashion... the helmsmen staring. Doubtless it could better be located elsewhere, somewhere less prejudicial to the passage of the pedestrian in the forceful swaying of this vessel.'

Neither Pat nor Duncan believed a word, not the smallest roll of the ship finding their attention for many an hour. Murphy returned with the coffee. He poured Simon's cup, and moved in haste and silence towards the door before he might be tasked with something more. 'Thankee...' said Pat in loud voice, determining on different tactics, a change to that subject which was ever dear to his steward's heart: the old saw was sure to divert his friend, '... and Murphy, will you look to Doctor Ferguson's coat in the morning? He has taken a fall whilst wearing it, and in the broad daylight it might be thought that he had stumbled into the bilges. I am sure the Doctor would much appreciate you favouring it with a wash... a goodly, severe wash... *the severest.*'

A rare smile from Murphy was immediately quashed by vehement objection; 'Oh it will do for a long time yet, it is only my second-best coat,' protested Simon; 'I wear it during my operations... the lesser ones that is, and... and doubtless when my apron becomes too much bloodied... there is a... a flow, a fluid transference... but I pay that no mind.'

'You will allow me to insist,' declared Pat, smiling wide, his overt laughter suppressed with difficulty, Murphy hovering with transparently keen interest.

'Here we are,' declared Duncan, tiring of the coat and interjecting, 'and we are speaking as if we are carrying all the ills of the world... but the plain fact of the matter is... we ain't. We will be here some weeks yet, no doubt, and then it is off, away to that *wild Atlantic stream*, to Biscay... and I don't care to remind you that our troubles when we were last there were greater than they are in this place. What do you say, Simon? Doubtless you collect the tempest, our near destruction? Yet here we are with nothing more than a hesitation, a worry... and let us cast that aside, for we know not our prospects for the morrow, but we are here... in the barky, in the dear *Surprise*... and with all our shipmates about us, and... and I am minded that there is not a deal in life that is ever more significant than that.'

'I am very sensible of your warm words, dear friends, I am so,' Simon nodded, 'and allow me to say that I am in the most humble and reverent respect of your kindness. Thank you... thank you both.'

Sunday 29th May 1825   23:00   *approaching Mount Athos*
A choppy sea, a fiercely blowing wind and blackness everywhere, save for the tiniest sliver of a moon casting the weakest glow of illumination as *Surprise* heaved to a league off the south-east tip of the mountainous peninsula. *Eleanor* left her to wait, the schooner hauling north a bare cable off the shore. They had sailed together and had made exceptional passage, blessed by a constant eight knots south-easterly wind since

departing Aegina. Pat had left Duncan, with Codrington, in command on the frigate, bringing Jason, Pickering and a score of Surprises with him on the schooner; his own barge, *Eleanor's* Deal cutter and *Surprise's* launch were all in tow.

'I do not much care for this caper,' muttered Pat to no-one in particular, his officers standing with him near the wheel. They had passed the lights of the monastery of the Great Lavra, its tiny rocky inlet of a harbour barely visible in the weak moonlight, sailing on for another mile and a half, keen eyes staring into the inky gloom, searching anxiously for the promised small strand.

'There!' exclaimed Pickering, pointing to what conceivably might be a lantern, low and near the water's edge.

'I see it,' murmured Pat, 'Let us take her closer.' Another five minutes passed; the schooner's men were finding her handling difficult in the still strongly gusting *scirocco*. *Eleanor* was rolling hard, her canvas all furled save for her solitary square topsail. Slowly she fought her way through the rough, rising swell in the shoaling of the water to approach the beach, still a hundred yards off, a lighter shade of shore just barely visible in the darkness, not the least protection afforded there from the wind and waves.

'Can you take her in a whet closer, Mr Mower?' asked Pat in doubtful low voice, his scepticism enduring and unconcealed, the obvious dangers of landing a small party on a hostile shore brewing a rising sense of apprehension within him.

'I believe so, sir.' With great skill, little spread of sail available to him and the feisty wind blowing as strong as ever, Mower brought *Eleanor's* bow round, coming back into the wind with a long, looping turn, the schooner immediately losing all way to bob and roll in the chop and swell some fifty yards from the strand. Her braces were slackened until her topsail flapped about with gusto, ropes and canvas cracking in the wind.

'Into the boat, lads!' shouted Pat, and a half-dozen of his men, pistols thrust into waist belts, cutlasses strapped to them, clambered down the side and into the barge as it rocked and crashed against the schooner. A struggling Jason was helped aboard. 'Pull! Pull for the shore!' cried Pat; the die was cast.

The fiercely volatile motions of the barge threw all about, rising and falling on the wave crests, rolling from side to side; it promised to be an uncomfortable pull. All hands set to, swiftly rowing towards the light on the strand. It was indeed a lantern, held high by a lone monk standing with obvious difficulty far out on the sand, the sea state volatile, the man's legs washed by irregularly breaking waves. 'A most determined fellow,' thought Pat. He gazed to the shore proper and could make out a half-dozen more monks in the shadows, standing ready with donkeys.

The boat's keel crunched into the sand and pebbles, Pat, Pickering, Jason and the Surprises leaping out, scrambling ashore through the surf, the boat rapidly hauled up onto the beach. The awaiting monks stood further back, dry and in mute welcome. The man with the lantern hastened across the wet strand to greet the arrivals, his fellows starting to follow but maintaining a cautious few steps behind him, the weak light of his lantern illuminating many apprehensive faces, the monks' themselves registering their own continuing uncertainty about who the arrivals might yet prove to be.

Pat and his men paced up the soft beach towards the monks. 'Mr Jason, kindly introduce us, if you will,' he murmured, his own men remaining mute, both parties staring silently at each other as they halted. A high state of nervousness prevailed within the Surprises, standing on the enemy-occupied shore in the dead of night and with no more than a few brace of pistols between them.

Jason approached the monk with the lantern who continued to stand a little prominent of his fellows. 'We are here at the request of His Highness, Prince Mavrocordato... We bear his communication and cargo. This is Captain Patrick O'Connor. We are here in the service of the Hellenic Republic.'

The ice was cracked if not entirely broken; the monk nodded with a ghost of a smile on his face; he shook hands with Jason and Pat in turn, though he said little more than his own name as introduction before turning to beckon his companions with a wave of his hand. Immediately the monks moved to bring the donkeys towards the Surprises, their task plainly understood.

'Mr Jason,' declared Pat, 'kindly explain that the gol... *the cargo* is still on the schooner; we will send for it now. Mr Pickering, be so good as to signal *Eleanor*, Mr Mower is to offload the ingots into the cutter and the launch directly. Now, what to do here?' Pat looked all about him, listening intently. Nothing could he hear save for the surf and the occasional snort from the donkeys; the monks remained silent, staring, watching. 'Mason, get along the strand for a cable or so to the south and stand watch; Tremayne, likewise, go to the north and listen out.'

It was an hour of enduring suspense before all the ingots were brought ashore, necessitating two trips with the boats, the weight of the ingots so very heavy. Jason strived to engage with the leader of the monks with little success, few words spoken and no clue offered as to the eventual sanctuary for the gold, even as Pat fretted, pacing up and down the strand. When the last of the donkeys was loaded with what seemed to Pat to be an intolerable burden, cursory farewells were uttered. The caravan plodded away into the darkness, and the Surprises hauled with weary arms on their oars to pull for the schooner, every man minded that would be the last anyone ever heard of the gold.

Wednesday 1st June 07:00   approaching the Cavo Doro strait

The strong south-westerly *scirocco* wind had not relented for even a minute and the return passage - directly south from Mount Athos - was proving to be an unremitting purgatory. Pat had calculated that progress might be measured at something no better than two knots, for *Surprise* was holding as close to the wind as she would stay. He stood on deck at the rail, warmed with coffee, and he stared all about him, hoping for a weather improvement as he waited for his first breakfast. Euboea's Cape Kafireas lay off the starboard bow, the island of Andros fine on the larboard bow, and *Surprise* was bearing directly for the Cavo Doro strait between the two. The rising sea swell made him uncomfortable, for it heralded - as he knew so well - the sure prospect of bad weather approaching.

Duncan stepped across to join him. 'I venture it will be a long passage to Cephalonia, sir,' he declared in friendly fashion, both men acutely conscious of extremely noisy squeaks of strain emanating from the mizzen topmast, under a deal of load as *Surprise* strived to make headway, no worthwhile alternative course available to her as she made for the strait, just a handful of miles to the south. That the frigate was patently struggling hard was evident to all aboard. The carpenter was a very worried man, fretting over the two repaired yards in particular, both considered to be greatly fragile.

'I dare say... if, that is, that mast and the yards hold fast... and the gods grace us with a more favourable wind,' Pat looked upwards even as he uttered the words, a particularly loud squeal from the mast remarked by all on the quarterdeck with rising unease.

'Breakfast is ready, sorr,' shouted Murphy, appearing from below and bellowing all across the quarterdeck, the helmsmen's heads raised and Pat irritated. His ire was immediately choked off by a shout from the maintop, 'Sails ahoy, larboard quarter!'

'Murphy, my glass... from the cabin!' cried Pat, the scowl wiped instantly from his face. From the vigorously rolling deck he could see nothing of the ships sighted, all far distant. Two minutes more of suspense passed until the steward returned when Pat gazed upon the horizon, his eyes straining in vain, still nothing visible yet. 'Mr Pickering, take the glass and call me when they are in sight. I am minded to take my breakfast. You have the deck. Mr Macleod, d'ye care to join me?'

'Who could they be?' asked Duncan, munching assiduously on toasted hard tack and sausages, seemingly oblivious to the uncomfortable motions of the ship, the table rising and falling with perilous instability, the frigate heeled well over, her bow repetitively rising and falling on successive wave crests with a thundering judder, timbers creaking loud everywhere.

'Miaoulis is coming from Calamata to Hydra,' declared Pat in loud voice, the wind gusting strong through the smashed stern gallery, 'It can't be him... and Sakhtouri is reported as being near Samos, waiting for any sighting of the Turk coming out from the Golden Horn. Perhaps it is his brigs? Of course, it may also be Johnny Turk... I venture we ain't seen the last of Khosref yet...

No, not by a long chalk. We will see more later in the morning. With this wind it will be as slow for them as it is for us. It seems they too, whoever they are, are approaching the strait. It will be some hours yet before we can make them out... put our doubts aside.' He drained his cup. 'Would you care for the last sausage?' Duncan nodded. 'Never any doubt there,' murmured Pat to himself. 'Murphy, pray cease scratching your head and light along another pot of coffee.'

At the solitary bell announcing the forenoon watch, Pat and Duncan stepped up on deck, the distant topsails of the converging squadron just visible, hull-down on the horizon. A mere five miles more to the strait between Andros and Euboea, and *Surprise* seemed to be slower than ever against the fiercely adverse gale-strength wind, only the most modest of progress reported by Pickering in the last hour. The strait between the two islands remained a close but taunting prospect. The general tension aboard ship was rising, the distant ships formerly reported on the larboard quarter were now off the larboard beam, undeniably converging even with the tacks forced upon them by the severe headwind, the newcomers also fighting against it to reach the strait and bear down on the barky from the east. Three bells and Pat, his uncertainty rising to a state of anxiety, climbed to the maintop himself and settled precariously on the platform with his glass.

The view in every direction was grey, the sky was streaked with low cloud and the sun's warmth had yet to influence the day; the drizzle of the morning was deteriorating and hard rain was setting in. He stared hard to larboard, to the emerging, closing vessels, their hulls at last become plainly visible. He could identify a razee, to his mind the chopped-down two-decker looking for all the world like... like what? He could not find the word on his lips; he cursed; she was perhaps the ideal of all ship types: as fast or nearly so as a frigate and near twice the weight of guns. He peered intently through the glass, wiping away the blurring rain every minute or so; there were at least two more frigates and they were accompanied by several score of brigs at the least. Worse, it appeared that astern of them were yet a further dozen vessels. His spirits sank in an instant, for such could not be Sakhtouri, who possessed nothing of the ilk of even a frigate let alone a razee, and even brigs in such numbers was but a Greek pipe dream. He strained his eyes to peer at the closest vessel, a frigate; staring hard he saw, proud at her maintop, flying bar straight in the fierce wind, the unmistakeable Turk red flag.

A surge of despair flushed through him in a sickening rush. The crudest, the most perfunctory of swift calculations had revealed to him in an instant the crushing conclusion: the wind being what it was, the Turks would be alongside within an hour or two; he doubted it would be longer. 'May God help us,' he declared vehemently, his words whipped away, unheard, in the fierce wind.

Wednesday 1st June 1825   10:30   *in the Cavo Doro strait*

Five bells stridently resonated all along the deck as if, to the many minds aware of Pat's observations, in announcement of imminent and cataclysmic doom. The leading Turk frigate was a mile off *Surprise's* larboard quarter and inexorably closing, her progress also much slowed whilst she too sailed close-hauled on her southerly course, and - similarly alarming for the men on the quarterdeck - half a dozen Turk brigs were moving to put themselves directly astern of *Surprise*, as if to block any intentions of flight, to thwart a drastic turnabout aided by and borne on the fierce wind. The most powerful Turk warship, the flagship, the razee of 64 guns, appeared to be struggling. She had lost her foretop yard, its sail hanging loose about the fore course, and, to Pat's gaze, the ship looked to be in difficulties, struggling against the extremely strong gusts, perhaps having turned into the wind a point or two so as to enter the strait before subsequently falling off; consequently she had dropped back from the van of her escorting squadron by a quarter-mile or more.

'We will hoist English colours, Mr Pickering,' declared Pat in matter of fact voice. 'Perhaps they will pass us by.' He did not believe such was likely, but he knew in his heart that few, if any, choices were left to him. Progress was excruciatingly slow and flight was not possible, the Turk brigs plainly would swiftly fall upon a *Surprise* turning back.

'Aye aye, sir. Dalby, fetch the colours.'

All along *Surprise's* larboard rail a hundred and seventy men gripped the hammock netting; they stared in trepidation and dismay at the oncoming enemy fleet: it would not be long before the leading frigate's guns would be close enough to open fire, if they were so minded. On the quarterdeck Pat and all his officers similarly stood gazing in silent assessment, not the least alternative coming to mind. The severe south-westerly *scirocco* was tearing forcefully at hats, wresting open jackets, lifting lapels, the crew's wide sailcloth trousers everywhere flapping in the fierce gusts, and the rain was setting in, heavier than ever, driven by the gale to penetrate the least chink in clothing armour.

Near the helm, Simon, increasingly wet, looked particularly glum, despondent even. The surgeon waited in mute trepidation for what his colleagues might determine as appropriate measures to effect escape, his own imagination not running to the slightest idea of how salvation might be gained; indeed, he could recall only the fighting exit from the Bay of Navarino when the barky had been in a more desperate situation.

'We cannot come about,' declared Pat eventually in sombre voice, 'having no sea room in our lee and with those brigs astern. We have no choice but to clear the passage... and fall off... to the east, when the wind will be on her beam or quarter... and, I venture, we will gain two or three knots.' All present simply stared in mute silence: that the Turk vessels in pursuit would also benefit from such a course change Pat had not cared to mention, which did not go unremarked, even by Simon, gripped by his own rising forebodings of what might be about to be unleashed upon his shipmates and himself, the fear of yet more blood at the forefront of his anxiety and his fervently whirring mind's worst fears going wholly unchecked.

'Mr Timmins,' shouted Pat, beckoning the gunner closer, 'Might there be any more of the incendiary shells left to us? We may have need of them.'

'Three are finished, sir, and four others require work.'

'Very good.' Pat turned to Pickering, 'Mr Pickering, what remains of the powder?'

'Perhaps the best part of the last barrel, sir... of that which Miaoulis gifted us... but - I regret to say - there is precious little shot. I collect two dozen or so of ball... but there is a plentiful quantity of grape.'

'Plainly we cannot fight that frigate, so many consorts so close with her...' Pat's sober conclusion was declared loud and with a bitter tone. Similar dismay and angst was endemic amongst everyone present. Pat continued, 'For 'tis plain we must be destroyed...' His voice tailed off, near indiscernible in the gale, his words whipped away by the wind, '... and so all that is left to us is to flee.'

Glum nods of resignation followed from all present. 'Mr Macleod,' the words were uttered by Marston, standing with Simon, the chaplain self-evidently dejected and anxious, 'If we are unable to gain a considerable distance... from the Turks... to flee... that is to say... with no... *no sea room* available to us... and neither can we fight... pray tell, what then is to be done?' All other officers politely looked away, leaving only Macleod to stare at the chaplain, for the question was banal in the extreme, embarrassing even.

A long minute of silence followed for all present before Duncan replied, as quietly as he could in the tumult of the wind, 'Then, sir, we must strike our colours.'

The chaplain was visibly shocked, horrified even, could say nothing more, and he looked down to the deck, the realisation striking him that everyone else already knew; such an entirely likely and distressing outcome had been plain to everyone but himself. 'Pray forgive me,' he whispered again to Duncan, 'May the Lord Almighty protect us.'

'Aye, indeed.'

'Mr Macleod,' Pat, thinking hard, broke the despondent hiatus on the quarterdeck after a minute, 'the topgallant masts are still housed abaft the topmasts?' Puzzled glances were exchanged between all in earshot.

'Aye, sir; main and fore, that they are. There is no mizzen t'gallant hoisted since the mizzen topmast was repaired.'

'Very well. Mr Codrington, send the men to the tops, hoist topgallant masts and haul in to a single reef the tops'ls.' Audible exclamations were evident from several men close by even in the wind's furore.

'In this strong wind, sir... *in this gale*... and whilst we are close-hauled?' asked Codrington, staring in open and very visible disbelief.

'Yes, yes... for sure they will be of no use at the present... that is plain to the meanest intelligence,' said Pat, scowling and looking to his officers, 'but they will be of the most precious value after we make our turn, south-east, to put the wind on her starboard beam, when we will need every knot to make our escape.' Pat wiped his face, the soaking rain cold on his chest and back. 'For the moment, if we do not clear the strait before the Turk and gain some headway, we are done for. Let the yards be braced but leave the t'gallants clewed up until we are ready for the hare to make her run.'

'Aye aye, sir,' Codrington nodded and turned to the bosun, who remained aghast, not the least appetite for sending men aloft in the gale, blowing ever stronger, and holding little or no confidence that the topgallants would endure. 'Mr Sampays, tops'ls... a single reef, if you please, and hoist t'gallant masts, brace their yards, t'gallants to remain clewed up!' Sampays, horrified, hastened away with a pained face.

BOOM! BOOM! The pursuing frigate, closing astern, fired her bow chasers, the shot optimistic and falling short, the splashes invisible in the rain and the strong swell. Pat stared through his glass: the Turk fleet was close, frighteningly so, and it seemed as if the sea was filled with vessels of many kinds: brigs, corvettes, frigates and the flagship razee. Three brigs were very close about the flagship, the razee no longer motionless but moving again. He hastily counted two score more brigs with her and a further, more distant dozen brigs following, perhaps two miles astern. With a sinking feeling he realised that *Surprise* would struggle to escape such an armada; indeed, he knew in his heart that she could not, for many of the pursuing brigs might be far fleeter of sail than the barky, in her present state of jury-rigged repairs; certainly the half-dozen swift corvettes he had counted would overhaul his ship before very long, even in the fiercely adverse wind which beset them all. Doubtless *Surprise* could inflict grievous wounds upon several of her pursuers before her powder was exhausted and she was overwhelmed, but such conduct was not looked upon kindly by captains who might lose men killed by a quarry whose prospects were negligible, whose firing was ultimately futile. No, surrender was staring Pat in the face, and he could see little or no alternative. For the moment he would strive to flee, but he dare not fire his guns, for such would certainly be an insane act, one guaranteed to adversely colour his pursuer's leanings, most certainly towards a very hostile view of the Surprises, which would be extremely dangerous were they to be eventually captured. Indeed, an enraged and victorious Turk captain might well justly condemn a number of his captured adversaries to death by hanging, Pat included, for opening and conducting an engagement with such hopeless prospects and wasting life.

Pat looked closer to home; near the stern rail Timmins was busying himself all about the two light chasers. He had loaded the powder and shot, for his mates were already pushing down with the rammers. Pat's heart missed a beat; he hastened to the gun where the master gunner was standing ready and he put his hand over the gunlock, 'Mr Timmins, you must not fire that gun!'

'Aye aye, sir, just readying it.'

Pat turned back to his inquisitively staring lieutenant, 'Mr Pickering,' he shouted, 'tell the men on the gun deck... no one is to open a gun port; make that clear to every gunner, I SAY THAT PLAIN: NO MAN IS TO OPEN A GUN PORT! There must not be any discharge, never the one!'

Surprise was very close to the southern extremity of the strait, perhaps a mere half-mile remaining before she could make her turn away from the wind, yet the leading Turk frigate had crept closer still, was only three cables astern of the barky, her smaller calibre bow chasers continuing to fire and the shots falling short by a bare few yards of *Surprise's* stern; their splashes were occasionally visible and Pat was much fretting for the rudder. Another tortuous half-hour, he reckoned, and *Surprise* could bear off to the south-east and into an open ocean of water before her, and with the wind on her beam she would be faster by a long mile. Such calculations raced again through Pat's frantically calculating mind even as he strived to ignore the churning, wrenching anxieties gripping his stomach. No, he reflected, that simply would not do; the ship in her present deteriorated state could not really bring that off: she would always be too slow compared with her pursuers, the fast corvettes astern of the pursuing frigate. The chilling conclusion, that one to which he kept coming back, the one which in his heart he knew already, brought him back to earth, fierce tension gripping tighter his chest, a band of steel tightening around his head: the hounds would be hard on the barky's heels all the way, snapping at them, firing, doing at least a modicum of damage and likely killing some of his men. The most acute danger was the rudder, exposed and fragile. His heart sank further and his breathing accelerated in short, sharp gasps. Neither could he return fire; he dare not, it simply was not done; the consequences might be grave indeed. He returned to his bleak and depressing ultimate conclusion of some minutes ago: he likely would have to strike his colours, but first he would try his last resort: pretend to be an English frigate. *Surprise* had the lines, for sure, and she had never returned fire; indeed, she had never opened her gun ports. But would the Turk captain be convinced? Composing himself to present some semblance of reassurance to his men, he strived for an authoritative voice, acutely conscious that he must preserve the spirits of his men, must keep them working to their common end, for a crew in disagreement, a crew who had lost hope, were in far greater danger of being killed. 'Gentlemen, the time has come when we must try our last remedy, the only one available to us. Mr Macleod, slacken the braces; we will bring her to a halt.' All about him cruelly shocked faces slowly folded to present a picture of extreme unhappiness.

Ten more minutes filled with grave anxiety and the wind seemed to blow ever more violently as *Surprise* rolled, rose and fell on the waves. The Turk frigate ceased fire and hauled alongside within another five minutes, her sails aback and heaving to just thirty yards off *Surprise's* larboard beam, all her guns run out, dangerous, threatening. *Surprise's* closed gun ports having never opened, and such being perfectly visible to the Turk captain, had probably caused him to direct his fire short even as he overhauled his quarry; that and the English flag at her mizzen top, whipping mercilessly in the fierce gale, now truly a tempest. An English frigate in these waters was not unusual, Pat said to himself, and the Turk too would surely know that.

Jason, interpreting for Pat, shouted through the speaking tube, 'Desist, sir, for we are English... ENGLISH, and we protest your firing.' The wind was so strong it was doubtful anyone on the near frigate could hear, and the Surprises waited, watching as the Turk prepared to lower a boat.

The half-dozen fast corvettes had also caught up; they were passing by and beyond the two stopped frigates, continuing to tack south-west with frequent short boards, and they were near to clearing the strait. *Surprise* and the Turk, their yard tips close to touching, were rolling vigorously on the severe swell, like bobbing corks on a windswept stream. The flagship, when Pat had last stared at it, was still a half-mile off and hauling towards them in short tacks, but now it too appeared to be motionless once again; indeed, she was beam on to the wind and rolling dramatically, the ship and her crew surely in the greatest of difficulties. Pat studied the scene intently and realised that the ship had lost all her topmasts; every one of them had been carried away in the gale; and now something more caught his attention, a small mystery presenting itself: at the tail of the Turk fleet several distant brigs were turning away, turning back. What did it signify? He could not imagine. He turned again to look at the adjacent Turk frigate, halted and rolling violently in the strong swell. Her own guns were all run out; he believed they were 24-pounders. At this range her firing would be devastating, she could not miss; her shot would smash straight through the oak of *Surprise's* hull without the least hindrance, sending showers of lethal splinters into his men. The Turk's boat was launched at last and was pulling towards *Surprise*, its crew struggling against wind and wave tops for five minutes of extreme difficulty until they hauled alongside, an officer climbing aboard with two companions; all looked exceedingly unfriendly, all were wholly soaked to the skin, very windswept and utterly bedraggled.

'Come, sir, to the cabin,' declared Pat with as much of a gesture to cordiality as he thought appropriate, the Turk officer and his aides a picture of misery and obliging immediately. 'Murphy, rouse out the coffee... as fast as can be. You may care to run!'

The Turks sat at the table, their oilskins liberally dripping water all over the deck. Pat hesitated: whether to protest their firing or make them welcome? Jason and Duncan were seated either side of him. The Turks sat opposite, in visible discomfort, their own formal introductions made, yet unintelligible to Pat.

'I am Captain O'Connor of His Majesty's Ship *Surprise*, gentlemen...' declared Pat as loudly and in as commanding a response as he could manage, Jason translating, '... on passage for the Ionians.'

Had the Turks heard him plain? Pat wondered, for they looked distinctly unimpressed. The gale wind was obtrusive, no glass remaining in the stern gallery, and all the sounds of the storm were carried into the cabin in a background cacophony. The moment seemed bleak indeed. A short pause and the Turk's leader, the lieutenant, spoke up, his voice betraying his deep scepticism, 'Captain, it has not escaped our attention that your ship evidences a deal of battle damage...' Jason translated.

'*Storm* damage... a severe storm it was... *the severest*,' Pat blustered, speaking louder, in a voice which even his friends would never have been convinced by, his plan already looking doubtful. 'Lieutenant... Lieutenant?' his recall failed him as Jason strived to translate in authoritative voice, although he was himself far from sure it carried the least conviction.

'Youzbashi Suleiman, sir; at your service.'

Murphy's arrival was most welcome to Pat as his thoughts continued to race: what more to say? What might be believed? The steward swiftly poured the coffee: thick, strong and Turkish, splashing much upon the table as he struggled against the rise and fall of the deck. Pat hoped the divinely smelling brew would be to the Turks' liking, for he could find no interest in it himself despite his mouth being so very dry. The deck canted severely, the ship rolling violently in the swell, and the coffee slopped about in the small cups, Murphy's spill streaking across the table to drip from the edge.

'We are an English frigate, sir, *English...* Lieutenant... *Lieutenant Sulibashi...*' declared Pat in strong voice, his mind made up; his last card, his only card, was certainly no ace. Jason gulped as Pat resumed, '... and I do not care to see you firing on my ship.' Pat spoke again in a louder voice, near shouting; it was all that was left to him, 'In fact I protest most strongly and... and it is sure that the authorities in Corfu will make the most serious complaint to the Porte.'

The lieutenant was unimpressed; he drained his coffee in one, setting the cup down theatrically and continuing in a cold, bleak voice, 'Then it is incumbent upon me to ask your papers, sir.'

The game was up. All present knew it, both British and Turks, for *Surprise* possessed no English papers, the First Lord never having the least intention of providing any. Such had been the Foreign Secretary's instruction, as Pat had always understood the case to be. Concerned for the prospect of just such an eventuality as this day had turned out to be, the English government did not care to admit their aid for the Greek insurrection. The hearts and minds of all the Surprises around the table sank like a stone. Was this the end, a life as Turk prisoners all that was left to them?

Chapter Six

Wednesday 1st June 1825   12:00   *in the Cavo Doro strait*

The fierce wind whistled through the smashed panes of the stern gallery, loud, cold and no aid to concentration. Pat stared at his own empty coffee cup, his mind in a frantic whirl: what to say? What to do? It was the most desperate of circumstances. Never before had he faced such a dire predicament. The Turks, polite but highly suspicious, simply stared and fidgeted; plainly they were uncomfortable too.

A long minute passed in silence, save for the wind, and all present reflected on the situation before them, not a word uttered. Pat was exceedingly uncomfortable and lost for words, the Turk lieutenant pondering his next move, the seizure of an enemy combatant something he had never done before; indeed, he had never in his dreams imagined doing so, and the moment was bearing heavy upon him, his own nerves taxed to the limit. He had no inkling that *Surprise* was bereft of ammunition and powder: would the English surrender, or would they seize him and try for fight and flight? Something must be done, something said; he began to rise from his chair, 'Sir, it is...'

He never finished. In that instant an enervated Codrington rushed into the cabin in great excitement, 'Sir, there is firing... FIRING... in the Turk fleet, in their train!' The boom of distant guns became discernible in the cabin, previously the vaguest of sounds which all had ignored until now, having been indistinct and unidentified, the distance so great, the noises unclear and distorted in the ferocious gale which was increasingly the most violent of winds. Few other noises were audible save for the constant creaking of the ship and the sharp, intermittent cracking noises from the sail canvas, all hanging loose. Every ear pricked up in an instant, every mind raced to a new level of alertness, the tension in the cabin soaring to new heights, all three of the Turk officers immediately and visibly exceedingly uncomfortable; as one they rose from the table.

'Gentlemen,' declared Pat with an avalanche of alarm surging through his every sinew. Rising from his chair he sought to preserve the customary polite formalities even as he stepped swiftly around the table to face the Turks, his thoughts racing in a confusing cocktail of rising faint hope; the tiniest glimmer of an idea was settling in his mind as the unexpected prospect of escape seemed to present itself: the meeting had reached the most surprising and unlikely conclusion. 'I beg you will depart for your ship,' he said, striving to keep his voice measured.

The Turks nodded, said nothing more; they hastened from the cabin onto the rain-lashed deck to clamber precariously down into their boat, rocking violently and smashing alongside a bucking, rolling *Surprise*, the gale having strengthened further during their brief visit.

'Haul on the braces!' Mr Macleod,' bellowed Pat, 'All hands about ship!'

Men everywhere raced to obey the supremely welcome order, three score heaving the yards round to catch the violent wind, frantically tying them off, a hundred more staring at the near Turk frigate to see what she would do. *Surprise* could not shift quickly for she would still be close-hauled, in fact as close to the wind as she could sail, perhaps just a few knots the best she might achieve until she had covered that final half-mile to clear the strait, when - more sea room available to her - she could turn east and better harvest the gale's brute force.

The Turk officers in their tiny boat were fighting hard in the swell to gain their own frigate, further away and now fifty yards off the beam, their boat hurled about on the wave tops in the most precarious, dangerous fashion. Pat, staring, wondered whether they would even make it back. *Surprise* began to shift, gaining a little way, painfully slowly, every man hoping that the Turk captain - having no knowledge of his lieutenant's investigations - would not open fire; at this point-blank range the absolute destruction of the barky was assured; there could be no salvation, none at all, if the Turk fired her great guns. Pat's heart turned over thinking about it. A near score of 18- or even 24-pounders, doubtless some double-shotted, at this short range would rip his ship apart with a single broadside, would kill scores of his men, and would render the barky unmanageable in one sickening great blast. He swallowed hard. He sought to dispel the vile image in his mind as *Surprise* struggled, making four ship's lengths before the Turk could resume the chase; thankfully, her guns could no longer be brought to bear, save for the smaller bow chasers once again. BOOM! Their first shot echoed out, the ball crashing through the fragile and overhanging quarter-gallery, the sound of smashing, shattering timber audible even in the fury of the tempest.

Pat, still very tense and miserably wet in the heavy rain, held firm to the rail and peered all about him, blinking the water from his eyes: those corvettes which had cleared the strait, passing by as *Surprise* had heaved to, seemed intent on their own tacking difficulties in the ferocity of the storm, and they were still bearing away, ever further south-west. Doubtless their captains were acutely aware that at every turn there was the very real prospect of falling in irons, becoming stopped with no longer the slightest way, when their vessel would be forced by the wind to an unwelcome direction, falling off with a long and slow turn being the inevitable consequence, and with little sea room that was not a welcome prospect, the island and its rocky shore near directly astern of them and so close. Pat was perfectly aware that the prevailing heavy weather and adverse wind made the smallest of forward progress exceedingly difficult for every vessel, but that might - *might* - yet enable him to save the barky. His mind whirred with numerous thoughts, some crystallising to the bare bones of ideas, frantically seeking the solution he desperately craved. At least those Turk corvettes showed no interest in his own ship for the moment, presumably content to leave matters to their sister frigate. BOOM! The Turk fired once again, the shot crashing into and bouncing off the hull quarter near the waterline in a visible, flashing ricochet, the thud reverberating throughout the near deck, the shot disappearing with a splash into the turbulent grey swell.

Just two hundred more yards remaining, Pat estimated - a mere cable - and *Surprise* could make her long-anticipated turn.

The Turk gunners were slow, for which the watching Surprises were very grateful; they reckoned they would have fired three shots for every one the Turk had managed.

Still close-hauled, that final cable before the much-anticipated turn seemingly taking an age, another two shots from the Turk's two chasers flew by. Pat was thinking hard, calculating swiftly, his mind awhirl. A minute passed and the sobering, brutal realisation returned to strike home yet again: *Surprise* could not escape simply with flight, it was not possible, the Turk frigate had proved to be faster than his own, likely because *Surprise's* hull was surely festooned with copious, slowing weed. He had no choice. His conclusion was the only one he could reach; he must embrace the most desperate of measures to save his ship and his men: he would shave the coast, continue her turn and put her between the island and the rocky outliers off the little port of Gavrio. At best, it was a dangerous manoeuvre which might deter the Turk from following; at worst, *Surprise* might ground on an uncharted shoal, one unknown to him, when his men would have no choice but to take to the boats and pull for the shore; such an escape in the boats would be exceedingly difficult, their prospects greatly uncertain in the ferocious gale and desperately dangerous, but perhaps such offered at least the slim chance of escaping captivity even if the barky was lost.

Pat swallowed hard, the boats could not possibly transport all his men, and a return to a stricken ship to fetch more in this storm was not likely to be possible; the thought struck him forcefully, was utterly depressing. Yet short of surrender he could see no alternative, the moment of decision was upon him, that moment was now, and an immediate choice must be made; he must choose immediately, time so short. At last the barky had appeared to have gained enough sea room to turn away from the wind, to put it on her quarter, the hope of gaining a slender few knots more was thankfully before them at last.

BOOM! The Turk chaser thundered; she was still there, plainly intent on the capture of her prize. Anxious faces all about the quarterdeck stared in very visible anxiety and Pat, biting his tongue, made his mind up, 'Mr Macleod, helm down a point. We are turning to follow the island coast.'

The turn began, the severe wind pushing hard on her beam. *Surprise* immediately gained speed, the Turk likewise, her own course also changed. Despite the danger of rocks and the close proximity of their pursuer, the spirits of the Surprises, every man on deck soaked utterly to the skin and all much dejected, lifted a little. Pat's intentions were communicated to them via his officers' shouts and from man to man, an understanding of his thinking becoming plain to all: the slim possibility of escape, albeit small, was a gigantic relief. At least the frigate still seemed to be their sole adversary: the remainder of the Turk fleet was either plodding on, south-west into the teeth of the gale, or, a little surprisingly, had still not emerged from the strait. Perhaps it remained in escort of the flagship in its disarray, in that confusion which Pat had glimpsed an hour before.

BOOM! BOOM! Both the Turk chasers fired once more, the shots smashing into the hull on *Surprise's* larboard quarter with violent reverberations felt throughout the quarterdeck. She finally completed her turn, her racing bolt for escape. Pat estimated she was - at last - making six or seven knots, likely the best speed she might make with her fouled hull and in a beam wind; whilst now the hoisted topgallants were making their contribution, as he had hoped. Despite this, it seemed to the Surprises that the barky had lost the smallest of ground to the Turk, trailing perhaps two cables astern.

With only one pursuer, should the barky haul out her guns? Pat pondered but dismissed the idea: they could not be brought to bear without abandoning his plan to seek refuge behind the outlying small islets. Perhaps the Turk might yet reflect on his prey, might conclude she was indeed English if, that is, her gun ports remained closed. It was an exceedingly slim prospect, Pat conceded, perhaps not truly a real one, but if the Turk did not give up the chase and if sufficient time passed with the Turk fleet sailing further away then he might himself reconsider use of his guns, but not directly, not now. No, manoeuvre was by far and away the best tactic for the present.

Five minutes had passed since the last explosions, when - BOOM! BOOM! - the Turk guns thundered again. *Surprise* had sailed at least a quarter-mile but in so doing had lost yet more yards to the Turk, the frigate still in dogged pursuit and plainly intending to continue to fire her chasers without let up. 'Helm hard over, Mr Macleod, EAST! Steer her into the islets there. Keep her course a cable north of the nearest one, d'ye see it?'

'Aye aye, sir, keep her a cable off the nearest, bearing east,' Macleod relayed the orders to the helm. A very wet Barton, his face drenched with rain, nodded his understanding.

'Mr Pickering, a man to the lead line, a constant call,' ordered Pat. The die was cast. The barky was making her further turn, coming round in a racing curve and gaining more speed as the wind now presented on her quarter; she must surely be making eight knots at least, thought Pat, brightening a little, the barky's speed still building, the gale now very much an ally. On she ploughed, faster and ever faster, nine knots perhaps as Gavrio port and inlet came up on her larboard beam, the Turk still chasing hard, much determined to catch her prize.

'Sails ahoy!' the shout from the tops, 'Starboard beam!' Pat shook the water from his glass to stare to the south, a glimpse of distant mast tops visible, nothing more. Who might they be? He had no time to consider that as the next shout from the man with the lead line at the side intruded into his thinking, 'Six fathoms!' There was, thankfully, enough water but without a deal to spare.

BOOM! BOOM! The Turk was firing again, albeit there was perhaps almost a half-mile between them now. Was the Turk slowing? Was he apprehensive of the water depth as the two frigates closed the nearest islet? 'Five fathoms!' came the loud shout from the side; the water was shoaling.

Pat was more mindful than ever of the draught of his ship and he cast his mind back: the Devonport men had measured it after the installation of the iron water tanks during her refit at eighteen feet nine inches, a trifle more than three fathoms; yet now she was lightly loaded, carrying near nil heavy shot; it might just give him a precious few inches more in the shoals. He possessed no greatly detailed chart for the islets, and consequently such sketchy navigation as was possible was very unclear to him, and any passage so close to the island would be precarious; indeed, there was a very real risk of grounding. However, he assumed that neither did the Turk possess a detailed chart, and her captain might not be so well informed as he was himself about the draught of his vessel. It was exceedingly thin ice they were skating upon, he admitted, but such was all he possessed to save his ship and his men from certain capture. BOOM! BOOM! On this occasion he clearly glimpsed for a fraction of a second the incoming shot from both Turk guns, flying directly at the stern, and he heard the smashing, crashing destruction as the balls broke the last few panes remaining of the great cabin's glass, smashed more of the gallery timber structure and thudded in a trail of destruction below his feet through the flimsy internal partition between the great cabin and the coach. He expected the shot to penetrate right through and fly down the gun deck, but perhaps it had not, for no shouts came from any injured men forward of the waist rail, but - it occurred to Pat - whether he would hear their cries in the enduring gale was doubtful indeed.

'Four fathoms!' the leadsman's shout was louder than ever, the shallow water shoaling further, the slim margin of safety much diminishing; the tiny islet of Plati, no more than a rocky outcrop, was looming fine on the starboard bow.

'Ease her a spoke; steer her a trifle more to larboard,' shouted Pat, striving to present a measured voice, although his thoughts were racing like never before. His words were whipped away by the wind, his hat long gone before them, his face a flurry of windswept and wet red hair. No matter, Barton was as dependable as ever, seemingly had anticipated the order and assumed Pat's shout had accorded with it, a slight but perceptible shift of the foc'sle resulting relative to the islet before their eyes. Pat nodded gratefully to his cox'n, never more cognisant of the unspoken understanding between them; George Barton truly was the man that his brother Brannon had once been, aboard *Tenedos* in a very distant past; in that instant, it seemed like a lifetime ago.

BOOM! BOOM! The Turk really was determined to capture his quarry, thought Pat, looking through his glass in careful study of the several islets before his ship, ever closer all about her.

'Three and a half fathoms!' the leadsman screamed his report, rising panic audible in his voice.

Perhaps, Pat wondered, he really had taken one risk too many this time. 'Keep her steady, Barton,' he screamed. Anxious, frightened faces stared at him all about the quarterdeck.

'A score of sail on the starboard quarter!' shouted the topman in a voice which was audible if indistinct in the wind, the strained timbre of his voice suggesting such was really too much to consider, what with an enemy fleet astern, a frigate closing on her and the barky herself near aground. Pat looked across, the approaching vessels - no longer distant - had gained miles very quickly, the gale on their beam fast driving them north-west, and they surely were coming up fast, more than a dozen of them visible, as the topman had reported. That they were certainly brigs he could now make out, but no colours were evident in the wild wind which was the gale, sheets of heavy rain a wet curtain between them and obscuring all detail.

'Three and a half fathoms!' the leadsman called again, the constancy of the depth something of the tiniest relief to Pat.

BOOM! BOOM! The thunderclap of the distant chasers was more muted. Pat reckoned the Turk frigate had surely slowed. She was firing now from a little more than half a mile astern, perhaps ever more cautious of the shoaling water. Despite the severe risk, *Surprise* continued to fly at eight knots, an exceedingly dangerous practice in unknown shallow depths, but there was no alternative, not yet.

'THREE FATHOMS, DEAR GOD!' the leadsman's cry was fearful, distressed, every man in earshot trembled internally, and then came the faintest of tremor as a deep shudder resonated throughout the hull, followed by a jarring, frightening judder for a few seconds, shaking all the decks and every man aboard presuming, indeed terrified, that she was about to run aground on the shoaling, sandy sub-surface or, worse, strike jagged, submerged rocks which must rip her hull apart. Pat was himself also frightened, fearing for the rudder, that part of his ship which sat the lowest, the deepest, in the water. He prayed that its hinges would not be damaged if it did strike, and he was never more conscious of the desperate measure he had resorted to: flight through the shallows. The fleeting thought occurred to him that he hoped Melville would never hear of the desperate last resort. He prayed that *Surprise* was drawing less water than the Turk. 'May Saint Patrick and all the saints allow us to bring this caper off,' was his murmured plea, his nerves thoroughly shot.

Simon, who had appeared on the quarterdeck some time previously and who was standing alongside Marston, both men the most anxious of spectators and holding firm to the mainmast in the still strong wind, was watching events with considerable trepidation whilst careful to keep out of the way of all others on deck. He had heard the panicked shout of the leadsman, his own fears rising. He stepped with difficulty past the belfry, Clumsy Dalby extending an inquisitive look; he stumbled as he crossed the gratings, Dalby hastening to seize his arm, to hold him up. 'Thank you kindly, Dalby.' Another half-dozen hesitant paces and he grasped the firmity of the mizzenmast with relief, looking all about him.

BOOM! BOOM! Pat, ignoring the Turk's firing, his attention until then wholly on the helm and the leadsman's call, turned briefly as his sweeping gaze caught sight of Simon. He discarded his surging irritation in a blink of his eye, concern for his friend seizing firm hold, 'Simon, what in all that is precious in the fair County Clare do you want up here? I beg you will go below, d'ye hear? We are under fire, and 'tis no place for you and Marston; go below... directly! I beg you will.'

'Four fathoms!' the leadsman's voice, only five seconds elapsing since the tremor, carried an audible deal of relief in it, every man in earshot profoundly thankful, many prayers offered to several personal deities.

'Bring her round, Barton; HARD OVER, SOUTH WE GO!' exclaimed Pat in full, shrieking voice, standing near the helm and waving his arm in the intended direction, a huge surge of relief coursing through his every fibre and his deep fears relenting in leaps and bounds.

There were no more shots from the Turk, who had plainly slowed and turned away before the Plati islet; the enemy frigate had shied off and come round a cable to the north to gain deeper water; doubtless her captain had also become frightened. Pat's last-ditch measure had worked, at least for the moment. He stared again at the oncoming northbound brigs, peering and squinting through his glass, two full minutes passing in anxious query, the rain making clarity difficult. 'Greeks! They are GREEKS!' he exclaimed with a loud cry, the spirits of every man on deck soaring high.

'Five fathoms!' *Surprise* continued her long, curving turn, coming close to the wind and so slowing rapidly to no more than two knots, her course set directly south, the far sixteen Greek brigs on her starboard beam. Thankfully the Turk frigate now seemed ever more distant and was seemingly moving away, sailing northbound at much greater speed to regain her fleet and flagship which, oddly, even now was yet to emerge from the strait. A little more than a half-mile further to the south and, his nerves settling, Pat ordered another change of course: to the west. 'Follow the Greeks!' *Surprise* came round fully into the wind, making the slowest of turns through it, every man believing she would be taken aback; but no, the frigate wavered and, infinitely slowly, a myriad prayers unspoken, her bow came through to complete her turn, the wind now on her larboard beam; a near stationary *Surprise* was bearing north-west and gaining speed once more, the Greek brigs already two miles ahead and heading for the strait, the Turk frigate a much diminished sight, her sails disappearing into the far distance.

Half an hour passed with *Surprise* chasing the Greek brigs, when the Surprises stared in shocked disbelief, the full width of the strait and the many vessels within it becoming plainly visible. For the most part the entire Turk fleet had succeeded in exiting the strait in the teeth of the gale, but they were plainly in action against another squadron of Greek brigs snapping at their heels. It was those brigs which Pat had seen astern of the Turk fleet several hours previously. However, those nearer Greeks which had passed the islets to where *Surprise* had fled from the frigate were also now closing on the Turk fleet from the south: the Turks were caught between the Greek pincers. The wind was on the near Greeks' quarter, filling their sails with the most ferocious, extremely powerful force even as the Turks still seemed mired in disarray, many struggling to make short boards within the broad strait whilst firing at the pursuing Greeks to the north, the gale force wind the difficulty for the seamen of both sides, the tempest as savagely extreme as ever, if not more so. The rain, driven hard by the gale, stung exposed faces, every man long inured to the soaking, no one giving it any mind; indeed, the Surprises had endured more pressing calls on their attention for some time.

Cautious, Pat kept *Surprise* at some distance from the looming confrontation on the Turk van. He had no wish to further endanger his ship. The flight through the shoals after the lucky escape from the Turk frigate hauling near alongside had scared him severely; indeed, he was not yet over that, and there was not a man aboard who had not been frightened in the extreme.

Another half-hour and the Greeks from the south began firing, every Surprise gazing in abject fascination. Of the half-dozen or so Turk corvettes which had cleared the strait hours before there was no sign. The topman declared - his words shouted from man to man - that he believed he could see them bearing off to the west, running as close to the wind as they could, perhaps bearing for the small port of Karysto on the south coast of Euboea. That the Turk flagship still remained in difficulties was plain to all to see, for she was mired, no way upon her at all, and only managing the most desultory firing at long range from her guns, the approaching Greeks ever closer. Eight Turk brigs had already closely engaged the Greeks, and the sea was criss-crossed with many and various other Turk vessels, brigs and corvettes for the most part, all striving to hold off the nearest Greeks from approaching closer to the razee and her charges of a dozen or so accompanying merchantmen.

The Greeks coming up from south and east of Andros possessed the weather-gauge, the gale at their back, which afforded them much superior speed and manoeuvrability. They used it to great effect, all the time firing at near stationary targets and, it seemed to Pat, getting by far the better of the exchanges. He marvelled at the Greek tactics; it had truly been a masterpiece of strategy by their admiral, presumably Sakhtouri, arriving from the east and splitting his forces, the north squadron being the decoy, to slow the Turks in an inconclusive rearguard engagement, to draw away the escort brigs. Little advantage was possessed by either side in the disadvantageous and all-powerful wind until the Greek squadron from the south had arrived in perfect time to capitalise on the Turk disarray and confusion, sweeping in with the wind greatly to their advantage so as to strike the Turks and their flagship from their other side. The Greek approach was hidden by the island of Andros until it was too late for the Turks, caught between two fires and their escape to the north obstructed by that first Greek squadron, whilst any movement to the south could only be slow, snail-like, and all the while buffeted by the severe gale, reducing progress to a crawl, and ever under bombardment. Sakhtouri had achieved a military masterpiece of strategy at sea, and all the Surprises marvelled.

Despite this, Pat, ever conscious of possessing so little powder, held off, *Surprise* kept far back, her position maintained two miles south of the fray, the wind sweeping away much of the sound of firing, but not all. The battle was reaching a crescendo, plainly many Turk vessels were striving to leave the scene in every possible direction; a dozen were bearing west for Karysto and many more - fighting brigs and lightly armed merchantmen - were picking a dangerous path through the southern Greek flotilla to try to sail on, south, and somehow escape the engagement, one which they were losing. Several merchantmen had already struck their colours. Another half-hour and the Greeks played their trump card: fireships! Two were burning fiercely, the flames very visible even at two miles. The first, ferocious, wild flames were roaring aloft, whipped to an immediate incendiary inferno by the gale and sweeping into the struggling flagship which was entangled alongside, the furnace roaring across the small gap to set alight all the Turk's sails in no time, a blazing beacon bright in the grey sky, and one which surely convinced every observer on both sides that the game was up for the Turks; it was time to save what remained possible, to flee as best they might.

A second fireship had grappled alongside that same Turk frigate which had pursued *Surprise*; the clashing confluence was large in Pat's fascinated gaze, and he marvelled at the speed of the spread of flame, for the Turk was quickly burning fiercely. Yet another fireship had struck a corvette, also near immediately set ablaze in the vicious wind. Four more *bourlotas* were also wildly afire, the group sweeping into the midst of the Turk fleet. The Greeks were surely having a field day, the weather conditions could not be better for their tactics, save perhaps for the rain. Pat prayed for the escape of their crews; indeed, he could not conceive of how they might escape in the ferocity of the gale; perhaps their only prospect was to be picked up by those Greeks to the north, for return against the tempest's raging strength was surely impossible.

Another half-hour and the wild, roaring flames were burning utterly unchecked on the razee, the Turk flagship. To every observer it was plain that there was no longer the least chance of putting them out, none whatsoever; perhaps there never had been once the fireship had crashed alongside, the wind so strong, the raging flame quickly spreading far beyond human resource and courage. Pat stared in some shock, his feelings mixed: deep satisfaction in looking upon the destruction of so important an enemy ship sat ill with his human concern for what would be many hundreds of men perishing in the fire, no real hope of escape, insufficient boats and wild waves all about the blazing wreck. In the next instant came the violence of the detonation of the Turk's magazine, the huge and expanding white flash casting aside the grey darkness of the enduring rain curtain; the deafening blast seemed to shake the strait itself, a huge fireball rising up from the wreck remnants to form a bright orange sphere which lingered for only an instant, burning fragments visible within it, all hurled up high into the sky, a rising pyre of black smoke within seconds all that remained, the swirling remnants swiftly blasted away in the sweeping ferocity of the enduring gale until, a mere ten minutes elapsing, not the smallest trace whatsoever remained of the flagship. All on *Surprise's* decks stared in a state of shock and horror: hundreds of seamen, five hundred and more, men much like themselves, had all been annihilated in the mere blink of an eye.

'There but for the grace of God go I,' murmured Marston. The chaplain, deeply shocked, had remained with Simon on deck, both men oblivious to Pat's call to go below. They were standing at the rail, staring, aghast and horror-struck.

Plainly the disaster had set back the Turk morale generally, for the battle as a whole rapidly ran down, the Turk survivors turning away as best they could and in every direction to run in utter disarray, no longer any collective cohesion, no command direction seemingly still existing. Several more merchantmen had been captured by the Greeks who remained in jubilant and undisputed possession of the stormy, aqueous field of battle.

From the quarterdeck and all along the sides, the Surprises watched in gaping astonishment the fleeing Turk armada, at least thirty brigs and transports flying south-east at best speed, the wind broad on their beam. Damage was evident on some of them, though most were largely unscathed, but all were plainly affrighted, no thought given by the armed brigs to the collection of survivors or the escort of their struggling merchantmen, many trailing in their wake.

In Pat's mind a rising mixture of relief and exuberance had come to the fore, had settled upon him, for none of his men had become casualties; the tension of the day was relenting its tight grip; the internal mental numbness and insensitivity of feeling - save only for the absolute concentration on his ship, on her situation, on the dangers presented before her and to her men - was thankfully fading. A blessed and welcome return to something more near a mental normality was creeping up upon him and, although it could not be said to be relaxation, he began to revel in it; he also firmly reminded himself that it would not be long before *Surprise* would find herself homeward bound; home, to her real home, to Falmouth. That was truly the most joyful of all his thoughts. Waves of relief were washing through him, the frightening and dangerous escape of his ship and men through the shoals was fading from his thoughts, and a tremor of relief had begun to beset him throughout his legs which he much feared might show to his men but could do nothing to halt. He leaned back against the mainmast so as to try to take the load off his legs and he nodded in encouragement to all his men nearby, no words could he find for several minutes.

An hour more and only Greeks remained in proximity. *Surprise* had turned about to run with the wind abeam, south-east once more and flying her Greek colours. Not that such was strictly necessary as she was by now well-known to all Greek combatants; indeed, she had fought with them on many an occasion, her usually powerful presence always very welcome. The ferocious wind, thankfully, was easing when Sakhtouri's own brig approached, the admiral keeping on parallel track a hundred yards off *Surprise's* beam.

Another two hours gone and the wind further diminishing, Pat, with Duncan, Simon and Jason, crossed by boat to board the Greek brig, Simon clutching his medical bag. Sakhtouri himself proudly welcomed them aboard and into the cabin where his steward served Turkish coffee and Greek brandy, a heady atmosphere of celebration endemic aboard the brig.

'I congratulate you, sir!' declared Pat in loud praise, Jason translating, for he marvelled at the absolute victory achieved and the tactics employed; he revelled much more in news of the brigs captured: five intact Austrian merchantmen; legitimate prizes, for all were discovered to be carrying war materials.

'Thank you, Captain O'Connor,' Sakhtouri's face glowed with pleasure, his delight never before so self-evident. 'I was in Samos when I learned that Khosref had put to sea and I sailed immediately.'

'I regret, sir, that my ship could offer no support to you during your glorious... your victorious battle... for want of powder and shot.'

'Then, Captain, you will allow me to gift you a plentiful sufficiency of powder and shot from our captures. Indeed, the first Austrian to strike her colours possessed of *thirteen hundred* barrels of powder.'

A sharp intake of breath from all the Surprises, 'Thirteen hundred barrels of powder!' exclaimed Pat, aghast, his eyes wide. 'I would never care to hazard my ship were she carrying that magnitude of explosive; why, it is akin to fighting a bomb-ketch without the mortar yet with a hundredfold more of powder.'

'Indeed,' murmured Sakhtouri with a doubtful look, 'and neither did the Austrians, for they gave us not the least hindrance in taking their vessel. From others we have gained a deal more of stores... and three dozen of siege guns with all their shot.'

'Did ye suffer many casualties, sir?' Duncan spoke up, 'We saw the explosion of the flagship and the firing of others.'

'We saw as we approached that the Turk flagship had lost her topmasts, all ripped away in the gale... plenty of confusion on her deck when we attacked her; she could not cut them away and cast them overboard quickly enough before my fireships came alongside her... and in the wind... well, that was that... she was doomed, no motion available to her.' The admiral paused in momentary reflection, such an event distressing for any sailor to contemplate. 'It is with considerable relief that I report only three of my own comrades were killed and four wounded.'

Pat exhaled audibly; *miracles do happen* was the thought that came to his mind.

'Admiral,' it was Simon's turn to interject, a little of anxiety melded with the concern in his voice, 'By your leave, it would please me to attend your men.'

'Thank you, Doctor Ferguson; that is most gracious. My aide will escort you.' The admiral nodded and his attending officer bowed his head to Simon, both men leaving the cabin.

'Captain O'Connor,' Sakhtouri continued, 'It is my intention to take my squadron south, to aid Calamata and revictual, to join with Admiral Miaoulis and thence to pursue the Turks. You will allow me to... *to suggest* that... when reprovisioned with powder and shot... you may care to accompany us.' The admiral's words were spoken politely yet in a tone which implied that he wished to make plain his intentions, his wish that *Surprise* should join with him. It did not go unnoticed by the Surprises. Not that Pat minded in the least, south was where he wished to go; at least going south he could continue to Cephalonia, the English haven of sanctuary in the Ionians, from where, when repaired, he would take his ship home to Falmouth. He nodded cautiously.

'That is to say, if it pleases you,' added Sakhtouri as an afterthought, scrutinising Pat's face, hesitant and plainly lost in thought, the admiral perhaps wondering whether he had overstepped his own small authority.

'Of course, sir, it would please me to join with you,' murmured Pat without a great deal of conviction and sinking his brandy, a degree of relief even now persisting with him after the near miraculous escape from capture, the tiniest of tremor in both his leg and voice; at least the former was beneath the table, though he could do nothing to disguise the latter.

The afternoon was near gone as *Surprise*, in the company of the Greeks, approached the north cape of the island of Syra, fine on the larboard bow, the wind continuing to ease, all vessels close-hauled and making little more than three knots. The smoke from a fire ahead prompted general interest and Pat took the frigate down the island's west coast, close in to the shore, deferring his intended change of course to the west. On they sailed for another mile until a tiny inlet revealed a far beach, small and sheltered within the curve of the tiniest of bays. He studied the fire through his glass, a mile distant. 'I venture 'tis one of the Turks which escaped earlier, wrecked and burning on the sands.' His murmur reached all on the quarterdeck, a surge of interest within every man, all staring towards the distant sight.

The Turk corvette was well alight, bright flames scouring her hull, her sails long crisped and powdered, her masts and yards blackening, dense smoke rising in a oily plume to be swept away over the island. Three score and more of men sat huddled on the beach, presumably the crew, watching their vessel burn.

They faced a doubtful future, thought Pat. The war had never seemed a merciful one, and the prospects for prisoners were ever exceedingly bleak.

At last he ordered the turn, *Surprise* beginning a long tack to the west before she could once more revert to her southerly track for Milos, all the Greek brigs a mile off her starboard bow. Pat presumed that their presence must have forced the Turk captain to put his corvette ashore rather than be captured.

In the evening, in the great cabin, the tumult of the senses having died down somewhat, Pat and Simon sat awaiting their supper. 'Pray tell, why did you come on deck and stay there?' asked Pat. 'I was more than a trifle affrighted to see you, I was so... the Turk firing.'

'I confess I was in some little anxiety those two hours or more... greatly uneasy and thrown about in the gloom... downstairs, and all the time wondering what was happening up there in the blessed sunlight... and whilst it appeared... *that is to say, it was the gossip down there...* that we were engaging in flight not fight... and I was wondering all the time if things were looking greatly propitious for our safe escape.'

'Believe me... and I do not care to dwell on it, flight was best suited to our particular circumstances... I cannot say fairer than that.'

'But tell me... I was a trifle confused... I had remarked as I ascended the steps that the great guns were never run out. Was it not in your contemplation to fire on that accursed fellow, our pursuer?' Simon, still visualising the Turk frigate in his mind, pointed towards the stern gallery, a glaring vacancy in the absence of all glazing, the wind gusting in with vigour, 'Were you not concerned... that vessel behind us... the obdurate malevolent that he was?'

'Perhaps things might eventually have come to that; it did cross my mind so,' Pat conceded; 'I dare say on those occasions when your back is really against the wall the time does come when it's time to turn round and fight.'

A rendezvous with Miaoulis, coming up from the south-west from a brief skirmish against the Egyptians off Cape Matapan, had united the two Hydriot squadrons earlier in the day to the south of Hydra. Subsequently, the admiral, on learning of Sakhtouri's own victory and Khosref's flight south, had ordered all the Greeks and *Surprise* to bear east, to the island of Milos for reprovisioning, the *scirocco* wind enduring still as a strong south-westerly.

Sunset, twilight fast approaching, and the great cabin was brilliantly lit by the low hanging sun in its brightly radiant entirety, all of it visible through the shattered remnants of the stern gallery, nothing of the glazing and precious little of the wooden structure remaining. Pat and Simon sat awaiting supper whilst sipping a thin Greek wine, breezy gusts blowing through the destruction with fierce gusto.

At last Murphy entered and presented the meal. Not a deal of interest was exhibited by either man at the table, and the steward, feeling slighted, exited with a barely audible grunt of dissatisfaction. The meal was eaten with little conversation, Pat seemingly content to devour his bowl of lobscouse, Simon picking disinterestedly at his, eventually pushing it away, near cold. He sat mute for several minutes, an ambience of discomfort, of unhappiness settling about the table generally, no attention given to the walnuts which Murphy had deposited with an air of triumph, the steward departing the cabin in disgust when no comment was offered. 'I am no great fist with... with table conversation,' murmured Pat eventually, '... but allow me to say,' he sighed, 'that you seem plentifully cast down this evening, you do so.'

'Oh, I beg pardon, brother; I was considering the works of the great classic writers... and was in contemplation of... of what extrapolations might be reasonable for the educated mind... in the matter of the present times for Greece, that is.'

Pat stared doubtfully, remained mystified, eventually offering his comment, 'I was a fair hand with Shakespeare at school myself.'

'I was speaking of Ovid and Homer most particularly.'

'Hmmm, I see,' Pat was not deceived. 'For a moment there I thought you were perhaps sleeping, I did.'

Perhaps it was his friend's implied tone of disbelief, perhaps it was simply the right moment arrived to raise the matter which sat heavy on Simon's mind, 'Listen, Pat... will I tell you something? I am already in a high state of anxiety... it has quite destroyed my appetite... that last battle ... the flames, the explosion of that flagship, and before that the tumult and terrible destruction at Modon. All before my own eyes it was... and I watched with a deal of anxiety...'

Pat looked up to a picture of apprehension and unhappiness on Simon's face; he decided in an instant to try and lift the mood, 'Why, until that day of the battle off Samos... last year, I had always held the opinion that you were fully a twenty-minute egg.' His jest falling on the stoniest of ground, sparking not the least response from Simon, Pat spoke again in softer voice, 'Go on, old friend; you do look low in your spirits. Please to explain.'

'I confess I am once more in constant dread of the new day... of every day... another day when I may be obliged to look to the bloody faces and bodies of a dozen or more men passing across my table. One, two or three presents a plentiful sufficiency for any black day, but I have, on several occasions, been pressed to attend six, ten, a dozen... a score sometimes and even more...' Simon's voice tailed off.

'Sure, it is ever the bloody business we are engaged in,' offered Pat weakly, striving to think of something more substantive, the smallest crumb of comfort, to offer.

'One matter in particular sits heavy with me. It is a torment which I find increasingly afflicts me in my sleep...'

'A particular nightmare?'

'Indeed, and I cannot shake it even... *I confess*... with recourse these recent weeks to a tint of the laudanum. It is the most vile of visions... so clear, so vivid... and I find it comes to me with a distressing regularity...'

'Please, do go on.'

'I am in the cockpit, wounded all about me... They are little more than boys... nineteen years old, twenty, twenty-one, all knowing precious little of the world... of life... some never likely to... and... and it is the world's pity... and it greatly pains me... that there is a choice to make, *one I must make*... the most distressing of selections...'

'Selections?' murmured Pat with a sinking, cold feeling.

'Who am I... to choose... *to decide*... who is to live... and... and who is *to die*?' Simon sighed, his crestfallen face a picture of painful dismay, of utter despair.

Pat stared at his friend. He had attended the surgeon's table in brief visit after many bloody battles, Simon and Marston, sometimes Jason too, working in the most horrible, foetid stench, the bloody buckets filled with amputated body parts: hands, feet, arms, legs and worse, much worse. Each and every time his stomach had turned with revulsion at the sights before him. It was, of course, an occupational hazard which he had always strived but failed to reconcile himself with, the inevitable conclusion always being his hastening away from the surgeon's blood and gore as quickly as he could, but then came the aftermath of thinking about it: his own nightmares would come, were always sure to arrive later, usually when he strived for sleep, always restless within his cot, no amount of liquor aiding him to find slumber at such disturbing times.

'I cannot attend more than one wounded soul at a time,' Simon continued in distressed voice, '... all brought to my table as they are struck down... but some, *later* arrivals, are in more pressing need of my attentions... *are in the most urgent need of surgery*... it is as plain as the day is long... and the dire choice is before my eyes... what to do?' A long pause followed, Simon plainly extremely disconsolate, 'What indeed am I to do?'

'Surely at such times Marston is... *will always be*... a help? You have oft remarked his skill,' Pat wondered whether his friend's description of a nightmare had been cast aside and the awful subject was founded in actual past events, real ones, and the horror was not really simply the nightmare Simon professed it to be.

A huge sigh, 'For sure Michael Marston is invaluable... There is not the least doubt of that, no. He is an accomplished surgeon of the first order... and I would not, in these dire days, care to be without him... and Jason too is a prized assistant... but on occasion there are sometimes a half-dozen unfortunates awaiting surgery, all of them in need of *my most urgent attention*... to save their lives... when both Marston and I are so... are so utterly devoted to the man before us on the table, and...'

Pat simply stared, words beyond his powers, the subject so utterly dreadful, so brutally dismaying.

'... and though I find I am increasingly these days in dread of the grinding of the saw... of the spurting crimson stream when severed limbs are coming off... I am so...

'Pat shuddered, a low exhalation escaping his lips.

'... I persevere, one man at a time, my attentions wholly for the poor soul before me... save for that crushing moment when another unfortunate is carried down, grievously stricken and little time remaining for him... *when I must choose*... to either set aside my present patient and turn to the newcomer... or continue with the man on my table... when I know... *I know* that the later man will surely be lost without the application of my knife... *my immediate application.*'

Pat continued to stare at his dearest friend in all the world even as his mind struggled to absorb an incoming tide of horror, a vision which he saw only too well. He wondered again: was Simon recounting a real event or had he returned to the nightmare? 'We must ever... *we can only* do our best,' he offered lamely.

'I will say... *in your private ear*... that I am cursed by a particular torment... I know I am dreaming, I speak to myself, I shout in my thoughts to remind myself it is but a dream; I tell myself I am not really there, but in that moment... in those seconds of being near to awakening... the horror of it all is overwhelming, terrifying... and... and it is with only the utmost difficulty that I keep my silence.'

Pat seized his friend's hand, Simon plainly in great distress, his eyes reddened with lack of sleep, 'Take courage, old friend.'

'Of course, I awake with a goodly tide of relief, but the vile thoughts... they remain in my head for hours... On those occasions I step upstairs... up to the deck... and I gaze into the darkness, thinking long... looking to the stars when bright in the heavens... Such is something of a reassurance, a reminder, something of a permanence... one not afforded to we humble mortals... Even - *I find* - I welcome the rain... warm and something of a notion of an embrace... and at such times, when in the quietude of the bright moonlight and the absence of the forceful billows, I lean for hours on the rail, looking up or oft simply to the track of white water running behind the ship in its procession beneath the moon or the stars... and I am, in those invariably, deeply, most profound moments... I am... I am ever in despair... I... I am in tears.' Simon swallowed and looked down.

Pat stared, feeling wholly inadequate; eventually, hardly daring to venture mere words, he spoke very tentatively, 'How do you feel at present?'

'Oh, the weeks passing... I have learned to come to terms with the hellish vision, and for much of the time I manage an accommodation with such black concerns, if perhaps a temporary one; that is to say... without a deal of the overt distress I was formerly afflicted by.' Simon's eyes moist, both cheeks streaked, he reached for his pocket to find a handkerchief.

Without further ado Pat stretched for the table bell, 'Hold fast, old friend. Let us enjoy a whet together and perhaps we will contemplate an attempt upon one of Boccherini's marvels... or perhaps that cheering little melody, *Bacon and Greens*, eh?'

However, the bell was unnecessary, Murphy entering in that moment, coming silently through the door with a look of abject concern on his face and bearing a tray with brandy. Pat presumed he had been eavesdropping, as was usually the case. He nodded his silent thanks and the steward departed, Pat pouring two exceedingly generous measures, one tumbler pushed towards his friend.

Simon, with not the least inclination to foray into music, to engage with his instrument, took a gulp, coughed, unaccustomed as he was to the strong, undiluted spirit, 'Even in those cases of the most grievously wounded of men... there is ever hope for many of them, though their prognosis is oft uncertain... and I am blessed with a brief flush of relief for all I have helped as they are carried from my table... perhaps their limb lost but their life no longer in danger... save for the uncertainty of the damnable infection.'

'Dear, *dear* brother,' Pat wracked his brain for suitable words, 'you have saved the lives of many a man who is here... *who is with us now* and serving aboard the barky. You have served us so well, all of us... since the day you and I met, and no man... to the well-thinking mind... could ever have done more... could have done the least thing more - *or better*; no surgeon would ever have saved more of our wounded; I have never... *never* myself... doubted that... *never a day have I doubted it.* Will you rest your mind on the rock of that so precious thought? So important it is.' After a long pause with no word from Simon, Pat persevered, 'By God, we need you, dear friend... we surely do. All our shipmates, our old stalwarts... all are *your* friends, *all of them* here in the barky, and every man, *every one,* has a kindly heart for you.'

A sigh and Simon gathered his thoughts, a modicum of restoration afforded by the brandy, 'I am much obliged for your opinion of me... I am so. Oh dear, what a misery I am become.' Simon stared at Pat, a silent minute more passing, 'No man ever steps in the same river twice, for it's not the same river and he's not the same man...' Pat staring, dumbfounded, Simon added, '*Heraclitus*... and neither am I, Pat... *neither am I* that man of those early days... of *Tenedos*... of years long gone.'

'And your home will always be too small to hold all your friends, so it will,' murmured Pat, rising to the philosophical challenge with a quote of his own recollection, 'My old grandma again, the blessed dear.'

The surgeon looked up to gaze directly at his captain, 'When will we see another day such as I fear... *that I see and feel*... in my nightmare? When, I wonder, is such likely to eventuate... and will I endure such a trial, for I fret so?' Simon exhaled deeply and continued to stare at Pat in silent supplication.

'Why, there's no need to fear the wind,' Pat had more than the firmest of inkling that he was far, far out of his depth, 'if your haystacks are tied down.' He strived for a smile, 'There, I'm coming it the philosopher.'

A weak smile and Simon grasped for the slenderest of lifeline, 'Would that be your grandma again? I suppose she also beheld the orbuculum in her hand.'

'The... *the orbu... obunculum?*'

'The crystal ball, the orb; and doubtless she foresaw the future within it...' The smallest flurry of despair returned, 'Do you see it? Do you see the future? Do you see *our future*, tell?'

'Oh... as for what the morrow will bring... eh? I am no... *no smoothsayer*, no Claire voyager - *Claire voyager*... a Galway man, eh! Hah! Hah! No, I am no voyeur... no damned crystal ball gazer myself, not at all.' Pat's weak attempt at humour faded and he continued in sombre tone, 'Indeed, I oft wonder... I do... in my own dreams... in the sleepless nights... *I am afflicted by them too, I am so...* and I wonder myself if - *that is to say what* - it is that may come...' A sigh and a pause, and Pat took comfort from a very large gulp of his brandy, his determination firming and his thoughts clarifying, 'Allow me to tell you this, old friend... Had Mavrocordato not asked, had we never set off to deliver his gold... *that damnable gold*... why, I venture we would now be in Cephalonia and doubtless enjoying a goodly ration of fresh mutton. Well, we are presently bound for that place, and I venture from there we will leave Greece and will soon be Falmouth bound, *Falmouth, eh?* What d'ye say?'

Simon appeared to be reflecting on this and said nothing more for several minutes until, after another sigh, 'It is my most cherished hope.' A pause, 'I do not let on to be a proper mariner, Pat... as you have doubtless remarked...'

'Never in life.'

'... but, tell me plain... it is my belief that precious Cephalonia lies in a generally westerly direction, does it not?' No reply and Simon continued, 'And I collect that you have oft mentioned that the sun, in the Mediterranean, sets *in the west...* or am I much astray?'

Pat stared, confused. He wondered what sparkling nugget of bright enquiry was coming; he spoke cautiously, without the least trace of humour, 'Indeed; that is so.'

'Then correct my ignorance if you will, dear, but allow me an observation: the sun is shining through the... *the rear* of this vessel, its illumination bright *in the west*... It came to my notice at supper a little while ago when I could not discern my sleeve in the soup, the sun in my eye... and... and forgive my conclusion if it is in the least erroneous, but have we not therefore turned about? Are we not proceeding in a... a somewhat *easterly* direction?'

Pat sighed inwardly, his mind wrestling with the simplest explanation he could think of for the technical necessities of long tacks or whether best to set such aside and explain Miaoulis's intentions of watering ship and victualling at Milos. 'It is in my contemplation to take aboard stores from the island we are nearing and then to depart, provisioned, for Cephalonia. A brief diversion it is... *the very briefest*, and then we will away.'

'And I have oft heard it remarked that the moon is made of cheese,' murmured Simon very quietly in a voice utterly lacking conviction, for many and various similar explanations had been vouched before on numerous occasions, and usually, in his experience, they came to nothing and often varied from the promised eventuality by a very wide margin indeed.

'Eh? Cheese?'

'Oh, please do forgive my tedious ramblings,' Simon sighed again and reconciled himself to what would be.

Sunday 5th June 1825   18:00   *Milos Island*

It was a jubilant gathering on Miaoulis's deck, evidently much drink having been flowing since noon, for the raucous noise had been remarked upon by all on *Surprise's* own quarterdeck for several hours before. The air was thick with the aroma of roasting mutton, a greatly anticipated delicacy, and one much to the taste of Pat's officers who had all come aboard to attend the festivities. They were warmly greeted by many Greeks with proffered gestures of friendship, with sincere and cordial words of grateful thanks, words which the Surprises could not literally understand but which were, in their meaning, readily understood by all; warm smiles, firm handshakes and exuberant greetings were offered in great abundance as Pat and his men made their way through the celebrating throng to the cabin, Miaoulis himself rising to welcome them.

The Greeks were revelling in tales of their recent two victories, quite splendid ones: Miaoulis's victory at Modon and Sakhtouri's in the Cavo Doro strait, vivid recounting of both successes expressed over the table with the most vigorous of explanations, all accompanied by loud oaths and vehement gesticulations, whilst much louder and similarly graphic demonstration was occurring out on the deck, the crowds of crewmen of many brigs mixing, the mood wholly exultant.

Simon too, the most minimal of deaths and casualties being a benign influence upon his unsettled state of mind - the barky's own wounded recovering well - had relaxed, greatly to Pat's relief, and doubtless this had not escaped Duncan's attention too, for he allowed himself an entirely unfettered onslaught upon the mutton, returning twice in person to the galley to make plain his inclinations for 'just another wee slice or two,' to the cook.

Miaoulis himself basked in the glorious atmosphere, in the coming together of Spetsiots and Psariots with his own Hydriot compatriots, all customary friction as was usual between the men of the different islands apparently cast aside in their mutual reverie; indeed, it had not escaped his earlier attention that he had rarely contemplated a combined force as large as his present armada, its morale so radiant and buoyant. Although he took nothing himself of alcohol, keeping to his renunciation of some years previously, he minded not the least the most severe depletion of his stores, for ideas were forming within his thoughts even as he relaxed amidst the loud reverie of his men, exchanging a word here and there, nodding in smiling encouragement to a storyteller, making a frequent compliment now and then to both his Greeks and the Surprises, all of which did not pass Pat's notice despite the mood of general relaxation settling so benevolently upon him too.

Another hour passed and three officers from a French schooner came aboard to join the party, graciously welcomed by two score and more of inebriated Greeks packing Miaoulis's cabin. The Surprises were slightly more circumspect with their own greetings, a hesitancy lingering which was founded on enduring recollections of the war against their former enemies, such memories still strong despite the intervening ten years.

Hours passed by in eating and drinking, and with the most cordial of loud conversation until, at the fading of the light, Miaoulis banged hard on his table to capture the attention of all present, the vigorous discussions faltering to an eventual silence. 'Gentlemen,' declared the admiral, 'We are here to replenish our stores, to water, to remedy those damages which may be repaired with what measures we are able to effect, yet this small island is not a place in which we will linger, for the Turk remains at large, is at liberty to fight another day. We have lost the great bay of Navarino...' a loud intake of many breaths, '... and doubtless Ibrahim will next attack Calamata... yes, I venture he will. Our brothers are also threatened at Messalonghi, and will be for as long as the Turk fleet sails in these waters.' The Greeks and the Surprises all nodded, painful memories of times in the company of Lord Byron flashing into Simon's mind. 'We have enjoyed two great successes in recent days... indeed we have; they have truly been days of glory, but the invader possesses of many more vessels. We are gathered here... *friends...*' Miaoulis looked all about him, his gaze fixing on the Surprises, 'Hydriots, Spetziots, Psariots *and Englishmen...* We are here together with an assembly of vessels in such numbers as we have rarely seen the like...' The cabin was silent, every man thinking hard as Miaoulis paused momentarily; 'I ask myself: can we stop the Turks *once and for all...* by destroying their fleet? We are seventy strong... and so it is in my intention to strike the Turk such a blow as he may never recover. Yes, our best chance is now!' Hearts throughout the cabin quickened, minds raced, blood rushed to heads and faces already reddened with drink, and men waited, hanging with keen expectancy on the admiral's next words. 'When we are finished here with our preparations, we will sail... all together... to find and finally... *finally* smash Khosref's fleet! What say you all?' With that Miaoulis smashed both fists upon his table; every glass was jolted, many spilling their contents, the admiral's determination dramatically underlined. From all around the cabin men shouted loud their support.

'Sir...' as quietude began to slowly return, Pat was the first to speak up; indeed, he loudly interrupted the still raucous and vigorous general endorsement of Miaolis's sentiments, 'Sir, where is the Turk? Have you any notion?'

'I venture he has sailed south... That was his direction when last sighted by a Hydriot brig. Perhaps he was bound for Candia... to Suda, to the safety of the harbour there. I venture that is most likely... and it is where we shall sail.'

'HEAR! HEAR!' Greek shouts resonated again throughout the cabin, a score of hands drumming loud upon the table.

Another hour passed with plentiful coffee served and more brandy consumed as minds tired and festivities wound up, and the French guests departed, affable farewells made and sentiments of support pledged as they took their leave.

Pat, with all his officers, emerged a few minutes later to the deck, grateful for the cooler outside air after the foetid heat and smoke of the cabin, the crew's loud and vigorous celebrations all about the brig's gun deck diminished but still ongoing. He stared over the side and all about the safe anchorage of the sheltered bay, the night air still mild. The light of a moon - a bare few days short of full - illuminated the calm, placid waters all about them, barely a breath of wind in the air save for a light breeze gusting occasionally, the edges of the limp, hanging sails flickering. His eyes wandered towards the French schooner; even in the dim light he could make out that preparations were being made to make sail. Why would that be? Pat asked himself. What conceivable urgency could there possibly be, to leave at midnight and with so little wind? 'Mr Codrington,' he declared, casting aside the soporific influences of the evening and injecting an authority into his voice, 'You are to board *Eleanor* directly, with not a moment lost.'

'Sir?' uncertainty and confusion in the lieutenant's voice.

'Haul anchor immediately the Frenchie departs... quietly does it, and follow at a distance. I am minded I wish to know where they are going. And when they do arrive, wherever that may be, you will return here at best speed to report. If we are not here then we will await you in Argostoli. Is that plain?'

'Yes sir,' Codrington strived to cast away the fog of liquor, Pat's tone of voice one he recognised would not brook further questions. He nodded, turned about and hastened for the side to clamber down into *Eleanor's* small boat.

Chapter Seven

The Austrian merchantman which had been stopped by the Greek fleet shortly after the dawn was *en route* for Alexandria from Calamata. Her captain reported the burning of Calamata by Ibrahim's army during the prior day, great fires raging throughout the town and a dreadful slaughter of its inhabitants on the streets - all visible with a glass from the deck of every merchantman - together sparking an immediate exodus by all ships from the harbour, nervous captains who had been taking onboard last minute cargoes taking fright and fleeing.

The calamitous news spread like wildfire throughout the Greek fleet, generating a surge of conflicting thoughts and emotions within all its men. Anger and a thirst for revenge appeared to be the primary emotions amongst the Greeks but there was also a parallel clamour to return home, to protect and safeguard their small and vulnerable island communities, the safety of which was very close to heart for Hydriots and Spetziots, cognisant of the Turk sacking of Psara. The personal and mental impact of that catastrophe was always in the thoughts of the Psariots, their own island having been destroyed the summer before, all their relatives either murdered or carried off as slaves; and so they were - at least to some small degree - better prepared to bear the shocking tidings from Calamata. The Hydriots and Spetziots were not so inured, and consequently an ambience of discord, understandably, prevailed amongst many of the Greeks, the Spetziots particularly. Indeed, Pat and Jason had returned to *Surprise* with the remarkable news of discontent arising even aboard the brig of Miaoulis himself.

Eleanor had returned to Milos three days beforehand, at midday of the 9th, to report that the French schooner had sailed to Suda, the port on the north coast of Candia. Arriving within sight of the harbour, Codrington had counted thirty-six Turk vessels anchored in some degree of disarray within the harbour:

Miaoulis had indeed correctly anticipated the Turks' destination. Codrington's report on his return to *Surprise* with *Eleanor* had raised a fervent storm of anti-French speculation throughout the barky, many an opinion vouching that the Frogs departing Milos aboard their schooner had surely gone to warn the Turk admiral, Khosref, who - conjecture and sight of a pennant flying atop one of the Turk brigs suggested - had escaped the burning of his flagship in the Cavo Doro strait.

Pat, with not the least delay countenanced, had despatched Duncan Macleod, Mower substituting for Codrington, aboard *Eleanor* to sail to Nauplia, to take news of the Egyptian sack of Calamata to Mavrocordato. Miaoulis was keeping a tight rein on all his own brigs and was seemingly unwilling to lose a single one for an unimportant errand, as he saw things; better to send news of a victory, as an attack on the anchored Turk brigs at Suda might well prove to be. The admiral, upon Codrington's report, had similarly wasted no time in hauling anchor, the entire Greek fleet departing Milos in the early afternoon of the 9th.

However, since departing the island, the weather had greatly deteriorated, the voyage towards Candia a gruelling and uncomfortable passage in heavy and persistent stormy weather, interminably slow and arduous in the teeth of a north-westerly *meltemi*, blowing hard on the starboard quarter, the exposed decks frequently shipping water and all present upon it miserable in their soaked clothing, the deck staying perpetually awash. On the combined Greek fleet sailed, Miaoulis paying no heed to any discontent, *Surprise* in train, southbound, the expected sighting of the peak of Mount Ida never occurring; low cloud, drizzle and spray persisted all about the dark grey sky.

On the quarterdeck Pat stood with all his officers, his sodden shirt sticking to his back. At least, so he thought, the wet would wash away the clinging smell of fear he felt sure was engrained within his shirt, for his own anxieties appeared to be ever stronger these days before every successive engagement. The noon sighting was an impossibility; not that anyone much minded, for there was a sense of approaching climax bearing heavy upon every man: if Miaoulis was right, if he was successful, if the remainder of Khosref's Turk fleet could indeed be burned, sunk and destroyed in the Suda harbour, then perhaps it might come to be a significant turning point in the war. Perhaps even Ibrahim, in his destruction of the Morea, might yet come to the realisation that, without sea supremacy, his very tenure on Greek lands might be in jeopardy. Pat stared all about him: Greek brigs in indistinct form in the near distance, all in various shades of grey through the dense spray, ploughed on, ever south.

'The magazines, Mr Pickering?' asked Pat, striving to turn his thoughts away from his wet discomfort.

'Both full aplenty, sir, and the ready-use cartridges are all filled.'

'Very good, and the shot racks... Mr Codrington?'

'Aye, sir; every gun is well served, a dozen of shot in the racks and plenty more below.'

'Very good. At least we will no longer be obliged to run away... to flee before the hounds.' Pat's satisfaction was plain in his declaration, loud and audible to all on the quarterdeck, which was as he intended, his customary confidence plain to all to see and hear; not that it seemed quite so emphatic to him personally, being greatly ensconced within his own private thoughts.

Simon did hear him, as did Marston and Jason, all three venturing on to the sacrosanct starboard side despite the vigorous chop and the recurring surges of spray as the bow dipped into successive troughs. All were keen to hear the smallest of thoughts that might escape Pat's lips and most anxious to understand what might develop, what could possibly be asked of them. Both Marston and Jason had stuck doggedly to Simon in all his waking hours for several days, a practice he had only slowly come to be aware of, Murphy having exchanged words with Marston, explaining Simon's enduring personal distress, his fears, for there was little aboard that did not reach the steward's ears, never far from the great cabin's door. Simon's friends sought to help him as best they might, at least to provide a sounding board and perhaps a few words of comfort; certainly that was the very nature of Marston, the chaplain's ear always open to every man aboard the barky; even Pat had benefited from his attention and words of support in the past.

'Michael Marston... Abel Jason, do not suppose I am some form of invalid; do you hear?' declared Simon eventually, his voice carrying the most mild tone of disgruntlement.

'I beg leave to differ,' whispered Marston, 'For the burden of our most recent times, thankfully whilst light, has served as a reminder of more onerous challenges, past ones which I myself do not care to dwell on, and doubtless... I dare say... you yourself are similarly afflicted. Is that not the case, dear friend?'

'Indeed, your distress... that is to say *your disquietude...*' offered Jason, his hand upon Simon's arm, '... has been remarked in several quarters, though I could not enlarge upon such confidences... as I am sure you will understand.'

Simon stared at each of his friends in turn, the realisation dawning upon him that denial would serve no purpose, would not be believed in the slightest. An awareness within him was developing that he was not the only man to have deep-seated fears of the next surgical burden and conceivably too the return of the trauma which had quite destroyed him once before after the second Samos battle; yet here, standing with him, were his stalwart friends, his brothers-in-arms, fellow medical practitioners both. Marston and Jason would be with him the next time, wherever and whenever that might be, and for that he was profoundly grateful, a surge of relief flooding his mind in that cathartic instant. He smiled at both men, he took their hands in turn and nodded his silent thanks, not a single word within his grasp in that so profoundly moving realisation.

Evening approached and at last Candia was sighted, the heavy weather persisting, white tops everywhere whipping off the waves in the fierce wind and the bows rising to fall with a crashing thud, the vibrations felt all throughout the ship as the hull fell off from every wave peak. The Greek fleet was holding off two leagues from the land, Miaoulis judging the strong wind - now a north-easterly - not helpful for his planned attack on the Suda harbour. Against the tempest he could not see how to evacuate his ships after an attack into the large anchorage, which was defended at its mouth by a fort, a smaller battery emplaced upon the island in the approach to the inner harbour. At least the Turks too could not escape the place; they were there, and they would would have no choice but to await the Greek attack, for doubtless the Greek fleet had been sighted by watchers on the surrounding low hills.

Monday 13th June 1825   20:00   *outside Suda harbour*

'The wind is dropping,' announced Pat, a crowd all about him on the quarterdeck, all eyes gazing towards the harbour, all minds gripped by a rising sense of anticipation. Excitement was growing apace with its close cousin, nervous apprehension. The Greek brigs - still seventy strong despite further reports of insubordination, the Spetziots proving to be particularly difficult - all remained present. It was a fleet of considerable firepower, one which could live up to Miaoulis's hopes, were it to fight determinedly and the weather not to stay their hand. The weather, however, did not seem to be in sympathy; indeed, the poor conditions had made it exceedingly difficult for the Greeks to stay all day on station, their small brigs rolling and bucking in the severe wind and seas. Their men waited patiently, keen expectation a strain on the nerves as the hours slipped by until, with less than an hour of light remaining, Miaoulis had judged the wind still too strong to begin any attack; such would have to await the morrow and - every man hoping - better weather.

Sunset, the wind ferocity much diminished, and Pat shared his supper table with Simon, Marston and Jason, *Surprise* holding station two leagues off Suda. Murphy served a roasted half-lamb, the sliced cuts, chops and joints all sitting on a bed of bright yellow rice, and the whole flavoured with an exceptional quantity of fresh herbs and spices, the divine fragrances of coriander within the rice and rosemary within the hot lamb maintaining their aromatic presence even within the meaty bouquet arising from the fatty juices of the roasted meat.

'This eats well,' declared Pat with huge satisfaction, nodding to his steward, Murphy hastening to refill the wine glasses. 'A gift from Miaoulis it was... a capital man.'

155

'What of our Greek comrades, sir?' Marston piped up, 'They have achieved two splendid victories, yet now... *so I hear*... there is discontent and - *is it true?* - even insubordination amongst the several factions. Why is that, tell?'

'As to that, I have precious little idea. Certainly, I have never met any men so greedy for applause as the Hydriot captains, and of their entire fleet their successes are due to ten or twelve good men, everybody else being a hanger-on... I have precious little doubt of that... and... and as for nepotism, why, every man of every crew is a relative... and so the crew's consent is always required for every task, though... *I will say...* on the other side of that particular coin... open quarrels are unheard of.'

Jason set down his glass, 'I have attended Doctor Ferguson when he has treated a goodly number of their wounded on several occasions... and I listen to their chatter. I will say that it strikes me that the Spetziots are inveterate grumblers, and neither is there any love lost between them and the Hydriots... I venture they have never failed their deeply ingrained inclination to disobey Hydriot orders. Perhaps there is the root of the insubordination we have heard spoken of today?'

'Indeed so...' Pat nodded sagely, 'I venture there is something in what you say, and what a contrast the Spetziots are with the Psariots... who are the bravest souls I have ever encountered. No longer do they possess of any home, their island being sacked... no longer any man, woman or child living there any longer; yet ever they display bravery... and always will support the Hydriots...'

'And consequently, the Spetziots don't like them either!' Jason laughed out loud.

'Yes, 'tis a rum band,' Pat laughed too, 'and no admiral of our navy would care to stand for it. There would by now have been a plentiful number of hangings, no doubt.'

All turned their attentions to the food, the rice delicious, the lamb sublime, juicy and full of flavour, the crisped fat particularly so. Murphy hovered about the table, the conversation in full flow, the steward maintaining a keen eye on the diminishing meat cuts, an anxiety to whisk away for his own attentions anything which might be left being at the very forefront of his thoughts.

'Simon, a glass with you!' declared Pat in loud voice, little spoken by the surgeon for much of the meal; indeed, he seemed to be brooding throughout it.

'Little do I know of the Greeks' internecine differences,' murmured Simon, 'my attentions being only for the wounds of those that cross my table, but... you will allow me to say... all of these men have my admiration, for of money they have none... of their prospects, all are uncertain, and the ships they serve in - *I have seen it with my own eyes* - are invariably inferior to those of their adversaries. It is a brave man that endures in such circumstances.'

'It is that,' agreed Pat in low voice, staring at his own men, the cumulative strain showing in their eyes, resonating in their voices since many weeks; many instances of that returning to his recollections even as he looked in discrete assessment at all his friends, a smile here, a short peal of laughter there; but to the close eye there was a small hesitancy about much of their movements, a slight waver in their hand as they raised a glass or reached for another slice of the succulently teasing lamb, a little of which was still present after the most generous distribution. For how much longer could they all endure? He had no idea save for an inkling of suspicion that it might be for a lesser time than he had always believed. Perhaps, like an ageing old horse, they were truly coming to the end of their useful lives as military men? Here and now seemed like blessed normality, as any casual observer might believe, but for all of them it really was not; it was a respite, an oasis of calm within a temporal storm of rising anxiety, and a short-lived one for all that. He turned back to his plate, his mind returning to an icy equilibrium, his own fears squeezed firmly back within their box and the lid screwed tight shut, his hand - a small waver about it, he noticed - reaching for another morsel of lamb. He determined to clutch at the flimsy and ethereal semblance of the appearance of calm for as long as he could, for never before had he contemplated his own self-delusion.

The stormy night relenting to the grey of a blustery morning and the wind having fallen further, to such a degree that it was little more than a breeze though still blowing from the north-east, Miaoulis at last ordered his attack. The Turks - all agreed that they had presumably been forewarned by the perfidious French - had reorganised their fleet into four squadrons, two each in the inner and outer harbours.

The leading Greek brigs exchanged a brisk cannonade with the outer Turk squadrons, within an hour forcing their outermost vessels to retire, to coalesce in the central deep-water channel. The fort on the southern approach and the tiny fortress on the island at the harbour mouth opened a brisk fire upon the Greeks.

'There go the fireships,' observed Pat, three old Greek brigs boldly venturing ahead of all their brothers. Two swiftly closed on a corvette which was rapidly consumed by the flames, the third, commanded by Politi, lost all way as the breeze failed, the fireship burning fiercely but all alone, her men taking to her launch and pulling for the nearest Greek brig, all the time being fired upon by Turks with small arms aboard a pair of scampavias.

In contrast to the prior two battles, the afternoon seemed to be moving exceedingly slowly. Partly it was the lack of wind; equally it was the inability of the Greeks to put more than their leading nine brigs into any position to engage with firing. Not that such was their usual tactic at all, for the Turks invariably possessed heavier guns, and so the Greeks generally contented themselves with a covering fire for their fireships, but without wind no opportunity was offered to them, at least none that the Turks could not avoid with defensive disposition of their own smaller vessels to head off any nearing fireship, whilst their own fleet fired upon those Greek brigs at the rear.

Three hours had passed after Pat's noon sighting when he regretfully concluded that the day would offer little success. Six bells rang out in a dolorous, mournful tone on *Surprise* as the feeble breeze expired entirely. From the quarterdeck, Pat and all his officers gazed at the distant harbour mouth where the brigs of all the Greek commanders, Miaoulis, Sakhtouri and Canaris, were now mired, utterly becalmed, along with six more Hydriot vessels, all in an increasingly perilous position with no means to shift nor to escape the firing of the fortress. Eventually the Greeks took to their boats and towed their brigs east and away from the Turk guns, the increasingly desultory and long range firing fading away as the hours passed until the yellowing sun eventually approached the low horizon, a distorted orb casting its diffuse and weak light through thin cloud. A strange sense of disappointment descended upon every Greek and every Surprise, only one Turk corvette having been destroyed. After the wildly successful destruction inflicted at Modon and the scattering of Khosref's fleet at the Cavo Doro strait, it was with deflated spirits that the Surprises sat for supper, the feeble dusk light settling upon them and bestowing an air of resignation to the end of the day.

'I saw much damage to Miaoulis's rigging,' remarked Pat.

'Indeed, and to many of the others with him,' murmured Codrington.

'What will be on the morrow, would you think?' asked Simon, the knot in his stomach relenting, secretly pleased that *Surprise* had played no part in the day, had suffered no losses, although ten Greeks had been killed. It was the price paid in lives for the burning of the Turk corvette.

'The weather... *the wind* will be the judge of that, I dare say,' offered Pat, as deflated as the next man by the near non-event, as all saw it, the much diminished frisson of fear within him flickering still.

Thursday 30th June 1825   11:00   *Nauplia*

'Welcome aboard, Captain Macleod!' came the shout in the delightful brogue of County Down from the officer hastening across the deck of the frigate *Cambrian*; 'Gawen Hamilton, at your service, sir.'

'Good morning, sir; Duncan Macleod, at *your* service,' a very tired Duncan shook hands.

159

'Come, let us go into the cabin and out of this fierce sun, when we will partake of refreshment,' said Hamilton, quickly assessing the greatly sombre mood of his visitor.

'Most kind,' murmured Duncan.

The stewards, two in attendance, served tea, coffee and sherry, a tray of marchpane biscuits accompanying the drinks. Hamilton nodded and they vacated the cabin, the two captains pausing for a few moments, sipping their drinks, a careful hiatus before the serious business began.

'Thank you for coming aboard, Captain Macleod. I arrived here only yesterday; indeed, my bargemen pulled me all the way from Hydra, my frigate becalmed there. My First brought her in only this morning. I bring despatches for you from the Admiralty and letters from London. But, how are you? How do you fare, all these months in this rum Greek business?'

'I hesitate to say a deal about it... I regret it is not... not...' Duncan halted, lost for words.

'Allow me to say that the First Lord himself, in recent despatches, has given me his explanation of your high personal standing with him and that of all your shipmates aboard *Surprise*.'

Duncan swallowed, such was praise indeed, 'I am much beholden to his Lordship in saying so.'

'I confess that I am myself sympathetic to Greek aspirations, though I endeavour at all times to respect both parties in this miserable little war with an absolute impartiality. Of course, one hears stories, tales of abominable events which strain such adherence to strictly neutral conduct but... *I dare say*... Boney too perpetrated his horrors.'

'Aye, indeed he did,' murmured Duncan, slowly chewing again on his biscuit.

'You will forgive me saying, sir, that you are of a... will I say, a... a much downcast disposition... Is there anything I am able to do... to offer, the slightest thing?'

'No, but thank you all the same, sir.' A long pause and Duncan spoke again, 'Aye, I am wearied of this war... of such abominations that you speak of. Until this week I had managed to preserve my sanity and a degree of support for the Greeks, I had so. Yet, such small measure of... of resolution that I still possessed was swept away in a single day this week... when it came to my eyes that I was... *had been* in sympathy with barbarians... vile brutes.... so greatly shocking it was.'

'Please... go on; to what do you refer?'

'It pains me so much to even recount these monstrous events... I was with Admiral Canaris on Saturday gone. We were walking along the quay on Hydra in the most cordial of discussion, his own opinions of the war and its progress being the matter of our conversation, and I endeavoured to speak with him about Miaoulis and their engagement at Suda on the 14th. The admiral had described the weather, a calm during the attack, which was aborted, and the great storm of the 17th which drove him away, all Greek ships scattered, Canaris and Miaoulis returning to Hydra a week ago. I was endeavouring to ask if he had any news of *Surprise.*'

'Was she there, at Suda with him?'

'Aye, that was Captain O'Connor's intention, after which he was minded to return to England, the barky damaged so when she escaped the great bay at Navarino.'

'Why, I have not seen her, but I am here only yesterday, a few hours before sunset. It was only this morning that we espied your vessel, *Eleanor*, at the quay... *Cambrian* too; and hence my message... my invitation to come aboard.'

'Allow me to say that I was much pleased to receive it, sir.'

'You mentioned the events of this week?'

'A great crowd gathered before Canaris and I as we walked the length of the quay... noisy, much anger evident and shouting such as might be expected from a mob. Indeed, it was a bloodthirsty mob, such a one as I have never before witnessed.' Duncan halted as if it was proving too difficult to recount the scene. 'Would you have a wee tait of something a trifle stronger?'

'Of course, would you care for a whisky at all?'

'That would make me very happy.'

Hamilton rang the little bell on his table and the steward entered immediately, leaving with celerity with Hamilton's request. 'You mentioned *Surprise*,' said Hamilton, choosing to steer for rather calmer waters; 'Where do you think she will be? What would Captain O'Connor be minded to do, where to go?'

'Oh, I dare say he will be thinking of Cephalonia, a safe haven for many pressing repairs... before a return to England.'

'Yes, that seems most likely.' A minute or two of silent evaluation and Hamilton spoke again, 'There is one matter that I must bring to your attention. The First Lord has mentioned to me that you enjoy the confidence of Prince Mavrocordato.'

'Aye, indeed we have shared many an hour in the most cordial of discussions. In fact, he was with me aboard the Greek brig, *Aris*, when we escaped the Bay of Navarino... and before that... when we were on the island, Sphacteria, the prince looking to the defenders... It was a hopeless task... every man lost.' Duncan shuddered, the ghastly events he had witnessed a still painful recollection.

'You were on the island?' Hamilton stared with incredulity.

'Aye, and a godforsaken hill it is too... We escaped the bay... under fire for four hours. Captain O'Connor, I am sure, was our saviour, distracting the Turks from a mile in our wake. Without the barky firing on those Turk vessels, I have not the least doubt that neither I nor the prince would be here today.'

'The prince is here?'

'He is, but I gather he is leaving Nauplia on the morrow. It was long greatly feared that the town would fall to Ibrahim's besieging forces, but... and much to the surprise of all, the Egyptian has lifted his siege but two days ago. The prince has asked me to carry him to Hydra aboard *Eleanor*... later this day.'

'You know that Kolokotrones has been released from prison in Hydra... Indeed, he was released some weeks ago; a date of the 28th May was mentioned to me in Corfu. It is understood that he has since assumed leadership of all Greek land forces.'

'Aye, I think that may be why Mavrocordato is himself intending to leave for Hydra; he does not care to meet the man.'

'However, I do believe that it may well have been the influence of Kolokotrones which has precipitated Ibrahim's withdrawal from the immediate environs of Nauplia.'

The steward returned with the whisky in that moment, setting down the tray. A slight bow to his captain and he exited the cabin. Hamilton poured a modest whet into his own glass and filled Duncan's to near the brim, his visitor plainly in an obvious state of anxiety.

'There is a Frenchman with Mavrocordato,' said Hamilton, 'The authorities in the Ionians have been intercepting his letters, reading them. It would appear that he is a spy for the French government.'

'What? His secretary is a Frenchie, Grasset.'

'No, not Grasset, another Frenchman; his name is in the secret memo... from the... *the authorities* in Corfu; I collect it is a Monsieur Théobald Piscatory. Seemingly he is in league with another Greek faction, that of Kolettis, a man of the Morea who is... so it is believed in certain quarters... which ones I am not a party to... is to some degree under *French* influence. I am come directly from the Ionians... to alert the prince.'

'Damnable Frogs!' Duncan took another large gulp of his whisky, little left in his glass. Hamilton discreetly refilled it.

'You were referring to Hydra, the quay.... with Canaris,' prompted Hamilton gently. 'Would that be... the mob that is, the event that has caused you such... such setback?'

'Aye,' Duncan's hand hesitated above his glass. He leaned back as if gathering his mental strength, the whisky untouched. 'As we approached this mob, such a cacophony of shouting, foul calls... before our eyes, from out of a building on the quay the crowd were dragging out Turk prisoners... two or three at a time...' An exceptionally large gulp from the glass, Duncan plainly in difficulties, and Hamilton could only stare. 'These unfortunates were hauled out and murdered before our eyes... axes, swords... pikes.... the bodies cast into the harbour water. More and more... out they came, some struggling, shouting, screaming, their blood flowing all over the quay... obvious it was to the poor souls about to be murdered, the hundreds of them inside becoming aware of what was happening... killings, scores struck down... not the least mercy offered...' An audible gasp of distress accompanied the look of despair upon Duncan's face and a horrified Hamilton could find no words. 'Canaris called for a halt, shouted... screamed at them... but they paid him no heed, ignored him... Angry words were exchanged, the admiral himself in great distress, aye... the man himself was in tears. I dragged him away with difficulty, no longer could we bear to see the ghastly events before our own eyes... and we hastened back along the quay, the screams of the dying following us for a mile... the worst mile of my life; aye, that it was... horrible... damn murderers, vile murderers... scum! Canaris himself said to me, "Today I am ashamed to be a Greek" as we left that place... as we left the... the terror behind us... nothing could we do.'

'I am greatly sorry for your distress,' whispered Hamilton, shocked and much set back himself at the horrific tale.

'Two hundred and fifty defenceless souls murdered... by vile brute beasts... *by animals!*' Duncan sighed, 'I collect something said by our lieutenant, Mr Pickering, a long time ago; it has always stuck with me; indeed, it was a quote which originated with Bonaparte himself... *"War is the business of barbarians"*. How true that is! I could not disagree. I ask myself, have I come to Greece to fight for such people?' This was declared in angry voice. 'No... I have not. I will no longer do so. I am going home... after I carry the prince back to that hell hole... to Hydra.'

'Then if it pleases you, I will be most grateful for the opportunity to speak with the prince before you depart.'

'Of course, sir; please do. The prince will be at the quay at 3PM to board *Eleanor*.'

'Then may I suggest we enjoy dinner here together? My chef has prepared a tasty morsel or two on my direction in anticipation of such.' Hamilton was much pleased to see a brightening in Duncan's face, his distress receding, the merest hint of a smile preceding his grateful acceptance.

It was 4PM when Mavrocordato eventually arrived at the quay, a train of a dozen followers accompanying him. Hamilton stared as a greatly impatient Duncan, anxious to make progress before the customary dying of the *meltemi* wind at sunset, assisted the prince down the ladder and aboard the schooner, the Scotsman listening attentively for the accent of any Frenchman other than Grasset, with whom he was familiar. The prince's secretary had also been with him on Sphacteria and during the flight of *Aris*. There was no other Frenchman, Duncan was relieved to conclude, and he rapidly introduced the Greek to Hamilton, the three of them repairing to the tiny cabin as Mower supervised an abeyance of the preparations for departure, the further delay countenanced by Hamilton's presence.

'Your Highness,' pronounced Hamilton, 'it is a great honour to meet you. Allow me to say I have long been an admirer.'

'Why, thank you Captain,' Mavrocordato beamed with obvious pleasure.

'Sir, I must report in haste, for I am aware of Captain Macleod's wish for a swift departure and his hopes of fetching Hydra in the daylight hours.'

'Please, Captain, do go on.'

'It is the understanding of the Ionian authorities that you are in recent times attended by a second Frenchman, Monsieur Théobald Piscatory.'

'I am familiar with the man, it is true.'

'He is, they believe, a secret service agent... a spy.'

'I see,' murmured Mavrocordato in undecided tone.

'A letter was intercepted... that is to say... it is believed that he has endeavoured to suborn your secretary, Monsieur Grasset.'

'Grasset?'

'May it please you to hear that Monsieur Grasset has had no truck with Piscatory...'

'That is certainly welcome news; thank you, Captain.'

'... and Piscatory has also been for some months in close contact with Kolettis...'

'That damnable rogue!' cried the prince, 'Why, that man has no more notion of the proper role of government than my dog!'

'That may well be,' said Hamilton as circumspectly as he could manage, 'However, His Majesty's Government wishes to aid your own honourable efforts in respect of Greek government and... and has no time for... *for bandits*.'

'Or for Frenchies!' interjected Duncan with feeling.

'Or Frenchies, indeed. In fact,' a weak smile and Hamilton continued, 'it is known to His Majesty's Government that Piscatory did meet with Capodistrias in Switzerland before he came to Greece and... and furthermore, that he has also been in contact with a known... a *well known* Russian agent in Greece.'

'With Capodistrias?' exclaimed Mavrocordato, 'With a Russian agent?'

'Yes, that is the case. Doubtless you are aware that Capodistrias was formerly in the service of the Tsar as his Foreign Secretary before he moved to Switzerland?'

'Yes, yes, of course; that has long been well known.'

'Sir, London is aware of the nature of *Russian* aspirations for the future of your country, for its structure as might emerge after the Turk is... is sent packing... and such as the Russians aspire to may not wholly accord with your own intentions. I am not, of course, privy to such detail myself, and I am here merely to state that His Majesty's Government is minded that these facts should be made known to you without the least delay. Hence my purpose in coming here in *HMS Cambrian*.'

'Thank you, Captain Hamilton, and I am greatly obliged to His Majesty's Government. In fact, of all the states professing sympathy for our cause, it has long seemed to me and to those of all who serve the present Greek goverment that England is the very beacon of inspiration for our future, for a democratic Greece, free of the Turk yoke... So much so that I am awaiting the finalisation of a letter from my government for carriage to London, for the attention of the English government, and it is my most earnest wish that Captain Macleod will convey it when it is ready.'

'Sir, it is an honour to be of the smallest service, and I have not the least doubt that your confidence in Captain Macleod is well placed. However, I must bid you goodbye without the least delay, for Captain Macleod is anxious to depart. Good day, sir; good fortune to you and farewell.'

The brief exchange of cordialities was swiftly concluded, Hamilton stepping up to the quay with his lieutenant, standing with his bargemen as *Eleanor* cast off, the schooner shifting quickly in the fresh breeze of the *meltemi* to the south.

An hour was spent in pleasing observation of the splendid views all about the schooner, Duncan and Mavrocordato relaxing, both entirely comfortable in each other's company, until they shifted to sit in the small cabin where a half-hour was spent much enjoying splendid Turkish coffee, open and conversational exchanges shared. The two had unwittingly forged a firm bond of friendship in the terror of their escape together from Sphacteria, Duncan having assisted the prince across the rocky island terrain and to the last boat escaping the shore for the Greek brig *Aris*, all the time under Egyptian small arms fire. It had been a close call, one neither man was ever likely to forget; certainly, the prince never would, and his gratitude to his saviour was deeply engraved, his voice carrying a warmth within it when speaking to Duncan on every matter.

'Your Highness,' Duncan broke the tranquillity of a reflective silence, 'you referred to a letter when speaking with Captain Hamilton...'

'Ah yes, the letter...' Mavrocordato nodded, 'It is a political motion, long debated, much argued over and near agreed after the most extensive consideration. Its arrival in London is of primary importance to Greece... is essential for our prospects and circumstances. I regret I am unable to speak of the contents of the letter... as I am sure you will understand... and it is my hope, *my sincere hope*, Captain Macleod, that you will carry this message to London personally... and with the utmost expedition... aboard your fine vessel.' The prince's face dropped as if in mute supplication and he stared hard at Duncan, unblinking, waiting for his reply.

'Sir, were the decision solely mine then I would, of course, be most happy to take your letter, I would...' Duncan set down his glass, 'However, I am obliged to speak first with Captain O'Connor. We believe it likely that he is in the Ionians, most probably at Cephalonia, at Argostoli.' Mavrocordato nodding slowly, Duncan continued, 'I venture that Captain O'Connor will not consider I am speaking out of turn when I say that I believe he will be greatly sympathetic to your request; indeed, it is exceedingly likely that he is himself preparing to take the barky... *HMS*... that is to say *Surprise*... home, home to England. In that event, the decision will be his as to whether to convey a message of such importance aboard *Surprise* or *Eleanor*. The schooner is little armed; that is not the case for *Surprise*.'

'Certainly, the letter must be safeguarded, its sanctity preserved.'

'If it pleases you, it would be prudent were you to provide *two* copies of the letter. If the missive is of the importance I am led to believe, then speed is of the essence, and *Eleanor* is particularly swift of sail... faster than the barky... than *Surprise*, she being damaged so.'

'I understand.'

'However, a copy held in the safety of *Surprise* would be no bad thing. There is... *I don't doubt that you know*... a deal of unsavoury nautical enterprises throughout all the Mediterranean waters, and *Eleanor*... an appealing prospect for any pirates she may encounter, though swift, is not assured of escape.'

'Very well. That would seem to be a sensible notion. The letter is not yet in my possession but I await its delivery to Hydra when finished and signed. It is expected any day.'

'Your Highness, may I beg to mention another subject?' Mavrocordato nodded. 'You doubtless remember the theft of the gold, the theft that never was... the kentledge... *the ballast ingots*... they being taken in error? You collect the two rogues, Peddler and Perkis?'

'I never actually met the men, no... for they had departed Calamata in that night, with the gold - as we believed. Thankfully your surgeon had ventured his opinion for shifting it elsewhere within your vessel... to effect a greater degree of stabilisation... if my memory serves me?'

'Aye, that was the case... We ne'er cease to laugh about that in the cabin these days - when he is not there of course. Hah! Hah! The very idea of Simon Ferguson advising on any matters of the barky... well, it is a hoot for sure, Hah! Hah!' Duncan laughed out loud again at the thought.

'Your surgeon enjoys the most excellent reputation amongst all the Greek seamen I have ever spoken with.'

'Aye, I don't doubt that, and with every one of us too; we are all much the happier in mind that he is with us. Indeed, I cannot conceive of losing him, though I do believe that he is, these recent months, finding the strains increasingly intolerable. There is a limit, as we have all come to see aboard the barky, to how long a man may endure.'

'I am sure of it... but, allow me to say, we Greek patriots consider that we are blessed that you and all your comrades are fighting in our service, fighting for Greece.'

'Thank you, sir, most kind. I was speaking of the two rogues, Peddler and Perkis. Have you any news of them, of where they went?'

'Precious little of substance save for a secondhand tale which was reiterated to me by an officer you may be familiar with: a Kasiot, Captain Zouvelekis.'

'Aye, I remember him well: a good man; he served with us all through 'twenty-four, but we have not seen him since.'

'He is now an agent of mine and travels wide all about the islands. He sends his compliments, Macleod, should I ever meet with you.'

'That is mighty good to hear, sir. I have a deal of respect for the man.'

'Seemingly he heard mention from an Austrian officer of a brig in Calamata that his friend, the captain of another Austrian merchantman, had conveyed two Englishmen to Genoa from Cerigo. It was around the time of the beginning of this month. Of course, we cannot be sure it was the two thieves, but I believe we can assume there is a degree of likelihood about the story for I have never heard a stranger tale from any of my sources about all the islands.'

'So, they have indeed escaped Greece and taken passage to Genoa... Well, well, well...' Duncan took a deep intake of breath,

'Then I venture they may at some time fetch home to England. It seems we may not have seen the last of the rogues after all. I venture Simon Ferguson will be keen to hear that.'

Four hours more and the schooner, moving gracefully with a pronounced heel, the stiff wind off her quarter, approached Hydra, the port looming large on the bow, the sun low, the sunset very near. Another half-hour, *Eleanor's* crew benefitting from the twilight, and she closed on the quay. The faint dusk glow was fast weakening and in the poor light no man could see what, floating in the water, the schooner struck several times, the gentlest brushes of mild collision registering with all aboard, everyone standing on deck, and all keen to step ashore. Just a few yards remaining and Mower brought her alongside with consummate skill, the Prince and his entourage standing ready to depart for the town. Duncan and Mower assisted the Greeks ashore and shook hands with Mavrocordato. Friendly greetings were exchanged, the prince pledging to return on the morrow with the letter he was finalising for carriage to London.

Total darkness was nigh upon them when Duncan's nose caught the unmistakeable, vile stench of human decay. He stared out over the placid harbour waters but could see little, near nothing, but then, in the illumination offered by Mower's lighting of the schooner's lantern, his eye caught the drifting flotsam, a mere five yards off the quay wall; he saw it for what it was: a floating corpse. His stomach turned and he near threw up, refraining with difficulty and discomfort. He sighed with a huge exhalation as if to clear the offensive smell from all his senses, pinched tight his nose and immediately beckoned Mower, when the two of them hastened off, towards the town, away from the reminder of the horror, his spirits sinking faster than the lead line.

Monday 25th July 1825   18:00   *Hydra*

Three weeks and more had passed in waiting for the anticipated Greek letter, the days spent in complete indolence with no further news from Mavrocordato about it when, unexpectedly, the prince finally appeared on the quay and was directed by

Reeve to the eatery to where Duncan had taken himself with Mower, for he could not bear, in the full daylight, sight of the obvious and great number of corpses floating all about the environs of the harbour. The lingering stench was scarcely any less unpleasant; indeed, with the passing of many warm days it seemed much worse every successive morning. On awakening on the first day after arrival Duncan had looked out from *Eleanor's* deck to a calm sea, only the mildest of ripples atop the water. The bodies of the unfortunate Turk captives murdered some weeks before had never been washed away; no tide of note and the subsequently generally benign weather with little wind had retained them within the harbour, scores floating still. He had gagged, his mind recoiling from the reminder of such cruelty, no Hydriot since the massacre caring to venture out, to recover the bodies for burial. 'Damn their souls!' he had shouted aloud in full voice, every Eleanor alerted, heads turning towards him both on the deck and all along the length of the quay.

Since that first morning he had consoled himself within the nearby watering hole, eating modest meals and drinking red wine with Mower, a score of locals taking their ease all about them and filling the small room, a dimly lit oasis of relaxation, one filled with the aromas of stale cooking oil, tobacco smoke, spilt alcohol and sweat. Duncan was entirely relaxed, if increasingly reconciled to no letter ever appearing, until the moment when they looked up to see Mavrocordato entering the tavern, accompanied by Grasset.

'Captain Macleod... and Mr... Mr Mower is it? Good evening to you both, gentlemen,' cried Mavrocordato as he entered. Cordial handshakes were offered all round and the new arrivals sat at the table with the Surprises. The waiter, recognising and much impressed by his illustrious patron, busied about them serving red wine, olives and fresh-baked bread. A pleasant but pensive half-hour passed with sips and nibbles, until the prince came to the point, the purpose of his call. 'I am here with the letter I referred to in Nauplia... It is from the provisional Greek government to the English government, and is at last concluded and recently signed. There has been a deal of disagreement about its contents, but I am pleased to say that it is finished. It is a missive of the utmost significance, the very utmost.' Mavrocordato spoke in hushed tones for it was apparent that every man within the tiny tavern was striving to listen, dignitaries never before being present in their humble refuge. Barely a one possessed the slightest grasp of English and greatly erroneous translations were being whispered from man to man, lips everywhere covered by hands, heads pressed close together. The Greek continued very quietly, dismissing the clientele from his attentions, 'It is also vital that the letter does not fall into the wrong hands, captured or lost... I cannot be plainer than that.'

Duncan nodded, 'With your permission, sir, I will return to Argostoli with your letter and seek out Captain O'Connor.'

'That is perfectly acceptable, Captain Macleod. When would it be in your intention to depart?'

'As this is plainly a matter of the greatest significance... to Greece, I will leave on the morrow, sir, at the dawn.'

'Excellent, Captain Macleod; I am in your debt.' Mavrocordato nodded to Grasset who extracted the precious letter from a goatskin satchel, passing it to the prince. It hovered for a few seconds only in his own hand before he pressed it into Duncan's, the Greek's demeanour grave, as if passing all the wealth of the world to another, nothing more spoken.

Mower glanced aside and formed the impression that every eye in the tavern was fixed upon the letter, every face blank, every hand holding a glass paused twixt table and lip. Men looked away as his ranging stare fell upon them in turn.

The table ensemble relaxed a little and the wine was followed by brandy, a hubbub of conversation returning in the tiny room until, an hour gone, Mavrocordato spoke of his own recollections of Sphacteria, much to Duncan's discomfort, the prince seemingly able to set the distressing memories aside as he asked Duncan's opinion on the island's defence, its failure, what else might have been done, renewed interest rising within all the tavern's patrons, a voluble translation rising on many tables as not a man left and each one ordered more wine, all determined not to miss a minute of this so very exceptional event.

Another hour passed in renewed recollections when, perhaps the prince's tongue loosened by the liquor, he touched upon the essential question, one which oft occurred in the thoughts of most Greeks even if, in political circles, it did not cross their lips, 'Captain Macleod, I beg a favour in asking for your opinion... your honest... *your forthright* opinion in this matter...'

Duncan nodded but said nothing. Mower had said nothing for an hour and felt wholly out of his depth; he was aware that all conversation in the tavern had halted once more but he could do no more than stare as a fascinated spectator himself, for no person of such standing as the prince nor anything of the like of the talk he had been listening to had he ever experienced before. Unnoticed at the table, the entire room had fallen into silence; eyes everywhere swivelled in discreet study of the conversation, for the sense of it had been generally grasped if not the totality or detail of the exchanges.

Mavrocordato, perhaps giving cognisance to the fascination of all present, resumed in a whisper, 'Greece is in the most exceedingly difficult dilemma. There are voices... I will speak no names... voices suggesting that we should come to an accommodation with the Porte... and give up our struggle.'

After the so shocking words, an absolute air of expectancy filled the whole tavern, and Duncan's heart missed a beat. His stomach turned over and he felt the rise of the acid bile within him, sensed the rush of blood to his head, and his mouth was dry in an instant. He remained absolutely motionless; indeed, he doubted he could move if he chose to do so. He held his tongue, his mind racing in anticipation of a question he realised was coming but which was as yet unasked.

Another minute and Mavrocordato, ignoring the attentions of a score of men, all obviously listening attentively and to the exclusion of all else, spoke again, 'In such times I confess it is a struggle to rid the mind of such unpleasant prospects, to cling to a singular determination... a determination to continue the struggle...' No word from Duncan, another minute passing and the prince at last put his question in little more than a reluctant whisper, 'Would you give any countenance to such a motion?'

173

Duncan heard Mower's sharp intake of breath at his side. His own mind raced and he could feel beads of sweat on his brow; his throat and mouth seemed drier than ever. He sensed rather than saw Mower, Mavrocordato and Grasset all staring at him, and he was oblivious to the other two dozen of patrons at the surrounding tables in the tavern's dim light. A few seconds passed as if an hour before he could find the words, ones which he had not the least difficulty in thinking; but of speaking, that was an entirely different matter. He hesitated, 'Sir... I am but a junior officer... one in a ship with precious little official standing, and my own opinion, I venture, is not worth a brass farthing...'

'Macleod,' Mavrocordato whispered, 'your opinion to me is worth all the gold in the world; I value none more... Please... go on.' Had the smallest of pin dropped it would certainly have been heard by all in the room, for not a sound was heard from anyone.

Duncan's resolution firming, he spoke again, 'Very well, sir... I will speak of words which passed between myself and Captain Hamilton of the *Cambrian*. Do you recall speaking with him in Nauplia?'

'I do indeed.'

The several discreetly spoken translations about the tavern being slow, whispers now abounded everywhere.

'These are *his* words, but they are ones with which I wholly accord.' Duncan paused for a deep breath, his mind momentarily flirting with the incongruity, the absurdity, of the moment: little more than two years before he had been about to take a Hebridean fishing vessel to sea, yet now he was here, speaking to the leading statesman of Greece, the great man himself asking his advice, the counsel of a lowly and humble Scot from Lewis.

An excited babble rose up throughout the small room, a score of chairs grated on the floor, all present swivelling towards Duncan. Multiple conversations were no longer whispered so much as spoken aloud, all pretence of disinterest being wholly discarded; every one of the Greeks present was staring with unconcealed and blatant curiosity.

Duncan, momentarily distracted by the rising voices all about the tavern, spoke up once more, louder, determination and conviction resonating in his voice, 'While there is a spark of hope, fight on, and when all is desperate... *when all is desperate...* then think of *foreign* assistance.'

Mavrocordato, until then a spellbound study in fascination, blinked, nodded his understanding. Silence having descended once more upon the room, the Greek spoke at last, 'If it pleases you, Captain Macleod, I asked your own mind.'

'Very well, sir,' a still hesitant Duncan began in quiet voice, 'Whilst ever there is a prospect of victory, however small it may seem, however dark the day... fight on.' Finding himself becoming impassioned, Duncan spoke up louder, the audience gripped, several concurrent translations about the room also rising in volume. 'Fight with every sinew, fight on with every weapon possessed...' Duncan found himself increasingly excited and near to shouting, the background noises ever louder, 'NEVER GIVE UP... and...' his final, excited exclamation, '...and never... NEVER SURRENDER!'

Mavrocordato, somewhat overwhelmed and wholly mute, managed a single nod before looking about him. Passionate voices were rising at every table until, spontaneously, every man erupted into loud shouting, all leaping to their feet and clapping with fierce applause, dozens of men moving towards Duncan and Mavrocordato to offer in their exuberance more personal and physical congratulations.

Mavrocordato rose from his own chair, extended his hand over the table. Macleod, somewhat taken aback by the loud acclaim from a dozen men standing all about him, reached to accept it. Without words, without ceremony, the prince leaned forward and seized Duncan's hand in both his own with an unrelenting grip. Mower and Grasset simply stared with wide eyes, amazed. A raucous further minute of cheering passed all about the tavern before it subsided and Mavrocordato mumbled the only words he could manage, 'Thank you... *thank you...* '

Chapter Eight

Sunday 31st July 1825   07:00   Argostoli port, Cephalonia

The dim pre-dawn twilight had begun to filter through the gratings and down the companionway steps a half-hour previously, the dark of the night gradually dispelled by the faintest glow of half-light, near-imperceptibly brightening until the dawn proper had arrived. The semi-conscious awareness of it awakened slumbering men all along the lower deck, men whose minds were well accustomed to filtering out the obtrusive bell until, a little after four bells of the morning watch, the men all about the lower deck were reluctantly stirring in their hammocks, initially reluctant to cede a slim comfort to the start of another day of back-breaking toil, until they remembered that such was not likely to be, not this day. Silently they clambered out from cramped, warm suspension, shook heads to better awaken bleary minds, stretched weary muscles to dispel the aches of the prior day, and hesitantly they traipsed the few steps to join their messmates sitting on their sea chests, low chatter prevalent, to await their breakfast of steaming hot porridge and its welcome internal warming of their bodies.

The greasy oatmeal gruel was consumed more slowly than usual with none of the customary haste of the change of watch in evidence. The hands were also much pleased that the cheese ration had been restored since purchasing had been enabled in Argostoli, and they nibbled on the precious shards of hard cheddar, only three months in storage *en route* to the island, still in delightful condition and a rare treat, knife points everywhere carefully prising out only the tiniest of green mould spots to throw to the waiting cat, staring silently in patient expectation. With pleasure they sipped the morning half of their grog ration, not so much diluted as usual - as many gratefully remarked - a rising sense of relief settling upon tired men, blessed hope once more extending its ethereal tentacles and coming afresh within numbed and fatigued minds, thoughts of home stirring as a beatific vision, one becoming ever clearer by the day; until, the porridge, the grog and the final delicious fragments of cheese all consumed, each man mentally conceded to himself that they were, at least, all together with their mates, and, if so ordered, the day's hard work would not be so bad after all.

Pat, feeling the happiest he had been for a long time, sat up in his cot and stretched out. Loud but indistinct noises of timber intermittently thumping upon the deck below his cabin had awakened him from deep sleep nearly an hour previously, but he had striven with limited success to continue dozing in a semi-conscious and contented relaxation, ignoring the bell and the muted sound of the pumps, a benign sense of well-being settling upon him. The brilliant illumination of the morning sun had filled both the cabin and his mind with a radiant sense of the new day, and a warming breeze wafted through the shattered remnants of the stern gallery, not yet repaired and not the least prospect of such until they reached Falmouth.

His mind briefly wandered back in review to the prior day, much thought given to when they might leave Greek waters. Not knowing when *Eleanor* might return from Hydra with Duncan, there had been much discussion about this at the supper table, Pat agreeing that *Eleanor* should leave without delay for home and without her consort, further repairs needed before *Surprise* could make her own departure. The past weeks of extensive repairs had near readied her fit once more for sea, sufficiently so for the Biscay passage, about which they all had reservations after the hurricane and near sinking of the prior winter.

Michael Marston had been powerfully persuasive in the cabin at supper, putting a profoundly well-argued and heartfelt case for allowing the men a break from the repairs, work ongoing continuously ever since arrival at the port many weeks previously. Pat had, reluctantly at first, conceded the traditional Sunday of rest when not at sea, eventually coming round to the conclusion, as the port was passed round, that perhaps it was, in fact, rather a good idea, for the men had toiled hard and unceasingly, and all had become visibly tired; Pat had seen many signs of that as he had toured the ship, the work to repair her damages never halting save for the hours of darkness when his men invariably slumped into an exhausted torpor.

It was an exceedingly rare event these days, thought Pat, when time could be found to hold the traditional Sunday church service aboard the frigate. As all aboard were ever aware, the barky had been most severely damaged escaping the bay of Navarino in May when, surrounded by a dozen Turk and Egyptian vessels, she had been cannonaded for four hours and longer, all the time under heavy fire, only the inaccuracies and incompetencies of the Turk gunners preserving her from absolute destruction. Time since had afforded opportunity for nothing more than exceedingly scant remedies, the most temporary restorations of only the severest damages. Hence all aboard, save for the wounded, were constantly engaged in heavy manual labour. It was an exceedingly strenuous task but one to which the crew had bent with unrelenting enthusiasm despite their own fatigue, deeply engrained since many months; for repairs completed meant departure, and such was the prevailing thought in the mind of every man. Yes, Argostoli represented safety, sanctuary and a welcome respite, albeit a temporary one, for it was neutral in the conflict, the Ionian islands being controlled from remote London since Bonaparte's demise. But home, home proper, was blessed Falmouth town. Even so, Argostoli was very much a welcome haven for the Surprises, for most men of the crew had much fraternised with the populace during lengthy spells in the port during the prior two years, the frigate first arriving in the beginning of August of 'twenty-three. Indeed, a goodly number of local young ladies were exceedingly pleased to see the barky's return, and several of them, who were oft to be found lingering all about the environs of the quay, were accompanied by the very youngest of Cephalonians, held tightly within their arms.

The authorities had once more turned a blind eye to the presence of an obviously battle-scarred combatant anchoring within the outer harbour, a blatant breach if ever there was one of the strict neutrality policy of the United Ionians. Fortunately, Napier, the island's Governor, had returned from London some two months previously, and he was increasingly and overtly recognised as a supporter of the Greeks, whilst his deputy, a most accommodating Ulsterman, Captain John Kennedy of the Royal Engineers, did all in his power to assist every one of O'Connor's requests, however obliquely worded they oft were, however inexplicit their careful presentations might be, the Surprises' explanations for this and that never detailed, nor indeed was any further clarification ever sought.

'Murphy! There you are,' Pat declared, still sitting on the edge of his cot, the steward bringing in the coffee, shifting about the table in lackadaisical fashion with scant interest, the pot set down with an indifference to a small spillage, his thoughts seemingly elsewhere. 'Tell Mr Pickering, there is to be no muster to divisions this day... though I grant you it is Sunday... and Dalby is not to ring the bell again until I says so. We will allow the men off watch to sleep a trifle longer... and... *Murphy*, are you listening?' Murphy halted. 'Please to rouse out and hoist the church pennant. I believe we will rig church on the gun deck this morning, in the full glory of the sunlight.'

'Well, anything else, sorr?' said Murphy with a sceptical look and a declaratory sniff.

'Pass the word for Mr Tizard and Mr Sampays.'

Murphy nodded and departed without a word. Hastily Pat dressed himself and, after the briefest foray to the quarter-gallery, set to to enjoy his coffee, its aroma utterly delightful; to Pat's mind it was the finest of starts to any day.

A cautious knock on the door and Simon entered with Marston. 'Pat, we are come to join you... if we may.'

'Please, come in, I beg you will... take a seat; there is fresh coffee here and, if Murphy is so minded, we may yet see a morsel for breakfast.'

Those men already up and about on deck had much welcomed, during the prior evening, the speculation about a probable day of rest on the morrow, their captain's demands upon them having been unrelenting from dawn to dusk ever since *Surprise's* arrival in Argostoli. Although his requests were always politely made and his explanations ever clear, so much so

179

that the men had set to every day with never a complaint, their minds were as one with their captain, their intentions the same: the speediest repairs would dictate the earliest possible departure to Falmouth, to wives, parents, sweethearts and children; that heartfelt aspiration was uppermost in all their thoughts, and every man had drawn on it for inspiration as he had laboured hard in the heat of the summer whilst heaving and shifting weighty timber, swathes of canvas, tar and rope all about the barky, the carpenter and his assistants never busier.

In the great cabin the carpenter and bosun arrived within minutes, both bleary-eyed and self-evidently still tired. On Pat's nod, not the least sense of urgency in his face, they stood at ease before his table. 'Gentlemen, it is in my thinking to speak with you later this morning about the repairs, how things are coming along. We will meet after church... at two bells of the afternoon watch and before I take my dinner. I would have some better notion of when we might depart this place when I speak with Mr Pickering and Mr Codrington later today.' Tizard and Sampays both nodded, their hesitant faces displaying a self-evident caution, a deep reservation. Pat continued, 'I am minded that we may still be here for some time to come...' More vigorous nods this time from the carpenter and bosun, '... and the purchase of a deal more of stores will be necessary before we leave.' Both non-commissioned officers remaining mute, Pat resigned himself to the discordant note within his mind and spoke again, 'Pray tell, I have been listening to the infernal pumps all morning...'

'The bilges are being washed clean, sir,' offered the bosun, his first words, 'The sweetening cock was left open all night.'

'I see,' Pat nodded, 'and the infernal thumping of timber striking all about the deck below my cabin?'

'The water rising, the rats began to rise up to the lower deck where the men made game of killing them.'

'Pestilential vermin!' Marston interjected, shuddering.

'There is a deal of unthinking hostility, of prejudice, against rats,' murmured Simon, all at the table nodding with no one attaching the least belief to their indications, 'and it persists so, even within the most intellectual of minds.'

Marston stared in shocked disbelief. 'Indeed, they had their uses... in the past,' ventured Pat with a thin smile.

'Uses? Rats?' the chaplain was perplexed. 'Surely not?'

'They did so. On long passages, the biscuit rotten - a weevil infestation is always remarked by the third month - the midshipmen would take to eating them, the hands too.'

'Oh, dear God,' Marston gasped, coughing up a spittle of coffee. 'Surely, they are ever the carriers of plague, the vile creatures? Never forget the Black Death... great multitudes of Christian souls dying.'

'Heathens too, I believe,' muttered Pat, mischievously taking a tiny pleasure in the chaplain's discomfort.

'I venture that it is far from sure that they were the culprits,' declared Simon, interrupting, '... the rats, that is; indeed, it has been my own thinking for some years that smaller creatures might be the root of such ills.'

'What smaller creatures?' asked Pat, his rapidly fading interest in rats flickering momentarily back to life.

'Lice. They infest the populace generally. I speak of people now... as well as rats. Why, I have oft observed them afflicting my patients... here, aboard this vessel... downstairs. It is a rare day when I do not see a one.'

Sampays and Tizard grimaced, and Pat instantly ceased scratching the persistent itch under his arm and determined to go for a swim at the earliest moment.

'I collect that it was also remarked by several surgeons in my past acquaintance,' offered Simon, 'that in such vessels where that particular practice... *I speak now of eating rats...* was indulged... then the incidence of scurvy was diminished.' He frowned, 'Though I would never care to countenance such a distasteful remedy.'

'Come come, Simon, eating rats a cure for the scurvy?' Pat laughed and slapped his thigh, 'And would you have us believe that we should nurture a fat pack for the cook, eh? Should I tell the lads that we will heave the salt pork over the side? Hah! Hah!' At this even the deadpan, staring faces of Tizard and

Sampays blanched, and Pat swiftly pressed on, 'Perhaps you will write to the Sick and Hurt? Oh, they will be pleased to hear that, I'm sure. Rats a remedy for the scurvy indeed!' He smiled, 'Though I venture there are plentiful rats to be readily found in London town, eh? Hah! Hah!'

'It is entirely true,' said Simon vehemently, never much caring for the scepticism of others when he spoke of matters in the medical line, 'I collect it was the observations of Dr William Warner, the surgeon of the flagship.' He scowled, 'We enjoyed many a speculative discussion about such inexplicables when I was at Haslar in the year 'thirteen... attending the sick. He was speaking of Dr James Lind's work with limes... It was they which gained the true measure of the scurvy.'

'Not the rats!' Pat laughed again.

'We scientists are accustomed to mystery... to scepticism... *and vexation*...' Simon directed a bleak stare at his friend, '... as we all know too well. Laugh if you will, but doubtless an explanation will emerge... in time.'

Silence; Pat failed to conceive of anything witty, of any further repost at all. Marston grimaced, the lingering vision of midshipmen eating rates perpetuating his excruciating difficulty.

'However, I am particularly pleased to hear that the men are exterminating the unwholesome creatures,' Simon continued, 'for they are ever infested with lice and fleas... and that is a sure harbinger of the ship fever... I scarcely need remind this august table that there can be not the least doubt of that. Will I presume that this fine vessel is now free of such vermin, Mr Sampays?'

'I believe it is, sir,' said the bosun with a beatific smile of relief, for he had heard about as much as he cared to hear, the attributes of rats leaving him greatly concerned, '... save perhaps for any that may have escaped to the orlop...' His customary mask of strain returned, '... or to the sailmaker's canvas rolls... though there be precious little of that left... and the men have shaken it out as best can be.'

'Mr Sampays, you mentioned the bilges filling...' said Pat, also tiring of the subject, for never in his career at sea had he found a ship entirely free of rats, '... the sweetening cock left open all through the night? Will I presume you have the boats prepared?'

Tizard laughed, the jest a welcome relief from rats. Pat himself was smiling broadly, and the bosun looked mildly affronted, 'On and off, sir... on and off. The men have set to with the pumps since dawn, sir, and the water level is dropping.'

'Very good. You are to scrub the orlop deck with vinegar and fumigate the hold with what is left of the sulphur when the bilges are dry and the pumps sucking,' added Pat, still cognisant of the discussion about rats, lice and fleas, the lice particularly.

'Aye aye, sir,' the bosun nodded emphatically.

'Gentlemen, until church then.' With a nod Pat dismissed Tizard and Sampays. Turning to Simon and Marston, he picked up the coffee pot with a feeling of small relief, 'Allow me to help you to another cup of this divine nectar... a Turk delicacy, I believe.'

A pleasant half-hour later and, on deck, Clumsy Dalby turned the glass and looked across towards the helm in obvious enquiry at his captain's staring face, when Pat shouted over from the wheel, 'Ring the bell!'

"*Ding-ding, ding-ding,*" four bells resonated loudly out and men everywhere poured from the companionways into a cordial and loud blather of a hundred voices all coalescing amidships on the gun deck. Lieutenants Pickering and Codrington stood at ease, awaiting Pat and Marston outside the coach as he stepped down from the quarterdeck. Eventually, all present, Pat nodded to Pickering and the lieutenant bawled out, 'SILENCE!'

The voices quickly died away, and Pat stepped alongside the capstan. 'Good morning, lads!' he cried, the answer a resounding barrage of confirmation from near two hundred happy souls. 'Doubtless you know there is yet a deal of work to do... to rectify the barky... and I venture it will be some days yet afore we haul her anchors...' A groundswell of murmured accord rose up, 'But... allow me to say... lads... you are doing a grand job, you are...' A louder confirmation followed this time, ' and you have MY BEST THANKS!'

The roar of acknowledgement filled the air, and Dalby, never slow to lead a cheer, stepped forward out of the crowd and turned to face the crew, 'THREE CHEERS FOR THE CAPTAIN! HIP! HIP!'

'HURRAH! HURRAH! HURRAH!' but the cheers did not stop at three, wild enthusiasm had taken its firm hold, Dalby waving his arms in complete abandon, and on it went, 'HURRAH! HURRAH! HURRAH!' until at last Pat, his face a beaming picture of unrestrained pleasure, raised his hands, the cheering dying away from the front.

'Thankee, lads. I am minded that no captain e'er had such a fine crew, I am ... and that was a sight to warm an Irish heart, so it was. THANKEE, all of you. Mr Marston will now lead the service.'

Marston stepped forward. From somewhere he had found a cloth of green velvet, which he laid over the capstan, upon which he also laid his Bible, the feeble breeze nothing of concern, though his thinning strands of uncut, long, grey hair flickered about his face as he looked up, gazed up to the heavens for a few moments as if in supplication, or perhaps in search of inspiration. Silence prevailed on the deck, for the chaplain too was highly respected. Every man knew that he was also a capable surgeon, had always worked with Simon when the shot was flying and the blood flowing; indeed, he was more customarily perceived as the second surgeon, more so than as chaplain, for many a man had been treated by him, and his surgery during and after *Surprise's* first engagement in Greek waters - Simon not being aboard at that particular time - had much endeared him to the crew. 'Let us begin today with a hymn,' he declared eventually, 'You are much familiar with... "When I survey the wondrous cross". We have all sung it many times.' A chorus of "ayes" and a general and strangely enthusiastic nodding of heads prompted Marston, in pleasant surprise, to initiate the singing,

'When I survey the wondrous cross,
On which the Prince of glory died...'

A deep groundswell of scores of voices followed the first two lines, albeit with nothing of the sound and skill of the least practised choir but with a unanimity, a sense of common contribution, carrying along the crew, even if, to the purist, it was greatly discordant.

'My richest gain I count but loss,
And pour contempt on all my pride...'

Pat, possessing not the least singing skill nor any training at all but finding himself entirely relaxed for the first time in months, sang out in strong voice, grimacing only slightly as he heard the loud and gravelly croaking from Dalby two yards in front of him,

'Forbid it, Lord, that I should boast,
Save in the death of Christ my God!
All the vain things that charm me most,
I sacrifice them to His blood...'

Blood, Pat shuddered involuntarily as he heard the vile word, his thoughts in an unwelcome instant flickering to an unhappy recollection of Simon's recent confession of distress. He tried hard to put that out of mind and looked all about him; every one of the men visible at the front of the assembly, he noted, was singing extremely enthusiastically, and many other heads everywhere were turning, the eyes of every man were looking all about their fellows, as much as he was himself; something, some feeling, something profound, had been discovered generally and was common to them all, and he found himself, mind and body, overtaken with a rising tide of relief, awash with the sensation of it, an utterly beatific relief, a sublime relief, one which had displaced all his long held fears in that moment of arrival, and he revelled in it, in the sweet sensation, in the overwhelming realisation of it. He smiled, without the least restraint, at all standing before him during the slight pause between the verses.

'See from His head, His hands, His feet,
Sorrow and love flow mingled down!
Did e'er such love and sorrow meet,
Or thorns compose so rich a crown?'

185

The final verse was nigh upon them, such being recognised by every man, and the singing had much risen in volume, Dalby ever louder, near shouting, his neighbours a little discomfited. The big man, having turned about, was waving his arms wide and high in encouragement of his fellows, eventually ceasing to sing himself to concentrate on his conducting; thankfully so, to the minds of the many who were near him. A rising volume, a determined embrace of the last verse of the hymn and every man sang up in stronger voice,

'Were the whole realm of nature mine,
That were a present far too small;
Love so amazing, so divine,
Demands my soul, my life, my all.'

The loudest applause ever heard on the deck heralded the end of the hymn, Marston entirely taken aback, marvelling in it, astonished, for such - the loud and enthusiastic singing too - had never happened before, his services generally being somnolent affairs of accepted routine, the men participating because it was the navy life, the traditional programme of Sundays, the event that preceded dinner and the dispensing of the second half of the grog ration. Smiling, he waved his Bible high above his head in gay abandon and in grateful recognition of his choir before thumbing to his intended reading, all present pleased to wait in splendid, mute contentment. A powerful feeling, a rising sensation of gaining a long-awaited release, was seizing upon every man present; anxieties were subsiding, fears fading, and joy - *sublime joy* - was embraced by all as it filled their hearts.

The last radiant vestiges of the sun were gradually disappearing, the yellow orb slowly sinking below the hill peninsula behind the town. The quay was the first to fall into shadow whilst sparkling remnants of silver light flickered for a few more minutes on the wavetops of the more exposed anchorage a half-mile and more to the north until, at long last, the final glow in the western heavens blinked out as if in reluctant gesture of farewell, the day's clarity of light ceding to the inevitable embrace of diffuse tranquility. Dusk had arrived, bringing its slower ambience of calm to settle over all the harbour; even the wind was only a mere weakling zephyr as *Eleanor* steadily closed in for the final quarter-mile approach to the quay in the warm evening air. All her crew were on deck and standing ready to bring her about, the schooner losing way in a graceful turnabout as she swung into the feeble breeze, slowing further until all motion was lost when the vessel was a mere five yards off. Her men prepared to throw her mooring lines, local hands already waiting on the quay to catch them.

'It is a considerable pleasure to be returned to this place, sir,' said a reflective Lieutenant Mower quietly, standing with Duncan near the helm. 'Many a month have I spent here... in reluctant immobility, recovering from my wounds...'

'Aye, I was here myself for some wee while... after my head was struck,' declared Duncan with feeling. 'Thankfully 'tis hard as oak, eh?' he smiled, tapping his forehead.

'... and I have the warmest affinity for this town, for these people; I do so; 'tis truly a precious oasis amongst the maelstrom of blood which is this vile war.'

'Aye, that it is,' Duncan nodded, 'and Kathleen is ever singing the praises of these island folk.'

'How is she, sir?'

'Much the better these recent months of this year, thank you; the consumption has relented, it seems, and we are ever hopeful that it may be held in check,' Duncan blinked, his eyes moistening, and he could add nothing more as his thoughts remained with his wife.

All along a distant *Surprise's* deck, the frigate gently rolling at anchor two cables out, men watched *Eleanor's* arrival, many waving their arms in greeting: their friends had returned, and the sight was an exceedingly welcome finish to their day of restfulness, supper eaten an hour before and the second half of the grog ration also consumed. Their weary bodies and minds had been recovering all day in the so rare and precious hours of relaxation, nothing more to do until the morrow except rest, the return of their shipmates a fine ending to an exceptional day, and hearts everywhere warmed just a little.

Aboard *Surprise*, two bells ringing out for the first watch heralded a modest supper being served in the great cabin. The cold remnants of a pie, fresh Sunday-baked bread and a Cephalonian goat's cheese were accompanied by the most generous of repeated port wine measures until the last of all stocks aboard was exhausted, the conclusion of eating swiftly followed by strong coffee and a sweet Greek brandy. Pat was revelling in the pleasure of the company of every one of his officers at his table. Even Murphy appeared to exhibit a rare state of satisfaction as he busied about his jovial charges, the liquor liberally dispensed and Freeman relegated to the coffee.

'What now are your intentions for us, sir?' ventured Marston as the amiable and informal conversations over the table reached a momentary common hiatus.

'I venture the carpenter and his lads must be afforded some days more to rectify her many and varied hull damages afore we risk the Bay and its tempests on our way home,' declared Pat, ears everywhere pricking up. 'Thankfully 'tis summer and we may pray Biscay will be more pleasant to us, eh? We will at least be blessed with the light of longer days, should we find she is not in kindly mood for our passage. Three or four days longer here and we will away, I dare say. In the meantime, *Eleanor's* cutter will come across to serve for the barky, only my barge still floating... and that with repairs that Mr Churchill would not care to contemplate. All the other boats are severely damaged, Mr Tizard yet to work his magic upon them.'

Steady, companionable drinking resumed, the customary order of the table wholly falling away to comments and questions from all, when, entirely unprompted by Pat, Mower spoke up, 'Sir, do you care to hear my poems of recent months? I have written two of them.'

'Why of course,' declared Pat in honest, generous voice, never holding much affinity for poems in his own mind but hugely pleased to see his most junior lieutenant in visibly fitter health and much restored in mind and body from his extremely severe wounds of the prior year; 'Please, let us hear them, Mr Mower.'

Mower pulled the poems from his pocket, 'The first, *Winter Homecoming*, harks back to our return to England last winter, to my fears in the worst hours of the hurricane... and then my feelings of relief for making home... home to precious Falmouth town.' Nods followed all around the table and a hush descended upon the cabin as Mower pressed on in quiet voice,

'In the midwinter frosts when the seas broke o'er the bow,
On the barky sailed, ever fightin' through the low;
Her deck canted over, her gun'ales deep within the froth,
Every man frozen to the bone, chilled in sodden cloth;

The gale growing stronger, her braces groanin' with the strain,
Homeward bound, the deck a misery in the freezin' rain;
The Dear Surprise making water, the ship a shattered mess;
The hurricane raging, hell approaching with the darkness;

The yards all struck down, waves everywhere raging white,
The last of daylight fading, despair coming with the night;
The bilge water ever rising, the boats all smashed away,
The sails long shredded, no hope left of seeing the new day;

Ever on we fought, until that fearful night was left behind,
The fears of all subsiding, hopes afresh astir in every mind;
And there in sight at last, distant off the larboard beam,
Blessed Falmouth town! For every man his precious dream.

The pumps a'workin' hard, the Black Rock at last astern,
As we reached the Carrick Roads, the barky made her turn;
The hated wind gone at last, we brought her about,
From hundreds along the shore, came the welcome shouts.

At last our familiar King's Road, no more the terror of the sea,
And so to the boats, every man pulling hard for the quay;
To the anxious arms of mothers, to families and dear friends,
Welcome tears of joy at last, the voyage at its blessed end.'

A momentary and thoughtful, reflective mood reigned at the conclusion and Mower spoke again, 'I rejoice so that it is where we are soon bound once more... all of us.'

'Hear! Hear!' declared Simon emphatically, his first words for some time.

'A splendid poem, Mr Mower, I congratulate you!' cried Pat, clapping vigorously to break the silent ice, all at the table joining in with enthusiasm, 'Very well done indeed... and your second poem?'

The lieutenant's face slipped back into the burden of long held strain. He sighed, 'My second poem is inspired, sir - if that be the proper term - by sad memories of my brother, killed aboard *Temeraire* at Trafalgar...' This was spoken in only a murmur, Mower still in quiet spirits, '... and by my own wounds of last year, at Samos, when - *I do confess* - I was mightily set back... I finished it whilst I was recovering in Falmouth town, ever wondering if I would return to serve again aboard the barky.'

All present were much moved by the poignant words and all minds raced with vivid, distressing recollections of the horror and the desperate hours when so many had been killed and wounded in the severe Samos battles. Quiet murmurings of encouragement were uttered by all around the table.

'Mr Mower... *James*,' pronounced Pat very gently, 'as long as I am captain and you are able to stand your watch, you will be welcome to ship with me, *with us*... you will. Have not the least fear of that... why, I venture you will ever be a shipmate, and you may set aside any other silly notions.'

'HEAR! HEAR!' came the resounding endorsement from all.

Mower nodded and smiled, 'Thank you kindly, sir.' He took a swift draught of his brandy and resumed in a more assured voice, 'This is my second poem, *The Tide of Life*...

I was born in Cornwall's haven, steeped in wet salt air;
As a boy I roamed the coast, every day with ne'er a care;
I fished the pilchard grounds, my youth a marvellous trance;
As a dare I crossed the Channel, sailed over to far France.
Happiness and hot summers, long days spent with my brother,
I cherish those memories still, I thought they'd last for ever.

As a young man I plied the oceans, the winds ever a merry
dance,
Whilst I served aboard the packet, striving for my chance;
Until pressed into a frigate, war a fright and thrill,
My brother lost to roaring guns, a bitter memory still;
Doubtless of great value are the blessings of the peace,
Boney gone at last, I was grateful for release.

My days afloat now but a memory, no longer any hope,
Not the least prospect of a ship, and all I do is mope;
Now too old to serve, I gaze across the chop and waves,
Sitting on the Falmouth quay, to sail again the dream I crave.
I cling to blessed recollections and will ever wonder: was I
wise?
Until that final day comes at last when I will close my eyes.'

'I... I commend you, Mr Mower... I do so,' said Pat with a
trembling inflection, thinking hard, his eyes taking in a deal
more of emotion from the eyes and faces of all present at the
table until, his voice firming, he concluded, '... though I do insist
you cast overboard that final verse... which - allow me to say - I
do not, myself, much care for.'

A staring, fascinated Murphy jolted himself back to the
present and hastened to refill the brandy glasses, Freeman
likewise the coffee cups, the two stewards making off to the
galley, their task done. The table relapsed into more jovial banter
until, midnight near, the cabin chatter slowing and one of the two
Argand lamps beginning to gutter, the smoky whiff of burnt oil
gave Pat his cue. He tapped a spoon on his glass, the repetitive
chinking catching the attention of everyone, the cheerful anarchy
of several conversations subsiding, 'Gentlemen, I could sit here
with you all for ever, I could so... but I am minded my cot is
desirous of my presence...' A low flurry of laughter followed,
even Marston admitting to himself with small reluctance that the
influence of drink had indeed reached his own mind, 'but before
we retire, before the end of this splendid day, allow me to speak
just a few words.' Silence and nods all evident about the table,

Pat resumed, 'Mr Macleod... *Captain Macleod...*' Exuberant and general laughter ensued for a second or two which Duncan, smiling, minded not the least.

Pat continued, 'My dear friend... *our dear friend...*' More laughter and even the lieutenants were emboldened to call out "Hear! Hear!" Pat resorted to his spoon once more, quietude quickly settling again, 'Our shipmate, Duncan here, is bearing a most important letter, a missive from the Greek provisional government to our own. It is incumbent upon us to carry this letter at best speed to London.' Every face at the table stared, all minds strived to throw off their gentle inebriation to focus, to concentrate, to listen carefully to something which all sensed was significant and which would bear upon their own situation. 'The barky being still so grievously damaged...' The audible sighs were general, '... it is in my thinking to send *Eleanor* with the letter. She will be far more fleet of foot than ever the barky will be.' Affirmative nods followed from the lieutenants. 'And so she will depart in the morning. *Captain* Macleod...' More smiles radiated from faces all around the table. '... and Mr Codrington will attend her.' Pat leaned towards his junior lieutenant, a brief hiatus following as all eyes followed his gaze, all present waiting for his words. Pat's hand was outstretched, 'Mr Mower... welcome back to the barky!' Hands beat upon the table, feet likewise upon the deck, and a loud and boisterous chorus of 'HURRAH!' resounded all about the cabin. Murphy's staring face re-appeared from behind the door.

'Thank you, sir!' declared Mower, smiling with obvious pleasure. He seized Pat's hand in his grip, the clenched handshake the finest confirmation of his welcome, his precious place restored.

'Gentlemen, we have experienced great dangers this voyage, seen more than our fair share of fighting... we have so...' Pat's voice dropped to little more than a whisper, 'I thank you all, every one of you, for your efforts... for your determination... to do your best... and I thank you most particularly for your loyalty, I do; with all my heart I thank you.' Tentative smiles all round within a pensive silence were the only display of a profound and deep satisfaction swiftly rising to consume the thoughts of everyone present. Each man was absorbing the striking sentiments flowing strong within, the briefest flashes of recollection of powerful events coming to mind, generally deeply unpleasant ones. No one had the least capacity for words and none were uttered, until Pat concluded in a rising, lighter voice, 'I think that will serve to bring our evening... and a joyous occasion it has surely been... to a fitting end. I bid you all good night.'

Tuesday 2nd August 1825   08:00   *Argostoli, Cephalonia*

On the quay, *Eleanor's* crew, assisted by a half-dozen Surprises, busied about loading a final few stores and the water casks, near all such completed the prior day for the passage home. Every man was in happy spirits, light-hearted banter was shouted from deck to quay and vice versa. A growing gathering of local Argostoli townspeople were standing and watching with keen interest, a few anxious young ladies pressing their attentions upon the more youthful of the Eleanors, great anxiety in their demeanour and voice. Pat stood watching with his officers, all come ashore from *Surprise* and all thinking of their own departure, still some days hence, whilst exchanging the odd word here and there with several of the town's merchants and dignitaries, a relaxed mood prevailing generally.

'You have the Prince's letter, Duncan?' asked Pat as they exchanged final words.

'Aye, and I expect to reach London well before the end of the month, the weather being with us. We will go there directly, we will pass Falmouth by... and bear up the Channel with not a moment lost.'

'Take great care. You collect that Khosref is back with his fleet and is besieging Messalonghi these past three weeks.'

'Aye, but we will be bearing south-west and be gone from his province in today's swift sailing. I am pleased to see the wind is with us, a northeaster.'

'Here is Simon's letter for the post when you arrive,' Pat shook hands with his friend, 'and my own, for Sinéad, if you will. Farewell, brother... and safe passage... *a swift one*. The barky will be leaving later this week.'

With a professed modicum of reluctance, to which no one present gave the slightest credence, and then without the least ceremony, Codrington called all the Eleanors to an alert awareness of the imminence of departure, and they boarded the schooner after final farewells to all those shipmates and local friends still on the quay, several young ladies in an emotional state. All the officers of *Surprise* shook hands with Duncan and Codrington, offered warm good wishes for the speediest of passage, and the mooring ropes were cast off without further delay. All the Eleanors stood on deck, shouting across the widening gap to those standing watching, the schooner immediately catching the wind to gain speed as she bore away towards the sea and home. From the deck of *Surprise*, a quarter mile away, as *Eleanor* passed by there came resounding cheering and vigorous waving of arms from every shipmate watching, near two hundred men thronging her side and all continuing to wave for several minutes until, the schooner shrinking to the tiniest speck in everyone's gaze, she tacked west around the end of the peninsula and was finally lost from sight.

Chapter Nine

The mood in the great cabin was more relaxed than anyone could recall all year, the prior day's departure of *Eleanor* being seen as presaging their own within a very few more days. The hull repairs, albeit still little better than temporary ones which no English shipyard would ever have countenanced, were completed to the carpenter's satisfaction, as were the rigging renewals, the latter more nearly resembling a proper job and finished to the very ostensible satisfaction of Mr Sampays who paced all about the decks with visible pleasure, his delight rubbing off on all he encountered. Indeed, Marston's Sunday of ease also appeared to have delivered a beneficial renewal of enthusiasm for work on the final few tasks remaining before Pat could contemplate the taking aboard of water for the imminent voyage.

News from the occasional merchantman arriving in the port during the past few weeks was less relaxing; indeed, it was greatly disquieting. All vessels coming from Corfu to the north or from Zante to the south, and encountering Greek fishermen and others of such ilk, had received reports of Khosref's large fleet of no less than fifty-five sail being anchored off Messalonghi. The stories were usually accompanied with sketchy tales of Reshid Pasha's attacks on the several islets about the lagoon there and his demands that the garrison surrender. Seemingly Khosref had brought flat-bottomed boats with which, for the first time, Turk troops could make passage within the shallow waters of the lagoon, all inaccessible to the Turk fleet. Only five days previously Sakhtouri's squadron had been sighted off the east coast of Cephalonia where, for several days, observers had watched the Hydriots race about the waters between the island and the mainland, fruitlessly pursued by Khosref's frigates. The Surprises paid this little mind, all considering their contribution to the Greek war done, wholly finished, the barky set fair for passage home, where her essential and necessary repairs could be carried out in proper fashion at Plymouth Dock, no one harbouring the least expectation of returning to the Greek fray.

It was therefore with some small degree of shock and astonishment that Pat saw Captain Zouvelekis enter his cabin as he was enjoying his supper, all interest in his fresh-cooked mutton vanishing in an instant as his thoughts flashed to a racing, all-consuming anxiety.

Simon, too, set down his knife and fork, blanched, and stared with a burning, fearful trepidation.

Pat rose from the table, stepping round to shake the hand of the Greek whom he had not seen since leaving Argostoli in October of the prior year after sharing the experiences of bloody battles to defend Samos island. Zouvelekis, a Kasiot, had served that summer as liaison officer for *Surprise* within the command of Miaoulis.

'Captain Zouvelekis!' Pat endeavoured to sound pleased; indeed, he was pleased - in the strict sense of greeting a former comrade - but the apprehension coursing all through him defeated his best efforts to present so, his greeting sounding anxious. 'I hope I see you well.'

'Thank you, Captain; I am quite well.'

'Allow me to offer you a whet... a morsel to eat perhaps...'

'I beg you will forgive me if I decline, save perhaps for a glass of wine. Admiral Miaoulis awaits my return... my earliest return.'

'Please, come and sit down.' Pat looked to Murphy, standing with keen interest at the door. 'Murphy, another glass and a pot of fresh coffee for Captain Zouvelekis... as quick as can be... you may care to run!' However, Murphy had already left the cabin, never caring for Pat's customary phrase whenever he desired urgency. Freeman appeared within the minute bearing the extra glass for the visitor, and Pat poured a generous measure of wine.

Simon, gathering himself at last, stepped round the table to shake hands with a still standing Zouvelekis. Both men much admired the other, but of words he could find none; tension had seized its firm grip upon him.

Pat pulled out the spare chair and beckoned the Greek to it, and he sat down himself in a visible state of anxiety. 'You spoke of Admiral Miaoulis...'

'Yes sir. I bear his words, news of his intentions for this day, for this evening and the morrow.'

'His intentions?'

'The admiral is minded to attack the Turk fleet, to drive them away from their blockade of Messalonghi so as to open passage for supplies for the garrison.'

'We have heard stories of Khosref's numbers, a large fleet, a powerful one... possessing of nine frigates... if the stories are to be believed.'

'That is entirely true. There are no less than nine frigates, a dozen of corvettes... many brigs... and the remainder are smaller vessels... schooners and the like.'

'And your admiral's vessels and numbers?'

'We are blessed, sir, with as strong a force as ever we have gathered: Hydriots, Spetziots and Psariots; all are here and Admiral Miaoulis commands forty brigs. There has been some dissension within the Hydriots, a refusal to sail without their pay being increased... I believe you heard of similar before the attack on Suda?'

'Yes, we had some notion of that.'

'It pleases me to say that such has been entirely resolved, sir, and the Admiral is desirous only of your own presence alongside his squadrons.'

Silence. The essential purpose of Zouvelekis, as feared, was revealed, and whilst it came as no surprise, the words of the request left both Pat and Simon in momentary shock. For once, Murphy's entrance was welcome. Pat waved for him to pour the coffee, all interest in wine and the unfinished remnants of his supper entirely gone.

'I see your ship is much repaired, a deal of new rigging and canvas all about her,' Zouvelekis spoke as gently as he could to break the ice; plainly his hosts' silence and their trepidation was clear to see; minds were surely racing, of that there was little doubt.

'Yes... yes...' murmured Pat, searching for the appropriate conclusion, for the words which would not come. 'She is much the better for these past six weeks here.'

'The admiral intends to take advantage of the coming night and to place his vessels to windward of the Turk inshore squadron so as to attack them at first light from the east.'

'And his intentions for *Surprise*? I would not care to hazard her in the shallows.'

'Khosref possesses of a sizeable fleet; if his inshore squadron is destroyed first, then - with the wind being an offshore one in the morning, as Admiral Miaoulis expects - the greater part of the Turk fleet can then be attacked with fireships.'

'I see, and it is an admirable plan, no doubt, but what of *Surprise*?' Pat pressed.

'Captain O'Connor, the escape of your ship from the great bay of Navarino, her firing of incendiary weapons and the flight of the Turk when she did so has, ever since, been the talk of every Greek seaman. Doubtless such is also the case within the Turk fleet. Admiral Miaoulis is mindful that even the presence of your ship, for she will surely be identified by every Turk captain as the fiery destroyer, will promote fear within every one of them... a great fear of you firing upon them with incendiary shells.'

'Hmmm...' Pat was unconvinced. Indeed, there had been no one at Navarino more frightened than himself at the peak of the conflict, his ship under the most devastating fire and surrounded by enemies, and with little wind to drive any escape. The prospect of any repetition, however small, held not the slightest appeal, and the Turks being reported as present in such great numbers was daunting indeed.

'Captain,' Pat's reluctance was plain to see and Zouvelekis played his last card, '... the morning wind being the usual north-easterly, all the Ionians are in close reach of the waters off Messalonghi and the entrance to the gulf of Patras. In the event of *Surprise* fleeing, sanctuary is close at hand, one where the Turk will never dare to follow.'

'Fleeing?' declared Pat sharply and with audible exception.

'I beg your pardon, sir,' Zouvelekis coloured, such was visible even beneath his tanned and weathered skin; 'I meant *in the case of being overwhelmed*... the Turk numbers being so many.' An uncertain silence enduring, Zouvelekis extracted a folded chart from his pocket and smoothed it out upon the table. 'Here is Cape Papas, on the southern side of the gulf, and here,' he pointed to Messalonghi, 'are the shallow lagoons and their islets, on which there are small fortified bastions, here at Vasiladi and here at Klisova within the lagoon... guarded by Tourlida. There are smaller ones here, here and here,' the Greek moved his finger about the chart. 'It is Admiral Miaoulis's intention to shift his fleet during the dark of the night to here,' he pointed to a point midway between Cape Papas and the fortified port of Patras.

'Would that be a position of great danger if the wind is not as the admiral expects, being within the narrows of the gulf?' exclaimed Simon, his first words since the Greek arrived. 'Why, would we not be stopped up in there, with no way out?'

'Indeed, that would be so,' murmured Zouvelekis, 'if the wind on the morrow is not the expected northeaster, but perhaps that is unlikely... The admiral is well acquainted with the customary winds of all parts of Greece... so many years at sea.'

Pat, his professional interest aroused, stared at the chart. 'Does the admiral have any particular interest for *Surprise*, tell? We are but a single ship and the Turks are fifty strong and more.'

'Sir, the Turk fleet - most of it - lies here in the channel midway between Cephalonia and Cape Papas, during the night. The Turk does not care for the proximity of the coast during the hours of darkness. When Admiral Miaoulis attacks from the east in the dawn hour, that will be where our approach will be least expected. With the advantage of the wind, fireships will imperil the Turk downwind to the south-west. The admiral is minded that the sight of *Surprise,* bearing down from the west, will greatly affright Khosref's captains... and so much the better for the success of our fireships.' Pat was thinking hard, Simon in silent dismay, and Zouvelekis pressed on, 'Captain O'Connor, it is not Admiral Miaoulis's intention, nor his expectation, that your ship will be more than a distraction... a powerful one. When battle is joined, it will be - as ever - our fireships which will deliver any victory that we may obtain... as we have seen these many times.'

Thursday 4th August 1825   08:30   *west of Oxia*

A hasty departure from Argostoli, steady sailing throughout the night all around the south of Cephalonia and then north-north-east, close-hauled for twenty-more miles during the darkness, and Pat brought *Surprise* round on an easterly tack to approach the island of Oxia, a grey shadow on the larboard bow in the twilight immediately before the dawn. If the Turks were indeed anywhere in the approach to the Gulf of Patras, Pat wished to remain undetected from their scouting vessels for as long as possible. For this reason and also wishing to be served by a beam wind when making the turn to approach Messalonghi, *Surprise* now hugged as close as could be to the island's south coast.

Every man of *Surprise* was on deck, alert, the topmen straining their eyes, staring in the weak twilight to the east, a low bass rumble of distant guns becoming audible on the larboard bow as the sun broke free of the land over the mountains of the Morea to throw its first bright rays over the water. Directly ahead at ten miles distance, the topmen could see the far Turk fleet, still indistinct save for the yellowing spreads of canvas atop many masts. *Surprise* sailed on, the north-east wind on her larboard bow just as Miaoulis had foreseen, but perhaps not as strong as it yet might become, the frigate making a steady four knots, holding as close to the wind as she could go.

Anticipation rising throughout the ship, a hasty breakfast quickly eaten, Pat gazed forward from his quarterdeck as Dalby rang four bells. The Turk squadrons were much closer now and fine on *Surprise's* larboard bow, a mere five miles ahead and bearing towards Patras. They were already engaged with the Greeks who were closing on them from the east. Miaoulis held the advantage he had sought in his stealthy night time approach, the wind astern. The long-range firing from both sides was general but thus far without the great intensity Pat had expected; plainly both sides were still manoeuvring to seek advantage. He stared all about the vista ahead: to the north-east was Messalonghi town, its extensive salt lagoons before it. His gaze focused on a burning Turk brig and another vessel, a schooner, run aground on the inshore mud all about the outlying islets of the lagoon. It seemed to him that the Greeks were indeed bottled up, as Simon had feared, for they had not, as yet, broken through the Turk inshore squadron of twenty-two sail, still doggedly blocking their westerly intentions. Worse, it looked to Pat as if Khosref's fleet was at last shaping up to counter-attack, forming three distinct squadrons: twelve fast corvettes on their right wing to the south, nine frigates and plentiful schooners to the centre - doubtless one would be Khosref's flagship - and all the Turk brigs were on his left flank, which was the nearest to the approaching *Surprise*, the frigate coming upon them slowly from astern.

Time was passing, noon was near and the sun, almost directly above them, cast little shadow over the deck. The nearest three Turk brigs were visibly turning, beginning to wear round to face towards *Surprise*, now only a half-mile separating them. The firing within the wider battle had become much louder in the last half-hour, the two sides engaging with close exchanges; the Greeks, as ever, were striving to keep a distance from the heavier Turk guns, enough to deny the lamentable Turk gunners the smallest prospect of smashing effective strikes upon the lighter Greek brigs.

At all her own guns, *Surprise's* men stood ready, all gun ports opened, the guns run out. The six weeks of recuperation in Argostoli had been immeasurably beneficial to his men, Pat saw that clearly, as did his lieutenants on the gun deck. Even two months ago the idea of bearing down on a vast enemy fleet as a single frigate all alone would have been inconceivable to Pat and all his shipmates, but here they were, doing just that. He marvelled in their situation: was it madness? Had insanity overtaken them all? What did he expect to achieve, for he had no

201

incendiary munitions left and possessed no sulphur at all to make any more?

The three Turk brigs had completed their turn and were propelled by the freshening north-easterly wind on their quarter, their convergence with *Surprise* being fast; only mere minutes were left before all vessels' bow chasers would open fire.

Pat stared beyond the brigs to the main battle; it was difficult to see the Greeks, the Turks in great numbers being between them and *Surprise*, but he could see flames atop three distant brigs. Perhaps Miaoulis had already set his fireships aflame?

Only a cable remained between *Surprise* and the nearest Turk brig. 'Mr Pickering!' cried Pat over the waist rail down to the gun deck, 'Fire when ready!'

Pickering nodded, turned about and shouted the length of the ship, 'FIRE WHEN READY!' The bow chasers opened up immediately, as did those of the nearest Turk, two shots whistling overhead and just to starboard. Fortunately nothing was struck at all on the masts, yards or sails.

'Mr Prosser! Barton!' shouted Pat, 'Stand ready - on my command - to come about, to wear ship to starboard!'

'Aye aye, sir!' both men acknowledged, all the helmsmen nodding emphatically.

'Mr Sampays!' cried Pat, 'Alert your larbowlins to haul hard on the braces when Dalby here rings the bell; he will not stop until she has completed her turn.' The bosun nodded, his face white: fiery destruction was nigh upon them, the fast approaching brigs only mere yards and precious few minutes away.

Surprise entered the Turk jaws, the leading two brigs beginning their pass abeam, one on each side, fifty yards off, the combined closing speed something of the order of twelve knots. From the bow the first guns to bear thundered in quick succession: *Venom, Dutch Sam* and *Tempest* on the larboard side; *Axeman, Nemesis* and *James Figg* on the starboard side. The brigs replied, shot crashing into the frigate's hull: the worst gunner in the world could not possibly miss at such short range.

Hurricane, Delilah, Vengeance, Pure Poison, Old Nick and *The Smasher* erupted with fiery flame, iron shot and prolific smoke. Pat stared to left and to right: his gunners had not missed either. Still the brigs came by on an unwavering course, their own guns roaring, bright flashes erupting, followed by the instant whistle of shot flying overhead or deep resonations as they smashed into the hull.

The Turks were amidships within seconds, and more guns flamed out: *Crucifixion, Hell's Mouth* and *Damnation* to port; *The Nailer, Salt 'n' Bile* and *Francis Drake* to starboard. The starboard side Turk brig had been struck hard; Pat could see that. Great sections of her hull on the level of her guns had been smashed away to leave an array of jagged holes all along her side; her hammock netting was near non-existent and all persons on her quarterdeck were in evident disarray.

The two Turks had almost slipped by when more of *Surprise's* guns began to fire: *Bill Stevens, Heaven's Gate and Devil's Tongue* added further destruction to the huge damage visible on the larboard brig; *Blood 'n' Guts, Revenge* and *In your Eye* roared to hurl brutally destructive shot into the starboard Turk; Pat stared, its mainmast was beginning to topple.

The aftmost four guns, *Daniel Mendoza* and *Billy Warr* to port, *Bull Horns* and *Mighty Fine* to starboard, and all the four quarterdeck carronades exploded with a final deafening thunder, and then *Surprise* was past and clear of the two Turks, the third coming on, fine on the starboard bow just fifty yards ahead and mere seconds away, all *Surprise's* gunners racing with desperate urgency to reload.

Pat glanced astern: the first two Turks were turning, coming about to the south; one conceivably might be returning for more. The other appeared about to lose her mainmast, leaning over in extreme disarray and imminently about to topple. All expectations of the Turks being affrighted by the mere presence of *Surprise* were plainly ill-conceived. Not that Pat had actually believed such would be the case, but his sense of duty had once again come to the fore, and he could never stand the thought of any mention of his ship, his shipmates, his comrades, his veterans *fleeing*; the very word was distasteful in the extreme, save for when not the least alternative choice was open to him.

The third brig began its pass on *Surprise's* starboard bow; *Axeman, Nemesis* and *James Figg* fired first; *Pure Poison, Old Nick* and *The Smasher* followed within seconds. The explosions rippled all down the side as *The Nailer, Salt 'n' Bile, Francis Drake, Blood 'n' Guts, Revenge, In your Eye, Bull Horns, Mighty Fine* and the two starboard carronades boomed once more, and then the brig, frightfully damaged, was past, swiftly opening a gap as she followed her fellows running to the south-west.

Pat stared towards the battle ahead; as far as he could make out through the dense smoke lingering all about the extensive mêlée of disparate vessels, Turk and Greek, it seemed that the Turks were turning about and disengaging. The Greek fireships had seemingly failed, Pat could glimpse one or two of them in the brief instances when he was afforded a clearer view of bright flames atop their masts, the fiery hulks drifting away without any victims caught within their grasp. 'At least Miaoulis has driven them away from Messalonghi... for the moment,' he remarked to no one in particular.

On *Surprise* sailed, converging with the larger Turk fleet for another ten minutes and half a mile, anxious glances directed at Pat from all on and near his quarterdeck, no man caring to speak, no one wishing to break his concentration, for he was plainly thinking hard. Eventually the master, standing nearest to Pat, coughed loudly and spat demonstratively before looking directly at his captain in obvious query.

'Mr Prosser, come about!' bawled Pat, scowling, his decision made; 'South!'

'Hard over!' cried the master to the helm, and he hastened to shout again towards the bow, waving his arm vigorously with his urgent indication of direction to the men standing ready at the braces.

The bosun was already hurrying down the side from the bow, having sensed the perceptible turn beginning, and he was shouting for all he was worth as he progressed along the waist to the frantic larbowlins hauling hard on the braces to tug the yards round, foretop first; on he rushed, arms waving, loud orders to his men, maintop next, and *Surprise* continued her turn, away from the wind and to the south, her bow coming round so slowly, rudder hard over and the deck canting ever further, all the gunners cursing as they strived to hold their guns, to prevent the starboard guns rolling out unloaded, every muscle straining to hold back two tons of iron.

Pat turned back to stare through his glass at the three Turk brigs, already a half mile astern. The first had lost its mast and was stopped. Its men were swinging axes to slash all restraints, others were striving to gather and cut that canvas away from those yards which could be reached. Plainly it was no longer any threat to *Surprise*. The other two had completed their own turns, south-west, and were fleeing, no longer any appetite for the fray. Pat's heart turned over within his chest, a huge surge of relief flushing all through him. The battle for his lads was over, finished. The barky had done all she could: he would not hold her to fight further; one solitary frigate could do no more. He collected his thoughts, his mind turning to look all about the decks in assessment of what damage had been inflicted, what casualties had been suffered.

The frigate continued her turn, coming all the way round to bear away to the west, towards Oxia, the deck stabilising, the gunners all along it breathing a sigh of relief, completing their reloading without the frantic desperation of before. The Turk brigs were receding towards the south a mile ahead and the main Turk fleet was two miles astern in *Surprise's* wake. Pat allowed an audible exhalation of relief to escape his lips, nodded to all about him near the helm, and he stared at the smashed and splintered fragments of wood strewn over his quarterdeck. He stepped to the waist rail and looked down the length of the gun deck: all seemed orderly save for similar splinters; cut strands of rigging were flapping in several places, but there seemed no corpses nor any badly wounded men lying anywhere on the deck. Perhaps, he thought, they had already been taken below? He hastened down the steps and stepped quickly towards the place he so very much dreaded: Simon's table. To his immense relief there was nothing of that atmosphere of fear and distress which he had so often seen during and after many a battle; instead, the ambience was calm, quiet, just a few groans and moans from wounded men sitting on the deck and awaiting their turn to see the surgeon. Pat nodded encouragingly to them as he stepped by. He stopped a few yards away from the two makeshift operating tables and watched for several minutes. Simon and Marston were busy strapping bandages around the bloody splinter wounds of two men, an occasional foray with the forceps necessitated for deeper and penetrating injuries, but nothing of panic, of urgency, was disturbing the surgeons' measured concentration. Pat could not see anything which alarmed him, and for that he was profoundly grateful. He approached closer to the surgeons, Simon giving him a brief nod as he completed strapping up his patient; Jason, helping him, stepped away towards Pat.

'How goes things?' asked Pat with the slightest trace of nervousness in his voice.

'A score of men are afflicted with splinter wounds...' whispered Jason, '... and Doctor Ferguson fears for the arm of one man and the leg of another. Both are stitched and bandaged... but thankfully not a one has been killed.'

'Thank God, Saint Patrick and all the saints,' blurted Pat, the welcome news such a huge lift, his anxieties receding like the ebb of a spring tide, his mouth as dry as a desert, the foul and bitter taste of burnt powder from the carronades' smoke lingering. His eyes watered in an instant, and he turned his face, looked down, in case Jason or anyone else might see the powerful wave of release surging through him and supplanting his burning fears even as his emotions raged through him like fire, wholly unchecked. His heart beat faster, his breathing came in short gasps; he nodded, turned right about and hastened back towards the companionway, wiping his cheeks as he paced up the enclosed steps in welcome seclusion, determined to take an age on each riser until he reached the quarterdeck, all the time engulfed within the overwhelming flood tide of his private relief.

The mood in the great cabin, indeed throughout the ship, was one of utter release, wholly unfettered and heartfelt. The barky had, once and for all, finished her duties and was homeward bound, so Pat had announced to all the crew, assembled on the deck as she navigated the passage between Ithaca and Levkada in the approaching sunset, a great swathe of red and orange brilliant above the western horizon and surrounding a diffuse, yellow sun, a distant and thin cloud hanging low above the sea surface. It seemed a fitting end to the day, and Pat's announcement had plainly been well received, an immediate lift in morale very visible to all, though his words had been welcomed by something of a muted cheer. Sheer relief was the weightier emotion, nothing much of overt indications of joy exhibited amongst the men. It had been a somewhat subdued closure to a day of great excitement, a day of danger, of battle, and fortunately one of few casualties. Pat, having made his announcement, hungry and exhausted, had retired to the cabin, to the enduring attentions of Murphy, Simon joining him for supper.

'We are truly finished here?' asked Simon for the third time in only a quarter-hour, sipping his red wine exceedingly slowly, near nothing of his supper eaten, the toasted cheese sitting untouched and fast cooling on the table, Murphy not troubling to conceal his scowl of disapproval.

'Yes, yes, I believe we are done,' came Pat's murmured reply, for that precious realisation was only now beginning to take root within him, his mind scarcely slowing since the engagement in the Patras approaches. 'The Turk brigs, whilst serving out no great damage, brought back to me that the barky has been repaired by Mr Tizard and his men in only temporary fashion, and there is a deal more of work for him to do now. Her remedy proper can only be achieved on the slip... in Devonport.'

'When will we reach home... Falmouth town?'

'Oh, as to that, I dare venture in three or four weeks... That is to say... *if* we are fortunate to be without the attentions of

Biscay at her worst, for I fairly dread the Bay crossing after... after last year.'

'I am wholly with you there, brother,' Simon sighed, a momentary flash of the horrific experience of the hurricane recalled, violent death by drowning seemingly come upon them all with the barky near to foundering; he shuddered. 'What of our Greek friends, the Turks in possession of all the Morea and seemingly intent on gaining Messalonghi next?'

'Well, they fled today, for sure they did, eh?' Pat smiled for the first time in the day, 'and there are but two more months of campaigning before Khosref most likely will return to the Golden Horn for the winter. If today was his best shot then I have no doubt that Miaoulis will preserve the town from his depredations.'

There came a knock on the door and Pickering entered. The lieutenant nodded to Simon and spoke to Pat, 'We are leaving the channel now, sir, Cephalonia is on the larboard beam, the point of Lefkada to starboard.'

'Very good, Mr Pickering. Our course is south-west,' declared Pat, nodding and cheering just a little. 'I will be on deck directly. Thank you.' Pickering bowed his head and left the cabin. 'Murphy, I am intending to take the air, the fresh air, the air of the evening. Will you kindly bring the coffee flask to the quarterdeck? Thank you.'

Murphy nodded and hastened away without a word. 'May I beg to join you?' asked Simon. 'Marston is attending the men, and thankfully we have no fears for any of them.'

'I would be honoured,' Pat nodded, smiled again at his friend and rose from the table. 'We will take my glass, and perhaps we may be blessed with a clear night sky... 'tis a long time since I passed an hour in the heavens. Let us go up.'

The twilight was enduring for a little longer, the distant extremities of Levkada to starboard and Cephalonia to port dimly visible in the weak, greying light, the still easterly wind a feeble shadow of its former strength at the peak of the day, and warmth still very much lingering in the air. *Surprise* was on an even keel and making, Pat estimated, perhaps four knots, wind astern. He looked about him: the mood on the quarterdeck was muted but relaxed, all on duty standing in contented mood near the helm. He nodded to each of his men in turn as he shifted to the stern rail. Five minutes more and darkness was come upon them in the east; astern the silver wake trailed behind in a visible straight line, phosphorescing its transient trace of recent minutes. Pat looked up: bright lights of many hundreds of stars were brilliantly radiating their presence, so greatly reassuring to him. He was still feeling subdued, relaxation proper not yet having reached him. In the western sky the weak and final vestiges of a purple light hovered in a low ribbon just above the horizon where the sun had made its farewell. A near complete silence abounded, the audible splashing of the wash alongside the hull and the ever present creak of the tarred ropes of the rigging were the only sounds intruding upon a total tranquillity, the realisation at last settling within Pat's mind that they were - *truly were* - done in Greek waters and finished with battle, bloodshed and gore. The rush of a sense of that quite overwhelmed him and he could no more take up his glass than fly up into the brilliant panorama of twinkling stars upon which his eyes were fixed. His mind had, at last, stopped whirling; his thoughts had, to all purposes, ceased their longstanding racing all through his head, and his heart was filled with a calm and peaceful serenity, absent since when he could no longer recall. A fixated Simon stood in silence at his side.

Sunday 14th August 1825   21:00   south-west of Cape St Vincent

Twelve uneventful days out from Argostoli in moderate winds and nothing adverse of note had arisen to slow their progress, until now. *Eleanor* was near becalmed in that dense fog which proliferates off the Portuguese south-west coast even sometimes at the height of summer when the warm and wet Atlantic westerlies come into conflict with the colder northerlies sweeping down from over the high Iberian plateau, an impenetrable murk and the air a stagnating dense wetness being the uninviting result for every mariner. The day had never been particularly bright, all the hours since Gibraltar being bleak, grey ones; overcast skies and damp were ever more prominent in the air, and all vestiges of warmth had ceded to the dim twilight, the atmosphere more akin to a wintry evening than an August one.

Duncan stared about him with great concern, no possibility of any noon sighting for the second day. His position for *Eleanor*, although most carefully calculated, left him with an enduring doubt about his longitude. With no prospect of any sighting of the coast in the fog and in the near complete darkness, he was inclining towards extreme caution. He stood near the wheel talking to Codrington in quiet voice. 'I am minded that we will maintain a north-westerly bearing... the wind on her beam, until daybreak.'

Codrington nodded, stared into the darkness, the very final vestiges of twilight serving only to emphasis the all-enveloping grey suspension of water all about them, which had not changed all day. 'Aye aye, sir,' Codrington nodded again.

'We must keep a careful watch. I widnae care to encounter any other vessel in this damn fog.' Duncan shivered as he uttered the cautionary words, rubbing the moisture away from his brow and eyes, the cold and wet so extremely uncomfortable after the dry warmth of the Greek spring and summer. The water droplets were everywhere suspended within the long stubble all over his face until, coalescing into larger drops, they ran through his beard - his neckerchief was already soaked - and then down his neck and chest. He strived to ignore the discomforting wetness, finally reconciling himself to enduring it whilst hoping, against all likelihood, for a dry, sunny day to come. 'Perhaps we will enjoy a warming wee dram, eh? Trannack, you may fetch the flask.'

Eyes all about the deck lit up; cold and wet furrowed faces broke into warming smiles, and heads nodded vigorously, sending showery cascades flying. Trannack disappeared below with alacrity, returning within a very short time with the whisky flask and a single large tumbler which was filled and passed round, every man enjoying a generous sip, Duncan himself draining the tumbler and refilling it, when it made the rounds for a most welcome second time.

Midnight and Duncan went below to seek sleep, laying fully clothed within his cot. Codrington and two men remained on duty. The schooner rolled gently on a modest swell, her fore and aft lanterns barely offering any light at all and, such as it was, their illumination offered only an indistinct glow, reflecting through the suspension of water droplets in the dense fog.

Sunday 14th August 1825   22:00   off the north coast of Africa

It was a clear and warm evening, the wind singing gently in its rushes through the rigging. Pat was greatly enjoying spending time on his quarterdeck with his glass. He stared for long minutes at the star-filled sky, thousands upon thousands of sparkling lights over Africa; Algiers was a day astern and Oran expected off the beam in the morning. At any moment he expected to be joined by Jason, for the man had much taken to the cordial hour it had become with Pat after the sunset, after all twilight was gone and before taking to his cot. He took a sip from his whisky flask, replenished in Argostoli and hidden from Murphy's search ever since within his chart table. The warming flow tasted wonderful, a smooth Islay malt, a gift from Simon, and a little smoky as he had much come to prefer. It was a delightful reminder of his youth and, albeit a far superior product, it invoked memories of the joys of illicit poteen. That particular treasure had been ever present in his grandparent's cottage, well concealed at all times in case of the Revenue inspection which never, to his memory, ever came.

'Ah, Mr Jason, there you are,' declared Pat with warm benevolence, pleased to see his friend emerge from the companionway as the memory of his grandma lingered in his thoughts, his delight in nostalgia slipping reluctantly towards regret: regret for the infrequency of his visits as he grew older; regret that he had never quite heeded her lessons and her advice as much as he might have done. That light of his life that he had not quite recognised at the time was long gone, and he missed her a great deal even after all these years.

Little more than one sleepless hour passing, all the time fretting with an undefined sense of disquietude, and Duncan, ill at ease, returned from his cot below to stand again at the helm, within a few minutes sending Tremayne to awaken all the men sleeping and to bring them too up on deck. They came up, bleary-eyed, tired, their enforced and unanticipated awakening most unwelcome. Searching stares were directed at Duncan, unspoken questions left hanging in the cold air. Eventually, all standing together near the helm, he apprised them of his purpose. 'Lads, I am minded that since we rounded that Portuguese Cape... St Vincent, aye... we are, for the first time, in the route of the Indiamen. I have known several of their captains, and they are forever in a damnable hurry, so much so that I doubt they will care to slow on their homeward bound passage even for this fog. Time is their currency, hurry is their byword, a day lost is a curse to them, and...' he hesitated, '... and I would not care to be below myself, nor to see any of you below, if... if one were to approach close: this vessel is so tiny, the Indiaman might not see us through the murk.'

Silence. The eight crewmen and Codrington shook off their great torpor to take in the unwelcome thought of being run down in the fog by a hastening merchantman, a leviathan in comparison to their tiny schooner. Doubtless any Indiaman would be anxious to reach home with its precious cargo and with passengers equally keen for best speed, all likely returning after many years in the Indies or the Tropics.

Duncan resumed, 'It is but a few more hours at this time of the year until the dawn.' His audience looking distinctly unhappy, he pressed on, 'Four bells of the morning watch, perhaps only five hours... until we will see what is all about us...' If - *that is* - the damned fog was to disperse; that was the thought he did not care to mention. 'So, lads, settle down up here, on deck...' Mute faces abounding, he spoke up, 'Am I plain?'

Nods and mumbled acknowledgements followed all round, deep dismay very evident, when Codrington spoke up, 'Dyer, go below and heat water on the stove. We will have a hot four-water grog ration to warm us.' That went down well, with more vigorous nods resulting from the men.

'Trannack, Tremayne,' declared Duncan, 'you are to launch the jolly boat.' All present stared in disbelief: launch the boat at an unknown distance from shore and in the black of night whilst amidst the thickest of fogs? 'You will leave her trailing on the full length of her line...' No movement from the tired men and Duncan, recognising their confusion, stepped forward, 'Well, must I do it myself? Mr Codrington, will you assist me?' This was spoken in very loud voice, Trannack and Tremayne jolted back to a more alert state from their tired and bemused incomprehension. Hastily they hurried off, midships, to prepare.

'Jenkin,' said Duncan in more measured tone, 'bring her round... into the wind. Allow her way to fall off while they launch the boat.'

'Aye aye, sir,' a tired Jenkin nodded. A few minutes passed with *Eleanor* rolling only slightly and drifting. Trannack and Tremayne, assisted by Chegwin and Hammett, lowered the tiniest of boats, large enough only for six men on the thwarts. *Eleanor's* former Deal cutter, a quite beautiful boat, had been passed to *Surprise*, the frigate's own boats being severely damaged in the escape from Navarino Bay. Duncan stared with some concern: it was, for sure, a very little boat; the exchange had been a gross and unavoidable economy, for he had never before seen a boat so small, scarcely larger than a dinghy. A few minutes passed and it went into the water, the four men returning to the weary gathering near the helm.

'Very well,' declared Duncan, 'Let us get under way.'

Monday 15th August 1825 01:30 off the north coast of Africa

Pat had failed to gain the relaxed state of sleep he so much sought; indeed he had coveted it for many a month; he stood at the side of the mizzen mast, his helmsmen and Mower casting sympathetic glances towards him every once in a while, his discomfit plain to all to see. Darkness was all about the barky, save for the stars: a million sparkling diamond lights, the moon a mere sliver of a bright crescent. Pat, in a mood of reflective introspection, again pondered the contribution of his men to the Greek cause: had one frigate really made a meaningful difference, the Turk fleet numbers so great? Had the sacrifices of his own men been worthwhile? Had they achieved anything truly significant? There were widows in Falmouth, bereaved fathers and brothers too, who might not hold the view that all their efforts and their losses - killed and wounded - had been of great use, of much value; indeed, how could they possibly judge? That was the most uncomfortable of all his thoughts, and Pat sighed. His mind returned to recollections of the Jelberts, father and son; both had been sterling shipmates at different times of his life and, sadly, both had been killed. His heart sank, he sighed again, rallied his thoughts to think of what was to be done, what must be done; and he came to a rekindled determination to seek out Mathew Jelbert's widow upon his return to Falmouth.

Monday 15th August 1825 02:00   *west of Cape St Vincent*

Eleanor was underway once more after a slow start to gain motion. The weak wind had picked up a little, Duncan thought, whilst the boat had been launched. Very tired, he was feeling that perhaps his caution had been excessive. He looked all about him: two of his men were at the helm; Codrington was striving to stay awake at their side, whilst the other six were dozing fitfully and uncomfortably, sitting back against the lee side: the warming grog had delivered its soporific effect, one which had facilitated a grudging accommodation with discomfort. More minutes passed and the wind continued to strengthen, a south-westerly bringing warm, wet air from far out over the Atlantic. Thankfully, thought Duncan, it was nothing of the ilk of the hurricane of the prior November, for he doubted that his own fortitude, mental and physical, could cope with another horror of that ilk. He looked up, gazed into the inky blackness. Had he heard something, the slightest sound, something indistinct but incongruous in the tranquil invisibility? No, it was merely his imagination escaping to run alarming riot; he dismissed it and allowed his mind to drift towards thoughts of his family.

Not too many more hours remained until the dawn, and Pat took bleak comfort from the thought. Pickering had spelled Mower at the end of the middle watch, the three together exchanging brief words, nothing of note occurring, nothing to report, Pat's lieutenants both urging him to take to his cot, his red-rimmed eyes never more prominent in their black hollows. He waved their polite concerns away, sleep beyond him; never before in all his years at sea had he been afflicted with insomnia. The watch system, even for officers, more often than not left all in a constant state of tiredness, even if it was not a great fatigue, and for the whole of his life at sea whenever he had reached his cot, even in the days as a young midshipman, sleep came to Pat near instantly, waking never a difficulty either, usually someone offering a gentle, waking shake of the shoulder. In his more senior years his steward invariably appeared with a steaming mug of tea or coffee, depending on the watch. However, in all the months of this year he had enjoyed neither blessed sleep nor the easy ability to rise from his cot with the former instant alertness he had ever been blessed with. He consoled himself with the thought that he would gain all the sleep and all the rest he required once the barky made home, once they reached Falmouth town. Simon had, several times, offered him a draught, a laudanum concoction, but he cared not for such artificialities, as he saw things, usually contenting himself with a generous brandy if the night was approaching or several strong coffees if it was not. For the present he felt oddly ill at ease despite being homeward bound, and that was most unusual, and he could not fathom it.

Duncan shivered, the cold night air chilling him after the long spell in the warmth of the summer in the eastern Mediterranean. His eyes ranged all about the schooner, his ears attentive for the slightest noise, for he could not throw off the most disquieting feeling that he had, an hour previously, heard something. What it was he did not know, and he strived to rack his brain, to recall the nature of the noise, to conceive of what it might conceivably have been. His men slumbered on, save for the two at the helm. Even Codrington had given up his efforts to stay awake and he sat in miserable discomfort upon the wet deck near the wheel. Duncan consoled himself that it was not long before the dawn, and then came the noise once more, an unsettling noise, a trifle louder than before, one he could not identify. He was instantly alert, looking all about him; the fog played tricks upon the sense of hearing, but he tried to identify the direction of the noise. With a rising sense of anxiety he wiped the cloying water droplets from his face, rubbed his ears as if such might aid his hearing; he looked around once more: nothing, not the smallest noise save for the gentle slap of wave on hull, and the rustling of the sails and rigging in the modest wind. *Eleanor* was making perhaps three knots, holding still to her safe north-westerly course, assuredly away from the perilous rocky coast of south-west Portugal. Then came the unidentified noise again. Duncan's mind raced to an instant alert; there was something out there, but what and where?

Monday 15th August 1825 03:30 off the north coast of Africa

'Young Mower reported you were up here,' declared a bleary-eyed Simon, stepping across from the companionway. 'Is there a particular notion afflicting you, tell?'

'Why Simon, what are you doing on deck at this hour?'

'I was attending my patients, Marston sleeping, when Mower arrived for his laudanum, a most modest dose, and one I am weaning him away from in gradual fashion. He does not care to tell you, but his arm wound still presents him with a deal of pain. I venture he starts each day with considerable fortitude.'

'He is the bravest of souls, I make no doubt,' declared Pat with a nod and a thin smile.

'And yourself?'

'Oh, I have not been sleeping well for some time. Doubtless that will change when we fetch home.'

'I confess there is one matter which sits ill on my own mind,' murmured Simon.

'Tell, if you will.'

216

'My old friend, Peddler... these recent reports of him and Perkis. It is conceivable that we will meet again in Falmouth.'

'Yes, that does seem possible... Please... go on.'

'Well, that he was away with the Greek gold, as he himself believed, sits ill with me, having known him, man and boy, since we grew up together in Tobermory.'

'Greed is ever a powerful influence... no doubt.'

'Yes, but as a youngster I never had a closer friend, and now I find he has let me down. What will I say to him?'

'Why, as to that, perhaps you will ask of him his account of events and then you may find out the true character of the man - if, that is, you believe the explanation he provides. I am minded that until faced with extremes, we do not see it... the real man; we never know until that moment, that time of decision, whether he is a man of integrity or proves to be a base, worthless creature, not worthy of our friendship or respect.'

'I am inclining to the view that he was influenced by Perkis into their deplorable... *their despicable*... attempt at theft.'

'That's as may be, but I am of the opinion that it serves as not the least excuse; a man possessing of honesty and integrity makes his own decision.'

Monday 15th August 1825 04:00   *west of Cape St Vincent*

Duncan had decided he had made his mind up: the noise he had heard intermittently was coming from the south-west. 'Listen,' he whispered to Teague and Jenkin at the helm, 'listen... there, d'ye hear it?'

Tired faces stared along Duncan's pointing arm. Utter blackness prevailed still, with not the least glimmer from moon or stars. Both men shook their heads.

'There it is again, louder,' declared Duncan in excited voice, 'Hear it!'

Codrington, observing the exchanges and Duncan's rising exasperation, hauled himself up from the deck and stepped slowly over to the helm; his gaze followed the still-extended arm; he listened hard. 'A ship's bell, might it be? 'tis muffled, more akin to a drum roll...'

Three minutes of rising anxiety and suddenly the bowsprit appeared a mere fraction of a second before the bow, the weak light of *Eleanor's* bow lantern illuminating the spray of the wash flung to both sides of the huge hull, and then the behemoth, as it appeared, struck hard against the schooner's side, neither Teague nor Jenkin afforded even a second to turn away. The schooner crashed over, her gunwhale pressed into the water, both the helmsmen thrown bodily overboard, as was Codrington. Duncan saved himself by seizing the topmast preventer backstay and holding it within both his hands as he was plunged into the water, the rope severely cutting him most painfully. Despite this, and struggling to breathe, he held on, clinging tightly with a desperate grip for what seemed an age until, his lungs bursting, the ship which had struck them passed by and, relieved of the pressure upon her own hull, *Eleanor* gradually righted herself.

Soaked, chilled and exhausted, sitting on the sodden deck, *Eleanor* still casting water to the scuppers, Duncan looked all about him: of Codrington, Teague, Chegwin, Jenkin and Tremayne there was no sign; Trannack, Dyer, Mason and Hammett were still there, flat on the deck against the side, all struggling for air.

'UP LADS!' screamed Duncan, 'UP!' He hauled himself to his feet, his sodden clothes a huge weight upon him, and he gazed astern into the darkness, but nothing could he see. *Eleanor* was stationary, rolling gently, stability had returned. 'HAMMETT! RING THAT BELL!' shouted Duncan. 'Keep ringing, don't stop! DYER, quickly, is the boat line still attached?'

'Aye, sir, the line is here, the boat is likely still with us.'

'Trannack, Mason, haul the boat in, make haste!'

Monday 15th August 1825 04:15 off the north coast of Africa

'Will we try for sleep?' ventured Simon eventually, both men tiring of their discussion about Peddler and Perkis, nothing to add, their only possible conclusion being to wait and see if they encountered the rogues in Falmouth. 'You look greatly tired, brother. Will I prescribe a modicum of laudanum? It will help.'

'I do not much care for the alchemist's black art, thank you; but perhaps there is a trifle left of the whiskey in the flask? Here it is... no, 'tis all gone.'

'I pass over you referring to me as an alchemist, Patrick O'Connor... *alchemist indeed!* Allow me to say that a deal of scientific minds have been brought to bear on perusal of that most valuable substance. Why, I have... at times... applied my own to study of its most beneficial medicinal properties, I have so.' Simon did not care to elaborate, a very substantial dose having proven invaluable to him for long spells after the distressing death of his wife, an addiction becoming the result, and that had taken several years to shake.

'Doubtless so,' murmured Pat. 'Tell me: when we fetch home... to Falmouth that is, is it in your intention to return to Scotland?'

'Yes, I believe so. I am minded to spend time with the woman who now possesses my mind, the treasure that I have found in Flora. Doubtless you collect my stated intention of a marriage proposal?'

'I do, but was there not some mention of that being scuppered by the law?'

'Indeed so; however, I am minded that a marriage elsewhere, in some... some more greatly enlightened province... will serve for me, and I must endeavour to see if such will be agreeable to Flora.'

'Ain't you getting a trifle ahead of yourself, old friend?' murmured Pat. 'After all, you have made no proposal as yet.'

'That's as may be, and we will have to see what will come, what will be... on my return to Tobermory and my... my proposal.'

Monday 15th August 1825 04:30   *west of Cape St Vincent*

'HAUL!' shouted Duncan, in desperate anxiety, ignoring the roaring pain in his hands and the blood flowing freely from them. 'HAUL!' The boat's line was collecting on the schooner's deck near the wheel, ten yards of it, twenty yards, scarcely much left to haul in. 'All together now, HAUL!'

At last came sight of the boat, and four of the *Eleanor* survivors still pulled on the line with furious determination, Hammett continuing to ring the bell frantically. The Eleanors stared: aboard the boat were three slumped men, the nearest an exhausted Codrington, still coughing water and unable to speak; Chegwin and Tremayne were also present and in similar but lesser distress. No sign was reported by either of them, in gasping breath, of Jenkin or Teague.

'Hammet, don't stop ringing that bell for even a moment,' shouted Duncan. 'Trannack, go below and seek dry powder for the chaser, quickly now. We will fire the gun if 'tis possible. Dyer, clean the chaser, a dry barrel and touchhole, as fast as ye can. Mason, let us see what can be done to get underway, to turn about; helm hard a-weather!'

Tense minutes passed with every man in great anxiety, desperate to find their two comrades washed overboard, as *Eleanor* gained way, came round in a turnabout to retrace her course, the wind now to starboard and Duncan careful to keep the wind forward of the beam, seeking to avoid lee drift. All aboard stared and shouted into the blackness, the bell clanging on and on in unceasing, raucous clamour. Plaintive stares were directed by all into the black darkness, a raging anxiety wholly consuming every man.

Five minutes, ten, fifteen; all passed so very slowly without any sighting of anyone in the water, and hope was slipping away, extinguished by a crushing sadness that cast down everyone; despite which they leaned as far over the rail as could be, the water calm, a placidity which was rare indeed. Duncan had shifted to the prow, so much the better to see anyone *Eleanor* might approach. He had already concluded that there was no hope: twenty minutes of even the slowest sailing - barely a knot or two being the schooner's best speed - suggested to him that she would have reached anyone still alive in the water, but no shouts had been heard in the moments when Hammet paused with his frantic ringing of the bell.

From below, Trannack sprang up in great alarm. 'She is taking water, sir!' he shouted in full voice, 'Mighty fast!'

Duncan hastened to the companionway, descended at the utmost speed to see for himself. The water was an inch above the lower deck boards. He knew in a cruel instant that it was all up, no prospect of saving her; no pump in all the world could hold back this tide; the merchantman which had crashed into her had undoubtedly smashed several of her ribs, and all the hull plating and the caulking was surely ripped away, so great the speed of the rising water. He stared for a few seconds, his mind awhirl, bubbles rising through the planking. He rushed back to the steps and scrambled back to the helm. 'Haul in the boat, lads; prepare to abandon ship!' Shocked faces stared; men stood immobile. The second calamity was simply too much to take in after the shock of the crash and the loss of two shipmates. Duncan's eyes registered the inactivity of his men; 'ABANDON SHIP!' he screamed in full voice, and then, with great dismay, he remembered the Greek letter, still packed below in his dunnage.

He hastened back to the steps, looked down with horror, utterly aghast: in the dim light of the solitary Argand lamp which remained above the water, it was plain to see that the level had already risen much higher. His mind raced, 'The damn letter!' he exclaimed. 'What to do about the letter?' It was now or never; he took a deep breath and plunged into the black water; it was numbingly cold, knee deep already: the schooner was sinking faster than he had believed possible. He fought on, pushed his way with difficulty through the water barrier, five yards, ten. The cold gripped all about him, every step harder than the last; the water rising swiftly to near his thighs, he pushed hard against the door to try to force it to open into the cabin, the water holding it firm. He tried again, despite a dimly aware sense of his strength ebbing as his body temperature plummeted. He was gasping for breath now, the exertion so severe; he heaved hard once more, but it was no use: the pressure on the door was simply too great, and now the water had reached his waist.

Alarm filled his mind. The feeling in his legs was fading, the sensation of numbing cold gripping him. He realised he must get out - *and quickly* - for there was no prospect of recovering the letter. There never had been. For the first time he felt fear.

The severe cold had chilled him further in the last minute to the point of leaving little sensation in his legs and none in his fingers. Struggling hard, every step near impossible in the deeper water which had risen to reach his chest, he hauled his trailing leg towards his body, extended the other a half-yard forwards; he was tiring fast. Only five more short paces remained to reach the companionway steps, but he was slowing; it was too far. His strength was dwindling; just two steps more, a final one; cold, so very cold; no feeling any longer within his legs, they were finished. The lamp blinked out and all was darkness. He took a deep breath - the air was so cold - and he gasped for another. The water was rising to his neck. Just one last step, only one, was needed to reach the companionway steps, but it was impossible. The water began to lap at his mouth, an inability to move even his head overcoming him, and then an involuntary pause. No strength left, not the least ability to move at all, the water rose above his head. Summoning all that was left to him of willpower, he commanded his body to try to jump up just a few inches with the last tiny vestige of his strength, all that was left to him, to try to get his nose and mouth above the cold grip of the water, to gain just one more breath, not the least of reserve left to him. No use: he could not move. Once more, he flailed his arms, no control over his legs left, and he rose a few inches, his mouth once again just above the water. His eyes were registering no more than vague shapes in the blackness, and he gasped a huge breath before sliding back to the vaguest sensation of the deck planking below him, his heavy clothing sodden and a tremendous drag on the slightest movement of even his arms. No energy left at all, his breath was finally failing him and his sluggish body had stopped moving. His limbs had lost all feeling and everything was becoming darker. Another half-minute passed and his thoughts slowed more, the cold exacerbating the lack of oxygen. So this was it, he vaguely perceived: the end; his struggle was over and he was not getting out. His mind was tiring, shutting down, nothing left to him at all of his last desperate breath and not the least energy to jump up again; every part of his body had become numbingly cold and his air was finally finished. He dimly perceived his legs beginning to give way underneath him, vaguely understood that he was falling back from upright into the grip of the numbing, deep cold of the water. His mouth was beginning to open involuntarily, the vile taste of saltwater striking his tongue, and he retched.

Monday 15th August 1825 04:30   off the north coast of Africa

Still two hours until sunrise and *Surprise* ploughed steadily on, the wind modest, the sea benevolently calm, a constant six knots maintained and a total absence of tension aboard the ship. Pat remained on his quarterdeck, talking to Simon, neither man feeling the inclination for sleep. A sense of something passing registered, something being left behind, a dimly dawning realisation that the future would be different, though neither man knew in what way. They leaned on the stern rail, occasional glances directed up, up to a brilliant star-studded infinity, ten thousand sparkling jewels spattering a blue velvet backcloth.

'Is it in your intention to return to Ireland? Are you minded to finish with this Greek venture?' murmured Simon cautiously, as if any question breaking the quietude might be considered unwanted.

'Oh, as to that, I am unsure. The First Lord and my cousin, the Foreign Secretary, may have further notions, but doubtless Sinéad will press me to stay at home in Connemara and attend the farm... and the mine... and precious little have we seen from that venture.'

'You are convinced still... about the mine, about its value... its riches?'

Pat leaned forward with a confident air exhibited upon his face, 'I believe I am, though perhaps a trifle less so than last year.' Pat's brow furrowed in Simon's close scrutiny, 'We are yet to reach the lode... the gold ore. It is certainly there to be found, somewhere... so I am assured.'

'And perhaps you should keep that proverbial pinch of salt at hand, eh?' Simon laughed. 'One might say that there are three uncertainties: woman, wind - which you are familiar with ... *in its several forms* - and wealth.'

Pat stared, unsure of whether Simon was making fun of him. 'There has been a deal of excavation... and great profit will be derived from even the thinnest of gold vein... so I am told.'

'I wish you well with that. A gold mine... I scarcely possess of a gold sovereign, and that landlord of mine may yet prove to be the unscrupulous man I feared him to be when I sold my house to him. I was inclined to the view even then that he appeared to be the grasping kind.'

'You do have funds for the present? You spoke of an account at the Plymouth Dock Bank... and doubtless we will receive some pay eventually for this... this rum Greek business.'

'Yes, I have no concerns for money, until... that is... when I have ceased these maritime crusades, finished with such as this Greek odyssey. I greatly doubt I will take to the sea again after I fetch home to Mull... save perhaps for attending my patients; though there are some of them, for sure, who I would never care to see again; a Mr MacKinnon of Jura is one such that springs to mind, a most miserable soul and one perpetually lamenting his lot.'

'Is there truly a living to be found there... in the Isles? They have always seemed to me to be a place of poverty, much like the west of Ireland... and these days I am minded that the sheep are considered to be of greater importance than the people. All of whom living within twenty miles of Claddaghduff would consider themselves lucky if they possessed of a single shilling.'

'Sadly, it is also the case in Mull... and much more so in other parts of the Isles; worse, it is rumoured that there are imminent intentions to clear the island of Rhum... to clear it of all souls living there! So it is said in a letter I have received from Flora. The kelp is everywhere finished and cattle prices are halved... and everywhere the sheep prevails.'

'Will you endure... up there?' asked Pat with more than a little concern for his friend.

'Change is assured and I doubt it will be for the better. Why, Caithness was cleared in eight years, every house burned to the ground, some with their inhabitants... unmoving, aged and infirm, incapable of rising... burnt within their beds... God forgive the vile tyrants! If the same happens in the Small Isles then I ... I will be in the greatest consternation. I have the deepest concerns for the impoverished souls living there. Great numbers of the clans' people are already leaving for Canada... for Australia. It is a bleak prospect, for sure; and what is to be done? I can think of nothing, and that fills me with an infinite sadness.'

Monday 15th August 1825 04:30   *west of Cape St Vincent*

His oxygen gone, unconsciousness near and his head below water as his body began to slip backwards, Duncan took an involuntary gasp, the last one of a drowning man, cold saltwater filling his mouth. Instinctively he snapped it tightly closed before more water could surge down to fill his lungs, and he bit harder on his teeth, a final vestige of determination taking feeble hold. And then, just as he was about to slip backwards to his death, to slump into the aqueous blackness, rough hands reached down and seized his shoulders; others grabbed his arms with the tightest of grips, Duncan no longer aware of the fierce exertions, and up, up he was brutally pulled, not the least care for any obstruction, until his head was sprung in an instant from the numbingly cold water, a great gasp of air taken as his body responded automatically. Up, up further he was hauled, higher, until his chest was out of the water. His lungs were violently coughing, his mouth was spitting great volumes, and his chest pounded as he took more huge gasps of air, no respite yet from the pull of his rescuers, up, up higher, until all his body was pulled out of the companionway; and then he was flung flat on his back on the deck, soaked, colder than ever he could recall in his life. He still gasped for air, and then he turned aside and vomited what seemed like pints of vile saltwater; but he was alive; it registered upon him in his confusion. He was alive!

Anxious faces stared down at him, not another second more of time allowed for him to further recover before he was seized up again and hauled to the schooner's side, passed overboard to waiting arms in the small boat, rocking violently with the gross overload. Duncan was barely aware of what was happening to him; he had great pains in his chest and his head throbbed as if having been beaten by a club; his frozen legs were of no use at all, no feeling in them or within his chilled arms. He rolled to the side with the last of his strength and vomited violently again. Firm hands pulled him up until he was sitting, held upright by Dyer and Mason, seated on the thwart, not the least of energy available to him; he coughed until all his chest ached as if kicked, all the time gasping for yet more air, continually retching as his lungs still strived to expel water that was no longer there, words wholly beyond him, his eyes registering only vaguely all about him in the diffuse moonlight.

The tiny boat, low in the water and ever in danger of sinking, hauled away, ten yards, twenty, the sea swell fortunately only gentle and just the slightest of wind. Through the wispy fog a distressed *Eleanor* was visibly and swiftly sinking, her deck awash, her sails hanging loose, flapping as if she was in her own panic; the old friend that the men always felt her to be now appeared to be fretting, and there was nothing to be done save to await the end. Trannack and Hammett ceased pulling, stopped as if to attend the final few moments, a reluctance to lose the nautical shipmate that all perceived *Eleanor* to be.

The fog was swirling thicker around the sinking schooner, her outlines barely visible and all detail fast disappearing. Duncan himself stared hard, mute, his reddened eyes smarting after so long in salt. He strived to make sense of all about him. He perceived indistinctly, no more, the schooner slipping down, down; she was finally going. Only her mast was still visible, and then she was gone, utterly. He looked all about him: cold water was sloshing over the tiny boat's gunwhales from within and without, only a few inches of freeboard remaining, the dinghy in danger of putting her side below the water. And then, no vestige left of his energy, more exhausted than ever he could recollect, soaked and utterly chilled, the onset of delirium came quickly upon him and he slumped into merciful unconsciousness.

Chapter Ten

Surprise passed the Black Rock and entered the Carrick Roads, a gentle south-westerly much facilitating her navigation; on she sailed until the Bar was directly abeam, when she made her tack, her course set, west, for her approach to Falmouth port. Just one more mile to go. Close-hauled, on she crept, slowing all the time until, all her braces slackened and no way on her at all, she dropped her anchors in the deeper water of the King's Road on the Trefusis side of the Penryn River, a great sense of jubilation gripping all on board, a realisation coming to them that they truly were home at last. The glorious sensation of their homecoming had settled upon all the crew as they had entered the Channel, and they hastened to lower her boats even as an armada of pilchard boats coalesced all around the frigate, joyful greetings of welcome extended from a hundred waving, shouting fishermen.

'Welcome home, sir,' declared Prosser, standing with Pat at the helm; 'Welcome home, Dr Ferguson; give you joy of it, sirs.'

'Thank you kindly, Mr Prosser; it is indeed a joy, I make no doubt,' said Simon, pleased and relieved, for he had fretted all throughout the Biscay passage, in fear of any repeat of the last crossing, in winter, the tempestuous fury of the hurricane never far from his thoughts. Vivid recollections of the fear and horror had eventually ceded to the grip of despair and the fading of all hope as everyone below deck waited for the inevitable sinking and drowning which they all felt sure was coming. However, these last few days of this particular Biscay voyage had been uneventful, the wind fair, the only moment of inclement weather being dense fog, persisting all day as they rounded Cape St. Vincent and lingering for much of the new day as they progressed northwards towards Lisbon; yet after that, once into the sunshine of the following day, the passage to Falmouth had been blessed with the most favourable of weather, with sunshine and gentle winds all the way, the Surprises revelling in it.

Two hours on and the wounded had all been conveyed aboard the pilchard boats to the quay, Pat's barge augmented by the cutter exchanged from *Eleanor* to carry the fit men of the crew ashore. Increasing crowds were gathering on the quays and strands as news spread throughout the small town. A mere dozen of the crew remained aboard to attend the frigate, Pickering with them, as Pat boarded his barge for the short pull to the quay. The welcome warmth of the summer day was persisting into the evening with a benevolent but diminishing radiance, sunset near and the waterfront in shadow, as Pat looked wistfully back to his ship. That she was *his* ship he felt acutely aware; that his crew were *his* shipmates was at the forefront of his thoughts in that moment. Painful recollections of their last homecoming intruded into his mind, greatly distressing memories of the many severely wounded men with him at that time so difficult to suppress; indeed, the images of too many comrades who had been left behind was hard, very hard, to bear. Many of their faces he could picture as if only yesterday. He saw, in his memory, the faces of cheerful shipmates as they had departed this very place, little knowing that they would never return. He shook his head, turned his gaze away from *Surprise* with conscious determination and he looked to the steps at the Customs House Quay, his barge fast approaching. At least this time the losses were, thankfully, far less, although one in particular had oft come to mind in his enduring sleepless nights on the passage home: the older Jelbert, *Mathew* Jelbert, was lost, and Pat reminded himself that he must seek out his widow and would do so on the morrow. Prosser would know of her, where she lived. He would speak to the master when he reached the quay, before a moment was lost; the necessity for such a visit had seized all his thoughts and it seemed, in that cold instance of reflection, in the moment of remembering his lost men, the most important thing in all the world.

Supper at the Royal Hotel was, in physical terms, the most blissful of relaxing evenings, and it would have been mentally so had there been any news of *Eleanor's* arrival in London, but no word of such had reached Falmouth, no news had arrived at all, neither by the Royal Mail coaches which arrived daily at the hotel nor via any vessel coming into the port from London, and that uncomfortable vacancy sat ill on Pat's mind, intruding into his thinking, ruining his pleasure in being home, at least as far as he considered the town to be his home. Far Connemara seemed ever more distant and remote. Not that he would, all things considered, ever conceive of himself as a Cornishman, but in all his time in the town he had been made welcome by every person he had ever met; indeed, even the grievous losses of the last voyage had not cooled the affection that the townsfolk generally held for him. He was seated with Simon, Marston and Jason, all enjoying a precious hour of warm, cordial amity around the table, the divine release from tension, from interminable strain, dawning slowly on each man. The most generous of beefsteaks were presented to them as soon as the first bottle of red wine had been downed, no man having the appetite or inclination to bother with the soup, a second bottle of red swiftly following its fellow. Oddly, he mused, there was no sign of Mower, who had also been invited. Perhaps, thought Pat, he had simply opted to stay with his family.

'Where is Sinéad, tell?' asked Simon, breaking Pat's train of thought.

'Oh, as to my dearest... she is in Connemara. I have a letter which awaited me here at the hotel. Naturally, she had no knowledge of when to expect our return and did not care to spend another summer away from the farm.'

'Then, allow me to ask... when is it in your thinking to depart for Ireland, for far Galway... to home proper?'

Pat sighed, 'First, I must speak with Duncan, to be sure he has delivered a most important letter to the First Lord...' Pat paused for reflection, 'There is also a copy of it in my possession, and I am minded to deliver that one too... deliver it myself: it must never go astray. I hope that in the morning we will find out where *Eleanor* is, when she is expected to return to Falmouth. I confess I had a deal of confidence that we would find her here already, plentiful time passing to fetch the Pool and return... she is so fleet of sail, but I venture she is likely tiding it down the Channel even now, coming back from London. I am minded that I will take the mail coach and ask of Admiral Saumarez in Plymouth. Doubtless he can avail himself of the telegraph and find out. It is in my contemplation to go there in the next day or so, but first I have a pressing duty to attend to.'

'A pressing duty?'

'Yes, I am intending to speak with Mrs Jelbert. Prosser has promised to escort me to her abode, and I am most grateful to say that Michael here will also attend.'

'I wish you well with that, brother. It is the most benevolent of gestures.' Simon sighed, as if imagining the meeting; he was sure it would be distressing. 'Allow me to help you to another glass.' He poured, not waiting for any reply, keen to move his own thoughts on, to steer towards a more tolerable direction.

'What of your own intentions, Simon? Are you returning directly to Mull?'

'In due course...most certainly; however, I am minded to stay here for several weeks yet, to attend the wounded... until they are all fully recovered or near so, no doubts lingering for the health of every man. Likewise, I also care to meet with those of our former... *our wounded* shipmates who did not join our voyage this time, to look to their recovery... how they are coming along. I dare say I will be away early in October, likely not later, and before the cold of the winter; I care not for the purgatory of a winter coach all the way to Glasgow.'

'Is all well with your home? That is to say... with your good lady friend... Flora?'

'I believe so. A number of letters awaited my own arrival here, several from Mrs MacDougall... and, I regret to say, one in a most remonstrative tone from my landlord...'

'Ahhh, yes… your landlord. I had forgotten that you were no longer the owner of your abode. Why is that the case, tell?'

'Oh, once it was. But in those years after our time at sea aboard *Tenedos*... ashore once more... the half-pay of a surgeon was precious little; I collect it was perhaps nine pounds a month... and, I confess, I had at the time a degree of debt.' Simon grimaced, 'I had expended much of what little I possessed in helping the sick folk of Mull... and of the outliers, Islay and the like. Hence, I was in some financial difficulties with the mortgage secured on my house, and so I made an accommodation with a man in Oban, a wealthy hotelier, who purchased the house and leased it back to me, albeit with a rather high rent.'

'You said *remonstrative*. Would you care to say more?'

'Yes, it seems that my rent payments did not reach Oban during my absence in Greece these past months. I will attend my bank in Plymouth to find out why at the earliest convenience. Thankfully, I am pleased to say, there were several letters awaiting me from Flor... from Mrs MacDougall... which were of a friendlier persuasion and... and I am minded that there will be the most cordial reception when I reach blessed Tobermory... yes indeed, and that is a warming thought... I am in the way at the present, in contemplation of that event, I am so.'

'Well, that is all to the good, I am pleased to hear,' Pat smiled, 'I must say I have a great yearning myself to see Sinéad, Fergal and Caitlin, I do... but none at all for the potatoes! *The potatoes*... Hah! Hah!'

Saturday 27th August 1825   09:00   The Royal Hotel, Falmouth

'Ah, there you are Mr Prosser,' cried Pat with a warm smile of welcome, the master entering the dining room as Pat's breakfast was concluding, Marston with him. 'Will we set off now?'

'Yes sir,' Prosser nodded, not the least trace of levity in his own gravelly voice; rather there was a determination, a fixed mindset, a steely resolution for a difficult task ahead. Pat's own smile melted immediately, his own thoughts focusing on the looming visit.

Together the three men left the Royal and walked the length of Church Street. As they paced in silence along Arwennack Street, their spirits sinking further with every step, Pat was pondering what to say. How would Mrs Jelbert be? They turned right into Hull's Lane and stepped ever more slowly up the hill, trepidation rising within Pat's mind, his stomach turning with a queasy feeling that had not the least foundation in his large breakfast, which by now he was much regretting eating. Another few yards on and so to the tiny, white-painted Hull's Cottage on the right near the top of the lane. Each man stared briefly, gathered their thoughts, their courage, and Prosser rapped on the door. They waited, a pensive minute, no man caring to speak to his companions; another minute and there came a creak as the wooden door shifted on its hinges. The door half-opened and a small lady gazed up at them with boundless distress and grave apprehension writ all over her tired face. Aged in her late fifties - it was hard to tell in the shadows and much of her face was shrouded by a close-pulled shawl - she looked carefully to each of her visitors in turn, in silence, her stare eventually fixing upon Prosser whom she evidently recognised, conceding a blink of her reddened eyes and a near indiscernible nod of greeting.

'Mrs Jelbert, I hope I see you well,' murmured Prosser, as brightly as he could manage without wishing to be loud; 'Here be visitors... Captain O'Connor and Father Marston... to speak with you... if, that is, you are so minded.' Prosser's voice tailed off as his own spirits failed him: Mrs Jelbert was plainly not well; not in the least could she be so described.

'Mr Prosser, how nice to see you,' the softly spoken and halting words were offered in genuine voice, albeit one of patently plain fragility. 'I am so sorry I have not attended the Chapel of late... I... I had been minded to await Mathew's return... that is to say... I...' Mrs Jelbert could manage no more, the tears began to flow, swiftly becoming an unceasing stream, and then her body was wracked by convulsions of sobbing. Pat and Prosser stepped forward quickly to seize her up, her legs plainly about to give way. They supported her gently back into the small living room, the interior light weak, the temperature cool. The tiny cottage was shaded from the easterly morning sun and gained no warmth so early in the day. They sat together around an old, wooden dining table, patiently waiting for Mrs Jelbert's recovery. Marston proffered his handkerchief, and the convulsions and tears gradually diminished.

A minute more passed and Marston spoke up with a tone of calming reassurance in his voice, the chaplain blessed with a deal of experience in such distressing circumstances, on and off the ship, 'Mrs Jelbert, we were all friends of your late husband... *of Mathew...* all of us; we were very proud to call him *friend*, we were so; and we are here today... here with you as *your* friends; we would very much wish to be thought of as such.'

A grief-stricken Mrs Jelbert nodded, for she could find no words. Her tears still running, still streaking her cheeks, she trembled as she dabbed at them with the handkerchief.

Pat spoke up, 'We are greatly sorry for your loss... Your husband was an exceptional man, one of the finest shipmates I ever served with, he was so... and... and I am minded that he will ever be with us... in our thoughts... in our memories as, in times to come, we go about the barky.'

A rekindled wave of sobbing from Mrs Jelbert, and Prosser interceded, 'Mrs Jelbert... *Emblyn*, my dear... we stand ready to help you in every way. Father Marston is here, a minister of the church... a faithful servant of God... and he will be with you *every day...* as will I... *as will I*, and Captain O'Connor will make all... all necessary arrangements as may be called for in the days, weeks and months ahead. Have not the least worry of that.'

Mrs Jelbert's frail face looked up for the first time since the tears began; she made a determined effort to hold firm, to stay the sobbing, her difficulty very evident to her visitors. 'Thank you all... thank you.' She could say nothing more.

Marston spoke up, 'Mrs Jelbert... may I call you Emblyn?' She nodded hesitantly, looked towards Marston, and he smiled encouragingly, 'Emblyn, my dear, it is my intention to be with you in these difficult days ahead. I hope you will allow me to wait upon you every day.' A cautious half-nod and Marston pressed on, 'I would speak with you about your necessities... provisions and suchlike, before we are in contemplation of attending to your intentions, which doubtless will not be clear for some little time to come.' Marston took her hand, squeezed it gently. 'We will face these troubles together... you and I, and... with the blessing and help of our Lord, we will endure. Be sure of that, my dear; have not the least doubt. Our Lord will be with us as we pass these difficult days together, you and I.'

Pat spoke again, 'It is in my intention to introduce to you a shipmate of mine and Mathew's... with your consent... a young man by the name of Mower. He was a particular friend of Mathew aboard the barky; indeed, the two were near inseparable in the latter months of our voyage until... until... that is to say, they were the best of friends; one might say almost like father and son. Mower has declared his wish to visit you, to speak of your husband... when it pleases you.'

Mrs Jelbert looked up to gaze at Pat for the first time since his arrival on the doorstep, 'Captain O'Connor,' she whispered, struggling to get her words out, 'Mr Mower... he was here yesterday evening... he brought the news of... of my husband; he sat with me all night until the dawn... when I tried for rest in my chair. He had not a minute of sleep himself.'

Pat simply stared, the explanation of Mower's absence at supper, the lieutenant invited, was revealed. Marston, still holding Mrs Jelbert's hand, spoke again, 'My dear Emblyn, you must be exceedingly tired, the need for sleep pressing upon you so very hard. I will sit here and keep you company for all of this difficult day. For the moment, I beg you will take this most modest drop of the laudanum which I have with me. I am, when aboard ship, also acting in the capacity of assistant to our esteemed surgeon, Dr Ferguson, and with his blessing I have prepared this liquid dose. Do you care to take it? It will help you sleep, and... my dear... sleep, *deep sleep*, is the most benevolent of all restoratives when we find ourselves in such hours of distress as the present.' Mrs Jelbert nodding cautiously, Marston pressed upon her a tiny flask, 'Here, drink it down, please; it will serve you well. You may gain a trifle of sleep... a little of rest.'

'Mrs Jelbert,' said Pat gently, after she had drunk it, 'I regret I must away today, to Plymouth... a most pressing matter is upon me... I am much dismayed that I cannot linger here... with you. However, Mr Marston ... *Father Marston* will attend you. I beg your pardon but I must be gone. Rest assured I will return to see you as soon as I am able.' Mrs Jelbert nodding, trying for a weak smile, Pat squeezed her hand gently and rose to move to the door, Prosser standing up to see him out.

'Thank you for attending, sir,' whispered Prosser.

'Here, take this,' murmured Pat, retrieving a two-pound note - which plainly had seen better days - from his pocket. He pressed it into Prosser's hand, 'It will serve for Mrs Jelbert's needs for the next few days, perhaps the immediate week ahead. I will visit once again when I return from Devonport.' He stepped out of the door, his thoughts awash with recollections of Mathew Jelbert, the late gunner's face vivid and prominent in his mind as he walked down Hull's Lane in miserable mood, picking up his pace along Arwennack Street as he determined that he must attend to the other matter sitting ill on his mind: *Eleanor* and her whereabouts. He hastened his pace and fairly marched along Market Street towards the Royal Hotel, intending to take the first Plymouth mail coach to leave from the Market Strand.

'I regret, sir,' declared the Royal's John Pearce, 'that you have missed the Plymouth Mail today; it left at seven this morning... and the next one is at seven *tomorrow* morning. It reaches Plymouth at half-past four in the afternoon.'

'Very well, that will have to serve,' Pat sighed gloomily.

The following hours of the morning passed in gloom and building frustration for Pat as he increasingly fretted about what might have become of *Eleanor* and her crew, Duncan prominent in his fears. Time passed so very slowly until, at 11 o'clock, he went to the temporary casualty station that, once again, the Wesleyan Chapel in the Moor had become, to spend a few hours with his wounded shipmates before dinner. He was pleased to find them in good cheer and recovering well in Simon's care.

Saturday 27th August 1825 14:00 The Royal Hotel, Falmouth

Simon had returned from the Chapel with Pat to attend the Royal for their dinner. The surgeon was relieved and grateful that, on the occasion of *Surprise's* second return from Greece, the casualties were neither as many nor as severe as the first time, which had been exceedingly distressing for every man aboard: more than two dozen shipmates having been killed and near three score wounded. Indeed, Simon had for most of the return voyage on that first expedition been near overwhelmed with the severest turn of depression, with grief, and the deepest feelings of personal inadequacy as a physician. Such mental discomforts had never fully dissipated, merely relented to a more tolerable level, one which he had come to terms with at long last.

They sat at the window table staring out at the persons passing along Market Street, coming and going from the Fish Strand Quay, as they waited for their roast beef.

'When are you going to Plymouth Dock?' asked Simon.

'Early on the morrow. There is a coach leaving in the morning from outside the hotel at seven o'clock. With a fair wind I will make Devonport before five in the afternoon; I hope the admiral may be found there on a Sunday... else I will await Monday morning to see him.'

'You are much downcast; I see that plain; should we be worried for *Eleanor* and her men? After all, she preceded our departure from Cephalonia by only two days. Is it not a trifle soon to be concerned? London and back must surely be at least a few days in time... and you have ever laboured to me the caprices of weather and tide.'

Pat stared at his friend, wondering where to start, Simon's grasp of seafaring never one of his strong points, nor indeed even one of his weaker ones. 'She is very fleet of sail... indeed, she can hold two points closer to the wind... can manage at least two knots more than the barky without luffing... on a bowline.'

'This bowline... I have heard you mention it a hundred times or more. Is it so greatly significant?'

No answer came from Pat, his attention entirely engaged as he stared through the window, a lone pedestrian approaching along the street. 'Look! Look there!' exclaimed Pat excitedly, pointing and rising from his chair to press his face to the glass. 'D'ye see who I see?'

Simon rose and stood alongside Pat; he peered through the window, 'By George, it is Peddler!' The pedestrian had by now reached the front door of the hotel and entered without hesitation, mere seconds passing before he came into the dining room. He halted, stared across to Simon and Pat, and hastened across the room, his hand extended, a broad smile on his face.

Pat was perplexed, thrown into confusion. Simon had no hesitations: his oldest friend since childhood, his bosom companion with whom he had grown up in Tobermory, had been lost and was found; indeed, he stood before him. Simon, his fears for his missing friend and all doubts about his integrity being swept away in an instant, seized and pumped Peddler's hand. Pat's handshake was far more hesitant, cautious, his own uncertainties about the character of Peddler not dispelled, but he was prepared to hear him out. The three men settled back at the table, Simon calling the waiter to order a third dinner, Pat requesting a bottle of red wine, preparing himself to hear Peddler's tale and wondering how credible it might be.

The wine arrived nearly immediately, the waiter pouring the first glass until, after a nod from Pat, he moved away. Simon and Pat did not touch their glasses, simply stared at the unexpected arrival and took not the least notice of the waiter, returning to lay out the cutlery, burning curiosity filling their thoughts. It was Peddler himself who began, 'I have but recently returned...' Only silent nods were offered in reply, and he continued, 'It was the most harrowing of experiences...' More nods followed. 'Perkis and I... we were kidnapped... on the quay at Calamata.'

The explanation was made, uttered in all its simplicity: kidnapped! Was it genuine? A perplexed Pat could find no words; his mind was a turmoil of doubt, indecision, uncertainty and calculation: could such conceivably be true? Kidnapped from the quayside only having just arrived, and with two and half tons of gold bars, twenty-four of them, a half-million pounds in value and concealed within iron plating to resemble ship's ballast, kentledge. Was such a story remotely credible? Pat held his tongue, took a deep draught, emptying his wine glass. He refilled without the loss of a moment and continued to stare with the utmost concentration at Peddler's face: was he telling the truth? Was it a lie? For once in his life he could not tell, could not make up his mind, and that unsettled him.

Simon was more gracious by far, speaking to fill the silence, one born of doubt, of scepticism, on Pat's part. 'Allow me to say, dear Benjamin, that I am delighted to see you, I am. To where were you abducted? By whom? For how long? Your escape, your release... pray continue.'

Peddler, the hurdle of trepidation and the doubts about whether his friend would believe him, both seemingly overcome, exhaled a long sigh of relief; he took a large gulp of his own wine, 'I had occasion to meet with Mr Prosser, just this morning on Jacob's Ladder... He was descending as I was half-way up the steps...'

Pat stared: was this irrelevance a diversion? He forced himself to find the minimum of sociability to make at least a half nod; Peddler was casting an anxious glance at Pat's face of fixated scrutiny.

'Mr Prosser declared that your vessel was returned, was here in the harbour... I confess I had not noticed... and that you were staying here at the Royal Hotel. Naturally, I hastened to find you immediately, old friend... and here I am.' A thin, tentative smile escaped Peddler and he looked up just as the waiter arrived with the steaming plates of roast beef.

Sunday 28th August 1825   17:00   *Devonport*

The Royal Mail coach had been exceedingly uncomfortable, near ten hours of jolting on the poor surface of the stony road. One of Pat's three fellow passengers had suffered exceedingly with flatulence, and the coach interior had been the smallest of space to share with such an unpleasant inconvenience, the atmosphere doing nothing for Pat's ruminations, Peddler's story at the forefront of his mind. Fortunately, after reaching Truro at 8:45, the morning had warmed sufficiently for Pat to leave open the coach windows, much to the relief of his fellow passengers, the guilty party never exhibiting the least contrition, and Pat strived to reach his conclusion: was Peddler lying? Precious little further detail had he added to embellish his account before he had hastened away, avowing an urgent attendance elsewhere, though where he did not care to mention. It was something of a small consolation to reflect that Simon had been much cheered to see his boyhood friend. At St. Austell at 11 o'clock, in the rising heat of the summer morning, Pat exchanged with an unknowing passenger with an outside seat, and felt guilty himself for all the three hours to Liskeard where the briefest of stops for a hasty dinner was made, ten minutes only being allowed whilst the sweating horses were changed. Torpoint for the New Passage was reached at 4:30 when a weary, much relieved Pat climbed down from the coach, his back and legs aching interminably. He stepped onto the ferry and waved goodbye to the coach driver. The ferry arrived in Morice Town fifteen minutes later. Stretching his stiff legs and bowing his aching back to aid circulation, to flex stiffened, tensed muscles, he pondered upon making an immediate visit to the port admiral. Despite it being Sunday, he decided that at least an aide might be present who would surely know from where to summon his absent chief - if indeed Saumarez was not to be found at his office. Casting aside his mental turmoil of doubt and indecision, he made his mind up; he rushed at the best speed he could make to present himself to the Devonport Dock Lines sentry. Finding no difficulty with gaining admittance, Pat being recognised by the guard, he marched on swiftly to the Admiral's office atop Mount Wise.

The view overlooking the Hamoaze was quite splendid, the afternoon enduring warm and bright, still three hours to sunset, but Pat gave that no mind at all, consumed with rising apprehension about his men aboard *Eleanor* and exceedingly anxious to speak with Admiral Saumarez as soon as possible. A knock, a few words exchanged, and the porter bade him take a seat in the waiting room, another half-hour slowly passing by as he sat waiting, staring at the diminishing coal fire, its original underpinnings of wood still present, smouldering and smoky. His patience was wearing exceedingly thin and he fretted as his nerves became increasingly on edge. With rising concern, he looked to his hands, noting with dismay that they trembled. Eventually, the Admiral's aide, Lieutenant Hemming, an officer known to Pat, greeted him most cordially and escorted him into the admiral's office. Saumarez himself was perfectly pleasant and apologised for keeping him waiting. The briefest of welcomes and preliminaries were rapidly despatched in monotone as if by rote. Plainly, Saumarez observed, Pat was here with some pressing purpose, presumably one of the utmost importance, judging by his visitor's evident anxiety. The admiral was perfectly aware of *Surprise's* mission to Greece. Saumarez studied Pat's face, staring closely at it whilst waiting.

Pat allowed his impatience to diffuse, his whirling maelstrom of fears and anxious thoughts to settle, as he welcomed the offer of coffee, the strong, bitter taste a divine and immediately successful restorative. A mere few minutes more passed so very slowly as a relaxed but curious Admiral Saumarez waited patiently for Pat to speak. 'Sir,' Pat drained the dregs of his cup and began, '*Surprise* arrived at Falmouth only on Friday but *Eleanor* - you will collect she was my own schooner and served as tender - had preceded her departure from Greece by two days.' The admiral nodded encouragingly and Pat pressed on, 'She is the fleetest of vessels and was bound for London... bearing a most important letter, one sent for His Majesty's government by the Greek authorities. Do you know, sir, is there any news of her arrival in London?'

'Mr Hemming?' Saumarez looked up and across to his aide, listening with great attention. The lieutenant was pleased that he had not been dismissed the room. Saumarez was minded that *Surprise's* endeavours were likely well known all throughout Morice Town by now, particularly after her refit, all the men at the Yard having cheered her departure, and presumably his aide too would have some idea of her purpose.

'None, sir; no news at all has reached us; I am sure that is the case... for I read the telegraph myself each day.'

'Very well,' the admiral paused only momentarily for thought, 'Will you please telegraph to the Admiralty and ask of that vessel... and... Mr Hemming... please to do so immediately; all other communications are to be held in abeyance, and explain in your enquiry that we shall refrain from all other telegraph traffic until we are in receipt of the reply.'

'Yes sir,' Hemming blanched: the telegraph traffic had never before been so suspended; such was simply unheard of. Sensing the gravity, the urgency, of the admiral's wishes, he nodded and turned about, hastening from the office.

'I am, sir, much obliged to you,' declared Pat with obvious relief, having himself come to realise that the admiral had ordered exceptional measures. 'Thank you, sir,' he added, 'I am in your debt.'

'It is not something that I could have contemplated back in Boney's day, O'Connor, oh no, but in the present times, as I understand matters, if His Majesty's Government cares to aid the Greeks... and your letter, as you say, being of the utmost significance, then I am sure it is for the best... such measures are warranted. Now, where are we? You mentioned possessing a copy of this valuable letter. Do you have it with you?'

'It has never left my possession, sir, since receipt of it in Cephalonia. Whether locked in my desk within the cabin or held close to my person. It is presently here, in my jacket.'

'Very good, and your intentions for this letter?'

'Sir, I am minded that it is incumbent upon me to deliver it personally to the First Lord. There can never be any doubt as to its whereabouts, and I do not care to hold it in my possession a minute longer than is necessary. Why, were it to be lost... what would the First Lord think of me?'

'Quite so, I see your conundrum. Allow me to suggest that we await the telegraph and what news may come from London. When we have heard what they care to report, we may take a decision founded on the urgency or otherwise of the situation. Do you agree?'

'That makes a deal of sense, sir,' declared Pat, a little of the sense of oppression, of responsibility, lifting from his mind.

'In the meantime, I am in the way for and about to enjoy my afternoon tea,' said Saumarez in kindly tone. 'You will allow me to say, O'Connor, that you look entirely knocked up; you have quite the palest of face and your eyes are shrunken into black sockets. A modicum of food would serve you well, no doubt at all. Would you care to join me, to partake of a morsel, a bite or two... I have Devon scones and clotted cream... with another pot of coffee perhaps... whilst we await the telegraph?'

'That is most gracious of you, sir; indeed, I would be exceedingly grateful for a bite. Thank you, sir,' murmured Pat with a surging wave of relief, the admiral's kindly words sending a flood tide of release throughout his very being, and Pat realising that he was ravenously hungry, having eaten nothing all day on the coach, Mr Flatulence having dispelled all appetite for the day.

Sunday 28th August 1825   17:30   The Royal Hotel, Falmouth

'After you had landed on the quay with the... *the presumed* gold bullion ingots, how... how... *precisely* were you accosted, dear Benjamin?' asked Simon tentatively, as if skirting any prospect of irritating his friend.

'The *presumed* gold?'

'Did you not know? Let us set that aside for the moment, I will return to that later. Please, continue with your account.'

'Why, we had barely seen Mr Mower withdraw with his men when, out from the shadows... *it was evening*... a more dubious set of ruffians I have never seen... appeared all about us; indeed, bandits might best serve as a description. They were brandishing... in the most intimidating fashion... long, curving blades... and all glaring with the most extreme hostility. Neither Perkis nor I could understand a word of what they shouted at us... but, naturally, the inference... *their meaning* was plain.'

'The inference?'

'Yes, step aside!' Peddler realised he had shouted, the attention of several in the dining room alarmed, and he hushed his voice to a whisper, '... and refuse at the peril of your life. Well, in fear of our lives, we did, and then the gold ingots were loaded upon mules, two dozen of them standing ready... also in the shadows.'

'But how did these.... *these bandits* know of your valuable cargo?'

'I have not the least idea, none whatsoever.'

'Mmmm, please continue.'

'A most brief spell of standing, waiting… in great fear and trepidation… whilst the mules were loaded, and then we were forced to accompany the train, off through the town and so to the hinterland.'

'I see,' murmured Simon, though he did not; the unanswered question was sticking in his mind, a significant mystery for sure. He drained his coffee cup, paused for thought for a minute, Peddler similarly sipping his own. 'After your... *your exodus* from the town, what then?'

'We were marched... *marched* into the hills for some considerable distance, miles it was... several days of brutal whipping... until we reach the most remote, the most desolate place I think I have ever experienced, rocks and crags abounding all about us... and we were accommodated within a cave.'

'You were released eventually or was there an escape?'

'Oh, I doubt there was any intention to release us, no, none at all, and Perkis suggested that were we to linger in that place then our murder was assured.' Peddler waved to the waiter. 'No, he suggested we endeavour to escape... and without delay.' The waiter arrived and Peddler spoke up, 'I am minded to take a brandy, a large one, if you please. Simon, dear friend... *old friend*, will you care for a libation? I confess...'

'You confess?' said Simon with a start: was the truth about to be revealed?

'I confess that the recounting of this dreadful experience is a burden, a taxing one indeed.'

'I see; well, perhaps I will take a sherry with you; yes, a sherry.' The waiter hastened away.

'At the coming of the third night... when we halted at last... we could not march another step; our feet were bleeding, our boots worn out... the bandits were drunk and sleeping after celebrations. We shifted out of the cave with the utmost caution and climbed the hillside as rapidly as could be, not the least idea of direction, and in the moonlight... *and precious little there was of that*... we kept going, on and on, never daring to halt, not looking back, mile after weary further mile, fleeing, until our feet refused another step. In the morning we sat for hours with them in the water of a stream, red raw, bleeding and swollen, in constant fear of the bandits catching up... but no, we never saw them again. We presumed that they had contented themselves with the precious treasure.'

243

The plate of scones had been eaten and another pot of coffee consumed when Hemming returned to the admiral's office. His bleak, grim face foretold the news, of which there was none, 'No report, sir, of the schooner's arrival anywhere on the Thames, nothing; most certainly no sighting in the Pool of London... and no one has reported to either the Admiralty or the Customs Quay. Neither, to the knowledge of the clerks at Admiralty House, has there been any report of her arrival in any other port.'

Pat gasped; his heart sank like a stone. His hopes were crushed in the bleakest of instants, hopes which he had nurtured for some time despite his better judgement, and his spirits returned to painful turmoil, to racing tremulation: was Duncan lost? Was it the case that one of his two closest friends in all the world was gone for ever, and with all of *Eleanor's* crew? He could say nothing in that bleak moment of utter despair and his mind was filled with the most crushing disappointment, far greater than he had ever known before.

'Thank you, Mr Hemmings,' declared Saumarez in gloomy voice, a long minute passing in total silence before he spoke to his aide again, 'I venture this calls for something a trifle stronger whilst we consider our position, Captain O'Connor possessing a letter which must go to London without the loss of a moment. Would you care to send word to prepare my cutter... and please to ask my steward to fetch a bottle of brandy, if you will. Thank you.' The admiral turned towards Pat, 'This is undoubtedly the most disappointing of news... Doubtless you will wish to take a moment to consider of your intentions.'

'I do not believe, sir... that... that...' Pat choked back his deep despair, struggled for a few seconds to find his words, fought hard within his racing thinking to set aside for just the immediate moment his fears for Duncan, for *Eleanor* and all her men. He forced his mind back to the urgency of the Greek letter. 'Sir, it is not in my contemplation to depart aboard your cutter. I am minded that we cannot entrust any vessel with the safety of this important communication; no, I venture... *I regret* I must take to the road.'

'Mr Hemming!' the admiral shouted, his aide entering immediately. 'Forget *Bramble*, Captain O'Connor will take a coach. Please endeavour to determine the departure times for London without the least delay... AND...' to the door closing behind a hasty Hemming, '... MR HEMMING!' The lieutenant reappeared. 'Please to arrange suitable accommodations for Captain O'Connor for tonight; *suitable*, that is, for the London coach as early as can be on the morrow.'

'Yes sir,' Hemming nodded and exited again. The steward entered, no words necessary, the ambience within the room obviously grim. He set down the tray and looked to Saumarez who dismissed him with a meaningful nod.

The admiral poured two generous measures and passed one to Pat. 'Here, please take this. I have found, myself, in past times that it steadies the nerves in such dire circumstances.' He offered a grim smile, Pat silent, obviously despondent and deep in thought. Nothing from Pat after another minute, Saumarez spoke again, 'I venture to suggest that, despite no news of your vessel... of your shipmates, it remains feasible... *entirely feasible* that they have fetched up upon some remote shore on the other side of the Channel and are, even now, striving to make their way home.'

Pat looked up, stared at the admiral, the man patently striving to assist him in the only way he could. 'Thank you, sir,' he murmured.

'After all, there ain't been any reports of storms either in the Bay or the Approaches, nothing of note, not a thing out of the ordinary... beyond the humdrum, no; and it seems to me that your man... Macleod was it? ... your First... was a perfectly capable officer; indeed, I have some notion, some recollection from reading the Gazette, that he was recently promoted Captain. Was that not the case?'

'He was, sir, yes; and - *for sure* - well deserved it was.'

'Good, then there *is* certainly *no doubt*; we will await news before we cast all our hopes overboard, eh, O'Connor?'

Pat found the admiral's words helpful, of some little cheer, and he endeavoured to allow the welcome theory to lodge within his conscious thinking; no, there had been no storms, none had been experienced by *Surprise* herself as she crossed the Bay, merely the dense fog which had been so inclement as she passed Cape St. Vincent. The admiral was quite correct. The slender hope firming within him, he looked again to Saumarez and lifted his brandy glass; his anxieties a very little diminished, he strived for a steady voice, 'Here's to you, sir; a long life!'

'Thank you, I take that very kindly. Here's our best wishes for your shipmates, O'Connor. May they be safe and well!'

'Thankee, sir; I wish that of all things, I do.'

Sunday 28th August 1825   18:30   The Royal Hotel, Falmouth

Simon was sipping his third sherry and finding his friend's tale fascinating. He gently prompted Peddler, 'And so, you had escaped... Please do go on. Here you are in Falmouth...'

'Yes indeed, and never more grateful in my life have I been than the moment I espied the town from the deck of the ship on which we arrived. It was a merchantman... brought us from Genoa. We had formerly escaped from the Greek mainland aboard a small sailing vessel, fishermen it was; they smuggled us - in the dark of the night to avoid the quarantine - to one of the more remote of the Ionians, to Cerigo...'

'Ahhh, Kythira.'

'Indeed, and from there a passing Austrian merchantman, taking on fresh water, conveyed us to Genoa.'

'Where is your friend Perkis?'

'He has gone to Exeter, to transact some business of a financial nature.'

'I see. Well, dear Benjamin, old friend, allow me to congratulate you on your miraculous escape from dea... from danger; I give you joy of your return to Falmouth.'

'Thank you kindly. I hope so very much that we may see greatly more of each other in the weeks and months ahead.'

'As do I, but you are to note that it is in my thinking to return to our birthplace, to Tobermory, before the winter. I have some duties to attend to... here, the wounded... for some weeks yet... and then I will be gone.'

'Well, here's Hemming. Let's see what he has arranged,' declared Admiral Saumarez, Pat feeling a little more relaxed, the admiral having inflicted grave depletions upon the brandy; deliberately so, thought Pat, though he had never demurred.

'Sir, I have arranged a room for Captain O'Connor at Elliott's Royal Hotel and an inside seat on *The Celerity* coach, departing at 6AM.'

'Very good, Mr Hemming, and that reaches London when?' asked Saumarez.

'At 8:30AM the following morning, sir, at the *Swan with Two Necks*.'

'Thank you; would you please ask my cook to set supper in train? I dare say Captain O'Connor might be minded to join me.'

'Thank you, sir; that is most gracious of you,' murmured Pat.

It had been the most momentous few days for Simon. The rediscovery of his old friend, Peddler, had been the most welcome event and entirely unexpected, for he harboured essentially not the least hope of seeing him ever again. He had given little credence to Duncan's reporting of the possible sighting of Peddler, supposedly in remote Genoa; no, Simon had concluded many weeks beforehand that he would never see him again, and that had been profoundly dismaying. Few boyhood friends stuck in his mind, very few; perhaps just one or two others from the earliest years of his youth; indeed, he could think of none with whom he had been so close as Peddler had been, and for all the years until maturity, when the two close friends, brothers in all but name, had parted to go their different ways. He sat on his bed at the hotel, pondering many and varied aspects of his life. His mind shifted to the uncertainty about *Eleanor*: had he regained one friend, one from the past, only to lose his dear friend of the present? Had that really come about? If such was really so, what could he offer to Duncan's wife, Kathleen? What might he say to that sweet child, young Brodie?

247

His thoughts shifted to a memory of saying farewell to her in the great cabin, off Gibraltar, on the eventful return voyage when *Surprise* had been so smashed by the hurricane. Fortunately, the families of Pat and Duncan had both boarded the schooner for the Bay crossing, *Eleanor* arriving safely several days before *Surprise*. He recalled that he had given Duncan's daughter the tiny Saint Christopher Celtic cross on a silver necklace which had belonged to his deceased wife, Agnes, the memory starting a tiny trickle of tears in his eyes. He rubbed them dry with his shirt sleeve and decided upon re-reading the first of the letters received from Tobermory, from Flora, a further small bundle of which had been awaiting his return. He had not written to her in reply recently, believing a perfect understanding of her feelings and the essential messages within her letters to be a prior essential, and so he determined that he must study all of Flora's letters once more, including the ones which had reached him in Cephalonia, before writing any further reply. He opened his tiny baggage chest, took out the precious first letter with a frisson of anxiety melded with something else, something undefinable, and he began to read,

My dear Simon,

I did not receive your letter my dearest until today. It is a week after your leaving Falmouth. I am writing in haste before I must away to church. Of course, your twenty pounds not having reached here this past week I could not send the papers and monies which you promised to Mr Salmon but they will be posted in the mail on the morrow for Oban. I have also received a letter from Mr Salmon today. He is inquiring after you and his rent to come.

I have found the tin box of your medicines here as you directed, and shall dispense its contents to your patients only as you have stated and await your further instructions. Mr MacKinnon will not have a boat bound for Jura to carry his medicines for a fortnight or three weeks, when he expects to have some sooner. He will doubtless complain again and request that I attend to your directions about his potions.

Mrs MacKinnon went with Mr Muir to Oban yesterday to fetch home poor Hamish McAdam. She says in a few days longer it is her opinion he could not have been moved, so I hope your medicine will prove of some use to him.

Mrs McGill wants two boxes of salts of Lemon.

Mrs MacCorkindale wants a bottle of the drops of Laudanum and two pints of your Healing Tincture.

I cannot omit telling you that the house roof is again leaking, and that the depredations of the incoming water at times of great rain is most rapid upon your front wall and floor — I shall walk over to the quay in the morning to speak of this with Mrs MacKinnon for she is the most helpful of souls and much laments your departure.

I observe despite mine and the girls' endeavours the black mould is beginning to spread, and Annag has kept it constantly scrubbed with water and salt during this warm Spring weather.

I have entrusted some small pieces of Linen I bought in Oban last week to the mail - hoping they will find you. If you take the trouble of looking for, and comparing this Linen with your present Shirts, perhaps you might be tolerably able to judge that new ones will be particularly desirable. I will make them and my cousin can procure it - the linen - beautiful for 4/- and 5/- per yard but advises me to wait a little until the seasonal summer cloth will reach Oban next month when a lower price might be obtained - for so she believes.

I think the ring that you sent to me is beautiful. It came quite safely. We are all in great admiration of it and I do not want anything more, either for myself or the bairns. Should we find a shortcome in our monies on another occasion, I am minded that Mr Salmon will become intolerant and may remonstrate with me. He has managed politeness in all our dealings until the last one when I was unable to pay his rent. Your letter and the twenty pounds you sent will remedy his concerns I am sure.

I am so happy to think you have found pleasure once more in the company of your longstanding companions aboard the vessel Surprise. I hope that my letter finds you well and with your friends in good heart.

The Children are quite well, but any expression or any fear that you may not return for a considerable time - or worse, melts Annag into a passion of tears, as she says 'she misses you so very much'. Rhona is too reserved to allow herself - at least with me - to be discomposed by such conversation.

I am greatly better since about the twelfth of this month after the illness - I do not care to burden you with it in my letter - but far from nimble.

I beg you will take great care in all your undertakings.

Until my next letter, my dearest, believe of me your truly affectionate admirer.

Flora MacDougall

Tobermory 22 April 1825

Simon poured himself a glass of port wine from a bottle secured from Murphy's predations within his baggage, a warming beverage to which he had much taken to of late. He focused upon the letter: *"my dearest"* was an exceedingly welcome turn of phrase, but then it did not - to his mind - sit so well with *"your truly affectionate admirer"*. Was that an inconsistency of wording or of feeling? He did not know. What *was* clear to him was the loss of his heart to her, and never before had he felt so inadequate: an impoverished and unassuming, plain man of modest stature, no pretensions of being handsome, ever the unruly dresser and never the least thought towards more fashionable demeanour. The ring had been appreciated - that was plain - but Flora had actually said nothing more about it; why was that? He re-read her letter for the third time in its entirety, the mention of illness striking a deeply worrying concern within his heart, a painful recollection of losing his wife to consumption striking him hard, and that it had happened whilst he was away at sea hurt him even now, after all these years. He desperately hoped that Flora had not contracted that awful disease. The mention within the letter of the damp and the mould flashed to mind and started a fresh turmoil in his thoughts. He must remedy the roof and without the least delay, but where to find the money? His account was not in great funds;

precious little, in fact, did he possess, but it might just see him through until the Admiralty paid at least something for the months spent in Greece. He sipped his port wine and resolved to put such thoughts and his reply to Flora aside for the moment. Perhaps in the morning, after he had returned from the Chapel in the Moor attending his patients, he would read the other letters again and, he hoped, all would help shape his reply.

Monday 29th Aug. 1825 06:00   Elliott's Royal Hotel, Devonport

Pat looked all about him: the horses' breath was steaming, the guard and driver were fussing with last minute matters, remonstrating with the final passenger about the stowing of his baggage. Stern faces indicated their anxiety and a wish to avoid the least further delay. He passed his small overnight bag to the guard for the roof and stepped up to his cramped seat within the coach, looking anxiously all about him to his fellow passengers, not caring for a repeat of the discomfort inflicted upon him on the Royal Mail coach from Falmouth: had they all breakfasted well? The sausage had been greatly tasty but, he reminded himself, that was generally so when it was high in fat. He hoped that his three companions, who nodded to him affably as he settled back within the padded bench, had refrained with similar and parsimonious zeal, having eaten just the four himself with his eggs and bacon: a quite modest breakfast when he was at sea; at least Pat thought so. He consoled himself with the small solace that at least the morning would soon warm, when the coach windows might be left open. He reached into his inside pocket to confirm to himself for the tenth time since rising that the all-important letter was still there. Not a minute more passed - after all, Pat reminded himself, this was *The Celerity* - and the guard blew his horn, the driver cracked his whip and, with a lurch, the coach started, the springs creaking in loud protest and the wheels click-clacking over the rough cobbles with small jolts shaking Pat's seat. They were off! In little more than twenty-four hours, most assuredly uncomfortable ones, he would find himself in London town and seeking out the First Lord.

'Ah, Marston, Jason, there you are,' declared Simon in cheerful voice as he strode down the side aisle towards the beds where the last remaining wounded crew members were accommodated. Only three men remained, the most severely wounded, and they were due to be shifted to their homes this day, a party of their shipmates expected imminently to aid their relocation. 'I hope I see you both well?'

'Thank you,' declared the two assistant surgeons in turn, Marston adding, 'Mr Prosser is expected within the hour with a half-dozen lads to aid the move.'

'Excellent, then I will look to our patients. Pascoe! How do you fare this fine morning? How is the leg?' asked Simon with a visibly enthusiastic countenance. Pascoe had nearly lost the leg to grapeshot, Simon's skilful surgery and dedicated aftercare preserving it through many weeks of the most doubtful prognosis and difficult recovery.

'All is well, sir, 'tis mended mighty fine,' Pascoe positively glowed, the anticipation of departing his sick bed a beatific stimulant.

'I will attend you these next few weeks. You are to endeavour for the shortest of walk each day... I do say *short*, do you hear?'

'Yes, sir, I will do so... and thankee, sir.'

Simon nodded; for the first time he allowed himself to feel the smallest sense of triumph, of personal gratification; Pascoe's leg - a worry for a long time - was beyond danger at long last, and he allowed himself, to only the tiniest degree, to accept the smallest feeling of rejoicing. He smiled at his patient, the expression a tiny reflection of his feelings enduring every minute since his breakfast, another of Flora's letters delivered by the Royal Mail coach. He moved on to his next patient. 'Hocking, a pleasure to see you on such a glorious day as we have. The chest is healing well, I find, eh?'

'Aye and the breathing is easing every day, sir, it is so.' The *Damnation* gunner had been struck particularly hard by a deeply embedded splinter, his life hanging by the slenderest of threads as *Surprise* escaped the Bay of Navarino.

'Take it steady; you are not to indulge in any exercise, not the least... and for some time to come... save for a walk to the table... and the seat of ease. Am I plain?'

'Aye aye, sir.'

Simon moved on to the last of the three. 'George Rowe, and how do I find you this fine morning?' The gunner smiled wide, great pleasure in his face. Simon resumed, 'Well then, I am minded that you will not be pitching up at Heaven's Gate for some time to come; rather, you will be at home... with your good lady wife and in time for dinner. What do you say to that?'

'Hah! Hah! Very funny, sir, thankee,' said the gunner, *Heaven's Gate* being his gun. 'I am mighty happy, sir, I am so; thankee kindly.' Marston and Jason both smiled, the gunner's evident pleasure was infectious.

'How is the hip? Can you stand?'

'Aye sir, 'tis still plentifully painful, and I do not care to think of hauling out the gun for some time, but I am able to walk... at least a short ways.'

'Well done. I will prescribe laudanum for the next few weeks; I am minded that thirty drops will serve, twice a day, and you are to endeavour to walk. A hundred paces a day will be plentiful. Is that clear?'

'Perfectly, sir. That will suit me just fine; I venture I will make the Fish Strand and take a seat there for the morning and watch the boats all day; aye, so I will.'

'Excellent, and you are to rest if ever it proves too much, at least these next few weeks. Now, here, drink this down; it will serve you well when Mr Prosser and his men shift you to your home in a little while. Rest as best you can until then.'

'Thankee sir,' said Rowe with an infinity of gratitude, lying back on his bed, Simon's constant care the support that had tided him over the fearful and deeply painful wound also inflicted at Navarino.

A noise from the door and Prosser entered with his men, all stepping promptly towards the patients and bearing stretchers.

'Good morning, Mr Prosser,' declared Simon in welcoming voice, 'It pleases me to say that all three of these men may be shifted. Most carefully, mind you. None is to walk.'

'Very well, sir.'

'Marston, Jason and I will each accompany one of them, see to their accommodations and attend them for an hour until dinner. None are to be anywhere other than on the ground floor, stairs may certainly not be contemplated for any of them.'

Tuesday 30th August 1825   08:30   *Piccadilly, London*

An hour late, a lame horse forcing a delay before Salisbury, and the coach limped in to reach the *Black Horse* where the ostlers rushed to effect a rapid change of team. Pat stepped wearily from his seat within the coach, welcoming an end to the discomfort and torture of unremittingly poor roads, with never more than a ten minutes stop as horses were changed. He had dozed through the blackness of the early hours but never gained sleep proper, his companions' awareness and excitability of reaching the metropolis waking him shortly after the dawn. Tired, he stretched every one of his aching muscles, thanked Saint Patrick to the high heavens that his companions had been of a quiet persuasion, thanked Jesus and Mary even more gratefully that none of them had exhibited the flatulence of the dreadful passenger on his journey from Falmouth to Devonport, and he yawned and shook his head. The guard passed down his small bag which Pat set down on the cobbles. He gave both the driver and the guard a shilling each, for which they thanked him with cordial restraint. He wondered briefly if he should have tipped more, but then they were gone, the driver cracking his whip and the coach pressing on towards its final destination at the *Swan with Two Necks* on Lad Lane. Thirsty, he stared into the windows of the *Gloucester Coffee House*, the appeal of a delectable hot coffee near overwhelming all other considerations, and he pondered briefly whether he might there indulge his desire for much needed rest and refreshment; indeed, Pat thought long and hard about such, for the appeal of breakfast was strong, his desire for coffee stronger; but no, he decided he must step out as quickly as he could for the Admiralty. He picked up his bag and reluctantly turned away to walk down St James's Street, his legs protesting and his dry throat inflicting torture upon him. He turned left into Pall Mall and, his aching legs relenting, another five minutes brought him to the Admiralty.

The uneven courtyard cobbles giving his weary leg muscles further discomfort, Pat gratefully entered the waiting room where the familiar face of Old Tom, the long-serving porter, looked at him with surprise. 'Are you expected, sir? Why, 'tis Captain O'Connor! Good morning to you! Come in... please... do take a seat, sir. It is good to see you again. Here, please to sit down. May I ask your business... I have no appointment listed for you today, sir?'

'Good morning, Tom,' said Pat, managing a weak smile in return for Old Tom's warm and genuine welcome, for they had known each other since Pat had first attended in the early days of his career; indeed, on reflection Pat had recollections of attending as a very junior lieutenant. 'I confess I have no appointment, no, but I bear a letter of the utmost importance which may be consigned only to the First Lord himself, no other may see it.'

'Very well, sir. If you care to be seated... through there...' Old Tom pointed to the small ante-chamber, the waiting room for the First Lord, '... in there, sir, the bosun's chair if you please, and I will endeavour to bring this to his attention. He has a most busy morning before him, his first visitor is expected in little more than a few minutes; you may have to wait for some time.'

'That is no matter. I shall await his pleasure.'

Old Tom stared at Pat, a memory of his own coming to mind, a recollection of Pat gifting him a gold two pound coin after his last visit. He brightened, spoke up with warm benevolence in his voice, 'Would you care for tea? No, I collect coffee it is! I shall fetch it shortly, sir.'

'Thankee, Tom; that would be heavenly.' Pat entered the small chamber, the bosun's chair as it was called since time immemorial; he recollected his last visit, the First Lord himself explaining his mission to Greece, its covert nature, the first mention of *HMS Surprise*. The proposed return to sea after years ashore had certainly been welcome, but he had been confounded utterly by the bizarre nature of the commission, not an official one, nothing to be said about it to any others - save for his crew and then only when they were at sea. Early May of 'twenty-three it had been, and he reflected on the many and varied experiences since then, two and a half years on; his thoughts wandered to the battles fought: they were bloody, desperate hours which he would never forget. He recalled once more, quite vividly even now, the faces of lost shipmates, his mind tumbling to a distressing recollection of the last ghastly few minutes of Old Mathew Jelbert on the quarterdeck, for that had scarred him, had burned the memory of those horrific moments within his mind for ever, of that he was sure; and then his thoughts turned to more immediate worries: what had happened to *Eleanor*? Where was his friend Duncan and his shipmates, including young Codrington?

The squeak of the door on its hinges interrupted his fretting and Old Tom returned, 'Here is your coffee, sir. His Lordship is aware you are waiting.'

'Thankee, Tom, I am obliged to you,' murmured Pat in grateful voice, the coffee aroma a perfect delight.

Fifteen minutes passed as Pat allowed himself the most modest beginnings of mental relaxation, the aches in his legs and his back greatly easing as he sat back in the upholstered red leather chair, sipping his second cup with infinite pleasure, and then, 'Captain O'Connor, sir,' Old Tom reappeared, 'the First Lord will see you now.'

Pat's pulse raced in an instant and all his small vestiges of relaxation were dispelled in a flash. He nodded and rose to follow the porter, up the stairs and so to Melville's office.

Lord Melville rose from his chair behind his desk and stepped around it to offer Pat his hand, 'Good morning, Captain O'Connor; I hope I see you well?'

'Thank you, sir,' Pat shook hands.

'Please, do take a seat. I have the busy morning of the year before me, Admiral Harvey is already awaiting my attentions -

and I do not care to leave that particular man waiting for long, no indeed!' Melville laughed, 'Heaven forbid, he might call next time with the duelling pistols... You know of Eliab Harvey... of *Temeraire* at Trafalgar? I collect he gave even Nelson a deal of trouble on that occasion, getting ahead of *Victory*, eh?'

Pat nodded but did not care to reply, Harvey was a noted firebrand, even in retirement, but he recalled that Collingwood himself had spoken well of Harvey's efforts at Trafalgar, and that was no small praise, *Temeraire* being struck hard in the battle and giving a fine account of herself.

'And there is a brace of senior captains due at any moment. Well, O'Connor, what brings you here? Pray tell. Naturally, news of your ship's return to Falmouth has reached me via the telegraph... and was there not some enquiry in these recent days from Saumarez down there at Devonport? Indeed, I gather that he ordered the telegraph silenced whilst awaiting our reply! Mmmm, most irregular, eh? Oh, d'ye care for tea, coffee?'

'Thank you, no, sir; I have been obliged by Tom, downstairs.' Without further ado and conscious that his time would be short, likely very short, Pat launched into his imperatives, 'Sir, *Surprise* is returned but her tender, the schooner *Eleanor*, has not, and that is of great concern... Captain Macleod and his men are missing with her.'

'That is a matter of regret... of concern... indeed it is,' murmured Melville with genuine sympathy, 'but I hardly think that such merits your visit... O'Connor... Plainly I can do nothing.' The First Lord paused to study his visitor, Pat's face betraying a deal of anguish. He resumed in more gentle voice, 'Was there not some mention of a letter, an important letter?'

'Yes sir. The letter was sent from Cephalonia aboard *Eleanor*, she being fleeter than *Surprise*... and it was only since fetching home to Falmouth that I discovered that she had never arrived, neither there nor in London... and no sign of her in Devonport. Hence Admiral Saumarez... I mentioned the letter to him... made enquiries of the telegraph.'

'I see, well that would seem to be perfectly well-intentioned, no doubt... but, this letter... what is the nature of it?'

'It is from the provisional Greek government, your Lordship, and of the contents I have no personal knowledge. I am acquainted... no more... with Prince Mavrocordato, who requested of Captain Macleod that he convey the letter to His Majesty's Government...'

'Yes, yes,' Melville interrupted, time pressing, 'but the letter... you said it was aboard the schooner... and she has not returned...'

'I possess a copy, sir, hence my visit. I do not care to presume upon the Foreign Secretary, albeit he is my distant cousin, and thought it appropriate to deliver it to you, sir.'

'Quite proper, O'Connor... Well, *where is it?*'

'Here 'tis, sir,' Pat extracted the letter from his inside pocket and passed it to Melville who stared at it for a long minute, unopened, his mind wholly focused on the implications.

Pat sat, his task done, but no satisfaction found in Melville's understandable comment on *Eleanor*. He knew he could expect nothing more. He racked his brain to think of the slightest thing he might suggest, but no ideas came to mind.

Melville rang the bell on his desk, and Pat concluded that his time was up, his dismissal coming, nothing more to be said.

Old Tom knocked and entered the room, and Melville looked up, 'Pray advise Admiral Harvey that I regret I will be unable to see him this morning, and likely not all day... Perhaps on the morrow? Will you look to my diary and see when the Admiral can be accommodated?' declared Melville, 'And, of course, do convey my regrets and apologies... *my profound and sincere apologies* to the Admiral, but... please to inform him... a matter of the utmost importance and urgency has come to my attention, a matter which I must bring to the attention of His Majesty's Government *and without the least delay.*'

'Yes sir,' mumbled Old Tom, looking shocked, for the First Lord to turn away a visiting admiral was simply unheard of, had never happened before in living memory, and he had himself served at the Admiralty for a long time, forty years and more.

'Come, O'Connor, I venture this matter demands that we step out immediately to see the Foreign Secretary... without the least delay.' With that, Melville seized his coat, retrieved the letter which he consigned to his inside pocket and beckoned Pat to follow him. At the bottom of the stairs they heard a beleaguered Old Tom being berated by an indignant Admiral Sir Eliab Harvey, and Melville turned away, hastening down the corridor towards another door, no intention of losing a moment to his irate visitor.

Chapter Eleven

Tuesday 30th August 1825, 10:30   Gloucester Court, Brompton

Lord Melville and Pat stepped out of the Hansom cab at the private residence of the Foreign Secretary. They were admitted immediately by the servant before being greeted by a solicitous Mr Lowrey, George Canning's aide, who escorted them without delay to the study. Canning, sitting at his desk, was much surprised to see the First Lord accompanied by his own cousin. He rose immediately, shook hands with both men and sent the servant for refreshments.

'Sir,' offered Melville, 'I beg you will forgive our intrusion, unannounced as it is, but Captain O'Connor has arrived in London only this morning and bears a most important letter, one for your attention alone.' He set down the letter on the desk.

'Lord Melville, it is certainly no intrusion; please give it no mind, not the least.' Canning turned to his cousin with a wide smile, 'Why, Patrick... the man himself! How good it is to see you again, dear cousin! Give you joy of your return! I trust you will afford me a few hours this evening to tell me all about your adventures?'

'Thank you, sir; I will be at your service.'

'Excellent. Gentlemen, if you will allow me a brief moment, I will look to this letter before we resume.' Canning broke the seal and opened the letter. He stared silently at it for several minutes, his face frozen into a severe scrutiny, an absolute concentration. 'Well,' he pronounced after five minutes, 'you were correct as to the importance of this letter, no doubt of that in the slightest... In fact, it must go immediately to the Prime Minister. I am not able to speak of the contents save that it is a matter for the highest authority to consider.' He looked to his aide, waiting impassively near the door. 'Mr Lowrey, please to summon a cab without delay. It is my intention to go directly to Downing St.' He turned back to his visitors, 'Gentlemen, we have a few minutes, that is all, and perhaps, Patrick, in that time you will tell me a little of how this Greek affair is proceeding? I ask no detail, merely your general impressions, if you will. It may be pertinent to my meeting with the Prime Minister.'

'Sir, the war is going exceedingly badly for the Greeks. On land they fight on, much as irregulars do, in the mountains, but never possessing of any military advantage and unable to dislodge Turk garrisons. The Greeks endure because they are able to resupply such towns and fortresses... where they do hold out... by sea, Admiral Miaoulis and his comrades providing sustenance and support which cannot reach the Greeks by land. However, at sea the Greeks can no more defeat the Turks than they can on land, for their vessels are no match for the Ottoman fleet, which possesses of many more and larger ships... with heavier guns. The Greeks gain victories only by their use of fireships alone, nothing more do they have to offer against the Turk fleet. They are saved, the Greeks that is, by the woeful Turk gunnery; indeed, such has also been the saving of my own ship.'

'Will they endure? *Can they*, indeed, endure?' Canning's enquiry was made with keen interest.

'Sir, the Greeks possess only brigs. They are converted merchantmen for the most part; and they are in need of heavier vessels - frigates and the like. Only with such can they consider of fighting the Turks, fighting - that is - in the accepted sense that any Royal Navy admiral might contemplate: not with fireships but with superior gunnery, with plentiful training *and with heavier guns*. The Greeks lack for all those things.'

'Lord Melville, are such things in prospect for the Greeks - better ships most particularly? I beg you will enlighten me... as far as you may know, for this letter will doubtless provoke the Prime Minister's most attentive interest, and such will include, *I have no doubt*, seeking such information.'

'Sir, the Admiralty is aware that the Greeks have sought to order new frigates off the stocks in New York. Doubtless you know that all English yards are prohibited from selling any armed vessel to them... a matter of politics and neutrality...' Melville did not expand on that, unsure as to what he might be allowed to say in Pat's presence. 'However, the contractors, Bayard and Howland, have indicated that their original quote for these two ships... fifty thousand pounds for each vessel was the figure... is being *re-evaluated*...' Melville's emphasis on the last word was spoken as if it was really a euphemism, '... and, so my agents tell me, the contractors are minded to increase this to a hundred thousand pounds per frigate.'

'The rogues!' Pat could not contain his disgust, 'Why that is monstrous... damnable profiteering!'

Melville said nothing but his face exhibited his agreement, a dour scowl lingering for several moments. Canning was more politely circumspect, 'I have little experience in such matters... but a doubling of price for any purchase hardly seems equitable... Indeed, it most certainly does not.'

Lowrey looked in again to announce that the cab was ready. 'Please forgive me, gentlemen, I must away. Lord Melville, doubtless the Prime Minister will wish to avail himself of your advice in the matter of the Greeks and their requirements for warships. I am minded that he may call for you later this day.' Melville nodded and Canning resumed, 'Cousin Patrick, it is in my thinking that I will return this evening for a late supper... *a very late supper*. In the meantime, my servant will make up the guest bedroom for you, and there will certainly be plentiful food in the larder to eat as you may care to choose. I hope you will avail yourself of it... the food and the bedroom.'

'Thank you, sir, most kind,' murmured Pat, a little overcome to be in such exalted company - the Foreign Secretary and the First Lord concurrently - and his personal opinion sought; indeed, this was turning out to be quite the day.

Friday 2nd September 1825 13:30 The Royal Hotel, Falmouth

'When did you return?' asked Simon of Pat as his friend sat at the table. 'You look exceedingly tired.'

'I am so... I believe it was about 7 o'clock this morning. I have been sleeping in my room until just now, until the hunger of the world set upon me. I left London on the Wednesday evening Mail, hastening back to see if there had been any news of Duncan... of *Eleanor*, nothing being known of them in London.'

'I regret to say that neither is there any news here,' replied Simon with a long sigh. 'Is there any hope for them, Pat... after all this time?'

'Admiral Saumarez was minded that they may have been shipwrecked... or at least *Eleanor* damaged... There were no storms in the Bay at the time, or perhaps they may have set into a port along the way... for repairs... in Portugal, Spain or France.' This did not sound convincing, even to Pat himself, and Simon's gloomy face did not dissuade him from that opinion; it was more than two weeks since the schooner might have been expected to make home. Her prospects did not look good. 'How are our lads?' asked Pat, seeking to change the subject and refusing to contemplate the worst.

'All are well; they have gone to their homes to complete their recovery. I am minded that every man will do so. Perhaps it is time for me to contemplate taking the Mail myself and returning to Mull? However, I will attend my patients for a week or two longer. You may call me pedantic if you will.'

'I was thinking more along the lines of *romantic*,' declared Pat, 'After all, there is a certain interest for you in Mull... is there not? ... And how, might I ask, are such things coming along, eh?'

'It is still in my intentions to ask for the lady's hand,' said Simon with a smile. 'Her more recent letters indicate nothing of a... *will I say*... discouraging note.'

'That is very good news, brother... the most splendid news indeed. I congratulate you... I do. How do you feel... in yourself? I was minded of our tribulations... our difficulties... in Greece; that is to say, *towards the end*.'

'I am sure I have great cause for thankfulness for... for likely gaining a new family... and a prospective wife that is goodness itself, with two healthy children that... with her care and her gracious example... can scarce fail to be like her. All my troubles in Greece seem light indeed when I look to blessed Tobermory and consider how well I am rewarded in finding them... so late in life... and after losing my beloved... *my dearest* Agnes... Flora is

Agnes come back to me... she is so. I marvel in that thought, I do. Indeed, it has sustained me in terrible moments.'

'I am mighty pleased to hear that and I rejoice in your good fortune... in your happiness, old friend.'

'What of yourself and our *Dear Surprise*? She has looked a forlorn soul these past days, near deserted out there, Mr Mower and Mr Pickering fretting about her damages. I collect, when they attended the Chapel before our patients vacated, there was some mention of Griping, of Spankers and Bumkins... or perhaps that was the infernal Bowline again?'

Pat smiled; plainly Pickering, the ship's jester, had been making fun of his friend, 'Oh, the barky... as for that, she must go to the Yard, to Devonport, for her necessary repairs; nowhere else will serve for that. I am minded that we will depart for that place before too long. First, I have every intention of seeking out a schooner or perhaps cutter to repla... *to stand in* for *Eleanor*, such that we may go to and fro Devonport without the cursed Mail coach. I am quite done with the infernal coach... thirty-four hours of assured discomfort from London. No, enough of that damnable carriage; it is the sea for me, *my world*, and a blessed boat for all travel. Will we look to a drink and then a bite, eh? What d'ye say to a bottle of port wine?'

'I would like it of all things.'

'Well, what other news is there?'

'Doubtless you collect meeting my friend Peddler... before you left for London... here in this room?'

'I do indeed,' replied Pat in dubious tone.

'He has provided a... a *fuller* explanation of... of the events in Calamata... the disappearance of the gold.'

'I see.' This was spoken in greatly doubtful voice. 'Fuller?'

'Yes. You will recall that he avowed that they were kidnapped...'

'Kidnapped... *Really*, Simon; do I look like I believe in the leprechauns?'

'There is, perhaps, a... *a modicum* of... of *possibility* in his explanation. Will you not grant him that?'

'And perhaps he also told you that the gold was hidden in a pot... and at the end of the rainbow?'

'I see you have doubts of the veracity of his story.'

'His *story*... yes, for that it what it surely is. I was considering of it during my coach journey. *Kidnapped*... in the hour of their arrival at the quay? Come Simon... in that same hour? How would the thieving brigands have known he possessed of two tons of gold, eh? Tell me.'

'For myself, I believe I am prepared to extend my goodwill, to give him the benefit of a... *a considerable doubt*, I grant you, but I just cannot conceive of the friend I grew up with, man and boy, selling me out, letting me down... betraying my friendship; no, that simply cannot be; I do not believe it.'

'Well, I see you will not be swayed. Perhaps I will hear Perkis tell of these events before we return to *my* verdict. Now, will we look to the dinner? Did I mention I am a trifle hungry?'

The waiter returned with the port wine, and Simon smiled, 'Allow me to pour you a glass of this delectable nectar.'

Sunday 11th September 11:00   *The Moor, Falmouth*

The service in the Wesleyan chapel had been exceedingly well attended, the returned men of *Surprise* joining close family members, relatives and friends to give thanks for their return. Mower had been invited to speak a few words once more and, despite offering no poem on this occasion, he had been warmly applauded. Indeed, the ambience of the event was relaxing, informal, a general air of contentment prevailing; for - at least for the moment - the town could enjoy a sense of being together. Mrs Jelbert had attended, sitting at the back with several other widows, a mutual support found in their common distress. Mower sat with them after he stepped down from the pulpit.

The service concluded, Pat and Simon turned towards the door and walked slowly down the aisle, their own thoughts filled with much concern for their missing shipmates of *Eleanor*, for there had still been no word. Pat had concluded that the worst had indeed occurred, but he could not bring himself to articulate his view to anyone; there had been too much distress inflicted upon his crew and their Falmouth families, and for the moment he preferred to set aside all thoughts of that nature. He clung to the fragile hope that perhaps the men of *Eleanor* might yet be found, even at this late hour; indeed, for much of the service that was the personal prayer that he clung to, oblivious of much of what was happening about him whilst sitting mute and inattentive, deep in his own gloom.

Outside the door, the congregation making their farewells to others in the gathering, Pat halted to speak to Mrs Jelbert, 'Mrs Jelbert, it is a pleasure to see you once more. How are you? How...' Pat's words faltered, wondering what to add.

'Captain O'Connor, it is a pleasure to see you... and may I thank you for the money that you have provided for me these two weeks gone? Thank you most kindly, sir, I am most grateful.'

'Oh, it is but a trifling sum, Mrs Jelbert. I hope it has helped in some small way; indeed, I am minded to establish an annuity... a most modest one... for you... when it is plain to me how to do so. I will be attending my bank in the coming weeks and will seek their advice.'

'I assure you that is not necessary, sir,' said Mrs Jelbert, taken aback.

'Mrs Jelbert... *Emblyn*, I assure you it is.'

'Captain O'Connor...'

'*Patrick*... you may call me Patrick, my dear.'

Mrs Jelbert stared at Pat for several seconds, mute, thinking hard, until she spoke up again in a low voice, 'You are a kind soul... an exceptional man... Thank you... *thank you.*'

'As was your late husband... A man, I am sure, neither of us will ever forget.'

Another long five seconds and a thoughtful Mrs Jelbert spoke again, 'If you have a moment, sir... may I introduce this young man? He is the cousin of my late son.' A lad of about fifteen, Pat judged, stepped forward to present himself, but said nothing. 'Go on... have you lost your tongue?' prompted Mrs Jelbert in encouraging voice.

'Beg pardon... Sir, my name is Jago Jelbert... cousin of Annan and nephew of Mathew. If it pleases 'ee, sir, I would wish to join 'ee... to join your crew.'

Pat was shocked to silence himself, a powerful surge of emotional feeling quite overcoming him as he remembered the youngster, Annan Jelbert, and his father, Mathew. He stared at the young man before him, his own difficulty plain for all persons about him to see.

'Beg pardon, sir, if I have offended 'ee,' Jago piped up.

Pat's mind whirled; why would a third member of the family which had lost two of its people already aboard *Surprise* present themselves with a wish to join, and what on earth did Mrs Jelbert make of this, grieving once again as she was? He temporised, 'Young man... Jago is it? The barky is once again in need of repair... she will sail for Devonport in the near days to come, perhaps to be laid up.' Jago Jelbert's face crestfallen, Pat relented, 'Have you any sea time?'

'I have served aboard the packet, sir, these two years.'

'I see, and your particular reason for wishing to join a warship?' Pat's voice softened, 'The packet is a safer prospect... as we... as we all know so well.'

'My uncle always said the town needs this ship, sir... come what may. I was too young when my cousin joined her, but it was ever my intention to do so, sir, to be with him; it was.'

'What will be is far from clear even to myself, I must say.' A pause for further thought, a minute slipping by, Pat impressed by the youngster before him, 'Very well... if the... *the authorities* are minded that *Surprise* will return to her... *her former duties*... I will ask Mr Prosser to send for you. I cannot say fairer than that.'

'Thank 'ee most kindly, sir,' young Jelbert beamed with delight and turned away to thank his aunt, looking on with the first small sign of pleasure for some weeks evident on her face.

'Young man!' declared Pat in loud voice, offering his hand.

Saturday 1st October 1825 09:30 HMS Surprise, The Hamoaze

'Will we go ashore presently, brother?' declared Simon with some little hint of anxiety. 'I am minded that I am done with

267

breakfast. I wish to look to my bank as near after the midday hour as can be. I doubt they will long remain open after that.'

'Of course. Murphy, please to ask Mr Pickering to lower the boat. Doctor Ferguson and I will be departing within the hour.'

'Yes sorr,' Murphy spoke in the gloomiest of tone, nodded and left without another word. The seemingly ever more likely loss of *Eleanor* and of the popular Duncan Macleod and their shipmates of the schooner had cast down the spirits of every man of the barky. Those few men present formed a skeleton crew to sail *Surprise* to Devonport. All of them were particularly set back, the decks having a feeling of emptiness with so many men absent.

'Are you... are you in funds?' asked Pat in nervous voice.

'There is a sufficiency, yes, though a trifle of pay for our Greek endeavours would not go amiss. The most recent letter I received from Flora indicated a perfectly unreasonable demeanour in the person of Mr Salmon...'

'Mr Salmon?'

'My landlord. He has refused to action the most pressing repairs to the house roof, alleging that it was something I should have informed him about before he bought the house. As I was serving aboard *Tenedos* at the time, I am minded that was impossible, and he is exhibiting, in this matter, the greatest degree of unreasonableness. It is my intention to send him thirty pounds to effect the necessary repairs.'

'What? *Thirty pounds!* Why I believe you could buy a house in... in... *up there* for such a sum! Is that not the case?'

'Perhaps so, I received only a trifle more than fifty pounds when I sold it to him, if my memory serves.'

'The grasping rascallion!'

'The boat is ready, sorr,' declared Murphy in baleful voice. 'Will 'ee be back for dinner?'

'Eh?' Pat turned his attention to his steward, 'No, no thankee, Murphy. We have business to conduct ashore and doubtless it will be the later afternoon, perhaps even the evening, when we return. You are to ask Mr Sampays to hold my boat at the quay.'

'Very good, sorr,' Murphy made as if to leave but turned back. He stared at Pat with the most downcast expression, 'Sorr, beg pardon... the men is asking of Mr Macleod... of his prospects, sorr.' A momentary silence, Murphy resuming in a whisper, 'Is he lost?'

Pat swallowed, Simon trembled, the longest three seconds of the world passing before Pat spoke again in a quiet, measured voice, 'No, Murphy, he ain't. It is in my intention to call on Admiral Saumarez this day... to ask of him if there be any news. Until we hear of a shipwrecked *Eleanor*... some evidence of the fact... Mr Macleod and his lads are with us.... *somewhere*; we just don't know where... *not yet*. Please to tell the men... Mr Macleod, Mr Codrington and their shipmates... all will likely turn up in Falmouth town afore we return ourselves.' Pat's heart sank even as he uttered the words, the unlikely prognosis rapidly becoming bleaker by the day. He endeavoured not to allow his despairing feelings to show, but he was far from sure that Murphy believed him; the steward managed an entirely unconvincing smile himself as he nodded and turned away to leave the cabin in patently plain despond.

Saturday 1st October 1825 16:00   *Devonport*

Barton and Pat's bargemen were awaiting his return to the boat, sitting in the early afternoon sunshine on the quayside. They had not expected to see him for some hours as he paced along the cobbles from the direction of the mast pond, deep in thought, his face expressionless, his feet - one slow step after the other - carrying him along in his dejection. They sprang up as he approached. 'Away to the barky,' was all he said, their spirits sinking like a stone, their hopes of positive news from Admiral Saumarez wholly cast aside in a terrible instant. It was a slow pull across the water, the bright sunlight reflections wholly in contrast to the mood, and not a word was spoken. Pat hauled himself up the ladder, turned about and shouted to the men in the boat, 'Back to the quay, lads; ye are to await Doctor Ferguson.' He waved them away and marched directly into the great cabin, nothing more said to anyone, looking neither right nor left, two score of inquisitive stares following him all the way. Murphy hastened into the cabin clutching the coffee pot within minutes, looked to his captain, took in the bleak countenance and did not dare to utter a word.

'Something a trifle stronger, Murphy, if ye will... Look to the brandy, that will serve; thankee.' The steward nodded and left, shocked.

Another half-hour and Pat heard the boat coming alongside. Simon entered the cabin within a few minutes, his face equally gloomy. Neither man spoke a word, and Simon sat down opposite his friend at the table. Pat indicated the brandy bottle. An attendant Murphy, hovering a yard away in nervous trepidation, poured another glass.

'Will I presume there is no news of our shipmates?' ventured Simon.

'No... but there is time enough yet.' The reluctant response was spoken with a deep sigh and Pat strived for a brave face, for both Simon and Murphy were plainly unconvinced. 'Murphy, will you ask Wilkins... 'tis a long time since breakfast and I think I am minded I will take a beefsteak for a late dinner; thankee.'

Simon nodded to the steward, 'A beefsteak will serve very well; thank you, Murphy.'

The two friends alone, Pat spoke up, 'You look greatly cast down. Was all as... as you expected... at the bank?'

'I regret it was not.' Simon spoke with difficulty, with reticence, 'I arrived outside a minute after three o'clock, a trifle later than I had intended, to find a small gathering of exceedingly unhappy persons, about a dozen... perhaps a score, all disgruntled, angry even. I made my way through them to the door to find it closed... locked... and a notice displayed.'

'Locked? The notice... what did it say?'

'That the bank had closed.'

'Early?'

'Closed entirely... has ceased trading only today.'

'What? The Plymouth Dock Bank! Closed? How can that be?'

'A further notice would be displayed in due course, announcing a creditors' meeting. Oh dear... I am mortally cast down. I am broke, Pat, entirely broke.'

'I collect I had, myself, a modest sum there... yes, perhaps in the order of twenty pounds. I suppose that is gone too... There was no indication of when the meeting might be?'

'None whatsoever.' Simon sighed, 'I no longer possess the funds to send to Mull, to Flora... for Salmon and the roof repairs; indeed, neither for the rent.'

'As to that, pay that no mind; I myself still do possess of funds at my *principal* bank... in London. We shall go there, to Pole Thornton, at our earliest convenience. Perhaps when I next attend the First Lord? He indicated that I would be required to be in London this month or, at the latest, next month. There is plenty enough of money at Poles to send the sum you indicated this morning to Scotland.'

'That is exceedingly benevolent of you, it is so, and you have my best thanks... but I cannot presume upon your generosity; certainly not.'

'Come, Simon, thirty pounds or so... 'tis but little more than a month's pay, a trifling sum it is. No, you shall have it, and I will hear no more of objections; am I plain?'

'I am greatly indebted to you, thank you.'

'No, you ain't, and let's hear no more of that. Now, I am to travel on the morrow... to a place on the river near Truro, Newham it is. Saumarez tells me they are near to completing a new vessel there, a sixty-eight foot, larch on oak, pilot cutter. Doubtless it will be of the size which is needed, that is to say which we and *Surprise* will need... as our tender for the barky; perhaps it may even be the ideal craft... she will handle rough seas and the like with no difficulties... and there is certainly something to be said for that... as we know too well. So I am minded such a vessel will serve most admirably...'

'You have given up all hope of *Eleanor* returning?'

'Perhaps that is the case, I regret to say... but I ain't given up yet on Duncan and the lads... no, not at all. It is plain that our schooner must at least have been damaged - *well, she ain't come back* - but how badly we cannot know. It is also the case that she may have made landfall before being wrecked... or her crew likewise may have fetched up on the beach. Let us hope that is the case. In any event, we must have a tender here. Why, I can no more consider of taking to the wretched Mail coach - *so damned uncomfortable it is* - than flying to the moon. Admiral Saumarez is sending his own cutter, *Bramble*, here in the morning, and we are to sail to Falmouth; and on the Monday we shall sail up the Fal River to Newham, where we will find the shipbuilders and the new pilot cutter. I venture she will be the sweetest of sailing vessels, her fuller keel providing that stability on a beam wind which *Eleanor* never greatly enjoyed. Why, I imagine she will be particularly fast too... *even on a bowline.*'

Simon looked up to reciprocate Pat's smile, 'Thank you, brother, and will we look to a drop of something before supper?'

Sunday 2nd October 1825 19:00   *Falmouth*

HMS Bramble approached the Green Bank quay as long shadows lay all across the water, their far edges near touching the Flushing side of the anchorage. The final vestiges of the sun glimmered in subdued welcome just above the rise behind Falmouth town. The men of *Surprise* were gloriously pleased to be back home, the barky being left in the care of Lieutenant Pickering and a half-dozen of the Yard's hands.

'Here we are, Falmouth town again,' declared Pat as loud as could be, as if such might stir the gloomy faces of his men to better spirits. Talk aboard had, for several hours across Start Bay, touched on the missing men of *Eleanor,* and the mood had become morose. 'Hear me, lads... LADS! My purse is at the bar at the Royal Hotel for the next few hours... D'ye care to join me for a whet, eh?' This, at least, was well received and a modest uplift in mood, though never reaching full enthusiasm, touched upon the men, and they set off with a brisk step along the front, Dunstanville Terrace soon left behind.

The twilight offered the faintest glimmer of illumination as they stepped along Market St. The recurring boom of a ship's gun sparked much speculation as they hastened along. 'Pray tell,

272

Pat,' Simon cried out in jest, 'Are we under attack? Are the Frenchies back?'

'Well... 'tis customary for a returning packet to fire one gun and then hoist her flag... but to keep firing... if - that is - *it is* a packet... 'tis a mystery, for sure. Doubtless we will hear of it later.'

Arriving in darkness save for the glow from windows as they reached the Royal, a homely warmth enveloped them as they all crowded in to approach the bar, a little more of good cheer coming upon them. Pat instructed the barman and soon every Surprise was holding a glass of ale, a hubbub of more jovial discussion taking hold, the roaring fire in the hearth disseminating its benevolent hot aura, and the fragrant aroma of wood smoke was endemic in the room, a comforting familiarity, and all - for the first time that day; indeed, for much longer - seemed well with the world.

'I collect this new vessel which you remarked upon,' prompted Simon at the bar, clutching his port wine, 'You have not explained, brother, how we are... *conceivably it is possible, I'm sure...* to afford to purchase this new... this new... this *boat.*'

'Eh? Oh yes... I will pass over you calling the pilot cutter a boat...' Pat smiled, a degree of relaxation coming upon him for the first time in weeks, 'Admiral Saumarez has pledged to provide the funds. From where I did not care to ask.'

'So we depart to see it on the morrow? Are you minded that I will accompany you?'

'For sure; after all you no longer have patients to attend. It will be a most interesting day, I have no doubt. A pot or two of coffee, a half-dozen of sausages, a brace of eggs and a rasher or two of bacon... and we will start the day well; yes, indeed; and we will board *Bramble* after breakfa...' Pat dropped his near full pint of ale as the front door swung open, the loud shattering explosion of the glass on the stone flags halting all the loud conversations throughout the room in an instant. Two score of faces stared towards the door, two score of men gasped with the most violent of shocks, a stunning moment of disbelief striking them all; and then came the jubilation, an unprecedented kick-start of joy surging throughout every heart and mind, a tidal wave of euphoria, of overwhelming relief and wildly surging emotion; all was unleashed in one sublime instant. And then the rush to greet the arrivals and the clamorous shouting began in a mad cacophony: 'DUNCAN!', 'MR MACLEOD!', 'HURRAH!' The men of *Eleanor* had come home at last.

Monday 3rd October 1825 08:00   The Royal Hotel, Falmouth

'You have a greatly wearied look, brother,' offered Simon, looking to Pat at the breakfast table; 'Will I ascribe that to a trifle of over-indulgence yesterday?'

'Eh? Over-indulgence? Will you please pass the coffee?'

'I collect you were remaining in the bar with an ever-increasing number of our joyful shipmates at 3AM when I retired... Why, I venture there was a hundred and even more... come the midnight hour, and a deal of complaints before that time from several of the other guests... You do collect the loud singing... somewhat raucous?'

'It ain't every day when... when you... that is to say... when the Eleanors come home... *the Eleanors came home, Simon...* They came back!'

'It was the most glorious of events, I make no doubt. Tell me, we are still intending to inspect the new vessel today?'

'Yes... yes, but I am minded that will be a trifle later in the morning... yes, that will serve. I have sent Murphy to tell the men of *Bramble* to look to the tide and to attend the quay with their boat at eleven o'clock.'

'Good morning, Captain O'Connor, Doctor Ferguson,' boomed the unexpected voice of Perkis, accompanied by Peddler. 'Give you joy of the return of your men.'

Pat looked up with bleary eyes. 'Why, thank you, Mr Peddler.' This was conceded in grudging tone.

'Gentlemen, please to take a seat, join us... do sit down,' Simon was more polite. 'Allow me to offer you coffee.'

Pat scowled, no one taking any notice. Peddler spoke up, 'Mr Macleod, is he well?'

'A trifle incapacitated this morning, I venture,' declared Simon with a smile, 'but otherwise, perfectly well; thank you.'

'Doctor Ferguson,' declared Perkis, 'We heard the news only this morning; Mr Prosser recounted the late arrivals of yesterday... the shipwrecked mariners... It is the most wondrous of events, is it not?'

'Indeed it is, Mr Perkis,' replied Simon, beaming.

'Mr Peddler has reported on the demise of the Plymouth Dock Bank on Saturday. Apparently, you spoke with him about the event yesterday... in the early evening when you returned from Devonport.'

'I did so,' said Simon, wondering where this was leading. 'We encountered each other for a brief moment in passing on the street outside. I will say... a greatly disappointing event it is too... and something of a minor calamity for me.'

'Doctor Ferguson, allow me to say that... that if there is anything with which I may help, then you may count on me; please do not hesitate. I have... will I say... *not insubstantial* financial resources available to me, funds which I can call upon - if necessary - at any moment.' A pause, Perkis turned to look at Pat, 'Were you affected in any way, Captain O'Connor... by the bank closure?'

Pat stared; his extreme hangover was clouding his clarity of thought. He looked at Perkis with an infinity of suspicion, 'Eh? Me? No... no, not at all.'

'Well, I can be contacted at any time... if circumstances change... with a message left here at the hotel with John Pearce. Good morning to you both.' Perkis and Peddler each made the most minor of bows to the table and departed.

'What was that about?' remarked Pat.

'Doubtless the benevolence of a kind soul... the influence of Peddler, my old friend.'

'Hmmm,' Pat growled, never more sceptical than that moment.

Monday 24th October 1825 11:00   *Seaford, Sussex*

Duncan Macleod paced briskly along Crouch Lane, his coat wrapped close around him, the temperature cool; his thoughts were filled with trepidation and not a small amount of anxiety.

The Foreign Secretary had requested his presence, had called upon a newly promoted Captain for advice, and that was yet another turn in his humble life which he would never have imagined only a year or two ago: such things simply did not happen to Lewis seafarers. His directions not being entirely clear, he stopped to stare at the impressive Stone's House, the name above the porch door revealing it was not his destination; he walked on to the next house, marvelled at the architecture, showing much of Dutch influence in the curving roof shape and the dormer windows, until his eye caught the nameplate: *Seaford House*. He had arrived. He knocked, a little nervously; he rapped harder on the brass knocker, and a minute more of waiting passed before it opened. A haughty and immaculately attired doorman stared at him.

'Captain Macleod for... for the Foreign Secretary,' Duncan's voice choked; he struggled to get his words out and he wavered anxiously at the step.

'Come in, sir; you are expected,' the servant said, thawing slightly.

'Ah, Captain Macleod,' the second man's greeting was in warmer tone, a handshake offered; 'I am Granville Stapleton, secretary to Mr Canning. Would you care to step into the ante-room here? Do you care for coffee... tea perhaps?'

'Thank you, sir; I would be most grateful for coffee.'

The servant hastened off and Stapleton resumed, 'Captain Macleod, Mr Canning is presently speaking with visitors and will call for you in due course; it may be a little while. In the meantime, please... make yourself comfortable; George will bring your coffee directly.'

'Thank you, sir,' Duncan nodded; he wondered how on earth he was expected to make himself comfortable. Here he was, quite probably in Seaford's grandest house, an impecunious mariner from the Hebrides; a man who, until two years previously, had been about to take command of a fishing boat. A fishing boat! Duncan laughed out loud at the thought, George giving him a quizzical look. He sat down, determined to relax, to calm down, and he paused to reflect on his miraculous escape from Death's near grip in the Atlantic waters, so recent, the thought even now profoundly disturbing. He shivered, despite the room's warmth. An hour passed in silence until the clock struck noon when the door creaked on its hinges and George returned to summon him to the exalted presence. He followed the steward to the drawing room and stepped cautiously over the threshold.

'Captain Macleod!' said George Canning warmly, shaking hands with cordial enthusiasm. 'It is so good to see you again. I understand from my cousin... Patrick O'Connor... in a recent letter of his these past few days, albeit brief... that you are most recently returned from Portugal... and from a shipwreck indeed!' Duncan still mute, finding the warmth of his reception a little overwhelming, Canning continued, 'I am greatly relieved that you survived.'

'As am I, sir... *as am I,*' Duncan replied, more than a little nervously. 'I came here directly I received your invitation.'

'Perilous, was it... the shipwreck?'

'Aye, indeed it was. We lost two lads, thrown overboard and never recovered; run down, we were, sir, aye, run down in the fog... off Cape St. Vincent... by a passing merchantman who should have reduced sail, no time to heed our bell, no chance to turn away... We were mired.'

'You took to your boat, I presume?'

'We were but a league or so off the coast when we took to the dinghy... Much overburdened she was too, aye... and we fetched up on the shore after a deal of time pulling hard... twelve hours it was... aye, and always bailing... near sinking.' Duncan looked downcast, 'I regret I could not save the Greek letter, sir.'

'We will pay that no mind. Your good friend and colleague, my cousin, Captain O'Connor, brought its duplicate. In fact, you are invited here to advise our discussion... about the letter, *the practicality in that environment of its proposals*. Mind, such is for your private ear alone.'

'Aye, sir; I understand.'

'I gather that you endured a difficult journey, on foot, to find passage, to return home from Portugal?'

'A trek it was, for sure; all along the coast, ne'er feeling well for a week after we sank... the saltwater... much swallowed... and near three weeks walking to Lisbon. We were aided by folk in the villages... the friendliest, the most helpful people of the world they were... gave us food, wine, aye. And then we took the packet to return to Falmouth. I venture it took us six weeks to get home...' Duncan smiled, 'Why, my feet have never hurt more!' Canning smiled too. Duncan was relieved to conclude his brief recounting of the epic journey. 'I am a mariner, sir, nae footslogger!' He laughed aloud, a wash of relief overtaking his chilling reflections.

The Foreign Secretary, recognising the release from tension and seeing plain Duncan's alleviation - very evident - joined in, patting him on the shoulder, 'Well done, Macleod! Come, come over to the window... and allow me to introduce you to His Excellency, Prince Lieven: His Imperial Majesty's ambassador...' Seeing Duncan's confusion he expanded, 'That is... *from Russia*... and Her Highness, Princess Lieven.'

Duncan's nerves flared to new heights: the aristocracy of Russia was being introduced to him by His Majesty's Foreign Secretary; he bowed, mute, several seconds passing as he stared whilst struggling to find the appropriate words, quite beyond him; until Canning, recognising his apprehension, interceded in helpful voice, 'Prince Lieven, Princess Lieven... Captain Macleod... let us take a seat.' He indicated the sumptuous leather armchairs near the fire, its flickering flames warming the room in the cool autumnal day. Duncan needed no such warmth; indeed, he found himself sweating, the exalted standing of his company stretching far beyond anything he might ever have conceived in his wildest flights of imagination.

Prince Lieven gazed at an increasingly uncomfortable Duncan all the time that Canning was talking, a scrutiny that was intense and not the least circumspect. Eventually he interrupted the Foreign Secretary, 'Sir, we have spent some hours speaking of His Imperial Majesty's proposals; will you now allow my wife to... in the most brief and... will I say... somewhat guarded terms... indicate our areas of interest to... to Captain Macleod?'

Canning nodded; Duncan swallowed, surmising that, perhaps, Lieven's examination of him was satisfactory.

Madame Lieven spoke up for the first time, in haughty and cultured voice, 'Captain Macleod, thank you for your attendance today...' Duncan nodded. Was the princess disdaining him? She exhibited a look which suggested such. She continued, 'I am honoured, together with my husband, to represent the Tsar's most benevolent interest in assisting our Greek religious compatriots of the Orthodox Church in their struggles against their Ottoman oppressors. The Tsar...*and I speak of matters...*' in a rising voice, '*... which are of the highest state importance and which may never be reiterated...*' Duncan swallowed and nodded again. 'His Imperial Majesty, is minded to offer his co-operation for any proposals which may be forthcoming from England... from His Majesty's Government here. The Foreign Secretary has graciously expounded only this morning his own thoughts on the matter... *in principle*... and has welcomed the offer of the Tsar... and so we find that there is prospect for common accord.' Madame Lieven paused to sip her tea and Duncan, entirely gripped, stared in mute fascination. She pressed on, 'It has been suggested by... by our sources, and I cannot speak of them... as I am sure you will understand...' Another mute nod from Duncan who hardly dared draw breath. 'It has been reported that Ibrahim... the Egyptian general in the Morea... is intent upon seizing the whole of the Greek population and intends... *I hesitate to reiterate mention of the most vile of schemes...* intends removing them to Egypt as slaves.'

Duncan gasped, could no longer hold his breath; 'The monster!' he exclaimed in loud voice.

'Indeed,' Canning spoke up for the first time in minutes, 'Captain Macleod, would you be so good as to opine on whether you think this despicable... this grotesque and repellent scheme could conceivably succeed? You have experienced the conditions in the region, the Morea particularly, and we care to hear the considered thoughts of a man such as yourself... a plainly level-headed man, as I hear of you from the First Lord himself... and, indeed, from my own cousin.'

Recovering, Duncan spoke up without hesitation, 'Sir, I thank you for the kind words, and I am gratified in your confidence in me... I will endeavour to speak of the... *the conditions* in Greece as I understand them.'

Chapter Twelve

Friday 2nd December 1825 7:00   *Westminster, London*

The public saloon of the Feathers tavern, off the Strand and within the Liberty of Westminster, was as dimly lit as ever, the wall-mounted gas lamps offering only a diffuse yellow glow, albeit they were complemented by the fire's flames, flickering brightly in the hearth and casting a benevolent warmth throughout the room, the welcoming spectacle immediately attracting the three tired and weary friends as they entered from a freezing street.

'I said last time that I would never take that infernal coach again,' moaned Pat, neither of Simon nor Duncan taking the least notice, for they had endured a plethora of similar complaints ever since the change of horses at Salisbury.

'Let us look to breakfast whilst there is the prospect of eating something hot and before all is sold,' declared Duncan with an audible degree of concern, 'for I am mortal hungry.'

'And perhaps we will allow ourselves a generous measure of that glorious beverage, coffee?' suggested a shivering Simon with great anticipation in his voice.

They set down their baggage, rubbed cold hands and settled into chairs at a table near the blazing fire, drawing powerfully, its radiant warmth restoring feeling to frozen fingers. The background clamour of numerous early patrons, all enjoying Mrs O'Donnell's hospitality, was a pleasant hubbub to the ear.

'Ah, Mr Macleod it is... Captain O'Connor... and, why, 'tis Doctor Ferguson himself!' The smile was beatific, the words effusive with satisfaction, Mrs O'Donnell positively gushing with pleasure. 'To be sure, 'tis all of you... the three old friends and all together, sorrs; and a grand pleasure to see you it is. Welcome, welcome back to my humble establishment. The girls will be along this d'reckly minute, sorrs.' She leaned over, seized Simon in her broad arms, squeezed him until he thought his breath must stop, turned to Duncan and grabbed tight his hand within hers, and then to Pat, a yet more fulsome greeting for an Irish compatriot, Pat near hauled up from his chair into her embracing bear hug from which she did not relent until the girls did arrive.

Macleod marvelled at his nieces, Sandra and Emma. The term *girls* seemed much a matter of the past, for here before him stood two sparkling princesses. The last two years had delivered a maturity, a filling out of the two little waifs that he recalled. Their own welcome for their uncle was emotional, both pressing themselves upon the man they considered their saviour, the man who had brought them as orphans to a new life in London. Mrs O'Donnell, ordinarily much leaning towards reserve herself save when immersed in the greetings of old friends, could only stand in a rapturous state of splendid gratification, ignoring the ever louder calls for service from all about the busy room.

'Mrs O'Donnell,' Pat interjected eventually, 'Would you be kind enough to serve three hungry gentlemen the best breakfast in the house?' He kissed the two girls on their cheeks. 'I am minded a pot of coffee, several of them, will answer the case.'

The breakfast was divine, a great tray of additional bacon pressed upon them, 'for strengthening the blood' said Mrs O'Donnell. The first pot of accompanying super-strength coffee was blissful, and a bottle of port wine too was consumed in mere minutes, the three close friends sitting back in pleasurable contentment as Emma served the second pot of coffee.

'We are here... in London town,' murmured Simon, 'and - *pray tell me* - what are your immediate intentions?'

'We are *summoned* here, no less...' declared Pat, '... Duncan and I. For myself, I am to attend the First Lord at his home at 3PM to speak of a particular matter, one on which he has not cared to enlighten me.'

'Aye, and I am to call upon the Foreign Secretary, likewise at 3PM,' said Duncan. 'And as for why... well, I have no notion.'

'You both do move in exalted circles these days, I must say,' exclaimed Simon, 'Perhaps now you have such influence – Hah! Hah! - you may care to mention the delay in receipt of our modest remunerations, for I possess of no more than the few shillings in my purse.'

'Never fret,' Pat declared in reassuring voice, 'It is in my intention to call at my bank on the morrow.'

'I sincerely hope that they are sound... will not follow my own bank into insolvency. It has become ever more plain to even me, the most innumerate of souls, that there is now a great pressure in the mercantile world; indeed, it has been suggested that this is consequent to the breaking of so many of these scheming stock company bubbles.' A momentary pause, 'Could you consider of going today, Pat... to your bank?' Simon spoke in nervous voice.

'No, I am so greatly tired that I must strive for a few hours of sleep before my appointment this afternoon. Tomorrow will serve to attend the bank. I have heard nothing of concern from Poles.'

'Aye, and I am also minded to take to my bed directly,' announced Duncan, rising. 'Will we meet for an early bite, a sandwich perhaps... before we go out?'

Friday 2nd December 1825 15:00 Arlington Street, Westminster

The servant ushered Pat into Lord Melville's study where the First Lord sat behind his desk studying documents and reports, his spectacles low on his nose as he looked up and above them to see his visitor enter. The room was lit by two gas lamps, the sun already behind and fading below the houses on the other side of the street. He rose and stepped round the desk to shake hands with a firm grip, as if bestowing confirmation of a sincere and genuine pleasure in his words, as he declared in a loud voice, 'Welcome, O'Connor! Good afternoon to you. Please, do take a seat.' He looked to the servant, hovering on the threshold, 'Edward, we will take coffee... and look to the kitchen for the marchpane biscuits, if you will.'

'Good afternoon, sir,' replied Pat, a fleeting recollection of his first visit to the exalted presence in his home coming to mind. That had been more than two and a half years ago, if his memory served him. Then, he remembered, he had felt himself a mere shrinking violet before this man, a bundle of nerves, of curiosity, tongue-tied and bewildered as he had first heard of his intended appointment to Greece, to serve a navy and country that had not

283

properly existed. Today, much water having flowed under that particular bridge, Pat felt more self-assured. He had done his job, had done all that was possible with a single small ship, with two hundred men; indeed, near thirty of them had died in the task; and what, he wondered, did the First Lord really know of it, of the efforts of his men, of the true cost, the price in blood. He sat, mute, waiting for Melville. Yet his host too simply stared, in silence, as if in further evaluation of Pat, a minute or even two ticking by, the ambience cautious, a goodly reticence evident on the part of both men.

Finally, 'I can tell you,' said Melville, 'that your service these two years and more... on behalf of His Majesty's Government's interests... in Greece... has been on many an occasion the subject of discussion between myself, the Foreign Secretary and even the Prime Minister; we have heard accounts... often no more than tales reiterated by merchantmen returning from the Ionians... of your ship's exploits. We have also received, from time to time, infrequent reports from your colleague, Captain Macleod. Allow me to say, *sir...*' Pat's heart leapt, the term had only ever been used before by the First Lord in remonstrance when discussion verged on heated, but this was not the case, the inflection was wholly different, an implied deference within it. Melville continued, 'Allow me to say that we have been exceedingly impressed by your application in this mission... and, of course, that of all your officers and men. I confess, O'Connor, that our expectations were... were *small*, our hopes... well, were modest... modest indeed. What could one frigate do against the might of the Ottoman navy and, lately, the Egyptian fleet come to aid its Turk overlords? We asked ourselves that question... and we had concluded that one frigate alone could be no more than a nuisance to the Turk, but... I have not the least doubt that the political importance attached to your mission was far, far greater than any reasoned military expectations of my own, yes indeed, and in that you and your men have excelled... *you have excelled, O'Connor.*'

Pat could only nod, striving to absorb the full flow of the First Lord's revelations, and then the door opened, the servant depositing the tray and biscuits. Melville, interrupted, simply nodded and the servant disappeared without a word.

'Your ship, your men, O'Connor, have demonstrated to the provisional Greek authorities the general leanings and indications of support which His Majesty's Government wishes to provide. Naturally, they grasp the notion that such support cannot be overt... no, there cannot be any rupture in relations with the Porte, not at all; but *covert* support, as you and your ship have provided - and as has been reported to the Ionian authorities from many a source - *covert support*, plainly demonstrable, has buoyed the morale of many a Greek captain in the battles in which you have fought. Indeed, we hear of many an instance where your ship has been particularly influential in such engagements.' Melville held up his hand as Pat sought to interject, 'Do you care for a modicum of refreshment, more coffee perhaps? A wee dram might be appropriate... indeed, I think it will serve very well.' Melville reached round and pulled a whisky bottle from his drawer and two tumblers; he poured a generous measure into his own and a substantially larger one into Pat's. 'Here you are, allow me to propose the toast...'

Pat raised the exceedingly well filled glass, 'Thank you, sir.'

'TO *HMS SURPRISE* AND ALL WHO SAIL IN HER!' declared Melville in exceptionally loud voice, the servant putting his head cautiously around the door.

It was almost more than Pat could manage, the emotions rising within him were so powerful. Valiantly - the surge of feeling was so strong within, almost overpowering, and his voice was seemingly no longer under his command - he whispered to begin with, 'To *HMS Surprise*... and...' At last he raised his voice, 'TO ALL WHO SAIL IN HER!'

A large gulp by both men and the First Lord swiftly moved on to pick up the papers he had formerly been reading. 'There... and now we will turn our attentions to another matter, one on which I seek your advice,' prompted Melville, Pat still in something of a daze. 'You may be aware of the New York shipbuilders who were commissioned to build two frigates for the Greeks?'

'Yes sir, although... was there not some problem arising when the price was doubled to a hundred thousand pounds per ship? Quite scandalous it was!'

'Indeed so, and it is reported that the price has been further increased... only last month... to one hundred and eighty-five thousand pounds each.'

'Outrageous!' cried Pat, shocked.

'Yes, it is, and there is now a deal of doubt that the Greeks can afford such an exorbitant sum; their finances are weak... are uncertain. No, there is the possibility that these ships will be lost to them. You have said yourself, I collect, that the Greeks are in need of bigger ships, heavier guns...'

'That is so, sir. I fear that when the Turks have learned how best to deal with the Greek fireships, which are their real weapon, indeed their *only* effective one... *if the truth be known,* then such ships as the Greeks possess will be seen as ineffective, powerless against the larger Turk frigates... and their few seventy-fours.'

'Then I will speak... entirely in confidence... of an offer which has been made by an officer who I believe you are familiar with... one who - if you will - is not presently held in great favour; indeed, there are some in... in political circles, will I say... who perceive him as some form of renegade.'

'Sir?'

'I speak of Cochrane, of course.'

'Ahhh...'

'Cochrane has returned from his service within the Brazils and has proposed to the Greeks that... that if he is provided with six steamships then he will enter their service and... and rid their waters of all Turk warships... thereby winning the war.'

'Steamships?'

'Indeed. Although, there is too Cochrane's stipulation of considerable personal remuneration... I collect he has asked for a payment of thirty-seven thousand pounds before he will begin, for his personal account... and another twenty-thousand when his efforts bear fruit, when Greece is independent.'

'Fifty-seven thousand pounds for his personal account?' Pat's mind boggled, for such a sum was unheard of; no Royal Navy officer had ever received such an advance. He recalled Simon's remark, to press for pay which was long overdue.

Melville continued before Pat could utter another word, 'Yes indeed, for his personal account.'

'Sir, one other matter comes to mind...'

'Speaking of steamships, I do collect a proposal from another officer, Abney-Hastings. He is no longer serving. He proposed an intention of procuring a steamship for Greece... which was an entirely admirable notion. It was a few years ago. I may have mentioned him to you before?'

'You did, sir,' Pat's reply was cautious: where was this leading?

'Is such possible, O'Connor? Can six steamships really win this war?'

Friday 2nd December 1825 15:00 Gloucester Court, Brompton

'Captain Macleod, how good of you to come up to London again, and so soon after your prior visit. I am indebted to you,' declared George Canning at the door to the drawing room. The Foreign Secretary seemed to be, as far as Duncan could perceive, somewhat disturbed, agitated even; there was no invitation to be seated this time; indeed, neither had Canning observed much of the customary proprieties nor offered refreshments; rather, he was disposed to get to the point as quickly as possible.

'Oh, pay that no mind, sir. I am in town with my friends, Captain O'Connor and Doctor Ferguson. We are minded to spend a few days together before Doctor Ferguson returns to Mull... for Christmas and the New Year.'

'Very good, an admirable notion, I'm sure. Tell me... *for I am pressed to call upon the Prime Minister within the hour...* and this is a matter I put to the First Lord only a very few weeks ago... You have a first-hand knowledge of the Ottoman fleet, of their capabilities and, perhaps too, some understanding of the morale of their crews, their men... Is that the case?'

'I have seen them fighting, sir; yes indeed.'

'Well, how would they fare... against... That is to say, were they fighting Jack Tar?'

Duncan's mind recoiled: was this a suggestion that the Royal Navy might overtly engage the Turks? He said nothing immediately and thought for a moment or two before offering a guarded reply, 'Sir, the Turks - to my mind - are not well trained. Yes, the Egyptians have received some French training and can serve their guns better than the Turks. We have a saying, sir, *if only the Turks did NOT aim their guns, only then might they be dangerous.'*

'Hah! Hah! Very good! So, you are minded that any Turk admiral would be plentifully cautious before considering engaging a Royal Navy ship?'

'Most certainly, sir... but there is the question of numbers. The Turk, particularly if joined with the Egyptian, enjoys a numerical advantage which the Greeks have certainly never challenged, and as for *our* navy, well, I cannot speak of that, sir.'

'In conclusion, Macleod, and I ask this of you *personally* at the bequest of our Russian friends... can the Royal Navy - *in sufficient numbers that is* - enforce an armistice? Would the Turks be so minded as to adhere to the imposition of such?'

Saturday 3rd December 1825 12:30 Lombard St, City of London

'I regret, Captain O'Connor, that the vault is empty, quite vacant,' declared Thornton in hushed voice in his private office, 'and this after one customer - *why, it was only this very morning* - withdrew... *entirely without notice...* his entire thirty-thousand pounds placed with us on deposit!'

Pat glared with a burning exasperation at the young man seated before him, 'Sir, surely you will... *you anticipate* deposits during the course of the day?'

'Most certainly, we do indeed. I am advised that we expect to receive some twelve thousand pounds of deposits today from our customary clients; however, we have been requested to pay out a further thirty-three thousand pounds of withdrawals - *and that excludes your own intended withdrawal.* It is entirely exceptional! I have known nothing like it before... It is quite unprecedented!'

'There is no other source of funds available to you?'

'I assure you... Captain O'Connor... that I have been scouring the City for further funds which I might borrow since that sizeable and unexpected withdrawal.'

'I see. It is a lamentable state of affairs, is it not?'

'Sir, I do assure you that this bank is solvent. We are dealing with a temporary crisis only.'

'Mr Thornton, since I have been, these past few days, in London, the talk of the town is of bank failures, and such tales are rife... RIFE! Why, only yesterday evening, at dinner, I could not fail to hear the loud voices of the adjacent table and their talk of - *I recall* - the failure of over seventy banks... *more than seventy!* How can I depend on your word, sir, that Poles will not likewise fail... HOW? When might I receive my money? Please to explain!'

In that moment a messenger entered after no more than a cursory tap on the door and bearing a note; he passed it to Thornton who broke away from Pat's glaring countenance to read it swiftly. 'Captain O'Connor, please excuse me for one minute. I must consider this note most carefully. It has some... *some bearing* on our mutual predicament. One moment, please.'

'Very well,' growled Pat, scowling.

Thornton looked up, 'This is good news. An old and valued friend of my father, John Smith, another banker, is minded to help us. I am called to wait upon him, to provide certain assurances as to the bank's solvency, when he may meet our requirements for funds requested today, that is to say... *as far as he can do so*. Would you be so kind as to await my return? I will be, *perhaps*, one hour, likely no longer. Mr Edmunds will ensure you will have tea or coffee, as you wish.'

Pat was dumbfounded; the prospect of recovering his money was uncertain, and recollections of Simon's cautionary words at supper resonated in his mind. He nodded with the weary and sinking realisation that, in fact, he had no choice, none at all. He looked up: Thornton had gone. He sat in sombre silence musing on his predicament. Simon had pressed him several times to come sooner, to seize his money before such as this might happen, but such urgings had been dismissed as verging on hysteria when in fact, as was perfectly plain to see with glorious hindsight, they were prudence itself. He cursed himself, accepted the coffee offered by Edmunds and determined to divert his thoughts towards other matters. Failing to do so, he reconciled himself to the suspense and distress of his predicament.

The door swung open; it was 3PM and Henry Thornton had re-appeared at last. He was accompanied by another man. Pat's nerves were wholly on edge. 'Captain O'Connor, there you are. May I introduce John Smith? I am pleased to say that he has provided limited... *limited* monies... such as are available from his own bank, Smith, Payne and Smiths... to tide us over the remainder of the day...'

Pat nodded and shook hands with the newcomer.

'... and at least it should just be possible to reach the end of our business day without refusing payment... that is to say, *save for yourself*.'

'That is hardly reasonable, Mr Thornton. I must protest.'

'Sir, that is perfectly understandable, and you are entirely within your rights to insist upon payment this very minute; however, I must tell you that if you do so then I must, in good conscience, refuse you and declare a formal default by the bank, when I will then close the doors. The bank, sir, will be bust.'

'That is outrageous!' declared Pat, his ire rising.

'No sir, it is the rules by which I must abide; I have not the least choice in the matter. However, if you are minded to bear with me, perhaps I can alleviate your concerns.'

'How?' demanded a very angry Pat.

'Mr Smith here has called upon me to attend a meeting at the Bank of England, at 8AM tomorrow...'

'On Sunday?'

'Precisely, and that is an illustration of the seriousness of this matter and of the Bank's approach in more general banking terms to a wider crisis. Mr Smith, who is exceedingly well connected, has indicated that the Bank itself is considering its position and may... *may* be minded to provide support.'

'The Bank of England?'

'Indeed, and in which case, sir, my own bank will demonstrate its solvency to you... when you may care to withdraw as much of your money as you wish.'

'Very well... I see I have no choice but to bear with you in this... this debacle.'

'Then that is decided. Captain, if I may, I would ask a favour, you being a military man...'

'A favour?' Pat could hardly believe what he was hearing.

'Yes, I believe it would be prudent to have an escort on the morrow; after all, I may be in possession of considerable funds upon my return from the Bank, *very considerable funds*. Do you possess of a pistol?'

'I believe I may find a brace at my lodgings.'

'Please to bring them. I will meet you on the steps of the Bank of England at five minutes to eight. And now we must look to today and hope that there are no further demands for withdrawals. Do you care to wait with me? We - *the bank* - are not yet safe... That is to say... if any significant and unexpected withdrawal occurs before five o'clock. I am minded that I will ask Edmunds for coffee... and perhaps something a little stronger. Would you care for a tint?'

The three men sat in gloom and despondency within Thornton's office, the coffee all drunk, the brandy bottle diminishing but providing not the least calming effect, the minutes ticking away so very slowly. The door had been propped ajar and the noises coming from the banking hall were audible in the small office. Every customer's request was listened to most attentively, every mention of the word *withdrawal* sending hearts racing and minds soaring to new levels of anxiety, even terror. On two occasions Edmunds looked in to declare that a deposit had been made, a small tide of relief erupting. At last, the clock chimed five and Thornton bolted from the office to slam shut the bolts on the front door; Edmunds swiftly rolled down the window shutters. Thornton turned about, his face a picture of abject relief; in slow paces he returned to his office, 'We have balanced the books! What a day! Captain O'Connor, I will show you out via the *back* door. Please to be at the Bank tomorrow -

on the steps - and, I beg of you, do not be delayed in the slightest. I bid you good day.'

Supper's main course consumed, Pat sat at the hearth in silence, staring into the fire's flames. Duncan too sat back within his own chair, clutching a generous glass of whisky. Simon watched with fascination, his gaze fixed on Pat. His friend's weather-beaten face, browned by long years on the quarterdeck in the full force of the wind, exhibited an unmoving expression of concern; indeed, Simon considered that he seemed more like the apprehensive father attending whilst the midwife - behind the screen - delivered his wife's baby. His demeanour for the past hour had been anxious, discontented, and it struck Simon that momentous thoughts must be turning over within Pat's mind, admittedly most likely very slowly, for his friend was no scientist or philosopher and had not the least pretension of being either; he was most certainly more the practical man.

'We have been in London for scarcely more than a day and you two are immersed in consultations with the higher... *the highest* echelons of society... save for the Prime Minister and the King!' exclaimed Simon eventually with mild disgruntlement, 'What are things coming to?' The supper was falling short of the convivial occasion he had much looked forward to all day. 'And you are both looking as miserable as sin. What ails you, Pat? Did you attend your bank?'

Pat set down his glass and looked to his friend with obvious dismay. 'I did...' His reply was offered in hesitant voice.

'And did you withdraw your money, tell?' Simon already suspected the answer.

'Not exactly...'

'Here be the cheese, sirs, and the port wine,' declared Emma in ebullient spirits, her great delight in seeing her uncle enduring still.

'Thankee lass,' Duncan smiled at her.

'*Not exactly...* Well, there is a deal of latitude in your answer, brother, which is not the characteristic I have come to expect of you in all these years,' said Simon bluntly, 'Certainly it is a rare occurrence when we are at sea.'

'I... I made an arrangement... with Mr Thornton.'

'An arrangement... for all love?'

'Yes, I am to attend him in the morning. I will not see you at breakfast. I must away at seven o'clock... or even before.'

'On Sunday... *Sunday?* But surely the bank will be closed?'

'Yes; however, there are matters... *wheels* in motion...'

'This is a rum business, I make no doubt. Will you return with your money?'

'Oh yes, for sure I will,' murmured Pat, great doubt in his mind. 'Now, allow me to pour you a glass of the sweet nectar.'

'Duncan,' Simon turned his attention to his other friend, 'What are *your* intentions for the morrow?'

'I am minded to accompany Pat... since I heard of his request of Mrs O'Donnell for my brace of pistols.'

'Pistols! *Pistols?* What's up? Pat, please to explain. Since when is it the case that pistols are taken to the bank? Are you considering of a robbery... not being given your money today?'

'A robbery! Hah! Hah!' Pat laughed and Duncan smiled with him. 'Of course not! A robbery indeed; how could you think of such a notion? No, I am to attend my bank's partner, to escort him and the bank's funds... There, are you satisfied?'

'I am pleased to hear it.'

'What of yourself? What are you minded to do on the morrow?' asked Pat quickly, much desiring a change of subject.

'I am crossing the river and, as I hear that you are in confident expectation of funds, I will take a cab... spare no expense. I trust I may still count on your offer of a modest loan?'

'Certainly, you may... and you are to consider it a gift.'

'I am greatly obliged... I am, but a loan it will be.'

'Please do not speak of obligation between us; what I possess is ever yours.'

'Well then I will give prayers for the success of your gold mine, for I am ever likely to remain the pauper, I am. The half-pay of a surgeon is the most modest of stipend.'

'Come, Simon... never fret in the matter of funds,' declared Pat, striving for a cheerful voice, 'Why, I collect never possessing a shilling in all the years of my youth... and here I am... swimming in the full tide of life... and with a gold mine.... *a gold mine...* Hah! Hah!'

Simon could not conceal a doubtful stare; he moved on, 'You asked of my intentions on the morrow... It is in my thinking to visit Greenwich... the maritime hospital. For some weeks I have been in correspondence with the consultant there, with Stephen Maturin, the great man himself. I have made an appointment to see him, and we are to dine together... to discuss the more recent developments in the medical world.'

'Very good,' said Pat, pleased to hear his friend's definitive plans, 'I collect the man served for many a year with Admiral Jack Aubrey... yes; indeed, they were with *HMS Surprise... twenty-eight*, the predecessor of our own barky. I would much like to meet that man myself... *Lucky* Jack Aubrey... and, most particularly, I do hope one day to share a table with him. I'm sure that he has many a tale to tell!'

Sunday 4th December 1825 07:30   Lombard St, City of London

There had never been the slightest prospect of Pat being late, rather he had risen well before the dawn, taken only coffee in the kitchen of the Feathers and set off as the sun began its mournful winter rise. Its puny early rays cast a diffuse glow through the fog rising off the Thames, albeit making little impression on the murk of the dense woodsmoke from many fires. Pat marched on; only with considerable difficulty had he dissuaded Duncan from accompanying him, thinking that perhaps *two* more persons, both quite obviously not bankers, might spark an objection at the Bank, whereas one might possibly pass scrutiny. He hastened down the Strand, bought a pork pie for threepence from a street vendor huddled over his fiery brazier, munched on it as he paced down Fleet Street, regretted the pie and its extreme fat content exceedingly as he stepped along Ludgate Hill and so reached the inspiring Saint Paul's cathedral. He pressed on at swift pace down Cannon Street, a burning indigestion paining him, and he arrived at the Bank rather earlier than strictly required. He watched the bustle of the City starting its day all about him as he stood alongside one of the columns of the impressive portico to await Thornton, the adjacent gas lamp post offering its small and yellow illumination, scores of passing clerks barely casting him a glance. He shivered in the cold air, and he drew his scarf closer about his neck, feeling the emerging stubble on his chin, for he had given no thought to shaving that morning in his haste. He pressed hard through his coat to remind himself that both pistols were still there: he had not dropped either as he had rushed through the streets. Pat glanced at his watch: it was 7:50AM In his tense state of anxiety, he strived to wait and to reconcile himself to the absurd venture, as he considered it to be.

'Captain O'Connor, good morning to you!' cried Thornton, arriving at last.

'Good morning to you, sir,' Pat offered pensively.

John Smith arrived within a minute and greetings were exchanged. Pat, feeling far out of his depth in such unfamiliar circumstances, pondered once again what on earth he was doing in such company.

'Come, let us enter; we are expected.' Thornton rapped on the smaller door to the left of the great central door and exchanged brief words with the doorman who admitted them, indicating where they were to go. They stepped into the Front Court, turned left into the Garden Court, crossing it to reach the Committee Room where another doorman invited their credentials. He looked doubtfully at Pat before allowing them in. The large room was splendorous, dramatic even; doubtless it was intended to be so, thought Pat as he marvelled at his surroundings. The clerk invited them to take a seat at the table. Neither Pat nor Thornton uttered as much as a whisper, and then the door at the far end opened and the Governor made his entrance, closely attended by another man, a dozen others in train. Pat, Smith and Thornton rose to greet them; hands were offered and shaken all round as the Governor initiated introductions, 'I am Cornelius Buller, Governor... this is my deputy, John Richards.'

'Henry Thornton, sir, and Cap... *Mr* O'Connor, my... *my principal clerk*; and may I present John Smith, an eminent banker who you may be familiar with.'

'Indeed, and these gentlemen are all those members of the Court of the Bank who are in London. Please, be seated and we will begin.' A moment or two passed as all sat down, when the Governor opened, 'I understand that your house... *Mr Thornton...* is in some degree of difficulty...'

'Indeed, it is, sir. Our coffers were entirely cleaned out yesterday. As we all here today are aware, there is a public sentiment building which is approaching, one might say, panic. Indeed, one of my principal and longstanding customers who has rarely, if ever, less than thirty-thousand on deposit withdrew every penny yesterday... *and entirely without notice.*'

'I see, and you are here to solicit a loan?'

'Yes sir.'

'Do you give your word that your house is solvent?'

'Most certainly, sir; and I have brought the most recent accounts of the bank with me.' Thornton passed them over and the Governor peered at them through his spectacles for tense minutes, eventually turning to John Smith. 'Mr Smith, I understand that your own bank provided support to Pole Thornton yesterday?'

'Yes sir, to the maximum extent that we were able. I am a longstanding friend of Mr Thornton Senior and have never doubted the veracity of anything he might say; indeed, I have formed the opinion that such confidence may be extended to his son, Henry, here before us.'

'That is most gracious of you, Mr Smith. Mr Thornton, may I ask: how many provincial banks are dependant upon Pole Thornton... and... I should say… *vice versa*?'

'Thirty-eight, sir.' There was a subdued but collective gasp all around the table followed by silence as the Governor assessed the implications.

'Might one suppose that Pole Thornton have little idea of the extent of their... *will I say*... the bad loans of these country banks?'

'That is the case, sir; however, neither are we dependant upon recovering any funds from them at all in the near future, if - *that is* - we can temporarily secure a loan from the Bank, a loan which is entirely backed by the assets of my partners.'

'And what magnitude of loan is in your contemplation, may I ask?'

'Four hundred thousand pounds, sir.' There was a much louder gasp from everyone present, many persons sitting up in their chairs, and the Governor blanched. Silence. Pat stared, such a sum far exceeded any number that had ever crossed his mind; such a magnitude would procure eight new frigates for the Royal Navy, if - he reminded himself - they were not to be built by those profiteers in New York. He stared at the assembly of more than a dozen of ageing, wizened faces; all their minds were transparently deep in some form of turmoil. How this would end he had not the slightest idea. His thoughts wandered to how he might help Simon if the tumultuous morning proved fruitless.

John Smith interjected; a brave man, thought Pat; 'Sir, may I say that the failure of Pole Thornton would occasion so much ruin throughout this land that such would be regarded as a national misfortune... and, from what I have seen of Mr Thornton... of his conduct, I am convinced that his bank can be saved and the crisis will pass.'

'Very well,' said the Governor eventually, staring at the principal supplicant, 'Mr Thornton, you shall have your four hundred thousand pounds by eight tomorrow morning, which I think will float you.'

The ensuing collective gasp far exceeded both the prior ones, for such was unheard of; never, in all its years, had the Bank loaned a sum of such vast magnitude to a private house; it was unprecedented, incredible. Pat simply stared, could not believe his ears. Thornton and Smith rose as one and bowed their heads. 'Thank you, sir... gentlemen!' declared Thornton, wholly unable to conceal his relief; he stepped forward to shake the Governor's hand. Pat rose hastily, offered an unthinking half-nod. One of his pistols tumbled from his waist belt and fell to the floor, rattling against the chair leg. Hastily he stooped down and thrust it into his boot, in hope that none might see it, and he followed Thornton and Smith from the room in great haste and without looking back.

Standing outside on the cobbles of Threadneedle Street, the trio paused to take in the events. Thornton whispered, his face frozen in a state of shock, 'I can scarcely believe it.'

'Congratulations, young man; your father would have been proud of you... had he been in there,' declared Smith, seizing and shaking Thornton's hand. 'Very well done, you spoke well, you did indeed.'

'I owe you my heartfelt thanks, sir; I have not the least doubt that your kind words swayed the case... no doubt at all,' said Thornton, plainly overwhelmed. He turned to a silent Pat, 'Captain O'Connor, it would seem that I have need of you... of your help... on the morrow, when I collect this... this large sum. Do you care to attend once more?'

Pat found his voice at last, 'Certainly I will, sir.'

'Thank you... thank you for attending... most kind, most courteous of you and, allow me to say, thank you again for your patience in this matter. All will be resolved tomorrow. I will see you here at 8AM once again. Thank you both, gentlemen... words are insufficient, you have my undying gratitude, you do.'

Pat retraced his steps of the morning, albeit at a slower pace, his mind whirring as he strived to fully comprehend what he had heard and seen before his own eyes: *senior clerk* indeed! He could not - Smith had warned - speak of the events to anyone and must keep all he knew entirely secret, for common knowledge of the events must spark a run on banks throughout the country. What might he say to his friends, returning with empty pockets save for his pistols? He laughed out loud at the recollection of dropping his pistol, passers-by staring at him, and he marched on in rising spirits.

Monday 5th December 1825 08:00   Lombard St, City of London

The doorman was expecting them and ushered Thornton and Pat through the Pay Hall, across the Bullion Court and into the Bullion Office. Governor Buller and his deputy stood ready at a small table, upon which Pat gazed at expansive bundles of banknotes the likes of which he had never conceived of, even in his most fanciful dreams.

'Good morning once again, gentlemen,' said Buller, shaking hands with Thornton and Pat. 'I do so hope that this will not overset you...' Both men stared as the Governor resumed, '... to see the Governor and the Deputy-Governor of the Bank acting as your clerks!'

Pat laughed, much to the amusement of the Governor and his Deputy; Thornton dared not. The notes were all counted and packed into a satchel. Thornton thanked the Governor, adding 'I must away in haste, sir, before my bank opens.'

'Very good, Mr Thornton; I wish you success. I think we may anticipate a degree of turbulence in the days to come.'

'I am sure of it, sir, but your help will surely ensure we pass through it. Thank you again.' They turned away, Thornton clutching the satchel.

The governor spoke up with the last word, 'Mr O'Connor, I trust you have brought your pistol... to ensure Mr Thornton's safe passage!' Buller and Richards laughed out loud, Thornton blanched, but Pat - taken aback - did not dare speak. They left as quickly as could be and hastened off towards Lombard St.

Back in his office, the banknotes safely secured within the vault and all his small staff marvelling at his success, Thornton opened his brandy once more, and without waiting for Pat's nod he poured two generous measures. 'Here's to you, my new clerk, Mr O'Connor!' Both men laughed out loud until Edmunds put his head around the door. 'Now to your funds, Captain O'Connor. You will not require your pistols!' Another round of laughter. 'I believe that you will accept that my bank is solvent?'

'Of course, sir, and I congratulate you on your success in this matter. In fact, I am minded that, on further consideration, I actually require but little of my cash at present...' Pat paused, 'There is the matter of funds to help my friend and - I trust you will help me - I wish too to establish a means to send to him a monthly sum, a... a modest stipend... to cover his living expenses, of the order of twenty-five pounds... and... and there is

299

also a widow of a shipmate of ours... in Falmouth, who I much care to assist.'

'Of course, we can arrange for local banks to disburse such sums as you stipulate in the amounts you desire.'

'Very good. Well, I will withdraw one hundred pounds today and I will write to you with the instructions for these arrangements in due course.'

Monday 5th December 1825 15:00   The Feathers, Westminster

'So, you see, Simon...' announced Pat in jovial spirits, '... all is well with my bank... and here is the money I promised you. Will seventy-five pounds tide you over for the present?' Pat pressed the notes upon the table, picked up his glass and drained the residue. The dinner being finished, appetites wholly satiated and the wine bottle empty, he waved to Emma, attending nearby. 'Another one, my dear, if you please!'

'That is exceedingly generous of you... It is so. I thank you most gratefully, brother. I believe that will attend to my roof and other pressing repairs... and the rent for a month or two.'

'And let us give thanks to Saint Patrick that I will not be beholden to that rogue Perkis!' cried Pat, slapping his hand on the table, a modest degree of inebriation creeping up upon him. The last few days of considerable anxiety were behind him at last and his funds were secure; a goodly degree of relief was settling within his mind, and it was increasingly exhibited in his voice and his demeanour, the table enjoying a grand spirit of bonhomie, long missing from the lives of the three friends.

'You were considering becoming beholden to Perkis? In what way?' prompted Simon, in fine mood and not the least bit inebriated, a degree of concern rising with his friend's words.

'Oh, that! Before we set off for London, Perkis had offered to purchase an interest in my gold mine... *to alleviate any temporary financial exigens... exergencies... emergencies* - so he said.'

'Did he indeed? And was my friend Peddler with him?'

'Oh yes, Perkis would take a forty percent share whilst Peddler - your old friend, *he laboured the point* - would take twenty percent... and such would ensure that I... that is to say *when counting on Peddler,* your old friend who could always be relied upon... that I would retain control of the mine.'

'In return?'

'Perkis promised me cash in the sum of two thousand pounds... even as he laboured the fact that no gold, as yet, had actually been found.'

'I am glad that you were not minded to accept on my account,' declared Simon, his concern and his ire rising strongly.

'I refused him,' Pat, increasingly excited in the matter of two men he did not much care for, was near shouting, and a number of patrons looked round. 'The man understands the workings of money, that is sure, and he possesses a considerable knowledge of investments, no doubt. He is said to have cleared thousands in the City, but I am convinced he is a rogue; indeed, I've never been more sure of anything!'

'Will we look to a drop of the malt, the brandy perhaps?' Duncan interjected, the subject holding no interest for him, 'I venture it may be our last dinner together for some time, eh?'

'Yes... Emma! There you are, my dear! We will take a bottle of brandy and another of the finest whisky in the house. Simon, I collect you are off... later today is it, to Mull, to your home and your beloved?'

'No, I had intended to take the *Express* to Carlisle, to leave at eight o'clock this evening, as you know, and from there to take the *Independent* to Glasgow...' Simon hesitated, 'However, I believe my plans can accommodate a minor delay. I am minded to join you in Falmouth for the forthcoming event of next week.'

Sunday 11th December 1825 09:30   Hull's Lane, Falmouth

The morning was clear but frosty as Mrs Jelbert, wrapped in a crimson shawl against the cold, stepped out of her cottage, Prosser and Mower at her arms, Marston and Pat one slow step behind. They walked in the sun's shadow down Hull's Lane and turned left into Arwennack Street. A dozen men, veterans of *Surprise* and *Tenedos* before that, both young and old, all greeted her with nods, *Good Morning* and encouraging smiles before joining her escort. As the party passed by the Customs House, the Collector, Samuel Pellew, stepped out from between the portico colonnades; he was accompanied by his brothers, Admirals Edward and Israel, and by Admiral James Saumarez, the three officers in full dress uniform, swords at their sides. All joined the procession, Edward Pellew exchanging nods with an astounded Pat. When the march reached Church Street, men adding to the numbers every few yards, the party was sixty strong. By the time Mrs Jelbert passed the Fish Strand quay, eighty men were in train, even more joining the procession as it moved along Market Street until, at the left turn into the Market, near a hundred and fifty shipmates of Mathew Jelbert came to a halt at the Market Place in bright sunshine. Pat, still in some astonishment, shook hands with the Pellews and with Saumarez, whispered brief words of cordial greeting all that he could find.

Silence. Breath steamed in the chilly air. Eyes blinked and looked away from the direct sunlight. Prosser whispered to Mrs Jelbert; Marston took her hand and spoke in quiet voice. Six, seven, eight hundred and more Falmouth people looked on, not a word spoken by anyone in the multitude to break the absolute silence, a huge air of expectancy prevailing, subdued and respectful.

Marston stepped forward and gazed all about him for a few moments before speaking out in loud voice, 'Good Morning people of Falmouth. I am the Reverend Michael Marston, and although I am not of the Wesleyan persuasion... as I know many of you are, I am an ordained minister of the Church. I too returned from Greece with many men of this town...' Marston paused to gauge the crowd's attention. The silence endured. All present appeared to be staring at him. He pressed on, speaking without notes, 'We are gathered here today for the special commemoration service for our lost comrades ... as you know... but first, before we go to the Chapel, allow me to speak of two men in particular who are, sadly, not with us... I speak of Mathew and Annan Jelbert... father and son.' A general murmur arose within the crowd. 'I am pleased...' Marston raised his voice, '... I am *honoured* that I served with both those men

302

aboard *HMS Surprise*. Young Annan Jelbert was a dedicated member of our crew... He never baulked at trying to learn something new and never hesitated to step forward when there was work to be done... and his father was the most exceptional man I believe I have ever met... He was always at hand to help a shipmate whatever the matter, the time or the place. We have lost two magnificent men...' At this point there was a huge groundswell of accord from the crowd, hundreds of voices echoing Marston's sentiments. A minute passed by as he waited for it to subside. Finally, he looked all about him once more and spoke up again, 'With me here today is another of my shipmates, a man you will be familiar with... having seen him in the Chapel at New Year's Eve... Lieutenant James Mower. He is also a Falmouth man... and was a particular friend of Mathew Jelbert's. He was helped by Mathew in his recovery from many wounds... and a bond was forged that will ever remain in his and in our memories. He would much like to say a few words this morning... Here with us is... JAMES MOWER!'

The applause for Marston's words was loud, the welcome for Mower was louder; as he stepped forward the crowd did indeed recognise him and erupted into the most energetic clapping of hands, which went on and on until the Lieutenant himself raised his arms in appreciation and supplication, the noise fading to silence once more. 'Thank you, friends, for that is what we all are here this morning... *friends*. Mr Marston spoke of my friendship with Mathew Jelbert. Allow me to say this: I would have been proud to call his son, Annan, brother. We exchanged words aboard ship, on occasion, and I did not know him as Mathew's son. Long before that... as a newcomer aboard *Tenedos*... I first made the acquaintance of Mathew Jelbert... *Mister* Jelbert... as we called him, for he was *the gunner*... and the gunner was something of a mystical figure for a young midshipman of twelve years old... Yes, I was but twelve when we first met. It was something of a disappointment to all of us... aboard *Surprise*... that Mathew did not return for our first voyage to Greece, and all of us - *every man jack aboard the barky* - was pleased to see him back for the second one... but now... *which we all regret so much...* he is gone for ever. For me that is a particular loss for... since I was aged but eight... when I was called *orphan*... in Mathew Jelbert...' Mower was plainly in great distress, his tears visibly flowing, and he struggled for his words, '... *in Mathew Jelbert*... I was sure I had found... found someone I... I could call... think of... as *father*. He will be greatly missed. Thank you all.'

The crowd erupted into a vociferous barrage of clapping and shouted greetings; loud calls of encouragement went on and on, several persons moving closer to shout consolations to a distraught Mower; others closed all about him, seized his hands, gripped his arms and shoulders. Mrs Jelbert, her own face streaming with tears, moved to seize the young Lieutenant in her own arms, the two hugging each other in tight grip.

Another minute passed in loud furore when Marston raised his arms once more, the crowd's applause dying away to an expectant silence. 'Friends, before we enter the Chapel for our Sunday service, we are gathered together for another matter of some significance, and so I present to you... the man who led us in our Greek ventures, the man who ... through his sound decisions and experience... saved the lives of those of us *more fortunate souls* who stand here today... He will speak a few words... I give you CAPTAIN PATRICK O'CONNOR!'

Pat stepped forward to thunderous applause, his grizzled veterans in particular welcoming him with shouts, whistles and energetic clapping. 'THANK YOU... THANK YOU.... GOOD MORNING TO YOU ALL! Shipmates! People of Falmouth town! Friends! I am but an honest sailor, yes… an old tarpaulin I am... and with precious few words to say, but I have something I believe you will care TO SEE... nearby. Will you care to come with me? A few steps is all; COME ON, COME THIS WAY, 'tis but a few yards.' Pat pointed back down the street, 'To the Market Strand... WILL YOU COME WITH ME? I beg you will!' He began to walk, slowly, a bemused Mrs Jelbert shielded from the crush by Mower, both close at Pat's side, the crowd talking about this unexpected event but shifting with him, a great mass of people of common purpose, loud, many of them shouting and hundreds talking at once. They shuffled along with a rising degree of curiosity until they faced the King's Hotel on the corner, where Pat turned left, a few yards bringing him to the Market Strand ope. The great throng pushed on, crammed ever tighter together in a dense squash, those at the rear shoving with gusto to see and to stare along the ope towards the sea. It was high tide and the shingle strand was underwater. The bowsprit of the new pilot cutter projected towards them, towards Market Strand.

Pat, the three admirals and all his own officers standing at his side, together with Mrs Jelbert, waved his arms; his veterans, old salts all, emphasised vociferously and with gesticulations to the multitude that he wished to speak once more. The hubbub gradually died away to an expectant silence and Pat shouted at full voice to reach the overflow of curious watchers, several hundred at the back having diverted to stand on the edge of Mulberry quay, only the highest part of that shingle slope dry, the rippling water washing its edge. He lifted both his arms in the air again and the profusion of murmurings faded away. He raised his voice to speak once more, just short of shouting, his words carrying with perfect clarity in the stillness of the morning air, the crowd all quieted, 'People of Falmouth... shipmates... friends all... we have, sadly, lost the barky's tender... the schooner *Eleanor*... but it pleases me to say, today, that here is her replacement...' A fresh murmur rippled throughout the crowd. 'Yes... a pilot cutter newly built these past months in Newham. It pleases me greatly to say that she is ready for service...' Pat, a little overcome and tongue-tied himself, paused and turned to his side, towards the three admirals all standing tall beside him, all of them dressed in their splendid, uniformed finery. They looked to Pat and nodded in encouragement. He took a deep breath and resumed, 'Yes, she is ready now... and I am proud... *very proud indeed...* today... to name her... in honour of a particular and most exceedingly special man... our lost but still revered shipmate...' He took the hand of an attentive but somewhat bewildered Mrs Jelbert in his own and he squeezed it gently. 'I name this vessel... MATHEW JELBERT!'

Bargeman.................weevil (usually in the bread and biscuit)
Blunties ....Old Scots term for stupid fellows
Boggies.....................Irish country folk
Bombard....................Mediterranean two-masted vessel, ketch
Bourlota .... an old brig converted to a fireship
Bower.......................bow anchor
Boxty........................traditional Irish potato pancake
Breeks......................Scots term for trousers or breeches
Bruloteer .... Ship's crew member on a fireship
Bumbo......................pirates' drink: rum, water, sugar and nutmeg
Burgoo.....................oatmeal porridge
Capabarre .... misappropriation of (usually government) stores
Captain's Thins........Carr's water crackers, "a refined ship's biscuit"
Caudle......................thickened, sweetened alcoholic drink like eggnog
Clegs........................Scots term for large, biting flies
Coddle.................... Irish stew-like dish of bacon, pork sausages and potatoes
Crubeens..................boiled pig's feet
Dreich.......................Old Scots for cold, wet, miserable weather
Drookit.....................Scots term for drenched
Etesian......................strong, dry, summer, Aegean north winds
Felucca......................small sailing boat, one or two sails of lateen rig
Fencibles..................the Sea Fencibles, a naval 'home guard' militia
Flat...........................a person interested only in himself
Flux...........................inflammatory dysentery
Frumenty.................a pudding made with boiled wheat, eggs and milk
Gabarre .... a sizeable three-masted merchant ship , sometimes armed
Gomerel....................a stupid or foolish person
The Groyne..............La Coruña in north-west Spain
Hallion.....................a scoundrel
Hoy...........................small (e.g. London-Margate passengers) vessel
Jollies.......................Royal Marines
Kedgeree..................a dish of flaked fish, rice and eggs
Kentledge.................56lb ingots of pig iron for ship's ballast
Laudanum............... a liquid opiate, used for medicinal purposes
Lobscouse................beef stew, north German in origin
Marchpane............. marzipan
Marshalsea.............. 19th century London debtors' prison
Mauk........................Scottish for maggot
Meltemi ....Greek and Turkish name for the Etesian wind
Millers......................shipboard rats
Mistico.....................similar to the Felucca sailing vessel
Nibby........................ship's biscuit
Praam .... flat bottomed boat, propelled by poles in shallow water
Puling .... whining in self pity
Razee .... a heavy frigate, formerly a two-deck ship cut down to a single deck
Scrovies   ....worthless, pressed men
Scampavia .... a long, low war galley
Solomongundy......... a stew of leftover meats
Snotties....................midshipmen
Stingo........................strong ale
Treacle-dowdy........ a covered pudding of treacle and fruit
Trubs........................truffles
Yellow jack..............Yellow fever (or flag signifying outbreak)

AFTERWORD - PTSD

If you are a serving military person or a veteran (or a friend or family member of either) who is in difficulty or affected by any form of distress, turmoil or anxiety, don't hesitate to seek help:

in the UK, contact **SSAFA**

the Armed Forces Charity

www.ssafa.org.uk/help-you/veterans

or

Combat Stress for veterans' mental health

www.combatstress.org.uk/helpline

email: helpline@combatstress.org.uk

The free telephone helpline is open 24 hours a day,

365 days a year

0800 138 1619 (veterans and families)

0800 323 4444 (serving personnel and families)

in the US, contact the Department of Veteran's Affairs

The National Centre for PTSD

www.ptsd.va.gov

call 1-800-273-8255

email: ncptsd@va.gov

Elsewhere, search the web and find your country's help providers.

Remember: courteous, caring people are standing by to help. There is nothing to be lost by calling. There is not the least shame in seeking help. There is no need to struggle on alone with PTSD difficulties. Call; you are not alone.

Printed in Poland
by Amazon Fulfillment
Poland Sp. z o.o., Wrocław

56196746R00190